Meredith Jaffé is the author of four novels for adults: *The Tricky Art of Forgiveness* (2022), *The Dressmakers of Yarrandarrah Prison* (2021), *The Making of Christina* (2017) and *The Fence* (2016). *Horse Warrior*, the first in a children's series, was published in 2019. She also contributed a short story, 'Emergency Undies', to the 2019 *Funny Bones* anthology.

She is the festival director of StoryFest, held on the NSW South Coast, and regularly facilitates at other writers' festivals and author events. Previously, she wrote the weekly literary column for the online women's magazine *The Hoopla*. Her feature articles, reviews and opinion pieces have also appeared in *The Guardian Australia*, *The Huffington Post* and *Mamamia*.

the tricky art of forgiveness

meredith jaffé

HarperCollinsPublishers

HarperCollins*Publishers*
Australia • Brazil • Canada • France • Germany • Holland • Hungary
India • Italy • Japan • Mexico • New Zealand • Poland • Spain • Sweden
Switzerland • United Kingdom • United States of America

First published in Australia in 2022
by HarperCollins*Publishers* Australia Pty Limited
Level 13, 201 Elizabeth Street, Sydney NSW 2000
ABN 36 009 913 517
harpercollins.com.au

Copyright © Meredith Jaffé 2022

The right of Meredith Jaffé to be identified as the author of this work has been asserted by her in accordance with the *Copyright Amendment (Moral Rights) Act 2000*.

This work is copyright. Apart from any use as permitted under the *Copyright Act 1968*, no part may be reproduced, copied, scanned, stored in a retrieval system, recorded, or transmitted, in any form or by any means, without the prior written permission of the publisher.

A catalogue record for this book is available from the National Library of Australia

ISBN 978 1 4607 6027 7 (paperback)
ISBN 978 1 4607 1365 5 (ebook)

Cover design and illustration by Darren Holt, HarperCollins Design Studio
Cover images by shutterstock.com
Author photographs by Rachel Piggott Photography
Meredith Jaffé's newsletter header by Michelle Barraclough, Fresh Web Design
Teacups and teapot by Seb Cumberbirch/Unsplash
Typeset in Bembo Std by Kirby Jones
Printed and bound in Australia by McPherson's Printing Group

*To my darling husband and gorgeous children,
who are my biggest supporters, not to mention a rich vein
of material!*

Part I

Everybody has a secret

Chapter 1

Now

Diana stands in the centre of the living room and surveys the extent of the task before her. There are stacks upon stacks of cardboard boxes as far as the eye can see. The sideboard is in three pieces, the reassembly of which is a job best left until Will's return. Her precious baby grand gleams like an oil slick on the pale blue sea of wall-to-wall carpet.

She bends over and scratches a sudden itch on her calf. On first inspection, the apartment had seemed rather spacious. All these months later, it's a tight squeeze. Bubble wrap and butcher's paper overflow the emptied boxes into which they've been stuffed. There are sticky balls of packing tape everywhere.

She scratches harder. Now she's made the itching worse. She follows the line of fire down to her foot and sees the source of the problem. Black spots hopping all over the joint. Sand fleas. She swears and stomps into the laundry, searches through the basket of laundry liquid, fabric softener, shoe polish and rags, and unearths the insect spray.

"'It'll be fantastic living by the harbour, Didi,'" she mutters, cursing her husband as she dispenses a liberal dose of poison over the carpet. "'Sunset walks on the beach, midnight swims.'"

If anything, spraying the little buggers only seems to make them jumpier. Diana gives her feet a quick squirt. On second thoughts, that probably wasn't the smartest move. '"Imagine waking up every day to the smell of the sea."'

Good point.

Diana opens the sliding glass doors and shoos out the toxic fumes. Stepping out onto the wide terrace, she inhales the salt-laden air. In all fairness to Will, she may not swim from one week to the next but the soothing sound of the sea and the tang of salt in the air go some way to make her feel better about the loss of Turpentine Street.

The view's not too shabby either. She leans on the balcony ledge and admires the sprawling Moreton Bay figs in The Green. They lend the park a certain gravitas, as does the quaint old-fashioned bus shelter nestled between the park and The Esplanade. Beyond, the harbour dazzles in the morning light. Diana concedes the point to Will. She *might* get used to living here. In time.

The packing boxes are a stark reminder that moving house is a monumental task — especially after the decades they called Turpentine Street home. And this apartment, despite its stunning views and yet to be discovered charms, is not home. Will it ever be? Hard to imagine at this juncture. Not now it's just the two of them.

She detours via the CD player. If she must spend her morning restoring order over chaos, then she cannot and will not do it alone. Diana loads the CD and skips to her favourite track, turning up the volume. Too early? Too loud? Who cares. She grabs the insect spray for a microphone and goes head to head with Peggy Lee. Singing the virtues of a boy she knows, she shimmies and twirls her way towards the bedroom, pausing to blow a kiss at her reflection in the hall mirror and tell that boy how she loves him so. There's a picture of Will on the dressing table. Diana picks it up and hugs it to her chest. As the song finishes, she gives a sweeping bow to the packing box audience and thanks them from the bottom of her heart.

Diana shakes off her kimono, shakes out her hair. 'Oh, that felt good.' A quick peek in the vanity mirror, such an apt name, shows her cheeks are pink and her eyes sparkle. A glimmer of her old self.

Once she's changed out of her PJs, Diana wanders back into the living room and turns down the volume. She surveys the boxes, each labelled with a list of contents. Lounge room: silverware, good glasses, cocktails. Not much point starting with that one given the sideboard is in pieces. The next box is labelled 'treasures'. That sounds far more fun. She peels off the packing tape and opens the flaps.

On top is an old pillowcase, inside of which is her Persian trinket box, covered in a pattern of deep-pink blossoms and gold filigree. Her grandmother kept it on her dressing table filled with necklaces and rings. When she was little, if she was very good, her grandmother, Clara, would let her slip on some of the jewellery, add a dash of lippie and a spot of powder on the nose, 'to get rid of the shine'. Nanna loved dress-ups almost as much as Diana.

Not being an everyday item, the trinket box has been packed for some months. Diana wiggles the lid until it pops off. The very first thing she lays eyes on is a birthday card. It's decorated with a hand-drawn pink unicorn, in the background is a rainbow and, of course, lots of butterflies. Inside are the words, *I luv you MUMMY!!!!* Diana laughs. All her life, Persephone has demanded centre stage, unlike her brother, Aiden, who was always Mr Chill. Written or spoken, her daughter's life has always been littered with capital letters.

Diana puts aside the box and pulls out a metallic-green picture frame rimmed in tinsel and fake snow. Aiden, dressed as an elf; he must be about four here. The teachers at The Village Preschool were masters of the innovative Christmas gift — handcrafted picture frames, tree decorations, and a million and one uses of dried pasta shapes — whereas big school was all about the Mother's Day stall. Diana rummages around among the ILOVEMUM picture frames, the soaps of dubious aromas, eyeshadows and lipsticks in shades that she wouldn't dream of wearing, even on stage, and some very dodgy jewellery. There's a tattered potboiler with a racy cover. Clear as day, she remembers Aiden grabbing her sleeve, explaining, 'Because you love reading, Mummy.' She did read it too, for his sake. Every card, every gift, she's kept them all.

She pushes the box along the carpet into the spare room. Everything she can't find a home for here will have to be stored in the garage. That can be Will's job. He's the hoarder in the family. It's bad enough she has to choose what stays and what goes. She keeps the trinket box, the picture of Aiden as an elf and one of Persephone in a Mother's Day frame and arranges them on the dresser in her bedroom. She's nothing if not even-handed.

A row of boxes line Will's side of the bed. That man has more clothes than her. She's half-tempted to leave his unpacking for him to deal with when he returns from his trip. After all, that's exactly what Fi would do if it were her and Richard.

'There's no point having all that capital tied up in the family home, especially now the chicks have well and truly flown the coop,' Fi had assured her over a light lunch at Carlo's.

The memory makes Diana wince. She hates having her family flung to the four corners of the world. If ever she's feeling a bit down, a little thought-worm whispers in her ear, *What have you done to deserve this?* Persephone and Emile in Edinburgh. Aiden, Anna and baby Lucas in New York. Her sister, Lydia, in Rome. Their mother, Audrey, now on the south coast — just far enough away to be inconvenient but not so far as to make a provocative statement. And to top it all off, Will constantly overseas on business.

Diana picks up the silver frame and strokes her husband's cheek. 'Have we made the right decision?' she asks the black-and-white version of her then much younger spouse. Such a handsome man. Look at that jaw! Who wouldn't want to kiss those lips? She certainly has, too many times to count.

Diana shakes off the self-pity, reminding herself that no one likes a misery guts. She returns Will's picture to the dresser. No matter how hateful it feels, the fact is, they have sold the family home and downsized to an apartment. She and Will are now officially Empty Nesters. She's bound to get used to it, in time.

Coffee. That will perk her up. Diana takes a fresh brew out to the terrace and breathes in the sea air. On the wrought-iron table is Ruth's housewarming gift. It's an orchid. Apparently it only flowers once a year, at night, but the payback is a flower so stunning and a scent to die for. Is there a metaphor here? Diana's been friends with Ruth long enough to know it will mean something. Diana prods the soil and wonders how often she's supposed to water the damn thing. Is she ready to assume responsibility for a gift that must be kept alive? At least it's a plant, not a pet.

Diana drains the mug. Enough of this procrastination. She's taken this Tuesday off precisely because she has mountains to do apart from all this unpacking palaver. Inside, she opens her journal and runs through her to-do list. She needs to talk to Royce Carmichael at the Beach Club about access to the venue the day before the Big Party, as well as arrange a time to do a stocktake of the club's crockery and the like. There's the photographer to organise and catering to be finalised. Diana's eternally grateful to the crew from The Village Providore. The food is pricey but excellent, and better still, they're a known quantity. Unlike the ladies from the Beach Club. Best not to go there. Suffice to say, club politics dictates she must walk the fine line of appeasement. On the plus side, she managed to secure a fabulous house up on the headland that sleeps twelve, so all the relos can stay in situ and catch up. No one's seen each other since Persephone and Emile's wedding the year before last at his parents' rather gorgeous seventeenth-century farmhouse. Although they did briefly cross paths with Aiden's terribly dull in-laws in New York when Lucas was born. Still, in a few short weeks everyone will be here for the Big Party and they can celebrate Will's 60th and their 30th wedding anniversary in style. Diana places an asterisk next to the last item: the Big Surprise.

There's a knock on the door. A disembodied voice calls out, 'Delivery for Forsyth.' She checks her watch. It's not even nine o'clock.

Diana traverses the chicane of packing boxes blocking the hallway and thrusts open the front door. The stairwell is empty. Not a sound, not a soul. How odd. Her bare toe stubs against a thick yellow envelope. Unsurprisingly, it's marked to Will's attention. Shouldn't she have signed for it?

She adds the envelope to the pile of mail next to the answering machine on the kitchen bench, careful to keep the newspaper article from last weekend's papers strategically placed on top. '60! A new lease on life' declares the optimistic headline. Buried within its columns is the bit she really wants Will to see — how at his age, men need to take charge of their mental and physical health, before it's too late. Maybe if he reads the glowing endorsement for regular medical check-ups he might heed their advice. He's certainly turned a deaf ear to any of Diana's suggestions, subtle or otherwise. Perhaps she's being harsh. Her hearing is definitely not as finely tuned as it once was — maybe Will's in the same boat. Mind you, Nanna Clara was a past master at selective deafness. A trait her mother seems to have inherited. Be that as it may, Will needs to make an appointment with their GP. After all, there must be some reason operations have ceased in the bedroom department. A visit to their doctor might eliminate any obvious reasons before either of them have to confront more delicate possibilities.

Diana returns to the bedroom and tackles the nearest box. Jumpers. Typical Will, he's just shoved them in and now they're all crushed. She takes them out one by one, folds and stacks them on the bed – a thick cable-knit, a range of light cottons and fine woollens, and a rather old-fashioned cardigan his mother made him that really belongs in the charity bin, but Will's loyalties have always run deep.

Her fingers brush against the soft cashmere of the fabulous shawl-necked sweater she bought him in New York when they went to visit Aiden and Anna after Lucas was born. She picks it up and buries her nose in the soft wool, inhaling Pears soap and an undernote of Will's scent. It's familiar and comforting and makes her yearn for his embrace. Closing her eyes, she rubs the cashmere against her cheek and another nugget of loneliness settles in her chest. Fi constantly complains she'd need a crowbar to wedge Richard out of his fancy Norwegian recliner. Whereas Will's brother, Ian, and his wife, Rebecca, are always at each other's throats. By that measure, Diana is lucky. Will travels too much for her to grow tired of his company.

She shakes out the sweater to fold it properly and a crushed ball of paper drops onto her foot. Diana picks it up and smooths out the creases. It's hotel letterhead. Somewhere along Orchard Road in Singapore. The paper is white and the hotel's name is in raised gold font. It's only a scrap. She turns it over and reads the words, *I FORGIVE YOU.*

A wave roils over her. Diana shoves aside the stacked jumpers and sits on the bed. She stares at the three words. A simple enough statement but not words Will has ever said. Diana shakes out the sweater again, hoping to find the rest of the letterhead and an answer to the question, what does this mean? But there's nothing.

Unbidden, Will's angry face flashes in front of her and she flinches, the memory still vivid after twenty-six years. She presses her fingertips to her lips, cool against the heat. Twenty-six years is a long time. A life time.

There's something she has to see. In the living room, she finds the packing box marked 'Photo Wall' and rips it open. At Turpentine Street, she carefully cut out a square of bubble wrap to fit snugly over the glass of each frame before wrapping it in a double layer of butcher's paper and taping it as if each were a gift.

Again and again, she digs a hole through the paper, identifying photos from her days in the band, the family snaps and long-ago holidays until she finds what she's looking for. Diana tears off the wrapping and takes the frame over to the light slanting in across the terrace. It's their wedding day. Here they are, just married in the back garden of the house in Turpentine Street. She was twenty-five with flowers in her hair and bare feet, one hand resting on the top of Aiden's head. Both of them cradled in Will's embrace. Their kiss caught for posterity. Carefree. Happy. She loved Will and he loved her. Life was that simple. Both of them certain of their choices and buoyed by the knowledge that today marked the beginning of the rest of their lives. How naive.

She traces the corners of Will's open smile. Those blue eyes twinkling. Father. Husband. Lover. The happiest man alive. Diana pulls the fragment of paper from her pocket. She runs a finger over the creases. It's Will's handwriting, the words written in capital letters. Shouty.

She catches her breath and holds it to ease the pain beneath her diaphragm. The ache is a familiar companion of her years. Diana is walking a tightrope strung between two buildings, high above the city. She daren't look down at the people so far away — so tiny they look like sand fleas jumping from one side of the street to the other. The only way to safely cross the chasm is to keep her gaze locked firmly at a point on the horizon.

Ask anyone and they'll tell you how easygoing Will is. He's a charmer, that's for sure. The perfect personality for a man who built his career in sales, earning his stripes in the family business as his father had before him, until the number-one job was his. But Will at home isn't quite the same version as CEO Will Forsyth. The financial pages describe him as clever and incisive. No mention at all of his need to control all the variables, to the point that it can be stifling. And definitely no mention of his jealous streak.

A tear plops onto the glass. Diana wipes it away. His hair was much blonder then and he wore it a bit longer than he does now. He still owns the suit in that photo. Unbelievably, it still fits him. What a shame she can't say the same about her wedding dress. To this day, he likes nothing more than to come home from work and swap his suit for a worn pair of Dunlop Volleys and a daggy pair of shorts. His idea of relaxing is a glass of red within easy reach of the stove or a barbecue, creating some feast.

Thirty years next month. *He's not the man I married*, pops into her head. No, but nor is she the girl he married. They've both made mistakes. Terrible mistakes. No amount of wishing 'if only' will ever take them back to those carefree days of song and laughter and flowers in her hair. But they made it. Albeit, patched together but they are here.

I FORGIVE YOU. Her heart lurches and she gasps. Diana flattens her palm against her heart and feels it pounding in her chest. They agreed. The only way forward was to never talk about what had happened ever again.

Diana takes her phone off the charger and copies the address of the hotel into the search engine. Just as she thought. It no longer exists, or rather not as part of the same hotel chain. If Will still stays there, they'd have new fancy letterhead. So, how long ago was this written? She scrunches it tight in her fist.

Thirty years is a milestone. They are holding the Big Party to celebrate. The family are flying in from the four corners of the world. The tightrope wobbles beneath her feet. The past must stay where it belongs. Diana must keep her gaze pinned to the horizon. The shame and loss is simply too much to bear.

Chapter 2

Then

Over the years, the story of how they met has worn smooth with the telling. Will never missed an opportunity to launch into the tale about how he fell in love with Diana feet first.

Her cue was when the questioning glances turned her way. 'Every word is true,' she'd say, picking up the threads. 'We were on holidays in the Whitsundays. Separately,' she'd add, emphasising the significance of this fact to the storyline. 'I was sitting under the palm trees reading a book. Anything to escape the horrendous heat and humidity.'

'It was love at first sight,' Will would interrupt, hand dramatically draped over his heart. Not happy until the audience chuckled in appreciation. 'Well, perhaps lust,' he'd murmur for Diana's ears only.

Then he'd reel in the crowd. 'Didi's right, it was as hot as Hades. I'd been for a dip and was walking back up to my hut when I thought I'd detour via the bar for a coldy' – here, he'd hold up his beer to demonstrate – 'and I went A over T.'

Nods of appreciation from the blokes, a few chuckles. The odd jealous glance from the wives because all the girls agreed,

Will was quite a dish. He held the audience in the palm of his hand, glued to his every word.

Diana knew the next bit off by heart. The first thing Will thought as he face-planted in the sand was, 'Shit! My beer.' The dropped bottle frothed like a mini Vesuvius. Will looked up and searched for the object that had sent him sprawling. He assumed it must have been a tree root but there, in front of his nose, a set of toes wriggled free from the sand like hatching baby turtles. Once he'd earned a laugh with that line, he had set the scene. 'My gaze drifted up, over shapely brown calves, the curve of her hips and a generous bust all packaged up in a black one-piece. And looking down at me was the most delectable creature I'd ever laid eyes on.'

*

They locked eyes and a buzz of electricity slithered down Diana's spine. A pair of eyes the same tropical blue as the ocean stared up at her. The man had impossibly broad shoulders. He picked up one of her feet and cradled it in his palm. Caught between alarm and curiosity, Diana held her breath.

The man brought her foot to his lips and kissed her toes. Then he beamed at her and said, 'I forgive you.'

By the end of the day, Diana had quietly packed up her belongings and moved into Will's hut at the other end of the long narrow beach, abandoning her at-least-ten-years-too-old-for-her actor boyfriend. The aging Adonis had managed to look heartbroken when Diana broke the news, but only for as long as it took him to register the young lady playing beach volleyball topless.

Within the thatched walls of their beach hut, Diana and Will found heaven. They barely left its confines, the geckoes and moths the only witnesses to their hungry explorations and late-night conversations. Will changed his flights so they could return to the city together. And when they arrived, they caught a cab straight back to his apartment. Diana stayed the weekend, then Monday came around and Will had to go to work. She lay in his bed, drinking the coffee he'd made her as she watched him knot his tie, marvelling at how handsome he was. When he left, she snoozed in the warmth of the sheets that held his scent.

Alone, Diana made a second cup of coffee and drank it as she flicked through his collection of LPs. Lots of jazz peppered the recent releases. Performers who'd stood the test of time like Peggy Lee and Dave Brubeck versus those who few would remember in ten years' time. A little buzz when she found an album that she also owned, reading the vinyl as if it were a portent of their compatibility. The bookshelves proved more slender pickings but he had a collection of movies, a lot of them black and white. Diana picked up the video on top of the pile, *Citizen Kane*. She'd never seen it. Putting it back, she examined the framed photographs on the walls. Most people had prints of Manhattan skylines or rain-washed Parisian streets. Not Will. Given the quality of the camera she'd seen him use on holidays, these were his. Portraits in preference to landscapes. Interesting faces that told a story.

Diana showered and dressed and set out to explore Will's neighbourhood. Her growling tummy led her around the corner to a strip of shops filled with cafés and bars, a delicatessen, a second-hand bookstore and a tiny hole-in-the-wall florist. She bought a selection of musty second-hand paperbacks from the three for five dollars display out the front and a bunch of the cheapest but nicest flowers she could afford. On the way back to Will's flat, she pinched some asparagus fern and viburnum from someone's hedge and transformed the meagre bunch of flowers into a bouquet which she placed on the tiny square dining table jammed in the sunny corner nook.

'Nice flowers,' he said that night, flinging his jacket and tie over the arm of the couch where Diana lay reading. He plopped down to undo his laces and kick off his work shoes, then he took her by the hand and led her into the bedroom. They made love as if they hadn't seen each other in weeks.

'Let's go out to dinner,' Will said once they came up for air. 'I feel like we should celebrate.'

Diana straddled his hips and threaded her fingers through his. She leaned down to kiss him. 'Or we could stay in and have an encore performance.' Will needed little persuading.

Although, soon after, they were enjoying tapas at the bar on the corner — the only place open so late on a weeknight.

'Try this,' he said, holding up a morsel of their famous chargrilled octopus. Diana took it from his fingers with her mouth, licking the oil from her lips. She watched him over the rim of her wineglass. It might have been the flickering candlelight that turned Will's blue eyes almost black. Either way, it seemed they were thinking the same thing.

Will called for the bill the moment the plates were cleared. 'I don't know about you, but I'm ready for bed.' On the street, he took her hand in his, giving it a small squeeze, as if to say, *I've got you. It's okay.* Diana felt a warm rush like he was keeping her safe.

*

It was a Thursday night and Diana's first gig since they had returned from the Whitsundays a fortnight ago.

'What should I wear?' Will asked, exiting the bathroom dressed in nothing more than a towel.

Diana lowered her compact mirror and returned the mascara wand to its tube. 'Well, I suppose you could go as you are, but I won't be much help to you from up on stage if the girls in the audience decide to eat you alive.'

Will dropped the towel and rummaged in his drawers for jeans. He held them up for her to inspect and Diana did her best to focus on the pants and not the model. 'They'll do.' Sadly, he popped them straight on. On the upside, he wasn't wearing undies.

Diana went over to the hanging rack Will used as a wardrobe. She flicked through the limited range of casual shirts: pale blue, pale blue with stripes, an obligatory garish Hawaiian number. 'Will, where do you shop? How can a grown man not own a single black shirt?'

Will produced an orange tie-dyed t-shirt from another drawer. 'Is this okay?'

It had seen better days, but it was preferable to the alternatives. 'It's perfect.'

At the club, Diana refused to let him backstage. 'Darling, please, this is work. I need to concentrate and you'll make me nervous.' Seeing his disappointment, she added, 'After we've finished the first set, I promise I'll introduce you to the band.'

She made sure to give him an extra-long kiss, which wasn't easy when she was lugging two dress changes and a makeup bag, then fought her way through to the dressing rooms to get ready.

'Ten minutes, guys.'

Diana peeked through the stage curtains and scanned the auditorium. It was a pretty good crowd. Thursdays were pay day and great for business. She spotted Will holding up the bar, some redhead making eyes at him even though he kept glancing over her shoulder at the stage.

Back in the dressing room, Greg, although everyone called him Animal after his counterpart in The Muppets, was on the couch with his tongue down the throat of his new girlfriend, Linda. Repulsed, Diana turned away. Jonathan sat in the corner, brooding over a rum and Coke, a lit cigarette dangling from his lips. Forever believing in his own mythology that he was one gig away from breaking into the big time. Playing lead guitar in a 1960s cover band? Hardly likely.

Michael handed her the set list. He liked to keep the show fresh, swapping out songs every so often or changing the order they played them. Diana didn't mind. He was a brilliant bass player and since no one else volunteered, Michael was also the band's de facto manager. It was him who'd dreamed up the name, the look and the playlist. Without him, they'd still be in the garage. Without him, she wouldn't have this gig.

She glanced at the opening number, 'I Heard It Through the Grapevine'. 'Cool,' she said with a shrug. Great song and something easy to warm up her vocal cords.

She hung up her outfits and scrutinised her makeup in the mirror, adding more blush and touching up her lips. 'How do I look?' she asked, twirling first one way and then the other.

'Gorgeous,' Michael replied.

She slapped him playfully on the arm. 'You didn't even look.'

'No need. You always do.'

She harrumphed but would never admit she was secretly pleased. Even though Michael wasn't her type, he was a bit of a chick magnet. Tall, muscular, with a mop of hair cut so his fringe flopped over his sleepy bedroom eyes. It drove women wild– they were always running their fingers through his bloody hair. And he knew how to play to an audience. But it was Will's approval she was thinking of. This was the first time he would see her in the spotlight – a far cry from the girl who preferred drawstring pants and loose t-shirts, if she wore clothes at all.

Michael clapped his hands. 'Showtime, folks.'

Diana waited in the wings as the boys went on stage and picked up their instruments. Even though they'd done the sound check earlier, Jonno and Michael played a couple of random chords. Animal hit the bass beat, a tap on the cymbals. The houselights went down as the stage lights went up. Michael and Jonno played the opening bars of the 'Peter Gunn Theme', earning a catcall and a wolf-whistle from the depths of the hall. When they'd done showing off, Michael looked to the wings. Time for Diana to make her entrance.

She walked on stage like she was on the catwalk, long hair swinging and showing off her dress, which tonight was a kaleidoscope of 60s psychedelia with way too many sequins. She waved to the audience, took her place at the piano, and leaned into the microphone.

'Good evening, ladies and gentlemen, we are Diana and The Somethings. Hope you have a great night.'

'I Heard It Through the Grapevine', a la Marvin Gaye's version, led to 'Son of a Preacher Man'. 'The Happening' followed by 'Colour My World' then 'Do You Know the Way to San Jose?'. Between each number, Diana scanned the auditorium. A flash gave him away. Will and his camera. Next she caught him crouched at the foot of the stage, aiming up and shooting beneath the haze of lights. And when she sang the opening lines of 'I Say a Little Prayer', she sang it straight to him.

The set ended with 'Love Child', the dance floor full. Diana gave it her all. Sweat ran down her torso, her fringe flicked salty droplets in her eyes. She didn't care, she loved every minute of it. This was where she felt most alive. Giving the audience what they wanted, connecting with them. The music brought them pure joy. The music gave her freedom.

*

An Indian summer passed in a blur of rehearsals and performing. Will at work, Will coming home, shedding his corporate skin, putting on jazz records, opening a bottle of wine, cooking them something delicious. One night they swam by the light of the moon at the crescent of a harbour beach secreted away at the end of a narrow street. Giggling and telling each other to shush so the people in the flats above wouldn't be drawn to their windows where they would see them, as slick as seals, bobbing naked in the sea. Afterwards, they ran back through the empty streets dressed in nothing but their towels, breathless with adventure, high on a heady cocktail of youth and hormones.

They tumbled through the door of Will's apartment and fell onto the couch, laughing. Will moved over the top of her and settled into her familiar curves. She adjusted her hips to take his weight, their chests expanding and collapsing, their eyes shining like stars in the night sky. Diana felt the heat forming, her body responding to the smell and touch of his. A shiver of anticipation. The taste of salt on his lips. The perfect fit of him. She locked her arms around his neck and her legs around his waist and drew him closer. The bright moon bathed the room in its magical light, the sole witness when their backs arched in unison and they cried out into the night.

Will rolled onto his side and propped his head on his elbow. He traced a pattern over her glistening skin, pausing to kiss the inside of her wrist, the dip in her collarbone. She half-heartedly brushed him off. 'That tickles.'

He kissed her lips then pulled away and frowned. The shift in his mood dragged her up from drowsy post-coital smugness to alert. He traced her mouth with his finger. Diana lay still, waiting, watching his chest expand as he drew breath.

'I'm afraid I'll have to marry you.'

Afraid. Why would Will be afraid of anything? She replayed the sentence, the laziness evaporating. 'Why?'

He sat up. 'I can't bear the thought of us being apart. Of losing you.'

The moonlight behind him cast his face in shadow but his meaning was as plain as day. Love had made him afraid. Love, giddy and exciting, like walking a tightrope high above the crowd in a circus tent, held up by their desperation that you'll stay lightly balancing on the balls of your feet, the wire bouncing beneath your weight, but knowing that a part of them would be thrilled if you fell.

Will fell, to his knees, squeezed between the couch and the coffee table. He clasped her hand in his. 'I love you, Diana. I promise I will cherish you and keep you safe until my dying day. I promise I will always be kind and never hurt you.'

At the tender age of twenty-three, Diana was unused to such adoration but she did recognise something else wrapped up in Will's proposal. Heartbreak, loneliness, falling in love and then right back out again. Every single time she stepped on stage, she ran the gamut of emotions. Poor Will was experiencing them for the very first time.

'Say yes, Didi. Please say yes.'

Diana scrambled to sit upright. She took Will's face in her hands, smoothing her thumbs over his stubbled cheeks. He was five years older than her. They'd only known each other a couple of months, yet somehow his proposal seemed daring, intoxicating. Except for Will, no one had ever treated her like she was the most amazing person he'd ever met. When she was with him, anything and everything felt completely possible. He was every song she'd ever sung. How could she refuse?

'Yes,' she cried, flinging her arms around his neck. 'Yes, yes, and yes again.' Excitement pulsed through her veins, her heart in tempo with his. When they kissed, Diana felt her future melt into his, and it astounded her how brilliant and right this feeling was.

In the blushing pink morning light, they drove over to Diana's share house in a less nice suburb on the other side of the city. Bless Will that he said nothing when they entered the shambles she called her room. He simply stood there holding open the garbage bags as she filled them with her possessions. When they were done, they lugged bag after bag to Will's old Holden. Diana returned and put her practice keyboard in its case and folded up the stand. She packed the sheet music in a folder and carried both keyboard and music to the car.

'One last thing,' she told Will. She dashed into the kitchen and wrote a farewell note to her flatmates. She knew she should feel bad for abandoning them but the truth was, there were a string of students who'd jump at the chance of taking her room and she'd outlasted countless more. She secured the note under the ant-ridden sugar bowl on the kitchen bench, placed a month's rent and her house key on top, then walked down the hall, past coats and hats and bicycles, and closed the heavy front door behind her. Just for a flash, Diana hesitated on the top step. She had no key and could not return even if she wanted to. But there was Will, lounging against the bonnet of his old Holden in his faded jeans, swinging his car keys around his finger.

'You ready?' he called.

Diana beamed at him and walked towards her future.

*

Autumn turned to winter. Diana lounged on the bed, twirling the one-carat solitaire ring that had once belonged to Will's grandmother around and around her finger, as she watched him dress for work. Singlet, boxers, socks, crisp business shirt, light wool suit pants, leather brogues. Good enough to eat.

'Come and watch me play tonight,' she said as he threaded cufflinks through his shirt sleeves. 'It'll be fun.'

Will met her eye in the mirror. 'I can't. I have a board meeting first thing and I have to present the quarterly sales figures. I'll need a clear head.'

She pouted but hid it in a flurry of slipping on her silk kimono and tying the sash. 'I promise we'll be home by eleven-ish.'

'You're never home that early.'

'That's because I have to get a lift home with Jonno or Michael and they always want a beer to wind down after a gig. If you come, we can leave straight after the van's packed.'

Diana squeezed past Will to get to the bathroom. She ran her fingers through her hair and wondered whether she'd ever pluck up the courage to cut it to shoulder-length. It took hours for her hair to dry naturally and blow-drying it made her arms ache. But along with the baby-doll dresses that sparkled and shimmered, kohl and false lashes and massive hoop earrings, hair to her waist were all part of the look. It took ages for her to get ready, unlike the boys, whose only worry was which colour shirt to wear with their low-slung pants.

She splashed cold water on her face and patted it dry, watching the reflection of Will tying his shoelaces. 'You know, you haven't seen me play in months.'

'Yes, I have. Twice. Once at The Lowdown and once at that place next to the brothel at the Cross.'

'Starlight City.'

'Yeah, there.' He straightened and slapped his palms against his knees. 'I've got to be up at the crack of dawn, Didi. I'm not a night owl like you.'

Yet she always made sure she got up when he did, even though she performed at least three nights a week. To be fair, she had dropped back to part-time on her music degree this semester. Between Will and playing, she was having too much fun to study. There was plenty of time for that stuff later, after she and Will were married.

Diana didn't want to fight with him, but just occasionally couldn't he take life a little less seriously? She knelt at his feet and placed her palms on top of his hands, forcing him to look at her. 'Pretty please, Will. Don't be such a fuddy-duddy.'

'Didi, it's a really important meeting. I need to be on my game.'

She pulled on the sash and the kimono fell open. She traced her fingers up the inside of Will's thigh. 'I'll make it worth your while.'

'Didi,' he croaked.

'And I promise we'll be home by eleven.'

*

At intermission, Will stood framed in the dressing-room door. Diana ran to him.

'How was it?'

'You were fantastic. I took some great shots. You should have seen you on "River Deep, Mountain High". Unbelievable.' He grinned at her, turning to Jonathan for confirmation. 'Wasn't she amazing?'

Jonathan shrugged and lit another cigarette.

'Amazing,' Michael echoed as he pulled his sweaty shirt off over his head and used it to towel himself dry.

'I'd better get changed too,' Diana said, shooting Will a look of apology, but he was staring past her at Michael. She sensed the shift in him. Knew it was because Michael stood there, shirtless, wearing languid insouciance like a cloak. She'd seen Michael half-naked dozens of times but Will hadn't, or rather, he had never seen her in the same room as Michael taking his kit off. And it seemed like Will didn't like it one bit. Diana saw what Will saw. Her alone in a room full of men. She risked a sideways glance at Jonathan. He'd noticed too, except he seemed to be enjoying Will's flash of jealousy.

Diana made a point of grabbing her outfit and disappearing into the bathroom. Imagine how Will would react if he knew she often changed in front of the guys. It meant nothing, she wore bikinis more revealing than her underwear. By the time she'd changed and freshened her makeup, Will had disappeared. Anger sparked but there was no time to dwell on it. Back on stage, they opened the second set with 'Signed, Sealed, Delivered'. Diana stood at the mic next to Michael, playing the tambourine. In between songs, she tried and failed to find Will. She searched for him as they packed the van, even asking Animal to check the men's toilets. Not a sign of him.

Without a word, Jonno hopped in the back with the gear. Michael opened the passenger door for her. As she climbed in, he squeezed her shoulder and she returned a weak smile. Michael got in the driver's side and slipped the new Elvis Costello album into the tape deck. He offered her a cigarette and she took it, even though she didn't really smoke. If she sang like Aretha Franklin or Ella Fitzgerald then maybe, but on the whole, she preferred to keep the temple pure.

It was around a quarter to twelve by the time Michael dropped her outside Will's. Diana waited until the van had disappeared before heading upstairs. No bar of light under the door to greet her. She slumped a little, then searched her handbag for the silver key chain Will had had inscribed with her name. Opening the door, she slipped inside, dumped her stuff and prepared to confront Will about his poor behaviour.

Will had his back turned to her and his pillow mashed into a lump beneath his head. Diana studied the rhythm of his broad shoulders, heaving in and out. He was feigning sleep, she was sure of it. Hurt and anger bubbled to the surface.

'Why did you leave?'

No response but he wasn't fooling her. In two steps, Diana was by the bed. She shook him by the shoulder, firm enough to mean business. 'Will, stop pretending you're asleep.'

In a flash, he rolled over. Diana stumbled backwards.

His eyes glittered in the half-light. 'No one likes to feel like the third wheel, Diana.'

'What?'

Will was the one who'd behaved badly. He left without even saying goodbye. 'I can't believe you would disappear all because Michael took his shirt off, *in the dressing room*! Where else was he supposed to change?' She had every right to be hurt. It's not like she'd been staring at Michael. It's not like he was doing it deliberately. But Will didn't see it like that. And she didn't need to be an anthropologist to recognise chest-beating when she saw it. So the question was, how much ground was she prepared to concede to keep the peace?

'I think you're overreacting,' she continued.

'Bullshit. Blind Freddy can see he fancies you.'

'Michael?'

'Yes, Michael.' Will shoved the pillow behind his head and propped himself upright.

Confusion made her pause. Diana knew what effect Michael had on women but she also knew it was all an act. He loved playing the rock star but away from the stage he was just a big softie. Yeah, he could take his pick of women but he always seemed to choose the ones who ate him alive for breakfast. As far as Diana was concerned, it served him right.

That Will could misjudge her so badly was just plain crazy. 'You're jealous of Michael?'

'He's got the hots for you.'

Diana couldn't help herself — she laughed, but it died in her throat when she saw the genuine hurt lash across Will's features. She perched on the side of the bed. 'I'm sorry. I'm sorry,' she said, and tried to grab his hand but Will was having none of it. He tucked both hands under his armpits like a small boy in trouble with his mother.

Poor Will. Diana had to save him. 'There's nothing for you to worry about where Michael is concerned. We're mates who play in a band together. I'm not even his type,' she added, thinking of the skinny Minnies that flocked to Michael wherever they played. Age never seemed to trouble him, but they all had that Mia Farrow elfin look. Michael wouldn't look twice at a girl like Diana.

'Are you planning to keep this up once we're married?'

Her momentary pity evaporated. 'I beg your pardon?'

'Maybe you should focus on finishing your degree instead, so you've got something for the future. You can't seriously be intending to play in a band forever.'

Diana's hand flew to her cheek as if Will had actually slapped her. 'Are you for real? You sound like my father.'

He squirmed. Good. He should feel uncomfortable. Who did he think he was, telling her what to do with her life? Maybe she didn't know Will as well as she thought she did. Their relationship was doomed if he thought he could dictate what she did and who with, and …

With a lurch, Will scrambled from the bed and disappeared into the bathroom, closing the door with a thud. There was the sound of the tap running and splashing water then the door opened and he stood silhouetted in the doorway.

'I'm sorry, that was completely out of line. I don't know what got into me.'

Diana leapt from the bed. 'No, I'm the one who should be sorry. I should never have asked you to come and watch me play. Look at the time. You'll be exhausted for your meeting ...'

Will held his hand up, telling her to stop. 'I've never been the jealous type.' He sounded shocked at this revelation. Watching his face was like fanning the pages of a book. Embarrassment on one page, hurt on the next. Vulnerability rivalling the urge to maintain control. Surprise that anyone, she, could reveal a side of him he hadn't known existed.

She had the overwhelming urge to comfort him, to take away his pain. All of a sudden, being on the moral high ground didn't feel quite so lofty or righteous. Here she was, angry at poor Will for thinking she was the kind of person who would play with his feelings. When deep down, he was worried that he loved her more than she loved him. She opened her arms and he fell into her embrace.

'I'm an idiot, I'm sorry,' he mumbled in her shoulder.

Will was not the only one acting stupidly. She had no right to be indignant at Will's behaviour. If she was honest with herself, a part of her relished the power of her attraction. And when it was on stage or making love to the one you adored, that was fine. But in real life, only a fool took credit for something that was an accident of birth. As her grandmother always said, good looks never made up for a lack of character. She had been careless with his feelings.

Diana took his face in her hands and looked him square in the eye. 'There's just you, Will. No one but you. Remember that.'

Chapter 3

Now

Falling in love was so long ago it sometimes feels as if it happened to someone else. Their first fight, if you could even call it a fight, was child's play. They got much better at it as the marriage unfolded.

Diana returns the note to the sweater, then the sweater to the drawer, and slams it shut. Marriages are like topography maps where the mountains are represented by flat ripples on the page. Unless you know how to read one, there's no real sense of the heights one has to ascend, nor the depths to which one can plummet. The scars, the pain, the sheer slog of it. Or the joys of reaching the pinnacle, seeing all of creation stretching out before you. That is what shapes any suffering into meaning.

She flattens the box and adds it to the pile growing in the spare room, then gravitates to the piano. She lifts the lid and runs her fingers over the keys. Peggy is singing, 'Is That All There Is?', which about sums up how Diana feels right now. She lightly plays the chords, just an echo beneath that stunning voice.

The song ends. Her ambition to clear the boxes from Will's side of the bed has dwindled. She goes to the kitchen, opens the fridge and takes stock. A container of marinated olives, a rind of blue stilton that Will is saving for some questionable future culinary delight. She settles on the other half of yesterday's baguette, the last of the bag of rocket and a slightly mushy tomato. The olives lift it from the mundane.

Mistakes have been made — by both of them. But the important thing to remember is that they got their relationship back on its feet. Diana scoffs. Listen to her, talking about 'the relationship' as if it were a separate entity. Me, Will and the relationship. It sounds like the title of a quirky rom-com for the older set. Something Nora Ephron might have written.

From this distance, it's easy to package up those dark dreadful days into a neat storyline. *Oh, we patched things up.* Nice and breezy as if they hadn't limped along for years, barely able to put one foot in front of the other. As if the guilt didn't just hang around forever.

Diana steps out onto the terrace and looks down at the mothers hovering around the swing set and the slippery dip — a view on the past when it was her and her friends. Chatting to Ruth and Fi, wiping noses, soothing scrapes, pooling plastic containers of snacks for morning tea.

On the final day at Turpentine Street, Diana stood on the pavement and watched the removal truck putter around the corner, filled with their earthly possessions. Farewelling Turpentine Street — with all its memories, the good and the bad — was like saying goodbye to an old dear friend. But it was more than that. It was severing ties to the house where they'd raised their family, where the doorjamb next to the spare loo bore indelible marks chronicling heights and dates in Will's handwriting. The spot under the camellia where first Lucy then Poppy were buried with full honours, followed by an afternoon tea of honey roll from the bakery and glasses of lemonade. Every time anyone commented on the magnificent profusion of blooms, she offered a little prayer of thanks to their long-departed cats.

Of course they weren't all fond memories but Diana had worked hard to tip the balance in their favour. The apartment on The Green will never be Turpentine Street. Even if she and Will live another thirty years, how can it possibly overflow with memories? No place to bury a beloved pet. With the children living overseas, there's little prospect of grandchildren stopping by. No, to her mind, moving to this apartment will forever be a formal declaration that she and Will are past their best-by date, just like that rind of blue stilton in the fridge.

Despite the unflattering connection, thinking of that lumpy old piece of cheese fills Diana with a sudden yearning for the sound of Will's voice. She picks up the cordless phone and hits speed dial. Fi thinks having a landline marks them as dinosaurs. 'And I ask you, who owns an answering machine in this day and age?' she's wont to observe with monotonous regularity.

Diana contemplates the proclaimed relic. Countless conversations have been recorded and erased over the years as she and Will spun in and out of each other's orbit, crossing continents and time zones. Wherever he was in the universe, Will remained tethered to her by this machine.

No answer. She hangs up, clasping her throat. It's like she's swallowed a pill the wrong way. That damned note is stuck there, haunting her every breath.

Diana regards the pictures she'd abandoned earlier on the dining table. Memories that tug at her. The sooner she's arranged the photos on the walls, the sooner the apartment will feel like a home. She picks one at random and unwraps it. It's of the children, in the paddling pool in the backyard. Persephone's wearing the yellow floaties she had insisted on, even though the water barely reaches the knub of her ankle.

A giant beach ball obscures all of Aiden except his skinny brown legs, while Diana kneels on her haunches, in oversized sunglasses and an enormous floppy hat. They're all laughing at Will, the photographer.

Nostalgia is making her teary. She props the photo against the wall and decides to ring Fi.

Unusually, she answers immediately. 'Fiona Sterling speaking.'

'It's only me.'

'Hello, only me,' Fi answers. 'I'm just at the club. I'm playing Bea Casters at eleven fifteen. Should be a doddle. Her backhand is pathetic.'

'Oh sorry, I won't keep you. I'm feeling a bit miserable and needed to hear a friendly voice.'

'Is it Will?'

'No, no,' Diana lies. 'I'm unpacking boxes and it's made me feel a bit blue, that's all. Moving into the apartment feels like such an admission that the children have gone. Forever. I think I'm feeling, dare I say, a bit … I don't know … old.'

Fi swears. 'Oh no you don't, you bitch. I was here first.'

'Pardon?'

'Not you, Diana. That first-class cow who runs the boutique opposite Samantha's salon tried to nab my parking spot.'

Diana listens as Fi gets out of the car and retrieves her tennis gear from the boot. The *cheep! cheep!* of the car locking signals Fi's return to the conversation.

'Right. I'm back with you. What were you saying?'

Diana quashes her resentment that she's competing for Fi's attention. It's par for the course, really. And the one positive is that the urge to vent has been replaced by the desire to finish the call as quickly as possible. 'I was saying, I am officially past my best-by date.'

Fi leaps in to rally her spirits. 'Darling, I can't believe what I'm hearing. House to yourselves? You and Will must be going at it like rabbits. Bea! Hello! Yes, it's marvellous we're up against each other today. Won't that be fun? Oh, you've put my name down for the doubles as well? Fantastic.'

Fi lowers her voice. 'Ugh. Kill me now. I'll have to take the net so I can cut Bea off with my volley. Let me dump my stuff and find somewhere quiet so we can talk properly.'

More rustling and helloing ensue before Fi graces Diana with her full attention. 'Between you and me, the best thing that happened to our marriage was the twins leaving home. Honestly, Richard is like a new man. Hard to believe, I know!' Fi continues the conversation as if Diana is contributing. 'I swear, I'm having some of the best sex I've ever had. As soon as those metaphorical apron strings were snipped, it's been on for young and old.'

This is an image of Fi and Richard that Diana can do without. It's astounding to think that Richard of all people has rediscovered his youthful vigour. Particularly galling given Diana and Will are not going at it like rabbits or any other feral pest for that matter. And the reasons why are not up for public discussion, even with Fi or Ruth.

'Coming!' Fi shouts to some distant member of The Village Ladies Tennis Auxiliary. 'Sorry, Didi, I'm going to have to love you and leave you. I'm due on the warm-up court. Wish me luck. If the gods are with me, I'll be rid of Bea Casters in two sets and can get to the smorgasbord before Fenella Clarke and her cronies devour the lot.'

Diana returns the phone to its cradle. She goes downstairs and checks their letterbox and finds nothing more exciting than the latest newsletter from the mob around the corner: Sea Breeze Retirement Village — Oceans of Care and the Wind in Your Sails. A neighbour passes, issuing a cheery 'good morning' and Diana's reply is equally upbeat. She watches the older woman march onwards in her culottes, sneakers and a zip-up polar fleece.

Diana scans the newsletter on her way upstairs. An article catches her attention. 'Are You Having a Late-Life Crisis?' Her thoughts drift back to Fi and Richard. Maybe selling off his magazine interests has given Richard a new lease on life.

The article goes on to state that one in three people over sixty experience a late-life crisis. Retirement, illness — it can all affect a man's libido. Or in Richard's case, fuel some deep-seated drive to make hay while the sun shines.

Diana closes the front door behind her. What if Will's lack of interest in the bedroom isn't because of a physical failing though? Thirty years makes for a long relationship. Plenty of couples split up once the kids are gone. Like that famous breakfast montage from *Citizen Kane* that shows nine years of marriage in two minutes. From cosy kisses and conversation over toast to cold war, glaring at each other across the length of the battlefield as they read rival newspapers.

Maybe instead of upgrading the sensible car and the aging spouse for better models, they're staying together out of habit. Because moving from Turpentine Street to an apartment on The Green is so much easier than arguing over who gets the fridge or the Margaret Olley.

They've already split up once. Back then, two months felt like an eternity, but it was a mere blink of an eye counted in marriage years. A tearful reunion ensued, vows made to never go there again, thick and thin, et cetera. Except there is now a note. Or rather, a fragment of one. *I forgive you.* What does it mean? The letterhead is ancient, so it could be a note from past Will. But if he wrote it recently, after twenty-six years, isn't it a little late for forgiveness?

After lunch, Diana tries Will's number again with the same result. Annoyed, she pours herself a glass of rosé and tells herself its medicinal therefore doesn't count. Still restless, she calculates the time difference between here and Edinburgh and rings Persephone, but the call goes through to voicemail. As she leaves a message, she remembers that Persephone and Emile are visiting his parents in the South of France for the long weekend. No doubt this entails enjoying vast quantities of Raphael's latest vintage and gorging themselves on Camille's legendary cooking. This is not just Persephone's enthusiastic opinion — Camille is an internet sensation.

Diana pulls up the YouTube app on her phone and loads the latest episode of *Real Women Can Cook*. She's addicted to it — fascinated and repelled in equal measure. There is Camille, with her trademark crisp white shirt under a bibbed butcher's apron. She wears her grey hair cut super short and spiky. A thick silver chain adorns her bare throat. The perfect blend of chic, like the French President of the European Central Bank, Christine Lagarde, meets Martha Stewart, without the criminal record. 'Bonjour, *mes amis!*' Camille beams at the camera. 'Welcome to my show. This week, we're all about courgettes. Let's cook!' And boy, can the woman cook.

Diana swipes the app shut. Her own cooking is the stuff of family legend too, but for all the wrong reasons. Will doesn't know that she secretly watches Camille's show. She's not stalking her acquired relative, rather it's a benign form of self-torture. He, on the other hand, shows no such consideration. Diana's often caught Will at it. A glass of red, the iPad propped up on the kitchen bench as he preps dinner, Camille blathering on about aubergines or filet mignon. If he catches her looking over his shoulder, he says, 'Don't persecute yourself, sweetheart.' Closely followed by, 'Oh that recipe looks good. I might try that.'

Diana considers calling Aiden but what would she say? As much as she adores him, having intimate conversations is not something they do. They talk about mutual interests, like music and Lucas. He sends her short videos of his son's milestones and weekend snaps of Anna pushing Lucas on the swings at the park or patting lambs at the baby animal farm. These days, their relationship is founded on regular Sunday catch-ups on Zoom and, more recently, emails about the party plans. He'd never understand a random phone call simply because she craves the comfort of hearing a familiar voice. Because she misses the squabbling, the laughter, the constant noise of a house filled with people. And now it's just her. And Will ... when he's here.

Wine in hand, Diana drifts back to the living room and considers the blank walls. The photo wall in Turpentine Street used to stretch the length of the narrow corridor between the laundry and the kitchen. None of these walls are quite long enough. She'll either have to cull the collection or spread it across two walls. She performs a slow pirouette. The baby grand is nestled in a shallow alcove to take advantage of the natural light from the terrace. It's an obvious spot to display some of the photos from her days with The Somethings. There are also some great photos of Aiden performing. Her favourite is one of him doing a tenor sax solo with the school band, and there's another fabulous one of him in the school production of *Jesus Christ Superstar*. He made a terrific Judas.

Inspired, Diana starts tearing butcher's paper off frames and sorting the photos into vanity pics versus family pics. She pauses at a lovely one of her grandmother, Clara, in a cloche hat and a sequinned knee-length frock pretending to play her trombone, next to a girl on piano and another with a bob-cut balancing a double bass. The Swing Sisters. Genetically speaking, Clara gifted her aquiline nose to Lydia and her musical talents to Diana. She places the frame next to a picture of Aiden.

It's the next photo she's been looking for. Backlit, sitting at the piano, Diana is in full flight, skin so slick with sweat it shines. Diamonds of light sparkle from her sequinned dress and her hair is so long it falls below the line of the stool. The muscles in her neck are taut, shadows against the light. Her hands thunder across the chords, her eyes closed in rapture, as she sings about deep rivers and high mountains. It was one of Will's best shots.

These days, her singing is limited to when she's teaching – the school choir three mornings a week, private students after school – and only ever to demonstrate technique. Except for the odd times she cuts loose around the lounge room, her performing days are well behind her. She lays the frame alongside The Swing Sisters. Poor Nanna ended up with terrible arthritis in her hands. Diana can just remember her still playing when she was very little. By the time she was a musician herself, her nanna could no longer play. It never seemed to trouble her though. Clara was always more than happy to keep the beat, tapping out the rhythm with her foot as Persephone or Aiden practised their scales.

The afternoon shadows are lengthening. Night comes early at this time of year. Diana walks around the apartment switching on the lamps to chase away the shadows. She hates the dark. When they were little, Lydia used to hold her hand and walk her to the loo if she needed to go in the middle of the night. Diana pours herself a second glass of rosé and takes it out to the terrace. The waves lap the shore — the quick inhale of the suck followed by the slow exhale of the surge. Nature's music.

She's glad now that she didn't get hold of Persephone. How could she explain why the note has upset her so much? The children are still too young to comprehend how marriages traverse such complex and treacherous landscapes. They are at the beginning of this journey, that even the shock of a first-born child — in Aiden and Anna's case — can't take the shine off. They still think they're clever and untouchable. Is it her fault for overcompensating for Will's constant absences? Should she have tried to make their young lives a little rougher around the edges? But Will would never have accepted that. Then after the split, when they got back together, they did everything in their power to make the children happy, or rather, to prevent them from ever being unhappy. It's not the same thing.

Diana has a sudden urge to talk to her mother, the only member of her immediate family within reach. She rings Audrey and arranges to come down for the weekend. A change of scene will be a welcome distraction. Who knows? Her mother might change the habit of a lifetime and share some useful advice. Wouldn't that be a turn-up for the books?

Chapter 4

Then

Diana sat across from the doctor, stunned by her diagnosis. 'Pregnant?'

Doctor Lavinsky was easily in her forties, with a sort of dishevelled elegance that Diana found reassuringly motherly. The doctor's expression was transparently cautious. 'You're only twenty-three, are you sure you want this?'

Diana glanced at the photo on the doctor's desk. Three girls, wearing school uniforms and Panama hats, lined up against a brick wall. She can remember doing the exact same thing at the beginning of each school year. Maybe Doctor Lavinsky was warning her about lost opportunities, but the doctor was wrong — on every count.

'Absolutely sure,' Diana said, a smile bursting forth.

Doctor Lavinsky used a cardboard wheel to calculate Diana's due date. She was nine weeks, which meant her baby was due in summer. Somehow, this felt appropriate and right.

'By my estimate, you're due around February fourteen, but Doctor Cash will confirm that,' Doctor Lavinsky said as she wrote the referral to the obstetrician. She passed it to Diana. 'What do you think the father will say?'

'He'll be over the moon.'

Diana filed the referral in the zip-up section of her handbag and walked to the bus stop. She sat on the bench and rested her palm against her belly. How perfect that this baby, conceived in love, should be born on Valentine's Day. It was a good omen.

By the time the bus let her off at the stop at the end of their street, she was convinced of this. She let herself into the apartment, went straight to the bathroom and stripped down to her underwear. She closed the bathroom door to examine herself in the full-length mirror, first from one angle, then another. She tried to imagine the baby growing inside her. Doctor Lavinsky had said that, right now, it was the size of a medium green olive and it was developing ears. 'But it won't be able to hear you until around twenty-four weeks.' The doctor had smiled. 'It still knows you're there though. It will feel you talk to it.'

As an experiment, Diana sang the opening lines of 'Close To Me' and imagined her baby's delight. She couldn't wait to tell Will. She dressed quickly and returned to the lounge, picked up the phone and punched in Will's number, impatient for it to ring.

'Good morning, Forsyth Medical Equipment, Will Forsyth's office. This is Kara.'

Diana replaced the handset. On reflection, perhaps it was best to tell him in person when she was sure to have his full attention. Except, he wouldn't be home for hours. She considered how to pass the time. Rehearsal was tomorrow, and she was on a study break. Diana roamed the room, too excited to sit at her keyboard. She'd put on some music instead.

Then inspiration struck. Good news deserved a celebration. Will always cooked for her — this time it would be her treat. And the perfect way to while away a lazy afternoon.

Galvanised, Diana surveyed Will's selection of cookery books and chose a slender volume with a colourful hand-drawn cover. *The Top One Hundred Pasta Sauces*. The author, Diane Seed, had helpfully organised the recipes by key ingredient. Simple. Bolognese. Everybody likes Bolognese. This could be fun.

*

Three hours later, Diana stood in the middle of the kitchen, wooden spoon in one hand, a scorched tea towel in the other, her heart beating a panicked rhythm in her chest. Across the bench were scattered empty tins of tomatoes, carrot and celery tops, the gold foil stock wrappers and the bloodied Styrofoam container the meat had come in. Soon, Will would park the car and walk up the street. As he approached the apartment block, he would smell smoke. Not the cosy woodfire kind, but the something-is-burning-that-shouldn't-be kind. She had opened every window but the charred smell stubbornly lingered.

It was a disaster. The kitchen looked like Diana had attempted to murder someone. A blood pattern of passata dripped from the splashback. Melted into the stovetop was the remains of the plastic spaghetti spoon, and next to it, the aluminium saucepan that was once Will's grandmother's where congealed pasta bobbed in an oily slick of tepid water. His cherished Le Creuset casserole dish was the source of the smoke. Diana had decided to have a shower while the sauce simmered. She thought she had turned the heat down low, but clearly not. If only she hadn't decided to shave her legs while she was at it. By the time she emerged from the bathroom, the Bolognese had developed a thick black crust and a smoke haze filled the apartment.

There was nothing else for it. Diana grabbed her wallet and fled to the local Indian restaurant. By the time she was on the return journey, trudging up the hill, bearing a shopping bag in each hand, it had begun to rain. She had not thought to bring an umbrella but then again, she didn't have a spare hand to hold one. To add to her misery, she was soaked to the skin. The only thing propelling her up this blasted hill was the hope that she might arrive home before Will saw the state of the kitchen.

But as she rounded the corner into Wickham Street, her aching shoulders slumped. Under the streetlight was Will's car. She glanced up at the flat. Through the wide-open windows floated the sounds of Dave Brubeck taking five. How apt. It was time for her to face the music.

At the front door, Diana put the bags on the mat and flexed her aching fingers. She was shivering so hard, she could barely get the key in the lock. She pushed open the door, just far enough so she could work out what mood Will was in and thus the extent to which she needed to grovel. He stood at the kitchen sink, a tea towel draped over one shoulder. To his left was a glass of red, and to his right, a mountain of washed dishes.

Diana shuffled the bags inside and used her foot to close the door. The wind caught it and it slammed shut. Will spun around.

'Where have you been? I was so worried about you,' he said, drying his hands and flinging the tea towel onto the now immaculate bench.

Holding onto her last skerrick of dignity, Diana passed him the shopping bags. 'Dinner.'

'Look at you! You're freezing.' Will grabbed the bags and put them on the kitchen floor then rushed to the linen press to fetch a fresh towel. He wrapped it around Diana, rubbing her like a wet puppy. His kindness made her start to cry.

Will pulled her to his chest and squeezed her tight. 'Oh darling, whatever's wrong, it's not worth crying over.'

'I wanted to cook you something special,' she sobbed, wiping her face on his shirt. 'To celebrate.'

'O-kay?' He relaxed his grip and Diana leaned into his embrace.

'And I've ruined your best pot.' She sobbed a little harder. What was wrong with her? Was it the hormones?

'Don't worry about it. I've put dishwasher powder in it. It'll be fine after a good soak.'

Diana sniffed and pulled away. 'Really?'

'Sweetheart, I've lost track of the number of times I've got distracted or left the heat on too high.'

She knew he was lying but she rewarded him with a small smile. How easily he made her happy.

He kissed her forehead and gently drew away. 'Go jump in the shower and put some warm clothes on. I'll go through these,' he said, indicating the shopping bags, 'and by the time you're done, dinner will be ready. Then you can tell me what we're celebrating.'

Diana returned to candlelight and Sade.

Seeing her, Will pulled a bottle of champagne from the freezer and poured them each a glass, using the good Wedgwood crystal he got for his twenty-first. He raised his glass in a toast. 'To us.'

'To us.' Diana took the smallest of sips, hoping it wouldn't damage the baby.

'Mm, nice drop,' Will said. He put down the glass to open the oven. 'We have butter chicken, samosas and Rogan josh for dinner, madam. Followed by mango sorbet, I believe.' He pulled warm plates from another shelf of the oven and smiled at her. 'A little of each?'

Diana was not hungry. Possibly nerves. After the fiasco in the kitchen, this morning's confidence had ebbed away.

What if Will thought it was too soon? Maybe he wanted to be married first. The flat was tiny. He was still working his way up the ladder and she wasn't within cooee of any ladder.

Will put a plate in front of her. 'Since you didn't answer me, I've given you a little of everything. I hope that's okay?' He sat opposite. 'Two four six eight, dig in, don't wait.'

Diana thanked him and picked up her knife and fork. She put them down again. 'I went to the doctor's today.'

'Why, what's wrong?'

This was more awkward than she'd imagined. She might be overjoyed but Will might be — what? The thought hit her with a jolt. *I can't not have this baby.* Diana slid her hand across her belly. 'I'm pregnant.'

Will's mouth opened but no words came out. A cool prickle rose up the back of her neck.

He closed his mouth and swallowed. 'How?'

Diana snorted. 'Seriously?'

He blushed. 'I meant, how many weeks?'

'Nine.'

'Nine. Wow.'

She pulled a face. 'That's it? "Wow"?'

Will picked up his glass of champagne. Put it down again. He looked rather pleased with himself, as if he'd performed the Christmas miracle. 'Yeah. Wow. Like wow, how amazing. Like, I can't believe it. Tell me everything.'

So she did, finishing with, 'That's about the sum of it.'

Will leaned back in his chair. 'February, hey? Do we know what we're having?'

Diana shook her head. 'We can ask at the ultrasound.'

'Or we could just wait to be surprised. What d'you reckon?'

A feeling of relief washed over her. Diana got up and went around the table. She sat on Will's lap and threaded her arms around his neck. 'I reckon we should go with the flow. I don't care what we have, as long as it has all its fingers and toes.'

He drew her closer. 'You're right. And, before you know it, it'll have brothers and sisters and we can make our own little Partridge Family.'

Diana threw back her head and laughed. 'Can you imagine?'

Will's lips were at her throat. 'And we'll have to practise lots and lots.'

*

The following week, Diana met her mother and Lydia at their favourite coffee shop around the corner from their family home. To celebrate the joys of a new addition to the family, Lydia gave Diana *The Complete Book of Pregnancy and Childbirth* by Sheila Kitzinger.

'As I'm training as a midwife, you can be my guinea pig,' Lydia declared, hoeing into her vanilla slice.

Diana flicked it open at random and lingered over the timeline of the developing foetus at the bottom of the page.

'I'm too young to be a grandmother,' Audrey fretted, toying with the edges of a slice of carrot cake.

Diana took a bite of her strawberry shortcake.

'I don't think you should be eating cake, full stop,' added Audrey, tapping Diana's wrist with her fork. 'Don't believe that nonsense about eating for two.'

'I hate to admit that Mother Bear is right but it is very easy to pile on the pounds when you're expecting. You'll have to breastfeed if you want any hope of regaining your figure.'

Diana wanted to say that she already felt like her figure was well and truly lost. When all hope is gone, why bother? 'The list of things I can't eat is ridiculous. The only thing raw in this is the strawberry. Surely that won't kill me?' Diana defiantly forked a giant mouthful of strawberry custardy spongey delight into her mouth.

'Don't listen to your sister. She's full of these new-fangled ideas on motherhood.' Audrey eyed the Kitzinger bible with contempt. 'When I had you two, it was evaporated milk in a bottle and look how well you turned out.'

'We're lucky we're alive. Remember,' Lydia said, adopting a perky smile, 'babies do best when it's breast.'

'Did you make that up?'

'Don't be stupid. It's from the pamphlet we give to expectant mothers.'

Diana regarded her elder sister with affection. Lydia had always looked after Diana's best interests. Yes, she was a first-class bossy boots, but her heart was in the right place.

Audrey, however, was not one to admit defeat. 'All well and good, but breastfeeding ties you down. At some point, Diana has to finish her degree. And let me tell you from experience, it's no fun lugging a baby everywhere. They have their own timetable, you know.'

'I thought you were a firm believer in the four-hour feed, Mum?' Lydia said.

Diana flicked to the chapter on breastfeeding. 'It says here ...' she began but Audrey cut her off.

'I know your sister thinks she's God's gift now she's a trainee midwife, but you might pay more heed to those of us who have practical childbirth experience rather than read about it in a book.' Audrey fixed a hard stare on her eldest daughter.

Lydia hooted with laughter. 'I don't think Didi needs advice from a woman who gave birth with her feet in stirrups surrounded by a bunch of med students.' Lydia paused long enough to demolish the rest of her vanilla slice, dabbing her finger in the flakes of pastry and icing sugar. 'If you book into my hospital,' she said as if she owned the joint, 'I'll make sure you get a spot in the new birthing suite. Low lighting, a bit of mood music, a nice big warm birthing pool. It's like a hotel.'

Diana squeaked in alarm. 'Birthing pool? That sounds disgusting.'

Yesterday, she'd booked her and Will into antenatal classes at the hospital. The nice lady at the desk had given her a handful of pamphlets to read in advance. Diana had expected pictures like the ads on TV for tissues and nappies — sweet little Labrador puppies and fluffy yellow ducklings. Not the startling image of a woman thrusting a plastic baby through a red knitted vagina.

She shared this with Lydia, who chuckled. 'All sorts of things are going to be excreted, Didi. The baby is only one of them.'

'Let the poor girl cross that bridge when she gets to it, Lydia.' Audrey pulled out a tube of lipstick, smeared on a layer and smacked her lips. 'Have you decided on names?'

'No, I've bought a book. Will and I are planning to read it together and decide.' A giant yawn overtook her and she gathered her things. 'I'm having a nap when I get home. We've got a gig tonight and I won't last the distance unless I sleep.'

Her mother gave her a sly smile. 'Sleep deprivation is excellent practice for when the bub comes.'

'Don't tell me that. I feel like I could sleep for a million years.'

Her body was doing things she'd never dreamed were possible, that she had no control over. It was not an altogether pleasant sensation. She'd never say this out loud, especially to Will because it sounded so awful, but sometimes it felt like she'd been taken over by a tiny alien.

*

Credit where credit was due, Will managed not to make a fuss about The Somethings. He and Diana had an understanding. He knew that she knew what he thought about her continuing to perform. Diana knew that he knew that she loved performing and couldn't bear to give it up. But unspoken opinions were not limited to Will and Diana. As the months ticked over, her tiny alien also made its presence known.

The first and most obvious way was via her wardrobe. Diana had invested in a pair of maternity overalls and these, along with one of Will's t-shirts, were what she wore pretty much every day. Performing was a different matter. She kept letting out as many of her costumes as she could but unless she wanted to ruin them, her options had narrowed. How awful that the lack of something suitable to wear might force her off stage. Diana resisted making the obvious decision, clinging to the life she knew for as long as she could. Until the decision was made for her.

One Sunday morning, Diana dozed, making the most of a lie-in after a late-night gig on the wrong side of town. She'd heard Will sneak out to the shops and return, soon followed by the aroma of bacon and toast. Her bladder demanded she deal with it and she reluctantly dragged herself out of her cosy bed. Yawning, she sat on the toilet and wadded up the paper. When she stood up to flush Diana screamed Will's name.

'What? What is it?' Will raced in, and she pointed at the bright red wad of toilet paper in the bowl.

'Oh. God. Do you think we should go to the hospital?'

'I don't know. I feel fine, I think.'

Will frowned, caught between wanting to solve the problem and having no idea what to do. 'But you shouldn't be bleeding, should you?'

'I'm going to ring Lydia. She'll know.' The decision made Diana feel less alarmed. 'It's not like I'm gushing blood. What if it's nothing?'

They sat together on the couch and Diana held the phone in such a way that Will could listen in.

'Hello?'

'It's only me. Sorry for calling this early on a Sunday. Oh?' She covered the mouthpiece and whispered, 'Lydia's just finished her shift.'

'I know,' Will whispered back. 'I can hear her.'

Diana pulled a face. 'Lyds, I'm probably overreacting,' she said in a tone that implied she'd be grateful if her sister agreed. She explained the reason for her call. 'Do you think we should go to hospital, just in case?'

Lydia yawned loudly down the phone line. 'When did you last have sex?'

'Pardon?'

'It's not a trick question, Didi. Have you guys had sex in the last twenty-four to forty-eight hours?'

Will nudged her side. 'Maybe,' Diana answered.

'Well, either you did or you didn't. Surely since you're up the duff you must have some idea about whether or not you've had sex.'

Sisters they may be, but did Lydia really need to know the details of Diana and Will's sex life? 'Assume we did.'

Her answer was met by the rush of running water followed by the sound of a kettle on the boil. 'Okay then, that's probably your answer. If it's only enough to wear a panty liner, there's nothing to worry about. It's just caused by irritation to the cervix. Hang on a minute.' The phone thunked against the bench, followed by a soundscape of cupboards opening and closing, water pouring, then a teaspoon stirring in a cup. Seeing

Will's face, Diana stifled a giggle. This kind of conversation with her sister was par for the course. Poor Will was used to people hanging off his every word.

There was a loud slurp followed by an 'aah' of satisfaction and Lydia was back with them. 'The other option might be a cervical polyp, which is harmless but can cause bleeding.'

'Should I go to the hospital then?'

'Not unless it's as heavy as a period. If it's still bothering you in the morning, then see your GP. But, believe me, no one wants to hang around the emergency department on a Sunday.'

'See, I told you there was nothing to worry about,' Diana said after she'd hung up. But it wasn't what she was thinking. She was thinking, *The tiny alien has decided to make its voice heard. It's telling me it's time to slow down.* The look Will gave her echoed the sentiment.

He came home early from work the following night, bringing her a large packet of dried apricots and a tub of caramel macadamia-nut ice cream. 'You'll have to roll me down the stairs to get me out of here,' she complained from where she lay on the couch, while opening the apricots. That morning the doctor had confirmed what Lydia had told her, but suggested she take it easy for a few days just in case, so that's what she was happily doing.

Will simply smiled and disappeared into the bedroom to change out of his work clothes. On his return, he sat at her feet and laid a hand towel and a bottle of very fancy-looking body oil on the coffee table. 'Pull up your shirt.'

Diana did so and exposed her growing bump. 'What are you doing?'

'What does it look like? I'm giving you and the tiny alien a massage.'

He slathered his hands with the oil, rubbed them together then laid them on her belly. 'Apparently this helps prevent stretch marks.'

'I think it's too late for that,' Diana murmured, letting herself sink into the couch. 'But it's nice of you to try.'

Will kissed her belly. 'Maybe if you followed the doctor's advice and slowed down a bit, I could do this every night.'

A little alarm bell chimed softly in the back of her brain.

'You're going to have to call it a day with the band at some juncture. And you've got enough on your plate with exams coming up as well.'

She tapped his hand. 'Women have had their babies and gone straight back to work in the fields for generations. I can manage.'

He stopped mid-rub. 'Didi, you had a bleed. I know what the doctor said, but that's no excuse to dig your heels in and pretend nothing has changed just to prove a point. The guys realise it's kind of inevitable.'

She threw an apricot at his head. 'Are you saying I'm no longer a groovy sex kitten?'

Will retrieved it and put it on the coffee table. 'Of course you are. But what I meant was, you have to set an end date. Otherwise, it's not fair on them. People like to know where they stand.'

Diana toyed with the idea of having another apricot but thought better of it. There was truth to the saying that you can have too much of a good thing. 'Soon,' she said, not wanting to concede that she didn't relish giving up what she loved, even if it was for a valid reason, even if it wasn't forever.

'Be warned, I will nag you until you do.' Will gently wiped the towel over her tummy then pulled down her t-shirt. 'Your body's telling you to rest. Things are going well for me at work, you should take advantage of it. Spend time getting to know him.'

'Or her.'

Diana hated to admit Will was right. Soon she'd be one of those women waddling everywhere. No one, including her, wanted to see her shake her booty in a maternity outfit. At a pinch, she might get away with a 1960s muu-muu, but Diana suspected she'd look more Mama Cass than Cher. Vanity? Absolutely, but it was an image she could well do without.

*

It took Diana a couple of weeks to build up her nerve — or, more accurately, to reach the point she realised it was never going to get any easier.

'The thing is,' she told the guys after rehearsal, 'singing is a physical act. The baby's putting more and more pressure on my diaphragm. It'll make performing too difficult.'

This wasn't strictly true. Singing was good for her breathing, and by extension, her circulation. Plus, the practice kept her voice in tune.

'I thought babies liked music. Isn't that why people put headphones on the chick's belly and play Mozart?' asked Jonathan.

Michael laughed. 'Where do you get this shit?'

'I would have thought the main issue was the risk you'd trip over the cables on stage and break something,' Animal threw in from the couch where he was rolling a joint.

'Please don't light that up in here,' Diana snapped. This wasn't the way she'd imagined the conversation going. The guys weren't exactly showing much sympathy.

'Are you kidding? You can't see for the amount of cigarette smoke in the venues. Every note you sing is full of that shit,'

Jonno said, removing a pack of fags from the sleeve of his t-shirt.

Michael indicated to Animal to do the right thing and take it outside. He smiled at Diana, the sort of smile she imagined a brother might give her, if she had one. 'If the change in your range is bothering you, I can transpose some of the songs a key or two lower. Or we can ditch them if they're getting too hard.'

Embarrassed, Diana pretended to organise her sheet music. She knew she'd lost some of her upper range and gained a few lower notes. To her ear, her voice lacked its usual brightness and her control was wavering on some of the harder numbers. But she thought she'd covered it up.

Jonathan ripped the tab off the can of a bourbon and Coke. 'Well, I hate to break it to you, sweetheart, but if you're leaving the band …'

'Taking a break from the band,' Michael corrected.

Jonathan shrugged. 'Same as. We'd better hold auditions.'

Diana's hurt quickly flared into anger. 'Don't beat around the bush, will you, Jonno.'

'Ignore him,' Michael implored.

Furious, Diana grabbed her satchel and stuffed the sheet music in, not caring one bit about crushing the pages. Anything to hide the tears burning her eyes. 'Nope. Jonathan's right. You can still be The Somethings. There must be plenty of singers out there who can step into my shoes.'

Drawn by the argument, Animal hung in the doorway. 'Hey, maybe Linda can take her place?'

'No!' they returned in chorus.

Animal raised his hands in defence. 'Okay, okay, keep your hair on. It was only an idea.'

But Diana couldn't resist a final stab at Jonathan. 'If they can't play the piano, then all you have to do is add another member to the band. I'm sure no one will mind splitting the fees five ways.' That wiped the smug smile off his face.

Michael gave her a 'thanks but no thanks' kind of look that made her feel a bit guilty. Unlike Jonno, Michael didn't rely on the band for an income, but it would fall to him to replace her.

Diana softened. It wasn't Michael she was mad at. 'When are we booked up until?'

He pulled a pocket diary out of his jeans and flicked through the pages. 'Middle of October.'

She tried not to sound like she was begging. 'Can the band take a sabbatical? I'm having a baby, not leaving the country. I'll be back in six months. Anyway, Animal and Linda are getting married in the new year. He said he wanted a month off for the honeymoon, right, Greg? And Michael, you said yourself that you've got three albums booked back to back. A break will make your life easier too, won't it?'

Michael nodded. Jonathan flicked his lighter and set the flame to his cigarette, inhaled deeply and blew out the smoke.

'Sounds okay to me. Guys?' asked Animal.

Diana waved away the cigarette smoke. Right now, she wished she could walk out the door and never come back but she would not give Jonathan the satisfaction. 'Think about it. I'll see you Saturday,' she said, grabbing her folder of music and waving over her shoulder.

The last words she heard Michael say were, 'Nice one, mate.'

*

Aiden slipped into the world on a summer night heavy with the scent of jasmine. Despite Lydia's pep talks, the antenatal classes and her avid study of Sheila Kitzinger's sage words, he arrived so fast Diana barely had time to light the candles in the birthing suite.

Lydia wouldn't hear of leaving her sister in the capable care of the midwives who were actually rostered on duty, and insisted on being there 'as backup in case Will faints'. This allowed Will to stay at the top end of the game and share plenty of encouragement while leaving 'the messy end' to the women in charge.

It was Lydia who swaddled the baby in a pale-blue wrap and passed him to his mother. Diana took one look at that mad thatch of black hair standing bolt upright from his tiny head, saw those bright brown eyes following her, and fell instantly in love. 'Hello, tiny alien,' she said, kissing his wrinkled little forehead.

Will leaned over her shoulder. 'He looks exactly like you.'

Lydia peeked too. 'You're right. He's got the same ginormous nose and sticky-out ears. Hopefully the poor thing will grow into them.'

Back on the ward, Aiden — as he was now officially known — lay in a clear plastic crib by Diana's side and slept off his ordeal. Will had gone home to sleep too but promised he'd be back in a few hours, and Lydia had to go to an actual shift. Diana was too wired to sleep. Instead, she lay there and marvelled at her creation.

The next morning, a midwife popped her head around the door. 'Just coming to check on Mum and Bub,' she said. She picked up Diana's chart. 'And how are you feeling?' But she didn't really listen to Diana's enthusiastic reply. It was all blood pressure cuffs and temperature-taking and 'Ooh, isn't he adorable?' when she looked at Aiden.

The woman smiled brightly, sterilising her hands and snapping on some gloves. 'Now, let's have a feel of your tummy and check on those stitches.'

Now she'd pushed out a baby in front of complete strangers, Diana no longer cared who looked at her downstairs. She and dignity had parted company, to the point she smiled back when the midwife lifted the sheet for a peek.

From somewhere behind Diana's bent knees, she heard, 'Oh, you must have Doctor Cash.'

Diana didn't know what to say. The woman was looking at her nethers, not the chart.

The midwife's head bobbed up. 'I can tell by the stitching. He's always so neat.' She snapped off her gloves and put them in the waste disposal unit. 'You should see the lady next door, split from one end to the other like an overripe melon. Lucky for her, she also has Doctor Cash. You won't even be able to tell by the time she heals.'

And here was Diana, resenting the obstetrician for only arriving in time to catch Aiden when he shot out. Maybe she needed to soften her opinion. Mind you, how long would she have to pee in the shower? Talk about peeing razor blades.

*

On Lydia's advice, for the first three months, Diana turned the clocks to the wall and curled up in bed with Aiden, sleeping the days away, waking for feeds. Will rushed in the door at night, rolling up his sleeves ready to run the bath and put dinner on the table. Restlessness soon drove Diana out of the small apartment, pushing Aiden's pram along the streets surrounding the harbour. Together they watched the ferries come and go, collecting the office workers and dispatching the ladies visiting town for the matinees.

In the wee hours of the morning, as Aiden suckled, she listened to the faraway clink of the yacht masts in the harbour and the sharp notes of the garbos banging bins. Precious times. She rocked Aiden to sleep, singing snatches of any old song that came into her head. His brain built tiny pathways on 'Mockingbird', 'Close to You' and 'Fire and Rain'. Crowd-pleasers for an audience that fitted in the snug curve of her embrace.

'Hey, how's it going?'

Diana was startled by Will's hand on her shoulder. She'd fallen asleep on the couch again. Out the window, dawn painted the sky in pretty colours. She looked at the bundle in her arms, her eyes alighting on the sweep of Aiden's eyelashes brushing his cheeks.

'Can I get you anything while I'm up?'

'A cup of tea would be great.'

He squeezed her shoulder and shuffled, yawning, into the kitchen.

Maybe it was the sound of the kettle on the boil or that he sensed the change in his mother's heartbeat, but Aiden stiffened and let out a short cry. Diana loosened the muslin wrap and he bunched his little fist atop her breast. Will put the mug within reach and hopped in the shower while Aiden fed and her tea went cold. Afterwards, he changed Aiden and tucked him into the cot jammed between the bed and the wall before a peck on the cheek and he was off to work. While Aiden slept, Diana showered and ate toast then sorted the never-ending piles of clean clothes. What didn't fit in the chest of drawers next to the stereo ended up stacked on the lid of her keyboard or stashed in a basket under the change table. It was hard to disguise how much the flat had shrunk. But that problem belonged to another day.

Chapter 5

Now

Diana decides to meander down the coast. In between packing up Turpentine Street, moving into the apartment on The Green, organising the Big Party, not to mention teaching, she has well and truly earned the weekend off.

It takes her all of about half an hour to pack. On a whim, she wraps two necklaces inside her jewellery roll and tosses them in her overnight bag. Who knows, Audrey might break the habit of a lifetime and suggest they go out for dinner.

By nine, she has parked outside the coffee shop and ordered a large takeaway cappuccino. While waiting for her brew, she rings Samantha and reschedules her brow, lip and chin wax to the following week. Diana is religious about her trips to the beauty salon. Her mother may consider it pure vanity but Diana's weekly appointments are the first line of defence in the inevitable slide into old age. If nothing else, Will appreciates her efforts.

Or does he? The thought stabs her in the heart. What if someone else is running her shellacked nails through the wisps of hair at the nape of his neck? Or worse, what if he's having an affair with some earth-mother type who not only shuns shaving but is equally dismissive about waxing? Diana has a vision of this husband-stealer, with her loose Indian cotton dress and no bra. Will, a sarong draped around his loins and nothing underneath. She'll be serving him a nut roast and he'll declare it delicious even though he hates lentils and has always viewed vegetarians with utmost suspicion.

'Diana, your cappuccino's ready.'

She grabs her takeaway and ducks outside, gulping in the fresh winter air until her heartbeat slows. *I forgive you.* Really? The way she remembers it, it was her who did all the forgiving.

Back behind the wheel, Diana is glad she's only staying with Audrey for two nights. Everyone knows fish and visitors go off after three days, even mothers and daughters who barely see each other from one month to the next. Mind you, Audrey has always been a somewhat absent figure in her life, if not physically then emotionally. For years, Diana convinced herself it was because Audrey ran a busy pharmacy and a household, since her father — like so many men of his generation — worked long hours and played golf all weekend. Beyond the obvious financial aspects, her dad's contribution to raising a family consisted of mowing the lawn and taking out the bins. But now she's older, Diana suspects Audrey's absentee parenting might have more to do with the fact that no matter how bright (Lydia) or talented (Diana), children were not scintillating company.

Beneath the brisk exterior, Diana has always sensed a simmering anger. That when her father suddenly died, it wasn't grief that made Audrey sell up the house and her business and take off travelling around the country. There was more to it than that.

Diana spots the sign indicating the turn-off for the coastal tourist trail and, on impulse, decides to take it. After all, she's in no rush, Audrey's not expecting her until five-ish. A leisurely drive along the coast and fish and chips for lunch sounds just about perfect. She and Will often detour this way and now, as then, she takes a walk along the beach after lunch to stretch her legs before getting back into the car. As an added bonus, Diana spots a roadside stall selling new-season strawberries and nectarines, and pulls over. She puts the mixed box of fruit and two jars of local honey on the back seat and grabs a strawberry to eat on the drive. The juice dribbles on her favourite silk smock but Diana is determined not to let it ruin an otherwise lovely day. When she hits town, she parks outside the pub and stocks up on grog — two bottles each of the ridiculously overpriced champagne, rosé and sauvignon blanc. Surely one of these will make her mother happy.

Once parked outside her mother's bungalow, Diana turns off the ignition and observes the house. The lights are not on. She checks her phone but there are no missed calls or messages. With far too much to carry, she'll have to make two trips. Shouldering her overnight bag, Diana puts the honey and fruit on the low brick fence and returns to grab one of the bottles of champagne.

She then moves her offerings from the fence to the wooden seat on the verandah and pauses to admire the front garden. It looks lovely with its winter-pruned roses and clipped camellias. In between, bulbs are already poking their heads out of the dark soil like little green sentinels, bursting with the promise of spring. Sadly, neither Diana nor Lydia inherited their mother's green thumb. Hands free, she approaches the cherry-red front door and gives the old-fashioned ringer two quick twists. It shrilly announces, 'Hello! I'm here!'

Diana waits. A thought darts through her mind like a fish in the shallows. Wouldn't her mother have an ear out for the sound of the car? In the gathering gloom, she switches on the phone's torch, picks up her overnight bag and the bottle of Veuve, and follows the gravel path around the perimeter of the house.

The side gate creaks open. Diana has an image of Audrey hiding around the corner of the house with a flat-bladed shovel over one shoulder like a baseball bat ready to be deployed against burglars. As a deterrent, she sings out, 'It's only me.'

But when she rounds the corner, there is no Audrey, with or without a shovel at the ready. Instead there is a volley of barking from Elsie the aging cattle dog, and Diana follows the sound through the raised veggie beds. When Audrey retired here, she repurposed the old drop box as a tool shed. Across the garden, a bare bulb illuminates the small space. Diana hears Bach's 'Brandenburg Concerto' playing on the radio. She pauses to listen. No. 1 in F Major or No. 2? She's not sure.

Diana moves closer. The light forms a halo around Audrey's head. She is working at the high bench — potting seedlings or similar — and Diana is aware of the hunch of her mother's silhouette. With a start, she recognises what was once called a Dowager's Hump. Then Audrey straightens and her mother's spine unrolls, her figure returning to its familiar shape – willowy, giving Audrey the illusion of height, with the same slender wrists and ankles she gave to Diana. But where Diana is olive-skinned, with black hair and brown eyes like her father, Audrey is sun-kissed and freckled. Her father used to sling an arm around the curve of his wife's slender waist and draw her to him, saying, *You look good enough to eat.* Audrey would laugh, her face opening up in a way that reminded Diana of that first bite of an apple. The crisp white flesh, sweet with juice, revealed.

'Mum?' she calls from the gloaming of the vegetable garden.

Audrey turns, not with the speed of surprise but slowly, as if she'd been aware of Diana standing there all along but wanted to finish her task. Elsie looks up at her mistress, her stumpy tail brushing the dirt across the concrete floor, her eyes liquid with love.

Audrey steps out of the light. 'Hello, darling. I wasn't expecting you for ages.'

'Actually, I'm bang on time.'

Audrey dusts her palms against her work pants and grabs a polar-fleece jacket from a nail behind the door. She slips it on and kills the light. Joining Diana on the path, she reaches up to brush warm lips against her daughter's cool cheek. 'It's lovely to see you.' The toe of her work boot kicks Diana's overnight bag. 'Is that yours? Goodness me! I thought you were only staying a couple of nights.'

Audrey picks up the bag and slings it over her shoulder, whistling for Elsie, and heads towards the soft glow of the kitchen. Diana trudges behind, once again a recalcitrant teenager dragging her heels behind the steady clip of a mother who always walked with a destination in mind.

Diana shakes off her childhood. 'I've brought champagne and some strawberries from a stall on the highway.'

'Strawberries already?' Audrey responds without breaking stride. 'I feel totally spoilt.'

Audrey turns the brass doorhandle and lets Elsie push ahead into the kitchen. The old dog trots across the faded linoleum to her bed and leaps up to it with a slight sideways shift of her hips, turns twice and lays her head on her paws.

Diana takes the bag from her mother. 'I'll just dump this in the spare room and fetch the rest of my stuff.' She feels the wall, searching for the hall light switch.

Audrey's hand moves past Diana's ear and pulls a cord. 'Have you forgotten? It's one of the old-fashioned ones.'

Diana walks the length of the hallway, flanked by the

formal lounge and the dining room. The cottage's two bedrooms are opposite one another at the front of the house. Facing the street, her mother's is on the left with French doors that open onto the verandah. The window above the doors is open. Diana goes in to close it against the winter chill. A quilted eiderdown is folded neatly at the foot of the bed, and a mountain of pillows conceals the wooden bedhead. A pool of soft yellow light illuminates a pile of books on what had once been her father's side. On the other bedside table is a pair of reading glasses and a flask of water. An envelope marks the place in a half-finished book. There is a tube of lip balm, hand cream and a tapering pile of coins arranged by size rather than denomination.

Diana pauses. The house had been in darkness when she arrived. The bedside lamp must be on a timer. That Audrey also doesn't like being alone in the dark sends a surge of sympathy through her.

'Hurry up,' her mother calls up the hall. 'I can't get the damn cork out of the champagne.'

'Coming.' Diana locks the casement window then draws the heavy drapes to ward off the cold before heading across the corridor to the spare bedroom.

She feels the wall for a light switch then remembers to look for a pull cord instead. A replica Tiffany shade in blues and greens casts the room in a sickly glow. The room is an exact replica of her mother's without the lived-in feel. The bedside tables are bare, as is Nanna's old dressing table. It has three bevelled mirrors and a stool upholstered in teal velvet tucked beneath. Nanna used to sit there like she was the queen of everything, slathering her face in Pond's cold cream, Diana relegated to the bed out of harm's way. She remembers the giant powder puff, the peculiar mineral smell of her grandmother's favourite lipstick, and always a bottle of 4711. Diana closes her eyes and presses the inside of her wrist to her nose.

'Diana? What's taking you so long?'

'I'll be two ticks.' She shrugs off her coat and hangs it in the wardrobe, then grabs the fruit and honey from the wooden seat outside and returns to the kitchen.

Audrey is rinsing produce in the deep sink — beetroots, shallots, coriander and rhubarb. Diana puts the box of fruit on the scarred wooden table next to a bottle of Cinzano and a bowl of lemons.

'Would you like one?' Audrey asks, draining her glass and reaching for the bottle. 'Sorry, I gave up on the champers. It gives me heartburn.'

'I brought still as well, if you'd prefer? I can run to the car and get it.'

Audrey throws a handful of ice into a tumbler. 'Aren't you well prepared?'

Unsure where that leaves her, Diana simply smiles. 'In that case, how about I help you prepare dinner.' Her smile falters. 'Unless you'd prefer to go out for tea? My treat.'

Audrey laughs. 'There's nothing decent open past eight at this time of year. I'm sure I can cobble something together from this lot.'

'Okay then.' Diana catches sight of her smock. 'Actually, would you mind if I quickly ran this under some cold water?'

'Be my guest.'

The laundry has an old double concrete tub and a washing line strung across one corner on which is pegged a pair of thick woollen socks and sensible underwear. Diana rubs at the stain with the sliver of yellow soap she found on the edge of the sink.

'How's Will?' Audrey calls out.

'Good. He's doing a quick round trip to see suppliers, then detouring via Edinburgh to see Persephone.'

Diana pegs her rinsed smock next to the undies and returns to the kitchen. Her mother has topped up her Cinzano. It would be far easier if Diana conceded to her mother's desires but, in a small act of defiance, she decides to open the Veuve. She refuses to dwell on the undercurrent of disapproval that runs through every conversation with her mother.

'I've never understood why you don't go with him. Yes, it would have been more trouble than it was worth when the children were young, but now? You should see the world before you're too old to enjoy it. It's not like you can't afford to travel.'

The cork pops and champagne fizzes over the edge of the bottle. Diana holds it over the glass and concentrates on pouring rather than answering her mother. Audrey is right on one count. Over the years, Will has done very well for himself but it's money hard earned.

She sips her champagne. 'Travelling the world as Will's handbag is not my idea of fun.'

'But you could spend time with Lucas while he's still young. You don't have to traipse along behind Will.'

'Aiden and Anna won't want me hanging around like a bad smell. And it's a long way to go for just a few days.' Fish and visitors. Diana downs a third of her glass in one gulp.

Audrey cracks eggs into a large ceramic bowl, one after another, single-handed. 'It'd be different with Percy. She'd appreciate an extra pair of hands.'

Diana's jaw tightens at the nickname Percy. 'Speaking of Persephone, she and Emile are spending the weekend at his parents. It'll do her good. I worry she's running herself into the ground.'

'Nonsense. When you're young is precisely the time to work hard.' Audrey scoops the broken eggshells into an old ice cream bucket then puts some washed spinach leaves in the spinner and gives them a whirl.

'Are you sure there's nothing I can do to help? I feel a bit useless just standing here.'

Her mother searches the room as she considers the question. 'I suppose you can grate the parmesan.'

Diana needs the distraction. She grabs a wedge of cheese from the fridge, the grater from the drawer.

Audrey passes her a wooden board. 'Which reminds me,' she says, reaching for a book from a shelf on the kitchen dresser. 'Percy sent me a copy of Camille's new book.' She holds it up for Diana to see. The smiling face of Camille adorns the front cover. She's holding a chicken — a live one, although who knows for how long? 'I presume she didn't bother sending you one.'

Stung, Diana snaps. 'Of course she did. Why wouldn't she?'

Audrey's eyebrows shot up. 'Really? Well, I suppose Will might find it useful.' She doesn't see Diana's scowl as she's bent over the cookbook, flicking through the pages. 'I made her Chicken Provencale the other night for the girls from bridge club. We all agreed it was a real treat. You must ask Will to make it for you.'

Breathe, she tells herself. It doesn't matter that the thread of the family running joke about her cooking skills stretches a long way back. It still makes her defensive, as if culinary skills are requisite for any woman worth her salt. Diana's gaze lands on the jumble of photos on the dresser. There's a large one of Persephone and Audrey leaning in cheek to cheek that Will took at Persephone's wedding. The pair have always been close. Grandmothering appeals to Audrey more than mothering ever did, perhaps because it requires far less dedication. Or perhaps

Audrey recognises herself in Persephone. They share the same high cheekbones and golden freckles.

'And choux pastry. Do you know, I always thought it wasn't worth the effort but Camille's goat's cheese and walnut gougères have completely converted me.'

Diana picks up a photo of the kids sitting on the merry-go-round at the park around the corner from Turpentine Street, all chubby cheeks and baby teeth. She goes to replace it and sees, tucked up the back of the dresser, a photo of her from her days with The Somethings. It's another one of Will's. She's seated at the piano, arms above her head, clapping the audience into a frenzy. Eyes rimmed in kohl, her hair swinging out behind her. Gosh, she was so slender back then. Of course, with the peculiarities of youth, she never thought so. Imagine if she'd known about what happens after babies and menopause have wreaked their havoc.

'Those were the days, weren't they?' Audrey says, closing the cookbook and picking up her Cinzano.

'Yep. They sure were.'

'Do you think you'll ever perform again?'

The question surprises Diana. Or rather, that her mother of all people has asked it. She laughs and replaces the picture. 'Well, I'd need a whole new wardrobe.'

Audrey puts a pan on the stove to heat up and fetches the butter. 'You're fifty-five, darling, not ninety-five. Live a little.'

Diana's eyes well with sudden tears. Is her mother right? Is she living life as if she's past her prime? Is that how Will sees her now? Diana clears her throat. 'I'd better grate that parmesan,' she says, and turns to the task so Audrey can't see how upset she is.

The butter sizzles in the pan. Audrey adds a pile of sliced mushrooms, shakes and stirs, then adds the spinach. Diana watches her from the kitchen table. Her strong capable hands.

She remembers her mother bent over the sewing machine late at night, whipping up costumes for drama eisteddfods using nothing but old dresses and scraps from a basket. Popping a cake in the oven for endless school fundraisers. Prepping veggies for dinner while Diana and Lydia grizzled over homework at the kitchen bench. Every task dispensed with calm efficiency. Yet never with any warmth, as if Audrey were performing the tasks out of a sense of duty without actually ever enjoying them. Then Dad died and Audrey packed up her perfect life and took off in the campervan.

'Do you ever miss Dad?' Diana asks as she passes her mother the grated cheese.

'Every day,' Audrey replies, pouring beaten eggs over the mushrooms and wilted spinach.

Diana gathers the silverware from the dresser drawer and starts setting the table for dinner. 'I can't imagine what life would be like should Will suddenly disappear.'

'Your father didn't disappear, darling, he dropped dead in court.' Although Audrey says it lightly, as if there was something slightly comical about James Roberts, solicitor, dying in the middle of a court appearance.

'I didn't mean it like that.'

Audrey pauses, glances at Diana in a way that makes her feel twelve again. 'I know you didn't, darling. You've always been careless with words.'

Diana breaks eye contact. 'I forgot the wine. Which would you prefer? Sauvignon blanc or rosé?'

'Neither. There's a bottle of Pinot already open. That'll do me, but you have whatever you like.'

It was a mistake to come here. Her mother is incapable of giving her the comfort she seeks. She's missed so many important milestones in Diana's adult life. Not necessarily the obvious ones — births, deaths and marriages — but the unspoken ones. The life-changing ones that happen in unexpected moments. Like when Diana needed her mother the most and she was in her mobile home on the other side of the country. And the anger sizzles — at Audrey for not being the mother she wanted, at herself for still longing for something her mother is incapable of giving.

Who's she kidding? She came all this way to tell Audrey that she found a note in Will's sweater and to ask her what she should do about it. But her mother's advice can best be described as brusque. Diana looks at the photo on the dresser. Now she remembers what song she was singing: 'These Boots Were Made For Walking'.

Chapter 6

Then

Will flew in the door from work far earlier than usual. 'I have a surprise!'

Diana and Aiden were on the floor in the process of building an enormous pyramid of plastic blocks. 'What kind of surprise?'

Aiden swiped at the blocks, chortling as they tumbled to the floor with a satisfying crash.

Will kissed the top of her head. 'C'mon, up you get. We need to get going.' He hooked his hands under her armpits and hauled her to her feet.

'Don't I get a clue?' she asked, wrapping her arms around his waist and kissing him properly.

He unclasped her hands. 'No you don't. There'll be plenty of time for misbehaving later.' He scooped up Aiden and blew a raspberry on his tummy. Aiden shrieked with joy. 'We've got to hurry. I want to get there before dark.'

Diana double-checked the nappy bag had everything she might conceivably need for an unscheduled adventure and met Will at the door. She passed Aiden a milk arrowroot biscuit.

'Now?' Will complained.

'It's either a quiet baby and crumbs in the car or a clean car and trying to drive with him screaming his lungs out. Your choice.'

He kissed Aiden's cheek. 'Looks like you win again, little buddy.'

'Can I at least ask where we're going?' Diana asked after she'd buckled Aiden into his booster seat and climbed in the front. She regarded her t-shirt — there was a milky stain over one shoulder and a patch where her boobs had leaked because she forgot to put pads in after her shower, a smear of Vegemite on one sleeve and a congealed patch of Farex where Aiden had thrown his spoon at her at breakfast. 'Please tell me we're not going out for dinner.'

'We're not going out for dinner.'

'Thank goodness. Otherwise I might have had to kill you.'

Will chuckled.

'Is there something going on at work?' Maybe he'd closed a big deal.

'Uh-huh.' Will concentrated on merging onto the freeway heading north.

'Well, it's too late to go to the zoo, so that can't be it.' Fish and chips by the harbour might be nice. Aiden could play in the sand and she could eat with both hands for a change.

'You'll never guess so stop trying. Just be patient for once in your life.'

'Ha! Says you.'

The next turn-off followed a winding road with looming Edwardian mansions and avenues of plane trees. Diana didn't know anyone who lived over this side, and she was pretty sure Will didn't either. It was a long way to come for fish and chips.

They turned onto the suburb's main street, lined with quaint cobblestoned footpaths, past The Village Bakery, The

Village Patisserie, and The Village Charcuterie. She presumed The Village Frock Shop was intentionally ironic judging by the window display. She'd be hard-pressed to buy anything in there for less than five hundred dollars.

They twisted and turned down a steep hill. Diana caught glimpses of the harbour and yachts racing in the dying light. A red-and-gold ferry chugged around the headland towards the jetty.

'Amazing, isn't it?' Will said, nodding at the water. He turned into a long narrow street and parked the car. 'This is it.'

Diana surveyed their surroundings, wondering where 'it' actually was. Almost identical weatherboard cottages lined the street. The one Will had parked out front of had a driveway running up the side of the house. A strip of manicured turf divided two cement tracks for the wheels. Parked upon it was an ancient but well-maintained, mustard yellow Mercedes Benz E class. An arbour of ridiculously pink roses framed the front gate and a riot of floral abundance thrust itself through the gaps in the fence. In the middle of the front lawn, a sprawling crepe myrtle rested its limbs in the graceful repose of a ballerina.

Immediately Diana thought of her grandparents. Her dad's dad was an active gardener and a proud member of the local gardening club. Her grandmother spent her retirement volunteering at the nursing home where she often took armfuls of her husband's flowers to 'brighten up the place'. This house oozed a similar charm.

Will got out of the car and went around to open the rear passenger door to release Aiden. He swung him up on his shoulders. 'Are you coming?'

Diana climbed out and joined him on the pavement. She looked around. Above the brass letterbox in the brick fence, a plaque read 'The Hillykers'. She'd never heard of them and couldn't recall Will ever mentioning anyone by that name.

Will pointed at the next house over. Now she was out of the car, Diana realised it had a For Sale sign erected in the front yard. The house was identical to the Hillykers' except it was in desperate need of a lick of paint to bring it up to the same standard. The garden fence was in the slow process of collapsing under the weight of a riot of honeysuckle. The foundations under the brick pillars at the front gate had cracks wide enough to stick your finger in. The whole lot looked as if it would tumble to the pavement any moment.

'What a shame it's already sold,' she said, nodding at the bright-yellow sticker plastered across the sign.

'Oh well,' Will replied with a dramatic shrug. 'Shall we go and have a poke around anyway?'

'You can't do that, it's trespassing.'

But Will and Aiden were already halfway up the front path. Diana trailed behind, not quite believing it when Will produced a set of house keys and slipped one in the lock. The door opened and he hit the switch just inside the door, illuminating a wide hallway with dark timber floors.

'Oh good, the power's on.' He put Aiden down and Aiden crawled off as fast as his chubby limbs could carry him. Will grinned at Diana. 'Are you coming?'

The house was a treasure trove of period features. Pressed metal ceilings, picture rails and fireplaces in virtually every room. Each time she entered a new room, all Diana could say was, 'Oh my goodness.' The only let-downs were the kitchen and bathroom, which were half-baked attempts at modernisation dating back several decades.

Outside, Aiden sat on the grass under a lemon tree gnawing on a piece of fallen fruit. Will swooped on him and removed it, with a 'Uh-uh, buddy.' Aiden went to cry in protest and Will passed him to Diana. 'I think he wants his mum.'

She rolled her eyes. 'Thanks,' she said, tickling Aiden's chin with the tail of her plait until he smiled again.

'You could easily put on another storey,' Will observed, scoping out the roofline and the large back garden. 'And there's ample space to open up the kitchen and lounge room into a family room.'

'Is there now?' Diana stared at him in disbelief but Will was having so much fun, she played along.

Back out on the wide front verandah, Diana let Aiden crawl around the timber deck. Night had well and truly fallen. Lights dotted the surrounding headlands. There was a thick shrug of darkness where the birds and wildlife lived in some of the best real estate in the city. She inhaled the fresh air and caught the tang of sea salt. It smelled divine.

Will wrapped his arms around her and rested his head on her shoulder. Diana leaned into him. 'This place is amazing.'

'I'm glad you like it.' A cruise ship, lit up like a Christmas tree, glided across the harbour. 'Do you reckon you could live here?' Will whispered in her ear.

'You're teasing me.'

'Maybe just a little.' He spun her around, and dropped a set of keys in her hands. 'How do you like our new home?' and Diana couldn't help herself, she burst into tears.

Chapter 7

Now

Diana opens the front door of the apartment and sags. What a shame the magic unpacking fairy didn't arrive in her absence, whisk everything into cupboards, get rid of the rubbish and store the flat-packed boxes in the garage before she left. Needless to say, this is because she *is* the magic fairy and the magic fairy wanted the weekend off.

She dumps her overnight bag in the doorway of their bedroom then moves into the kitchen where she divests herself of the four remaining bottles of wine and one of the jars of honey. On second thoughts, she puts the two bottles of rosé in the fridge. Yet again, a weekend with her mother is driving her to drink.

Diana flings her coat and scarf over the back of a dining chair and prises off her leather gloves. She hits play on the answering machine, hoping at least one of the two messages will be from Will since her mobile phone had been conspicuously quiet all weekend. Mind you, it would have been awkward to hold a normal conversation with her mother hovering in the background, and downright rude of her to talk to Will when she was her mother's guest.

Not that she needs her mother's permission to talk to her own husband. And yes, a psychologist would have a field day analysing the intricacies of her relationship with her mother but that's never going to happen. Diana can practically hear Lydia laughing at her. Although, no doubt her sister is tucked up in bed with her latest squeeze in her Rome apartment, doing who knows what rather than thinking about Diana. Her sister goes through men at a rate of knots. It's commendable Diana even remembers Armando's name. No, she's being unfair. He's been around a good twelve months. Long enough for her to know that he's a painter — walls, not canvases — although to hear him talk about it, you'd swear it was the other way around.

'Darling, it's Fi,' plays the recording. 'I've just left a message on your mobile as well, so if you've already heard it, delete this one. If that makes sense.' Diana winces at the loudness of her friend's voice, as if she is addressing an auditorium of slightly deaf shareholders at the annual general meeting. 'Anyway, quick reminder. I've booked a table at twelve at The Boatshed for Ruth's birthday. It's just the three of us, which will be lovely. I can't stand hangers-on.' A pause ensues then Fi adds, 'Unless there's anybody else we should invite? I didn't think of that. Does Ruth have other friends? Feel free to change the booking if anyone springs to mind. It's in my name. Otherwise, I'll see you tomorrow. And try not to be late!'

Diana hits delete with slightly more venom than required. Fi's always having a dig about her tardiness even though Diana is rarely more than five minutes late, ten at the most. Fi says it shows disrespect for the value of other people's time. None of this would be an issue except for Fi's policy of always arriving fifteen minutes early. The upshot of which is that combining Diana's five to ten minutes and Fi's fifteen means between them they've clocked up almost half an hour in lost time. This has remained a bone of contention for decades and promises to be so until they're parked in wheelchairs sharing a sneaky bottle of Veuve in their sippy cups at the Sea Breeze Retirement Village.

Diana hits play again. 'Hey hon, it's me,' booms Will's voice. 'Sorry I haven't called. I lost my phone. Well, I thought I had, but don't worry, I found it again. Although I can't find my charger anywhere.' There's banging in the background that indicates he's packing as he chats. It's a familiar soundtrack that has underscored years of messages and conversations with Will in various hotel rooms and airport lounges. 'I had dinner with Percy and Emile on Thursday night before they left for France. She sends her love and says to tell you they both can't wait to come home for the party. She looks wonderful, but tired. The hospital works her too hard. Anyway …'

Diana tuned out to the rest of the message; she knows his sign-off by rote. He sounds completely normal and the depths of her gratitude for this both galls and pleases her in equal measure. Here she is getting herself all worked up over nothing. A man engaged in an extra-marital affair doesn't ring his wife and rabbit on about inconsequential nonsense, does he? On the off-chance she might catch him, she dials his number.

'It's only me,' she says, surprised when he answers.

'Hi. Did you have a good weekend?'

'I went to visit Mum.'

'Guilt trip?'

Will, as usual, has hit the nail on the head. Or at least, this particular nail.

'Anyway, is there a problem? I need to get my skates on. Do you want me to pick up some Frangelico in duty free?'

'Sure. Why not? It never goes astray.'

The familiar rituals honed over thirty years comforts her. She has worked herself into a tizz about a scrap of paper. It could mean anything and nothing. In her heart of hearts, she knows Will loves her and she loves him. Menopause is playing its usual tricks, making her anxious and paranoid. All couples have their ups and downs, their successes and tragedies. Their marriage is no different.

'I'm looking forward to seeing you,' she says with feeling.

'Yeah. Me too. The old body clock doesn't reset like it used to. I miss sleeping in my own bed.'

Poor Will. She can't believe he'll be sixty next month! It used to sound old, now it just sounds alarming. 'You'll be home soon. Why don't you take a couple of days off and relax?'

'We'll see,' he says. 'Look, I really do have to go or I'll miss my flight. I'll ring you when I land.'

It niggles Diana how Will refuses to slow down. He measures himself against the pace he maintained in his thirties but he's not thirty anymore, not by a long shot. It's time he started winding back and developing new interests. Another thing to add to her list of Tactful Conversations I Must Have With Will. Diana glances at her watch, looks wistfully at the fridge door. Is it too early for wine? She thinks not.

*

No sooner has she returned the bottle to the fridge than the home phone rings. 'Mum, it's Persephone. You sounded upset. What's wrong?'

Did she? Diana frowns and sips her wine. Yes, she supposes she was. Time to deflect. 'Oh, I was just having a moment. I'm tired of unpacking boxes and coming home to yet more boxes to unpack, and I miss your father.' She starts at her final words and realises that yes, it's true. She misses Will. All of a sudden, her deflection seems a little less like a white lie.

'Good. How are the plans for the party going? I know you and Aiden are up to something but he won't tell me a single thing,' she complains.

Persephone sounds twelve again. Diana recalls the memory with fondness. Braces on her teeth, tearing through the house off to hockey training or swimming squad or debating. A whirlwind of activity and breathless with the joy and wonder of it all. Diana has always been slightly in awe of her sporty, smart daughter. How on earth did such a magnificent creature spring from her loins?

'Mum? Did you hear me? I said, did you receive Camille's present?'

Diana blushes. She's tuned out again. Her focus is shot, not to mention her memory. Well, short-term memory. For a while there, she started worrying she had early onset Alzheimer's, but then some neuroscientist on the radio said she needn't worry until she found her car keys in the microwave or her phone in the fridge. Good to know in advance. Apparently standing in the supermarket aisle wondering what you came to buy is par for the course.

'Yes, yes, sorry. It arrived a couple of weeks ago. Didn't I tell you?' This time her vagueness has nothing to do with post-menopausal muddle. How could she forget when she opened the package and discovered a copy of Camille's cookbook, inscribed in her trademark flourish? 'I'm still trying to fathom why Camille sent it to me. Surely by now you've told her about my prowess in the kitchen?'

'Of course I did, but I don't think she believes me. Her show's called *Real Women Can Cook*, Mum, what do you expect?'

There's not a trace of sympathy from Persephone, who, thanks to her father, *can* cook. Her current obsession is mass-producing macarons in unusual flavour combinations. Apparently she finds baking relaxing.

'Just try something simple like the omelette *fines hêrbes*. That way, when you see her at the party, you can genuinely put your hand on your heart and tell her you've made one of the dishes.'

A snort escapes before Diana can contain it. 'For heaven's sake! Callously tossing out "just make an omelette *fines hêrbes*" as if any Joe Blow can whip one up. Remember who you're talking to.'

Between Will, Audrey and Persephone, it seems the entire family is determined to rub her nose in it. Although, to be fair, Diana does have begrudging respect for Persephone's French mother-in-law. Unlike Diana, Camille has reinvented herself now she's post menopause and child-free. And it is rather awe-inspiring the way she flits about her immaculate provincial kitchen in her efficient Gallic way — decimating onions, carrots and celery into neat dice like one of those fancy chopping gadgets.

'Well, I hate to break it to you, but Dad's already been posting on his Insta account and tagging her. Camille thinks he's some sort of demi-god.'

Will and his Instagram account. Anyone would think he invented social media the way he goes on about it. He calls himself Willfulfoodie and thinks it's a witty play on words. Mind you, Diana is more surprised at how many followers he has. Who'd have thought photos of food would garner so much interest. Still, as far as time-wasters go, it's harmless.

'At least tell her how much you love the book. Camille made a point of saying she went to the post office personally to send it.'

Diana's tempted to make some smart remark but she bites her tongue. As soon as they hang up, she pounces on the damn book and hides Camille in behind Will's stash of *Gourmet Travellers*.

It's so annoying when people expect you to be grateful for a gift when it is patently obvious they have not spared a single thought about what the receiver might actually want. She sent the woman a thank-you card, what more does she want? Then again, by the time Diana's finished embellishing it, this will make a terrific story to share with Fi and Ruth over lunch tomorrow.

Chapter 8

Then

The Hillykers were there to welcome them almost the moment the removal van had rounded the corner. Mrs Hillyker had baked a passionfruit sponge to mark the occasion and, not to be outdone, Mr Hillyker brought over a jar of his pickled beetroot and a bunch of silverbeet tied up with coarse string.

'We've lived all our married lives in Turpentine Street,' Mrs Hillyker informed them once Will had cleared the dining table and offered their visitors the chairs. Will and Diana leaned against the kitchen bench. Aiden was more than happy on the floor.

'That's amazing,' Diana replied, putting the kettle on to boil. Luckily, she'd had the foresight to pack the kitchen essentials in a single box and store them in the car boot. One of the many advantages of having Aiden in her life — she had become much more organised.

'It's such a brilliant day, why don't we take this outside?' suggested Will, which was much more tactful than admitting that the current dining setting was cramped for two, impossible for four.

'What a lovely idea,' replied Mrs Hillyker, gathering up the cake and passing the basket of crockery to Will. Diana filled the teapot and Mr Hillyker kindly offered to carry it, leaving her to scoop up Aiden and bring him out into the sunshine. Will followed with the basket of crockery, the chairs and the tiny dining table, which he placed next to their even smaller outdoor setting that Mrs Hillyker had requisitioned as a side table for the cake and accoutrement. Diana plonked Aiden on his blanket in the dappled shade of the gnarled old lemon tree.

'Shall I be mother?' Mrs Hillyker asked, proceeding to cut generous slabs of cake that filled her delicate floral plates. 'Have you any milk or sugar, dear? If not, I can pop home,' she added as she began pouring tea. Diana dashed back inside to find them.

Mr Hillyker passed Will the largest slice and his eyes lit up at the plate-load of confection held together with passionfruit curd and cream and slathered in icing. He broke off a piece with his fingers. 'Sorry, I have no idea where the cutlery is,' he said, turning on his most charming smile.

Mrs Hillyker waved him away. 'Never you mind. We don't stand on ceremony, do we, Charlie?' she said with a nod to her husband.

To prove her point, Mr Hillyker took a bite and sucked icing from his thumb. 'Delicious, my dear. You've excelled yourself.' In an aside to Diana, he added, 'You should be honoured. Esther doesn't break out the passionfruit sponge too often these days.'

'I'm guessing you're no longer working?' Will asked.

'I used to be a stockbroker but these days I content myself with breeding budgerigars.'

'And spending way too much time watching Test cricket,' added Mrs Hillyker, handing Diana a cup of tea.

'What about you, Mrs H? Have you also retired?' she asked.

If the shortened moniker offended her, their new neighbour didn't show it. 'No, no. I haven't worked properly since we had the children. For a while there, I was the canteen manager at the primary school but when they upgraded the systems, I said to myself, Esther, that's your cue. Time to move on.'

'Ya!' Aiden shouted. Everyone stopped to look at him. Clearly thrilled he'd captured their attention, he shouted again. 'Ya! Ya! Ya!' Diana spotted the cause of Aiden's excitement. He had one chubby fist shoved in his mouth but the other he waved frantically in the general direction of a stinky bitzer that had snuck into the garden.

'Roger, sit!' commanded Mrs Hillyker. 'Don't mind him, he loves babies.'

Wisely, the old dog sat just out of arm's reach but close enough to keep a benign eye on the flailing bub. Even so, caution prevailed and Diana scooped up Aiden and fussed over wiping the drool from his face. When she was done, she carried him over to his father and dumped him on Will's lap.

'And when is this little one due?' Mrs Hillyker asked, pointing in the vicinity of Diana's stomach.

'Oh, I'm not pregnant,' she replied, a little flustered and awkward on behalf of her new neighbour. Will raised an eyebrow in her direction and she frowned in reply, giving him the 'I don't know what she's talking about' look. Will responded by raising both eyebrows.

Mr Hillyker chuckled. 'You better watch Esther, next she'll be making you take off your engagement ring and wafting it over your tum-tum so she can tell you what sex it is.'

'Shh, Charlie. Don't be rude.' Noticing Diana's horror, Mrs Hillyker patted her arm. 'Don't worry, dear. I'm only a yoo-hoo over the fence. You'll be fine. We had three under four at one stage, didn't we, dear?'

'Speaking of which,' said Will, rescuing Diana from further embarrassment, 'what can you tell us about the local schools?' That was all the prompting the former canteen manager needed to share a lifetime of insider knowledge.

Will laughed about it after the old couple left, although quietly, in case their voices drifted over the fence. Even so, Diana declined a glass of wine with dinner and detoured via the pharmacy on the way to the supermarket the following day and bought a testing kit.

It turned out that Mrs Hillyker was a wise woman. Diana was not only pregnant but once she figured out the dates, she realised the new baby was probably due in seven months. When she calculated the age difference, Diana gasped.

Straight after breaking the news to Will at work, she called Lydia. Her sister hooted with laughter. 'Thirteen months apart? Ouch.'

'I know, right? Breastfeeding is supposed to stop you falling pregnant.'

'How can you be so naive? Surely you knew it was an old wives' tale.'

'But Mum told me!'

'Well for a practising pharmacist, she should know better. For future reference, about the only way breastfeeding stops you getting pregnant is because you're too busy to be getting up to mischief. The rest of the time, it's open slather.'

Diana spent the rest of the day in a daze, wandering about the house, worrying about the logistics of having two little kids to manage — cots, prams, clothing. The first thing she said when Will walked in the door was, 'We'll need to buy a second car.'

To which Will responded, 'Not before we're married.'

Diana went to protest but Will cut her off. 'No more excuses, Didi. I know you didn't want to be pregnant in the photos but my parents will never forgive me if we have two bastards.'

'Will!'

He laughed. 'The only reason they're still talking to me is because we had a son to carry on the family name, and fortunately for us, Ian and Rebecca seem to be taking their sweet time producing grandchildren. Two kids out of wedlock might be pushing my luck.'

But she forgave him for being so old-fashioned because it was impossible to argue with Will, especially when he wrapped his arms around her and touched her in ways that melted all resistance.

*

They married in the garden in spring. Diana wore her hair loose and long, intertwined with flowers, her feet bare at Will's insistence. Aiden wore a lopsided crown of flowers on his head. He kept pulling the flowers out and stuffing them in his mouth. Audrey, whose job it was to take charge of him for the day, calmly pulled them out again and threw them into the bushes. Diana couldn't have done anything about it anyway — it took all her willpower not to be ill all over the front of her diaphanous white frock. When Will swooped in for the big pash to seal the deal, she had to hold her breath and think of peppermint tea.

'Made an honest woman out of you at last,' said Will's mother, Marianne. She softened her words with a peck on the cheek.

'Welcome to the family.' Will's brother, Ian, started off shaking Diana's hand but then pulled her in and gave her a big hug. 'Not that you weren't already, of course. Now it's official.'

His wife, Rebecca, smiled and offered her cheek. 'Only just in time though.'

Will's father, Alan, was over by the drinks table with Lydia. She was regaling him with some story that had him in stitches.

*

By the time they arrived at the hotel, Diana was dead on her feet. Will — because he really was the most wonderful man in the world — insisted on filling the enormous bath with bubbles and cancelled their restaurant booking in favour of room service while she soaked. They spent the one night of their honeymoon curled up in bed watching a romantic comedy until her new husband passed out, snoring loudly by her side. While Diana fretted about how Audrey was coping with Aiden, or rather, how Aiden was coping with Audrey, Will slept like a log.

Chapter 9

Now

Diana arrives at school early on Tuesday morning for the first choir practice of the week and, being Tuesday, that means it's the Amberside College Senior Choir. Her main aim today is to select the two soloists for the school's centenary celebrations. As choir mistress, she's already decided on the new girl, Juliet, but is yet to be persuaded that Thea is up to the task.

She pastes on her brightest smile and claps her hands to garner everyone's attention. The chitchat diminishes. 'Ladies and gentlemen, when you're ready,' she calls out in her most authoritative voice. The auditorium falls quiet. 'Just a reminder before we start, I'll be dedicating the last half hour of this rehearsal to auditions for the solo parts for the school concert. Those who don't wish to try out will be free to go.'

Diana stands tall and straight and draws the attention of the sixty members of the choir. She addresses a pretty girl with long blonde plaits — angelic voice, brain like a sieve. 'Thea, please make sure you come in on the third beat of the second bar. Watch for my cue.' Diana holds up her hands, makes sure all eyes are on her, then brings the choir in.

After choir practice, she pops into the staffroom and submits the online eisteddfod application for the regional battle of the school choirs. It's not really called that, obviously, but it may as well be. Amberside College has won first place in the junior and senior sections for the past five years. Or, to put it another way, ever since Diana took over from the retiring choirmaster. She, and the school, have a reputation to uphold.

After leaving the school grounds, Diana starts up the hill on the long walk up to The Village. Lunch with Fi and Ruth means she needs to earn dessert, so no car for her today. Diana checks her watch and shifts it up a gear. She has ten minutes to make her salon appointment, then just enough time for a quick coffee with Michael before catching up with the girls for lunch. She's been looking forward to seeing him all week. It's a rare day she can entice him over to her side of the harbour. And coffee with Michael is just the tonic the doctor ordered.

Diana opens the salon door and sets the little bell tinkling.

'Hello! How are you?' Samantha stands at the front desk where the appointment book lays open next to the computer. 'Lip, chin and brow wax, yes?'

Diana examines her nails. She broke one opening the second bottle of Veuve at her mother's. She's gnawed the polish off another. Diana holds up her hand. 'Actually, can you fix these instead?'

Samantha beams at her. 'For you, yes. Always. Take a seat. Take a seat.' She bustles Diana over to the small table near the window and leaves momentarily to fetch a tall glass of green tea that carries the faint scent of vanilla.

From here Diana has the perfect view of The Village main street. She can see all the way down to the toy shop on the corner and all the way up to the kitchenware store that Will cannot walk past. He has a thing about their Egyptian-cotton tea towels.

Samantha sits down and settles her half-moon glasses on top of her face mask.

'How are the kids?' Diana asks. 'How did Lily's exams go?'

'Good, good.'

Diana has been coming here since Samantha took over the salon when Persephone was in preschool. Samantha is only a few years younger than Diana and still has a son in his final year of school and a daughter, Lily, who is in her first year of uni. The children are the glue of their friendship. Samantha and her family have just returned from visiting relatives in Vietnam, and Samantha shares her news while she repairs Diana's damaged nails.

Back out into the sunshine, Diana heads down the narrow walkway between the beauty salon and the homewares store towards a tiny café tucked in the corner of the square away from the wagging tongues of the main street. Its petite tables, cutesy wrought-iron chairs and yellow-and-white striped awnings remind her of Paris. The moment she sees Michael, joy bubbles to the surface.

He turns and smiles that same easy smile she knows so well. He stands up and when she is within reach, he clasps her hands and pulls her to him, kissing her on both cheeks. She breathes him in — a blend of lemon-scented washing powder, soft cotton and wool. His scent floods her with memories, the years fall away, and Diana sheds her skin.

He pulls out a chair for her, saying, 'I've ordered your usual.'

She has no sooner sat down than a waitress arrives with a cappuccino for her, a short black for him, and a saucer of Diana's favourite pistachio shortbreads.

'Thank you,' she says with a smile, directed at the waitress but really meant for Michael.

'You'll never guess who I ran across the other day,' he begins, pulling out his phone. Under the table, their knees brush; neither pulls away. He scrolls through social media, past photos of him in the studio posing with musicians or caught at the sound desk in the middle of a recording session.

Diana recognises a few familiar faces but there's plenty of new talent too. 'You've been busy,' she comments.

'Yep, plenty of work going around if you want it.'

'Don't be so coy, it doesn't suit you.'

'Here.' Michael turns the phone around so Diana can see the screen. Judging by the haircuts, it's an old photo. In it is a man, a woman and three kids lined up in descending order of height. A fourth child straddles the man's shoulders. All six are identically dressed in the club colours of their favourite team, complete with scarves and a couple of flags bearing the club emblem.

Diana looks at Michael. 'Am I supposed to know who they are?' One thing's for sure, they're not relatives of Michael's. And if they were, their fashion sense would be enough for him to disown them.

'You really don't recognise him?'

He's leaning so close she can see the tiny mole in that spot where his earlobe meets his jaw. 'I feel like this is a trick question.' She wraps her hand around the phone to bring it closer rather than get out her glasses. Michael doesn't let go. His hand is warm and familiar beneath hers. She studies the people. Middle-aged, overweight — not that she should talk. The man is going bald. The kids share the mother's widow's peak. 'I give up.'

A triumphant grin lights up Michael's face. 'It's Animal.'

'What? No!'

'And Linda from the bank. See? She wasn't joking when she said she wanted four kids.'

'I don't believe you.' Diana zooms in on the couple and shakes her head. 'Well, who'd have thought.'

'Is that the best you can do?'

Diana presses her palm on Michael's bare forearm, still sinewy and strong under his trademark flannelette shirt. 'Alright then. Try this on for size.' She affects a shocked tone worthy of a reality TV show host. 'Oh. My. God. How can that be Animal? Beneath all that chunky man-jewellery and those tight shirts, he really was just a bank clerk all along.'

'Too right. I bet he still dines out on his days as the drummer for a rock band.'

'We were hardly a rock band. More like lounge music.'

'Oi! That's harsh.' Michael nudges her.

The ladies at the next table are doing that thing where they're pretending to look past Diana and Michael to the pet shop window, but Diana is familiar with the ploy. She and Michael are drawing attention to themselves.

She lets go of his arm, whispering, 'Tone it down. People are staring.'

'In that case,' he says, barely skipping a beat, 'how about this?' Before Diana can register his meaning, Michael kisses her. It's a proper kiss. On the lips. Astonishment renders her speechless.

He pulls away. The way he's looking at her, Diana knows he's gauging her reaction. He's crossed a line. They both know it. The trouble is, she's not sure how she feels about that.

'You saucy wench!' he says, squeezing her kneecap.

Diana yelps and the moment vanishes. She presses a hand to her burning cheek and laughs to cover her embarrassment. 'You've lost none of your charm, young man.'

'Not so young anymore, my love,' he replies, adopting a mock-sad expression.

She sighs. 'No. None of us are.'

Michael leans back in his chair and looks around for the waitress. 'Do you want another coffee?'

'No, I have to go. Fi is always early.' She gathers her handbag and slips on her sunglasses. Michael is staring at her, appraising her. 'What?'

He shrugs. 'Nothing. Well, not nothing.'

Diana tenses. Is he going to say something about the kiss? Surely he realises that the worst thing they can do is talk about his faux pas.

Michael leans his elbows on the table, closing the gap between them. 'Have you ever thought about us getting back together? The band I mean. Or, at least, you and me.'

'You mean to perform?'

'What else would I mean? Don't you miss it?'

She thinks about the baby grand sitting in the apartment on The Green. It needs to be tuned after the move but in truth, she's in no real hurry. 'Oh Michael, I don't know. I think the late nights would kill me these days. I don't sing much anymore.'

'What a waste.' And the way he looks at her, into her, Diana isn't entirely sure he just means the singing. She breaks eye contact and searches her voluminous handbag for her wallet. She offers Michael a fifty-dollar note. 'Sorry, I don't have anything smaller.'

He looks offended and waves away the cash.

'Alright then, but next time it's my shout.'

Michael stands, putting a twenty under the saucer. 'How are you placed next week?'

'Um, maybe Wednesday, if that suits?'

'Sure. My schedule's pretty light on until early next month, so I can move things around.'

'Shall we meet at yours?'

Michael smiles his sexy sleepy smile. 'That'll be easier. Text me.'

Then he's gone, winding his way between the little outdoor tables, thanking the waitress and disappearing down the alley back to the main street.

Diana checks her watch. 'Shit. I'm late.' She scrambles to her feet, mentally ticking through the options. Should she text Fi, call a cab or just hoof it? She'll never make it by twelve. Bloody Michael. Time flies whenever she's with him.

She's trying to text and walk when she feels a hand on her bum. 'Your place or mine?' hot in her ear. She spins around, expecting Michael. Thank God it's not. But worse, it's her brother-in-law.

Diana steps away, pressing a hand to her heart. 'You scared the crap out of me, Ian. You can't go around sneaking up on women. Does the term "hashtag Me Too" mean nothing to you?'

Her sarcasm runs off him. 'Becks is having lunch with a girlfriend, Will's away. The stars have aligned.'

Diana doesn't dislike Ian but she's never been overly fond of him either. For starters, he is a shocking flirt and he's the only man she knows who can make a five-thousand-dollar suit look like a sack of potatoes. Maybe that's a bit harsh. He must be on a diet, he looks like he's lost a bit of weight. 'As it happens, it's Ruth's birthday. Fi and I are shouting her lunch.' She makes a point of checking her watch. 'And I'm late.'

'My car's just over there. I can give you a lift.'

Diana hesitates, weighs up her options. 'Alright, but keep your hands to yourself or risk losing them.'

Ian's midlife crisis is parked in the council car park behind the library. In ten minutes, he's dropping her outside The

Boatshed. As Diana waves him off, she smooths her tangled hair. Lucy Jordan might have wanted to ride in a sports car through the streets of Paris but Diana hates convertibles — they play havoc with her hair.

She pushes open the heavy wooden door of the restaurant and spots Fi sitting at a sunny table overlooking the marina. Trust her to have nabbed prime real estate.

'You're late,' Fi says, putting down an enormous glass of wine and air-kissing Diana's cheeks.

'Sorry, I got caught up.' She spies the bottle of wine in the ice bucket. 'Can you pour me one of those while I duck to the loo? I'm busting.'

Weirdly, on her way back she sees Rebecca. Although not all that weird, really. The Village isn't exactly heaving with nice places to eat. There's a rather ordinary Mexican on the main drag, Carlo's obviously, and that lovely little café at the nursery, if you only want a salad or a bit of cake. On such a delightful day, everyone flocks to The Boatshed.

Diana detours via Rebecca's table, where Rebecca is sitting alone. Judging by the way her sister-in-law is watching the front entrance, she's keen for her lunch date to arrive.

'Hey Becks, fancy meeting you here,' Diana says.

There is a flicker of eye contact, the faintest of smiles. 'Indeed.'

'Ian told me you were out to lunch. Good on you for taking some time out for yourself on a workday.'

Rebecca glances at the front entrance then back to Diana. 'That's one of the advantages of running my own show. I can suit myself.'

The temptation to tell Rebecca what she really thinks is hard to resist — that her sister-in-law derives a great deal of pleasure from organising all those fundraising balls and corporate golf days. Loves how everyone fawns over her. In the end, Diana goes for something more anodyne. 'Well, I won't keep you. Enjoy your lunch.'

Rebecca fails to answer. Her gaze has drifted again to the front entrance. As Diana walks away, she steals a peek and spies a woman carrying a hefty briefcase. Judging by the very expensive suit, this is not the typical uber-rich bored housewife Rebecca usually courts.

The moment she's seated and sunk a decent slug of wine, Diana shares her encounter with Fi. 'Yet again, I'm reminded how little I enjoy my sister-in-law's company.'

Fi holds up her wineglass and points at it. Somewhere over Diana's shoulder, a waiter fetches another bottle.

'You're not working?' Diana asks.

Fi shakes her head. 'I'm done for the day. Horrendous board meeting this morning. Honestly, whoever thinks being a company director is a doddle has never tried to wrangle a room full of old private-school farts.'

But aren't you married to one of those old private-school farts? Diana thinks but doesn't say. Far be it for her to judge. Not to mention that Richard and Will were in the same year at school.

Fi's eyes linger on Rebecca and her companion. She twiddles with the pearl earring dangling from her lobe. A matching string of them, the size of Maltesers, adorns her throat. They look fabulous, especially with the signature Chanel suit. 'Why would Rebecca be having lunch with Georgina Templeton?' Fi suddenly asks.

'You know her? Who is she?'

'Depending on who you ask, she's a family lawyer or a piranha — take your pick. Trouble in paradise?' Fi muses.

'I don't think so.' But how would Diana know? She and Rebecca have never shared marital confidences. Will certainly hasn't mentioned anything either and Ian would definitely confide in him. 'Maybe Becks is organising some corporate love-in?'

Fi snorts. 'Ian's always been a player. It's one of the main reasons we broke up. As impossible as it is to believe now, I used to be the insanely jealous type when I was young. She'd have her work cut out keeping him on a leash.'

'Really?' Diana finds that next to impossible to believe about Ian, even taking into account the hand-on-arse incident this morning. 'In my experience, the touchy-feely types are usually guilty of little more than making monumental fools of themselves.'

Fi gives her a withering look. 'Number one, a woman with your natural charms has a skewed view of normal male behaviour. And number two, Ian and I were an item for two years — I am well aware of his failings.'

'Hello! So sorry I'm late.'

'Happy birthday!'

'Happy birthday, Ruthie.'

Cheeks kissed, Ruth plonks into the third chair just as the waiter arrives with a fresh bucket of ice and a cold bottle of wine.

'Oh my goodness,' Ruth says, beaming up at the handsome young man — young enough, Diana notes, to be her son. 'You read my mind.'

The cheeky sod smiles at her, jiggling those sun-kissed curls that are just begging for some young thing to twirl her fingers through.

'Cute,' Ruth murmurs as Blondie disappears. She takes an enormous gulp of wine then lets out a giant 'aah'. 'Now, what have I missed?'

'We were just trying to figure out what possible connection there is between Rebecca and Georgina Templeton,' Fi says, tilting her head in their direction, and explaining the lawyer's professional expertise.

'I've always felt kind of sorry for her,' Ruth says, scooping up a handful of ice from the bucket and dropping it in her glass.

'I can't imagine why,' says Fi, over Diana's 'Which one?'

'Rebecca, of course. Imagine wanting to have kids and then finding out you can't have them? I've always assumed that's why she started fundraising for children's charities — you know, channelling her energies in a productive way. I mean, housing orphans is a pretty generous thing to do.'

'You never told me that was why she went into charity work.' Fi pins Diana with a laser-like stare.

'It's not really any of my business, is it? We don't talk about that kind of stuff.'

'But you're family.'

'Only on paper.'

Fi reaches for the wine. 'As I was saying before you arrived, Ruth, Ian's always thought with the wrong end of his anatomy. Looks like his bad behaviour is catching up with him.'

'I don't know about that.' Ruth holds out her own glass for a top-up. 'Marriages end up on the rocks for all sorts of reasons. Infidelity is usually a symptom something else is wrong in the relationship. Ian might be completely blameless.'

I forgive you. Diana regards her sister-in-law with fresh eyes. What had turned her into a class-A bitch? If Fi is right, has the effort of forgiving her husband's peccadilloes placed too much strain on Rebecca? There's a thought. The public face of marriage is never a true yardstick of what's really going on. Look at her and Will.

Blondie hovers within their line of sight, his iPad at the ready. Diana takes the hint.

'Let's order, shall we?' she suggests, thankful when the conversation moves on to topics a little less close to the bone.

Chapter 10

Then

Diana's back room had turned into a crèche. Aiden sat in his playpen, absorbed by a fly crawling up the railing. Ruth, her friend from mother's group, sat on the couch breastfeeding Harry and talking to Fiona, whose two-year-old twin boys had spent the afternoon doing their level best to wreck the joint. And because Diana didn't know Fiona very well, she had to put up with it. Right now, one of the twins had discovered Aiden's xylophone and, exhibiting absolutely no sense of rhythm, was bashing out a tone-deaf version of 'Twinkle Twinkle Little Star'. Fiona was man-handling the other boy into a highchair while he did his best to resist. Lydia, who — being childless — was here as an act of pure love, had positioned herself behind the kitchen bench, as if it were some sort of safety barricade. Or because it was closest to the grog. Audrey, as per usual, was late. Much to Diana's relief, Mrs Hillyker had declined the invitation but only because her sister was in town and they were going to see the new stage production of *My Fair Lady*. Surrounded by such chaos, the idea of sitting in air-conditioned comfort sounded heavenly, even at the price of putting up with all that rain in Spain nonsense. On the dining table sat the remains of a large cake she'd ordered from The Village Patisserie for the baby shower, the word 'Congratulations' now collapsed into the cakey wreckage.

Exhausted by this child-wrangling masquerading as a party, Diana lay prone on the couch, where she'd been trying to catch the faintest whiff of a breeze. So much for holding the baby shower early to try to escape the heat. The trouble was, now she couldn't seem to get up.

'Are you right? Do you need a hand?' asked Fiona, grabbing Diana's forearm in a vice-like grip and hauling her upright.

Gratefulness superseded humiliation. Truth was, Fiona was here under protest. Will went to school with her husband, Richard, and the couple had recently returned after five years in Hong Kong. Will said she was lonely and needed friends.

'But she was born here,' Diana had argued, annoyed that Will seemed to think she had time to babysit a grown woman. 'Surely she has friends of her own.'

'Maybe her husband insisted it's *you* who needs a friend,' Lydia had replied when Diana had whinged about it. Diana's horror amused Lydia no end. 'Cut her some slack. Some people take longer to warm to.'

Aiden picked up a board book and began punching the large pink button on the cover over and over again, making it moo like a demented cow. Diana grabbed it off him and exchanged it for the one about a hungry caterpillar. Aiden kicked up a stink so she relented and passed it back.

'What do you do when you're not doing this?' Fiona asked, sweeping her arm to encompass the room of mothers and babies.

'I sing in a band.'

'Oh.' Fi almost choked on the word. 'How do you manage it?'

'Same way you do, I guess,' Diana replied with an even smile.

'No, I meant, lucky you.' Fiona pulled a bib over her son's neck and took the lid off a container of pumpkin mash. 'Pulling billable hours for a big-six accounting firm is possibly the most boring job ever created. But my cunning plan is to stick at it until I'm fifty and leverage myself into a company directorship. I'm betting that by then, they'll all be screaming for women on boards.'

'Wow, that's real long-term planning.' Diana had her doubts though. It was hard to envisage this woman as a company director as she tried shovelling mashed pumpkin in her son's mouth while he was having the time of his life spitting it right back.

Very soon now, she'd need the loo. At this stage of her pregnancy, this required strategic forethought. The first challenge: going from sitting to standing. Diana leaned forward and observed her feet. They reminded her of those bloated puffer-fish carcasses that wash up on the beach. Her last salon pedi was ages ago. Will, sweetheart that he was, had made a valiant attempt. Clearly, he'd never been a child who could colour between the lines. 'I can't even wear shoes anymore.'

Lydia rattled the ice in her G&T and drained the glass. 'I told you, soak your feet in Epsom salts for half an hour then massage in some arnica oil.'

Lydia was the only one drinking. The bottle of champagne meant to shower the baby's head remained firmly corked and floating in the ice bucket.

Leaving the safety of the kitchen, Lydia plumped up a cushion and put it on the coffee table. She picked up Diana's feet and plonked them on top. 'Keep them elevated.' Then she grabbed a banana from the bowl on the kitchen bench and passed it to her. 'Eat this.'

'I'm not hungry.'

'Eat it. Bananas are full of potassium. It'll help balance your salt-to-water ratio.'

Diana began peeling. 'When I was pregnant with Aiden, I put on ten kilos of which he weighed four. This time, I put on ten kilos in the first trimester. For one scary minute, we thought we were having twins.' Diana realised her faux pas. 'Sorry, Fiona.'

'None taken. I agree, it's totally terrifying,' Fiona said as she removed a blob of pumpkin from her hair.

'Maybe it's because you're having a girl,' Ruth suggested.

'Not according to Mrs H. She swears it's a boy. She also predicts that Will and I will have three children.'

Lydia snorted. 'I'm sorry, you're taking the word of an elderly woman swinging a ring over your belly as gospel, are you?'

'I didn't say I took her seriously. It's just a bit of harmless fun.' With concentrated effort, Diana planted her feet and launched upright. 'I'm off to the loo. Can I get anyone anything while I'm up?'

Receiving a universal no, Diana waddled to the bathroom and slumped on the toilet. To get up again, she gripped the handrail thoughtfully installed by the previous elderly owners. Since the day she managed to snap the last toilet seat in half, she'd been extra careful when sitting and standing. Every time she used the bathroom was a fresh humiliation.

When she'd told Will, to his credit, he managed not to laugh. 'You broke the toilet seat? How? I mean, what?'

'Because I'm a fat marshmallow,' Diana had wailed.

'Oh, sweetheart, no you're not,' he had valiantly protested, attempting to console her with a hug. 'You're a gorgeous pregnant woman.'

Diana refused to be jollied out of the pleasures of wallowing in self-pity. However, she did capitulate when Will suggested she have a lie-down and he'd bring her a cup of tea. Then he took Aiden with him to The Village hardware store and bought a replacement seat.

He had looked so pleased with himself when he showed her the new toilet seat. Unfortunately, the less attractive side of Diana had leapt to the fore. 'Did you deliberately buy the cheapest, nastiest one you could find? Is this your idea of being funny?' she'd sniped.

'That's all they had,' poor Will had protested.

'What? They only stock cheap plastic pink toilet seats? You couldn't have bought a nicer one in white?' continued nasty Diana.

'But this matches,' Will had replied, bewildered and desperate to appease the savage beast.

Diana flushed the toilet now and let the cheap plastic toilet seat drop. It rattled in a flimsy fashion when it hit the porcelain rim. At least it would be easy for the kids to use.

She washed her hands with intense focus, avoiding her reflection, but accidentally caught a glimpse when she grabbed the hand towel. The horrid creature stared back with its extra chin and inflated cheeks pillowing piggy eyes. *What if I never lose this weight? What if I look like this forever?* This time, she didn't need anyone to remind her of the inevitable truth. She had to break it to the boys.

Diana waddled back to the party to find her mother had arrived, looking very chic in a black pantsuit and spotted silk blouse tied in a bow at her neck.

'Darling, look at you,' Audrey said, catching Diana's elbows and leaning in to kiss her cheek. 'My goodness, you're positively blooming. How many weeks now?'

Diana pulled away. 'Twenty-five.'

'Is that all? I thought you were further along than that.' And with that, Audrey flitted away to talk to Lydia, leaving Diana and her mutinous body reeling.

Audrey's arrival seemed to signal Ruth's and Fiona's departures. Diana didn't blame them. By the time Diana had waved them off from the front verandah, Audrey and Lydia had cleared space on the kitchen bench and were pouring the champagne.

Exhausted, Diana returned to her spot on the couch.

'Good news,' said Audrey. 'I've found a buyer for the pharmacy, so this afternoon I signed a contract to put the house on the market.'

Diana and Lydia shared a look. 'Great news,' Diana managed.

'Gee, Mum, what's the hurry?' Lydia added.

Audrey looked from one daughter to the other. No one said a word but all three women were thinking about the recently deceased James Roberts. Just not the same thing.

'And I brought these.' Audrey delved into her handbag and produced several glossy brochures.

'Mobile homes?' asked Lydia.

Diana waved from the couch. 'Let me see.' Lydia sat beside her and together they flicked through the pages. Aiden wanted to look too but Diana lifted the brochures above her head, as if they themselves were worth a cool couple of hundred thousand.

Audrey sloshed more champagne into her glass. 'Enough about my life. What's going on with you girls?'

'I'm quitting the band.' The words were out of her mouth before Diana could catch them. 'I mean, for good.'

'Well, that hardly constitutes news,' Audrey replied.

'What? Why?' asked Lydia.

Diana burst into tears. 'Because I'm too fat and I'm too tired and I can't face it. It's all too hard.'

'Oh Didi.' Lydia enveloped her in a hug and let her sob on her shoulder. 'It's the hormones, darls. I promise you'll be back to your old self as soon as bub pops out.'

Diana lifted her tear-stained face and looked at her swollen ankles. 'I can't even fit into my costumes. Last week I tore a seam on my favourite dress.'

'Not the emerald?' Lydia said as if they were discussing jewels, not dresses.

'Yes,' Diana sobbed.

'Bugger. Is it repairable?'

She shrugged — 'I don't know, probably' — and dissolved into more tears.

'Stop acting as if your life is over,' Audrey interrupted with a tsk. 'The trick is to reinvent yourself.'

Bracing himself on the couch, Aiden stood unsteadily and handed Diana his blankie. She pretended to wipe away her tears and gave it back to him. Satisfied, Aiden handed it to Lydia, who continued the pantomime. Then he turned and tottered towards his grandmother.

'What was the point of finishing your degree if you never use it? You should take up teaching. It's quite amenable to small children.' Audrey snatched Aiden's sticky paw moments before it grasped the knee of her black crepe pants.

'You sound like Will,' Diana said.

Audrey downed the rest of her glass. 'What does that tell you then?'

*

Diana parked the car where she could see the entrance to the rehearsal studio. She wanted the whole band there so she could break the news and get it over with in one fell swoop.

She had decided not to tell Will what she was up to. Better to present it as a done deal. After all, it was her decision to make, not his.

She practised what she was going to say while she waited. 'I don't think it's fair on you guys to have to depend on me coming back at some point. It's better if I quit and let you find someone new.'

Animal wouldn't care. He'd just been promoted to branch manager and Linda had made it quite clear that she wanted the kind of husband who mowed the lawn on weekends, not played drums for a bunch of wannabes.

Jonathan sauntered up the street and hung outside the rehearsal studio while he finished his cigarette. Diana drummed out a rhythm on the steering wheel. 'C'mon, Jonno. Get inside,' she muttered. Now she'd made the decision, she couldn't wait to say her piece and get out of here.

The moment Jonathan flicked his cigarette in the gutter and entered the rehearsal studio, Diana was out of the car. Despite her determination, she felt ill and she knew why. This wasn't baby sick, it was guilt. This was 'Am I making the worst decision of my life?' sick. She loved performing. It was more than the band. It was being up on stage, the audience looking back at her, the emotional connection, the physical exhilaration. There was nothing else quite like it.

Diana didn't even pause to put down her bag. Plastering on a brave smile, she came right out with it. 'I'm quitting the band.'

Animal stared at her. 'What, you mean permanently?'

'Fuck that.' Jonathan walked straight out.

'It didn't have to be this way,' Michael said as the door slammed.

'What way?' she asked.

'Why didn't you talk to me first?'

Diana had meant to break the news gently; instead she'd blurted it out like some kid. Now Michael looked how she felt and she released the truth. 'Because I didn't want you to talk me out of it,' she said softly.

'We could have taken a few months off like we did when you were pregnant with Aiden, built it up again when you were ready.'

It hung between them. She knew he wanted her to change her mind. She wanted to change her mind, if only not to see him hurting.

'Did Will finally get his way?'

A slap in the face. 'I beg your pardon?'

'C'mon, Diana. Will's made it clear from day one that he hates your involvement with us. The baby's just an excuse.'

'That's outrageous and hurtful, and completely beneath you.'

Silence. Michael picked up his guitar and put it back in its case. Animal got to his feet. Diana blushed. She'd forgotten he was sitting there.

He grabbed his keys off the speaker. 'I'll get my drum kit later, yeah?'

'That'd be good. I'm here all week.' The door shut. Michael gave her a sheepish grin. 'That was awkward.'

'You're telling me.' Diana didn't know how to end the conversation. Walking out like the others — leaving Michael alone — seemed unfair, but it wasn't her job to comfort him. She was Will's wife, not Michael's girlfriend. She adjusted the strap of her handbag. 'What will you do?'

He shrugged and switched off his amp, disconnecting the leads. 'That's not really your problem, is it?'

Diana cried all the way home.

'I just hope to God that I don't spend the rest of my life wondering what would have happened if I'd stayed,' she said to Will later after they'd put Aiden to bed.

He sat on the couch and eased off his sneakers. 'A door closes, a window opens, I guess.'

Diana sat at the other end of the couch and put her feet on his lap. Will took the hint and massaged her instep. She laid her head on the armrest and closed her eyes. 'I'll miss the band.'

Will rubbed a little harder than he ought to. 'Everything happens for a reason, Didi.'

She thought of Michael's parting words. 'Well, at least now you won't have to work around my schedule,' she said lightly to disguise the hurt.

'You won't hear any complaints from me. Now Dad's retired and I'm CEO, I'll be glad to have you watching my back.'

*

Persephone, goddess of spring, arrived on a chilly autumn night after sixteen hours and much pain relief. She was born contrary, thinking night was day and day night. It was to define her life. She would become the child who could drive Diana to her wit's end, but the day she was born, Diana looked into those eyes — the same tropical blue as Will's — and forgave her daughter everything. It set the tone for their relationship.

Chapter 11

Now

At lunchtime, Diana ducks out of school to make her appointment with the president of the Beach Club. She crosses The Esplanade then follows the wide footpath away from the netted baths towards the low-slung red-brick box with its wide verandah and rolling lawn that merges into the sand. To an outsider, the clubhouse is an anachronism — a knockdown job not worth saving. But locals know the continued existence of the Beach Club is a reminder that no matter how much The Village may have changed over the years, its values remain the same.

The closer she gets, the shoddier the building appears. She can't understand Will's loyalty to the place. It was he who insisted they hire it as the venue for the Big Party. Diana tried to dissuade him, suggesting The Boathouse as the obvious alternative, privately thinking it'd be less work for her, but selling it as a far more impressive location for their overseas guests. To no avail. Will's commitment to the clubbies far outweighed the practical considerations. Practicalities were Diana's department. Lucky her.

She walks up the new concrete path towards the club's entrance, shaking off her defeatism. As Lydia often says, when life gives you lemons, open the gin.

Royce Carmichael rounds the corner of the building wearing a towel slung around his neck and his budgie smugglers slung low on his hips. His enormous belly is first to greet her.

'Diana, darling, how are you?' he booms, extending the hand not carrying his cap and goggles.

They shake, then Royce bends over and retrieves the key to the front door from the wheel hub of his car. It gives Diana a full view of the name of the village emblazoned in club colours on his bum. He opens the security gate and ushers Diana inside. 'Ladies first.'

She peers around the gloomy interior. The place is all shabby and no chic. What sort of miracle worker does Will think she is? This is more Rebecca's department, not hers, but she'll ask for help over her dead body.

'Give me a tick while I get some gear on,' Royce says, disappearing in the direction of the men's changing rooms.

Diana gravitates to the glass folding doors, the club's saving grace — they open onto a spectacular view of the harbour. For all its faults, the Beach Club is angled in such a way that from the inside, it feels as though you're in the middle of nowhere. No hint of the mansions crowding the hills, just uninterrupted glittering harbour, white sand and sandstone cliffs covered in bushland.

Out on the lawn, club members are rinsing off under the outdoor showers or limbering up in preparation for a plunge in the icy winter waters. This is Will's crew. The people he swims laps of the harbour with in the early dawn, racing every Sunday, summer or winter.

'I wouldn't skip it for the world,' he often says, although sometimes she wishes he would. She misses lying in on a

Sunday morning, like they used to when they were young. After all, there are other things to do in the early hours that don't even involve getting out of bed.

'Morning, Di,' bellows one old salt, hand raised in salute.

'What have you done with Will?' calls out another.

'Done a bolt, has he?'

'That's alright, I'm always here for you, dear,' says Ralph Jordan, grinning at her, revealing his long yellow teeth. 'You've just got to say the word,' he adds with a lascivious wink and they all roar with laughter.

Diana presses her fingers to her lips and blows him a kiss. 'Ralph, darling, you're first on my list.'

Maybe that's the key. Will is a citizen of the world, wheeling and dealing, living the five-star lifestyle. But here among this motley crew, in this decrepit building, is where he feels accepted for who he is, and who doesn't crave a sense of belonging?

'There you are. Thought I'd lost you.' Royce strides out onto the lawn. He's changed into an old polo shirt with the name of his former company in faded letters on the breast pocket, and a pair of work shorts. He carries a manila folder labelled 'Forsyth's Party'. He balances a pair of chemist-shop glasses on the end of his nose and fumbles through the paperwork. 'Now, you want us to do the catering, is that right?'

Diana's heartbeat immediately kicks up a notch. 'No, no, that's all under control,' she assures him, forever grateful to The Village Providore. 'I was hoping to check if there's enough glassware, crockery, serving platters, that sort of thing. Perhaps I can take a peek in the kitchen, do a bit of a stocktake in case I need to ring the party-hire company?'

Royce's bushy eyebrows disappear into his hairline. For a brief moment he looks flustered, but he quickly recovers and peers at her with the sharp-eyed intensity of the corporate Mr Fix-it he once was. 'What about some music? Shirley Cosgrove's nephew moonlights as a mobile DJ. He'll play whatever tunes you like.'

'Again, we're good on that front. I'm not sure if Will told you but our son Aiden is coming home for the party. I've put him in charge of the music. He knows our tastes.' She shrugs in a way she hopes conveys *Isn't that sweet? I couldn't possibly disappoint him.*

The reality is that Diana and Aiden have been having a ball spending large chunks of their weekly Zoom meetings collating a playlist of old favourites. In between, Aiden sends frequent emails reminding her of songs she's forgotten all about. It takes her straight back to New Year's Eve parties at Fi and Richard's. The tag-team effort getting the kids bathed and fed and ready for bed so the adults could let their hair down. Richard used to spend months making mix tapes. Every chat with Aiden is a trip down memory lane.

Royce's steely gaze softens into a more pleading one. It ages him ten years. 'I was hoping to provide a bit more than the trestle tables and the fold-out chairs, love.'

He's angling for a slice of the action and Diana knows precisely why. The membership fees barely cover the bills. There's no spare cash for repairs, let alone the full-scale renovation it really needs. The Big Party is the answer to some of the club's prayers, or at least Royce's.

Bloody Will. Diana resents being put in such an invidious position. How does she get out of this politely? By lying, of course — it's the only way.

She leans closer, as if sharing a confidence. 'Between you and me, Royce, it's my daughter's mother-in-law. You see, she's quite the sensation in French cooking circles. She's posh.'

Diana indicates this with a flourish. 'I feel compelled to put on something a bit more high-end than what we'd normally go for.' She's lying through her back teeth but Royce seems hooked, so she keeps going. 'Otherwise I'd absolutely *love* the Beach Club to provide a barbecue.'

The word defeat, however, is not in Royce's vocabulary. 'I don't know, Di. I reckon a barbecue would give her an authentic Aussie experience. If you want to go a bit posher, Mary makes a mean devilled egg, and her potato salad is the stuff of legends.'

Before her eyes flashes the Beach Club Christmas Party, Mary passing around her tray of devilled eggs with their ridges of carefully piped filling, speckled with festive green chives and paprika. They were delicious, but Diana can't imagine a fancy egg is going to impress someone of Camille's calibre.

Diana smiles. 'Gosh, that's very generous of you. Though Mary's already quite busy with her volunteer work, not to mention running the croquet club. I couldn't impose on her further.'

Royce waves away her concerns. 'You'll need a birthday cake too. Will loves Mary's pineapple upside-down cake.'

Alarmed at this fresh assault, Diana starts to babble. 'Oh golly, yes! You're right, he does. I think it's the amount of rum she uses. But, I'm so sorry, I've already ordered one of those slab layered cakes from the patisserie. I need something that can feed a cast of thousands.' Well, forty.

The look on Royce's face makes her feel like a complete bitch. Will always says he's going to run for club president himself when he retires. How would she feel if some latter-day Diana thwarted Will's genuine desire to help? It's not like Royce is begging in order to line his own pockets.

She decides to grease the wheels. 'Will and I have discussed it' — complete lie — 'and what we'd like to do, as an act of good faith, is to make a donation in lieu. Would a thousand dollars cover it?'

Royce might be old but the former chairman of one of Australia's largest listed companies is not stupid. She can see his brain ticking over, no doubt thinking of the missing roof tiles or the concrete cancer in the men's changing rooms. 'Make it two K and we have a deal.'

Diana stifles a sigh and offers her hand. 'Deal. Now, I have ten minutes before I'm due back at school. You'd better show me this kitchen.'

Chapter 12

Then

'C'mon, Aidy, please let Mummy help you put on your shoes.'

'No! Want that one,' he said, pointing at his Thomas the Tank Engine gumboots.

'Sweetheart, it's going to be stinking hot today, you can't wear gumboots to kindy. Put your sneakers on for Mummy, please.'

'No!' Aiden kicked out and caught Diana in the stomach. She flinched and told herself he hadn't meant to hurt her. He was three, for Pete's sake. She took a deep breath and tried not to look at the clock. The nine o'clock news had been and gone. She'd promised to meet Ruth at The Green at half-past. And because Ruth was incredibly well organised and serene, despite having three boys under six, Diana did not want to be labelled a flake by her.

'Aidy, darling, I'll make you a deal. How about you wear your gumboots to kindy and I'll put your sneakers in your bag in case you change your mind later?' Diana picked up the sneakers and tucked them in the side pocket of his Thomas the Tank Engine backpack. Given the sneakers were also covered in tiny Thomases, this felt like an irresistibly persuasive argument. She poured diluted apple and blackcurrant juice into his Thomas the Tank Engine thermos and slipped it into the side pocket. Juice was a treat beyond his wildest expectations. If a sneaky juice didn't clinch the deal, nothing would.

Aiden watched her with those enormous brown eyes of his, silent, then slipped off the couch and ran over to his gumboots. He flopped on the floor and slid them on his feet, the wrong way round, but Diana was past caring. She helped him stand up and put on his backpack. He swayed as he adjusted to the weight but Diana wouldn't dare offer to carry it — nothing came between Aiden and Thomas.

Job done, she swooped on Persephone and swung her onto her hip. Diana didn't bother with niceties such as shoes or a clean face. She had precisely seventeen minutes to get Aiden to kindy and meet Ruth. If she floored it, she might just have enough time to grab a coffee. A large one.

Aiden's preschool was tucked in a corner next to the oval. The moment Diana opened the gate, Aiden took off, discarding his backpack as he ran, barely hampered by his gumboots. Diana scooped the backpack off the ground, hung it on his hook and put his lunch box in the basket. When she signed him in, she felt the twinge. Every single time. And every single time, it made her cross with herself. Other mothers seemed more than happy to see their little soldiers and princesses charge off into feisty independence. Was she the only one who wished Aiden exhibited any separation anxiety? Not bawling his eyes out like little Samuel Hooper, who clung to his mother's leg as if it were a piece of flotsam in the shipwreck of life, but a modicum of sadness every once in a while might be nice.

Persephone plonked herself in the middle of the big kids in the sandpit. She filled a dump truck and drove it over to a giant castle that was under construction. It was a glimpse of the future. Next year, Persephone would be here for real. No chance of abandonment issues there.

'Persephone, time to go,' she called out.

Persephone frowned at her. 'Mummy!' she exclaimed in a stern voice.

'Rufus is waiting for us.'

At the mention of her best friend's name, Persephone scrambled to her feet and ran over, trailing sand like fairy dust. More sand in the car — Will would be ropable.

*

Because they were late, Diana had to park ages away from The Green. It took some talent to extract Persephone's tricycle from the boot where it had ended up jammed between the stroller, shopping bags, Will's fins, and two large green garbage bags filled with Aiden's old clothes. She'd been meaning to give them to Ruth for months but kept forgetting. If she remembered later, she'd drive over to wherever Ruth had parked and give her the hand-me-downs.

Persephone took off on her tricycle, her little legs pedalling like mad, the pink glittery ribbons on the handlebars flaring in her wake. 'Persephone, stop at the coffee shop,' Diana yelled after her. She had no hope of catching her. She was not one of those yummy mummies jogging past with their new-fangled three-wheeler prams. It seemed lycra and leggings were de rigueur, not drawstring pants and a shirt of dubious cleanliness.

'I'm so sorry I'm late.' Diana passed Ruth a hot chocolate. 'This is my way of apologising.'

'You mean, your way of not feeling guilty because you needed coffee,' Ruth replied, extracting the marshmallows. She sucked them down and licked her fingers. 'Hmm, always the best part.'

Diana eyeballed the kids. Every piece of equipment was crawling with toddlers. 'Yeah, sorry. Aiden insisted on gumboots.' The caffeine hit her and she felt instantly better. 'Do you know, before I had Aiden, I'd never have imagined that simply getting dressed and out the door was a major achievement.'

'But not exactly a highlight,' Ruth said as she laid out a series of plastic containers. 'Cut-up watermelon. Rice crackers. Little homemade berry muffins. What have I forgotten?'

Diana contributed a container of strawberries, another of halved seedless grapes, mini yoghurt pots, and a bottle of diluted apple and blackcurrant juice. 'Look at us. Living the high life,' she joked. 'All we're missing is the champagne.' She took the lid off the container of strawberries and offered it to Ruth.

She waved them away. 'I'm trying not to snack. I swear I've put on ten kilos eating kids' leftovers.'

'I don't know how. Your three must run you ragged.' Diana ate a strawberry. She didn't add 'on your own' out of deference to Ruth's recently acquired single status.

Ruth shrugged and ferreted around in her enormous bag. 'You do what you have to do, don't you?' She pulled out sunscreen. 'Rufus Baker,' she bellowed. 'Front and centre, now.'

He scrambled to his feet and ran over, leaving a perplexed Persephone alone on the see-saw. Rufus held up his moon-face and barely even squirmed as his mother applied a liberal amount of sticky fluid to his cheeks, ears and neck. He giggled when Ruth tickled him and set him free, saying, 'Off you go, munchkin.'

'I wish mine were that well behaved,' Diana said, watching him run back to his bestie.

'The secret is setting the right expectations. I expect them to come when they're called and do what they're asked and they all know there will be consequences if they don't comply.'

Diana suspected there was more to it than that. As an experiment, she called Persephone over and waved the sunscreen bottle in an authoritative fashion.

'No!' came the response from the sandpit.

Ruth giggled. 'It takes practice.'

Diana decided to change the subject. 'How's the new job?'

'Pays the bills.'

Ruth had just started part-time as the school counsellor at Amberside College, the K to 12 co-ed private school that backed onto The Green. Since Dave decided he couldn't hack being married with three robust little boys, Ruth had stepped up to the plate.

'But are you okay? I mean, I know you don't have much of a choice right now, but are you enjoying it?'

Ruth smiled. 'What's not to love? I'm like the plumber with the leaky tap — brilliant at solving everybody else's problems. And I'm fantastic at keeping teenage girls' secrets.'

'I've always blamed Will's constant travel for me staying at home. If you can work, what's my excuse?'

'Don't be so hard on yourself. There's plenty of time — the kids are still little.'

'You and Fi have kids the same age.'

Ruth changed tack. 'Except it's not so practical to go back to performing, is it? You could turn your hand to teaching. I know it's not in the same league but I think you'd be brilliant at it.'

Diana peeled the wrapper off a teeny raspberry muffin and bit it in half. Her mother was always on at her to do something with herself. 'Maybe.'

*

On the weekend, Diana and Will christened the newly completed deck and the new barbecue. Will was in his element, a glass of red in one hand, tongs in the other. Diana nursed a cold glass of rosé and picked at the olives. The conversation with Ruth had stuck with her. She'd been waiting all week for the right moment to broach the subject with Will. The kids had both crashed after a morning at the beach and a long lazy afternoon stretched ahead of them. Now was as good a time as any.

'Did I tell you I've put Persephone's name down at preschool for two days a week next year? Family members get first preference so she should get a spot.'

'Do you think she's ready?' Will put the corn on the grill, fiddled with the gas until he was happy with the temperature.

'She'll be nearly three. It'll be good for her.' This was harder than she thought. She knew damn well that her staying at home suited Will down to a tee. He could either make this easy or difficult. It was the first time she'd tested these waters. She took a sip of wine to fortify her resolve. 'It'll give me time to do something for myself.' She paused to let that idea sink in. 'I thought I'd go back to singing.'

Will put down the tongs and turned around. He did not look happy. 'How will you manage the late nights?' he eventually asked.

Diana laughed, mostly in relief. 'Oh no, no, no. Not performing. Those days are long behind me. I meant teaching singing.'

He relaxed, which she found just the teensiest bit annoying. Why was *he* the only one entitled to a career? There had never been an actual conversation about the division of labour. Because he earned more money in a year than she would in a lifetime, Diana kept house and raised the kids. As if being there so he could walk out the door and jump on a plane at the drop of a hat counted for less simply because it carried no monetary value. Without her, Will would be stuffed.

More to the point, her sense of self-worth couldn't be measured by the balance in their joint bank account. Truth was, if Diana thought she'd get away with it, she would go back to performing. Teaching singing was a compromise, a small tilt at reclaiming her identity. That simple gesture, relaxing his shoulders, the moment Will realised he wasn't going to be inconvenienced, turned an idea, a question, into a fact.

'We can easily turn the sunroom into a studio. I'll be home for the kids and it won't interfere with your travel schedule. Once they're both at big school, I'm sure Mrs H would be over the moon to lend a hand.'

Diana waited to see which way Will would jump. Inside, she was pleading with him to be reasonable. How could he complain? She'd be teaching children, not hanging out with a band. No late nights, just a sensible, grown-up day job so she wasn't the only one of her friends without a toehold on independence.

Will moved the kids' sausages to the cooler part of the hot plate and turned the steaks. 'I suppose a bit of extra cash might come in handy.' He took a sip of wine. 'Especially if Persephone is starting preschool next year.' Diana felt herself teetering, waiting for the balance to shift. Then he said, 'If things take off, maybe we can build you a proper studio.'

She leapt to her feet and threw her arms around his neck. 'Thank you, thank you, thank you.'

'Why are you thanking me? I haven't done anything.'

She moulded herself to Will's torso and kissed him in a way filled with the promise of more to come later. He didn't need to know what she'd really been thinking. That she thought he'd put his needs ahead of hers, and how desperate that made her feel. 'For being you, that's why.' She kissed him again.

Will put down his wine and wrapped his arms around her. 'Those steaks have got about four minutes.'

Diana raised her eyebrows in mock horror. 'Will Forsyth, are you suggesting a quickie?'

For an answer, he pulled on the drawstring of her pants and they fell around her ankles. He gently pushed her backwards until her bottom nudged the new outdoor table, which turned out to be the perfect height and remarkably fit for purpose.

*

Diana couldn't wait to tell Ruth. Next time they were at the park, she shared the story with her, although she skipped the bit about the sex. Since poor Ruth wasn't getting any at the moment, it seemed unnecessarily cruel to remind her.

'Once you're up and running, you should talk to the school. Amberside could do with some fresh blood in the music department. The choirmaster is a lovely bloke but a hopeless teacher. If you were head of the choir, the kids would be lining up to audition.'

'Slow down. Beyond prac teaching, I've never taught a day in my life. I might be terrible at it. And I'm not convinced I can juggle everything as efficiently as you do. I think your choirmaster's job is safe for a while yet.'

Ruth began packing up the detritus of morning tea, tipping the fruit into one container, rinsing the others under the tap. A single apple and cinnamon muffin remained. Diana watched her, waiting to see if she would pack it, offer it to her, or eat it herself.

'Actually, I've got an even better idea,' Ruth said, picking up that morsel of deliciousness. 'Why don't you advertise for students in the school newsletter? I'm sure they will flock to your door.'

Diana pounced on Ruth and extracted the muffin. 'I'm saving you from yourself,' she said, then ate it before Ruth could protest. 'But you, madam, are a genius.'

*

Diana had the floorboards in the sunroom sanded back and resealed, returning them to a lovely warm reddish brown. In between naps and preschool, she painted the walls sage green. She even let Persephone and Aiden paint their own patches in the corner.

'Is this going to be our playroom?' Aiden asked, painting his hand with the brush and planting it on the wall.

'No, darling,' Diana said, wiping his hands clean. 'This is going to be Mummy's playroom.'

Once the second coat was dry, she set up the electric piano at one end of the room and moved a potted bamboo into a corner where it would catch the morning sun.

Thanks to Ruth's brilliant suggestion, Diana advertised in the school newsletter and had three students for the start of the new term. 'I feel like a bit of a fraud putting credentials after my name,' she confided to Lydia when she came to inspect the makeover.

'Blame Dad. He was the one always banging on at us about doing something useful.'

'Yes, but you did, Lyds. Remember he used to tell me, quote unquote, that just because a university education was free didn't mean I had the right to pick something as flaky as music.

The only reason I tacked on a diploma of education was to mollify him. Never in a million years did I think I'd use it.' She straightened the frames of her degrees. Diana Forsyth, Music Teacher. BMus. Dip Ed. 'It makes me feel strangely proud.'

'So you should be.' Lydia walked the length of the sunroom, nodding her approval. 'You've done a great job, sis.' At the opposite end, she sat at the piano, getting a different perspective. 'You know what you do need though?'

'What?'

'You need to put up some pictures.'

Diana examined the walls, bare except for her degree and diploma. 'Hmm, I thought the same thing. I'll pop into that shop in The Village and see if they have anything suitable.'

Lydia spun on the stool and frowned at her. 'God, you're an idiot sometimes.'

'What do you mean?'

'You don't need to *buy* pictures. Will must have boxes of the bloody things. All those photos he took of you and The Somethings. Put them up.'

Diana blushed. 'I can't do that.'

'Why not? They're perfect. Pictures of you performing are way more impressive than the bits of paper,' she said, flicking her fingers at Diana's qualifications. 'The kids will think you're cool and seeing you in action will inspire them to greater heights.'

Diana shared the idea with Will that night while he was making moussaka and she was half in the bathroom keeping an eye on the kids.

'I think it's a great idea.'

'Really? You don't think it sounds a bit, you know, vain? I mean, no one wants to see me from yonks ago. It feels a bit try-hard.'

Will gave her a look remarkably similar to Lydia's that afternoon. 'You loved performing with The Somethings. It was a huge part of your life. You should make it work for you.'

He put the moussaka in the oven and grabbed her hand. 'C'mon, I'll show you what I mean.'

They stood at the entrance to the narrow corridor that ran between the kitchen and the spare loo. On the inside doorjamb of the loo, Will had marked the ascending heights of Aiden and Persephone every three months, starting from their first birthdays. The last mark proved Aiden was having a growth spurt.

'We can put a selection in the sunroom, then put a whole lot on that facing wall between the door to the sunroom and the spare loo. It'll be kind of like your resume, except in pictures. Plus, you'll be able to charge more.'

'Well, when you put it like that,' she said, keeping a lid on the sarcasm.

It went straight over Will's head. 'Problem solved. I'll sort through my shots on the weekend. When's your first student?'

'Monday afternoon.' Just saying it set off the butterflies in her stomach.

'And you know what?' he said, heading back to the kitchen. 'Once they hear you sing, you'll be turning them away in droves.'

Chapter 13

Now

On Wednesday morning, Diana drives to the other side of town. Since her meeting with Royce a week ago, she has barely had a moment to think between unpacking, choir practice and party planning. She makes her way over the bridge and along the freeway that winds through the cityscape beneath all those tall towers of tiny apartments that have sprung up since she lived out this way. She takes the turn-off that bisects the enormous park and the bay filled with cruising yachts. Rows of terraces and workers' cottages line the hilly streets. They've all been dolled up since her day. And why not? Fabulous view of the bay and the city skyline, walking distance to the theatre district, cafés and restaurants on every corner. If they'd bought an apartment here, Will would be a stone's throw from the airport and she'd be in heaven.

Off the main street, she squeezes into a space outside a tiny terrace. She loves this house. It has French doors either side of a wooden front door that is painted bottle green with an enormous brass knocker. Out front is a gorgeous little courtyard with a tumbling fountain and hedges reminiscent of French topiary. It's next to a garden slightly larger than a house block with a timber bench built around the girth of an old shade tree. A little wrought-iron fence hems it in and, as Diana walks past the gate, she reads the sign declaring this to be the Harriet Penske Memorial Park. Whoever Harriet was, she very generously gifted the neighbourhood some extraordinarily valuable breathing space.

A man brushes past her and Diana automatically steps aside. A small dog trots along beside him — a white whippet covered in splodgy caramel spots. It wears a smart navy tartan coat trimmed in red and is attached to the man by a matching lead. Once he has closed the gate behind him, he unclips its lead and the dog bounds across the grass, desperate to explore. The man sits on the bench beneath the tree and fiddles with his phone, ignoring his dog's toilet break. If this was The Green, Diana wouldn't hesitate to remind him of his duty but since she's not on home turf, she glares instead. The man points the phone at her. There's a distinct whirr and click. Unnerved, Diana turns on her heel and hurries off.

Her destination is a warehouse a few doors up. The signage declares it was once Smith & Sons Footwear but like so many inner-city warehouses, it is now a blend of apartments and office space. She walks up the gravel driveway under an arched portico and presses the buzzer. The security door clicks open. Inside the foyer, Diana presses the number four and while she waits for the lift, she touches up her lipstick and smooths a damp finger through her eyebrows. A yap startles her. It's the man from the park. He's standing outside the warehouse complex, on his blasted phone again. The lift bell dings, the doors open and Diana scurries inside.

Michael must have heard the lift because the door to his apartment is already open.

'I've just had the strangest experience,' Diana says, entering the apartment as if being chased. She heads straight for the kitchen bench and deposits herself on one of the bar stools and her handbag on another. 'I was just standing there, admiring that little park down the road from you, when this guy turned up and took my photo. Don't you think that's weird?'

Michael kisses her cheek. 'A bit. Are you okay?'

'Yes, I'm fine.' Diana bites her lip, thinking. 'The strange thing is, I feel like I've seen him somewhere before. I just can't put my finger on it.'

'It'll come to you. Coffee?'

He doesn't wait for an answer. The reservoir is already full and the machine is on.

Diana unwinds her scarf and stuffs it in her handbag, shaking her hair free from her collar. She needs a moment to recover her equanimity. She watches Michael playing barista. He's wearing black jeans and a soft moleskin shirt over a t-shirt. No shoes despite the cold. His hair is still damp from the shower. With a start, she realises he's only just got out of bed despite the fact it's nearly lunchtime. Has he had company? Worse, is she intruding?

Michael pours warm milk into her coffee, spoons over the froth and dusts it with a tiny shake of cocoa. 'There you go,' he says, sliding her cappuccino across the bench.

Diana has had plenty of time since her last coffee with Michael to think about that kiss. She's been from one extreme — dismissing it as her reading far too much into it — to the other, wondering why Michael would suddenly declare an interest after all these years. Sex is the one thing guaranteed to ruin a friendship, and they've been friends for too many years to risk that. He must know this as well as her.

Diana sips her coffee. She can feel Michael studying her. She has to get this off her chest. 'Before we go any further, we need to talk about last week.'

He leans against the bench and smiles at her in that sleepy sexy way of his. 'Which bit?'

Cheeky sod. He's determined to make this as hard for her as possible. 'When you kissed me, Michael,' she says in her best teacher's voice.

'You want me to do it again?'

'No. Don't you dare.' She laughs. 'I'm not here to flirt with you and you know it.'

'Are you sure about that?'

'We're friends, Michael. I'm married to Will. Thirty years next month.'

'I know. I was at your wedding, remember?'

She smiles. 'I do.' Diana plays with her cup, twirling it clockwise, anticlockwise. What is she trying to say? 'Thirty years is not to be sneezed at. Not that you'd know. Your threshold of interest is about thirty days.'

'More like thirty minutes.'

She snorts and wags her head at him. 'Way too much information.'

To avoid looking at Michael, Diana looks around the apartment. He's lived here the entire time she's known him. Long before this part of town was trendy, he bought it for a sum that would now be considered a song. Back then it was barely habitable. In the alcove where the bookcase is, used to be Michael's waterbed. She smooths her hands across the stone bench. It took him years to get around to building a kitchen. Michael mostly eats out. The place still has the bachelor feel. Diana looks at him and tries again.

'Marriage is different from how you imagine it will be when you start out. It takes a lot more fortitude, sheer bloody grit some days.' The urge to cry threatens. 'Will still travels a lot. A lot. Sometimes for weeks at a time.' Diana stops in her tracks. Michael doesn't need to know how lonely her life often is. If it weren't for work, some days she wouldn't even get out of bed, especially now the kids aren't around. She misses Will when he is not there but when he is, more and more she feels that she and Will are on different paths. He doesn't know what she does when he's away. She has no idea what he does. Diana thinks of the note, that blasted note, and she wouldn't be thinking any of this right now if bloody Michael hadn't kissed her.

The tears fall. 'I'm sorry, I don't know what's got into me. You don't need to hear this rubbish.' Her voice catches, the sheer strain of trying to hold this all in. She dashes her hand under her eyes. 'You know, I think it's moving house and the party.' Diana finds a tissue in her bag and blows her nose. 'Ignore me. Just for future reference, you can't go around kissing me like that, okay? Look what you've done. I'm a wreck.' She laughs at her feeble attempt at humour.

Michael puts down his empty cup and comes around to her side of the bench. He takes hold of Diana's hand and helps her off the stool. The warmth of his touch almost undoes her.

'C'mon, you gorgeous creature, I know exactly how to cure what ails you.' He doesn't let go — she willingly follows, and when they enter the room, she is relieved when he shuts the door behind them.

Chapter 14

Then

Diana had tied herself in knots trying to work out which photos belonged in the studio versus those better hung in the corridor. 'I'm leaning towards group shots of the band,' she said to Will patiently standing there, hammer and hooks at the ready.

'They're buying *your* services, not Michael's or Jonathan's or Greg's,' he countered.

She winced. 'That doesn't sound too great.'

He shook his head in that irritated way of his. 'You know what I mean.'

She went to check on the kids and by the time she returned Will had hung a close-up of her in full flight with her boobs practically falling out of that little black sequinned number.

'Will! I'm teaching kids,' she protested.

'Teenagers,' he corrected.

Now, every time she saw herself, she cringed. Best not to look. But she had to admit, it was good for business. Eventually, she even saw the funny side of it.

Take today, for example. She had the first lesson with a new student, which meant a first meeting with a new mother. These women were a breed unto themselves. They liked to come and chat with her before they handed over large sums of money for one term's fees. They'd walk into the studio, wafting over to check out the qualifications hanging on the wall, as if it were a mere passing interest. Then their gaze would drift towards the block of photos and from that point on, Diana could almost write the script.

Pause. Step closer. Crane forward ever so slightly to better study the photo of the glamorous woman wearing a full-length dress split to the thigh. Diana's face in profile, eyes closed, microphone at her lips, hand raised in supplication. A step back. A glance at Diana, who pretended to be arranging sheafs of music on the stand while she kept the first-timer in her peripheral vision. Never sure if recognition might morph into *Oh my, she looks so different now*, versus *Wow, she looks amazing*. Fortunately for her vanity, the reaction usually veered towards the latter. Otherwise, she would have made Will swap the photo for another.

Move on to the next photo, a shot of the whole band — Diana had insisted. 'I can't say I was part of Diana and The Somethings and there's no Somethings. It's ridiculous.'

This picture was Will's concession. He'd taken it from below the stage, framing her, front and centre, tambourine above her head, hair swinging out behind her as she glanced back at Michael, stage left. Jonathan lurked in the shadows stage right, next to Animal in a spray of sweat that glistened like raindrops.

A finger-tap on Michael with his bulging biceps. 'Is this your husband?'

'No, my husband doesn't play an instrument.'

'Handsome devil though, isn't he?' So predictable.

At this juncture, Diana invariably said, 'Well, shall we start the lesson?' Then she'd smile brightly at the mother until she, however reluctantly, tore herself away from stickybeaking and promised to pick up Susie, Sarah or Samantha in half an hour.

And that's how the word got around. Given The Village was a close-knit community, it didn't take long. Even more surprising, Diana took to teaching like the proverbial duck to water.

She closed the door on her last student of the day. Ellie was a talented singer but her work ethic let her down. Singing would never be more than a hobby unless she sharpened up her act. It had been a long week. Diana was glad to turn off the studio lights, close the door and walk back into family life. 'Hello, Mrs H, how are you?'

Mrs Hillyker was wiping down the kitchen benches. There was no evidence of what the kids had had for dinner. The empty washing basket declared that a load had been hung out, another brought in, folded and put away.

'You really don't have to do that,' Diana protested.

'Nonsense, I may as well make myself useful while I'm here. I've been banished from playing Snakes and Ladders because I win too much,' she said with a smile.

'Let me guess. Persephone?'

'Correct.'

Diana stuck her head around the doorway into the playroom. Aiden was glued to the television and Persephone was playing Snakes and Ladders by herself. Her little face lit up when she saw her. 'Mummy, play wiv me.'

Diana sat at the tiny table. 'I like your hair, Persephone. Did Mrs H do those plaits for you?'

Persephone's hair had been washed and braided into tiny plaits that would make her hair go all crinkly when Diana undid them in the morning. Mrs Hillyker had parted Aiden's hair on the side and combed it flat, and Diana could see Mrs H's own boys back in the day. All that was missing was the thick tartan dressing-gown and the matching slippers.

'You go, Mummy.'

Diana rolled the dice and let Persephone move her piece along the board because it was good for her to practise her counting. She made no comment when, accidentally on purpose, her daughter slid the piece a spot too far and she missed the ladder. In another year or so she'd nip this cheating in the bud but it amused Diana no end. The fact this was a game about vice and virtue made Persephone's behaviour even more hilarious.

On impulse she called out, 'Can I interest you in a glass of wine, Mrs H?'

Mrs Hillyker walked past, arms filled with Aiden's sheets. 'That would be lovely, dear. Just let me pop these in the machine and I'll be right with you.'

Up the ladders, along the rows, and down the snakes until Persephone declared, 'I wonned, Mummy.'

Diana looked at the board. Amazingly she seemed to have slithered down a long snake and was back on the first row. 'Well done, darling. Mummy's going to have a glass of wine with Mrs H now. Why don't you ask Aiden to play?'

Aiden didn't even take his eyes off the screen. 'No. She cheats.'

'No, I don't! Mummy.'

Diana kissed her tightly braided head. 'Yes, you do, but that's okay because you're very little.'

'No, I'm not!'

Diana raised her hands in surrender and escaped. She poured two glasses of chardonnay then dug around in the fridge and found dolmades and olive tapenade. Perfect. Finish these off and dinner was solved.

'Now I feel quite spoilt,' Mrs Hillyker said, observing the hastily arranged antipasto platter to which Diana had added a packet of crackers. 'Cheers.' She lifted her glass and took a sip. 'Ooh, just what the doctor ordered.' Mrs Hillyker took another, somewhat larger sip.

Diana couldn't agree. The wine tasted corked. She checked the label on the bottle. The vintage was only a couple of years old, so that couldn't be it.

'Are you alright, dear? You look a bit pale.'

'Do I? I'm just tired. It's been a big week.'

Mrs Hillyker made soothing noises. 'It's hard on you with Will always travelling. You need an extra pair of hands.'

'Why when I have you?'

'That's very kind, but I really think you should invest in a cleaning lady and start sending Will's business shirts to the drycleaners.'

'My mother said the same thing.'

'Wise woman.'

Diana smeared olive tapenade on a cracker and offered it to Mrs Hillyker.

'A bit rich for my taste, dear. You have it.'

With a shrug, Diana popped it in her mouth. 'I don't know, a cleaning lady feels a bit decadent. It'd be different if I worked full-time. To be honest, I think I just hate housework. It's so unrewarding. No one is ever going to write on my gravestone, *Here lies Diana Forsyth who never once failed the white glove test.*'

Mrs Hillyker chortled. 'True, but I thought young Will was doing well these days, or well enough. Charlie always says there's no point having money if you can't palm off the jobs you hate.'

A ginormous yawn caught Diana short and Mrs Hillyker put down her glass of wine. 'Time for me to go.'

'No, no, sorry. I don't know what's wrong with me. I slept like a log last night. Maybe that's the problem.'

Mrs Hillyker's gaze lingered on Diana's tummy. 'Don't tell me I need to press that ring back into service.'

'Goodness me, no! Two is enough. I'm just starting to get my life back. I don't need another baby.' Diana nudged the glass of wine towards her neighbour. 'Don't go. I enjoy your company.'

But Mrs Hillyker was having none of it. 'Nope. Charlie's stomach will think his throat's been cut. I'll win the Lotto before he ever works out how to cook his own dinner.' She looked around for her coat and slipped it on. 'Do you need me on Monday?'

Diana slid off her stool. 'If you don't mind.'

'Of course not.' She popped her head into the playroom. 'Goodnight, you two. God bless.'

'Nigh, nigh, Mrs H.'

'I'll let myself out.'

Diana returned to the stool and her glass of wine. On impulse, she tipped both glasses down the sink. She'd never much liked chardonnay anyway.

*

When Will walked in the door the next afternoon, he looked like death warmed up. After he'd thrown his briefcase and jacket on the couch, and torn off his tie, he went straight to the fridge. He pulled out a beer, twisted off the top and chugged it down like it was lemon squash.

He grabbed a second beer and took a long draught. 'Do you want a glass of wine?'

Diana watched all this from the kitchen bench where she was in the process of assembling fruit salad and ice cream for the kids' dessert. She shook her head and pointed at the glass of sparkling mineral water. 'Having a day off.'

'Hmph,' was the reply. When he went to the wine rack, alarm bells started ringing. This wasn't just a bad day at work — something was seriously wrong.

Whatever was brewing, the kids didn't need to witness it. While Will opened a bottle of cab sav, Diana took dessert to the table in the playroom and let the kids eat it there. Afterwards, she raced them through their bedtime routine. Only once they were tucked in bed and she'd delivered an encore performance of 'A You're Adorable' did she return to tackle Will about his mood.

He sat at the kitchen bench, the bottle of cab sav now half empty, a plate with pâté and wafer biscuits in front of him. Diana sighed. She'd been looking forward to seeing Will. She had news of her own. Now she'd have to keep it under her hat.

She wrapped her arms around his shoulders and nuzzled his neck. He relaxed into her embrace. Whatever or whoever had upset him, it had nothing to do with her, then.

'You going to tell me what's going on?'

He rubbed his fingers along the worry lines in his forehead. 'I've had a shit of a week.'

Blind Freddy could spot that from a mile away. Diana tried again. 'What's happened?'

He poured himself another glass of wine. 'Forsyth Medical Equipment has received a takeover bid from Holworth and Harrow.'

'What? The American firm?' Poor Will, his whole body language spelled defeat. Her heart went out to him. 'That's terrible news. Can't you stop them?'

'That's the sixty-four-thousand-dollar question, or more like the twelve-million-dollar question.'

'You're pulling my leg.'

'Nope. We'd be rich.' But the way he said it told her everything she needed to know.

How many nights had they lain in bed, fantasising about the day some multinational would come knocking on the door and make an offer too good to refuse? *Imagine what we could do with three million bucks,* he would say. Because that was the biggest number they could get a handle on. *I could retire at forty and we could just rack off and travel without a care in the world.*

And Diana would laugh along. There'd be talk of villas in Tuscany, nights at The Ritz and dining in Michelin-starred restaurants. But it was a dream, they both knew that. Yet here they were with twelve million dollars on the table. Life-changing.

'I started working for my pop in the school holidays when I was sixteen.' Will reached for his glass of wine. 'Went to uni, then when I joined the business, I was determined to turn FME into a major player. My pop, bless him, hated taking on debt but you can't be in medical equipment business these days without it. I've worked my arse off for that company, like Dad did before me. We did it to build something, not to sell it.'

Diana knew all this — she'd lived this story. Now Alan had retired, Will worked horrendous hours, often dealing with paperwork well into the night. By Sunday afternoons, his mind had already switched to work. She worried he'd put himself in an early grave if he kept up this pace. She'd congratulated herself for not marrying a man like her father, yet she saw about as much of her husband as she ever saw of her dad. 'What does Ian say?'

Will shrugged. 'Not much. He reckons we should reserve judgement until we receive a formal contractual offer. You know Ian. Always the lawyer.'

'The devil is in the detail.'

'Precisely. He reckons it might just be a shot over the bow, to see how we react.' Will sandwiched pâté between two wafers.

'Are you sure you don't want something proper to eat?' Diana asked, worried he needed more than pâté to soak up the alcohol.

He shook his head. 'I've asked Ian and Rebecca to come over for lunch on Saturday. Mum and Dad too. We need to talk about this as a family.'

'How long do you have?'

'The offer stands until the end of the month.'

Diana did the maths. Eighteen days.

She went around the other side of the bench, pulled out a board and grabbed a loaf of bread from the freezer. Cheese toasties it was. Her signature dish.

Diana sliced cheese and buttered bread, contemplating the weekend ahead. How would the family react? Her bet was on Rebecca urging Ian to take the money and run. About the only thing that woman got passionate about was money. When Lydia ran away to join Médecins Sans Frontières, Diana had fleetingly hoped her sister-in-law might go some way to fill the gaping hole created by Lydia's sudden whim to save the world. Not that Diana was fooled by this burst of noble sentiment. Lydia's decision coincided with meeting Gabriele the Italian gynaecologist. Diana gave it six months.

She shoved the plate of toasted sandwiches in front of Will and he hunkered over it. Not a word of thanks. Diana checked the clock on the oven and wondered what the time difference was between here and Nigeria. She missed her sister terribly.

*

Everyone sat out on the deck at Turpentine Street. Diana brought out a platter of various dips and crackers and put it in the middle of the table, just in time to hear, 'I said to Ian, the first thing that has to go is that kitchen.' Rebecca turned to Diana, no doubt in a bid to gain solidarity for her argument. 'I mean, hanging pot racks and a copper rangehood, I ask you. And those kitsch glazed tiles. Ugh.' The last accompanied by a dramatic eye roll.

'Do you know, Alan and I have had the same kitchen since we bought the house forty years ago,' came from Will's mum. Marianne's expression declared 'Extraordinary!', as if there was nothing wrong with a kitchen that screamed 1960s glamour. 'Everything old becomes new again. We'll be back in fashion any minute now.' She cocked her head at Rebecca, reminding Diana of a bright little sparrow who'd spotted a tasty worm. 'It's amazing what a lick of paint and a new set of curtains can do to freshen up the look.'

What Diana would like to know was how on earth Ian and Rebecca could afford yet another new house. Given the brothers earned similar amounts, Ian and Rebecca must be up to their eyeballs in debt. This deal on the table isn't even a week old, yet Rebecca was already spending the money on renovations.

But she kept those thoughts to herself and smiled instead. 'I'm the worst person to ask. We've been in Turpentine Street three and a half years and still haven't got around to briefing a builder about the extension.' Two against one was never fair, except when it came to Rebecca.

'You're not drinking?' Marianne asked when Diana topped up her wine.

'I've got a bit of a headache, I thought I'd take it easy. I might have one with lunch.'

Marianne's gaze flicked to her tummy and her expression told Diana her excuse didn't wash.

'It's been a big week,' Diana added to underscore the veracity of her statement.

'It's not the end of the world if you're expecting again,' Marianne continued, turning her bright sparrow eye on Diana. 'If this deal goes through, it certainly won't be a financial strain.'

Her mother-in-law's kindness drew out a more honest answer. 'It's not the money. Between teaching and the kids, I'm flat chat. It would be one more thing I'd have to squeeze in. I know that sounds awful.'

Marianne shook her head. 'Not at all, I know exactly what you mean.'

'If you don't want another baby, maybe you could give it to me.'

Stunned silence. Diana replayed Rebecca's words to make sure she'd heard her correctly. Ian and Rebecca had just gone through another devastating round of IVF. Via Will, she knew Ian had had enough. Apparently Rebecca was furious because there was no medical reason why they couldn't conceive.

The not knowing must be hard on Rebecca. To be consumed by the desire for a baby when people like her and Will seemed to spit them out like orange pips. Diana erred on the side of kindness. 'Like I said, I have a bit of a headache. It must be the stress.'

She swept her arm around to encompass the family gathering. The men clustered around the barbecue, buried in discussions about their future, the women relegated to the outdoor table out of the way. Persephone was having her afternoon nap. Fi had taken Aiden for the afternoon. 'One less thing to worry about,' Fi had said, locking in Aiden's booster seat between her two boys. Aiden, itching to clamber in between Ollie and James, didn't even wave goodbye as Fi drove off down the street.

Rebecca shook her head, a sharp angry gesture. 'It's really not complicated. I say take the twelve mill and run.'

'Except it's not your place to say, is it?' Marianne replied, sweet as sugar. 'Ian is the shareholder, not you.'

Rebecca shot daggers at her mother-in-law. 'In our marriage, Ian always considers my opinion.'

'More fool him,' Marianne muttered under her breath but not quite softly enough.

Diana attempted to pour oil on troubled waters. 'I don't think any amount of money would make Will feel okay about selling the family business. Their pop built it from scratch. Alan has steered it through some lean years. Will's put his heart and soul into it. It's almost like another one of his children. He can't bear to let it go.'

Rebecca's lips thinned and, too late, Diana realised her gaffe. It was like that bloody comedy. *Don't talk about the war!* Trust her to put her size eights straight down her throat.

Marianne patted her hand. 'This whole business is quite upsetting.'

Diana nodded, swallowing against the lump in her throat. She moved on to safer ground. 'What do you and Alan think?'

'We'll be guided by what the boys want. Alan's no longer captain of this ship and he has to abide by his decision to not interfere.'

Diana suspected Marianne had had to remind Alan of his promise. At his retirement dinner three years ago, she had been bursting with joy, telling anyone and everyone who'd listen that she couldn't wait to have her husband back. She'd spent months planning that first overseas trip and they hadn't stopped since — an African safari, an Alaskan cruise and a trip on the Orient Express.

She leaned over and hugged Marianne, squeezing her tight enough to elicit a 'goodness me' from her mother-in-law.

'Well, this will be interesting then, won't it?' Rebecca added, unmoved by the show of affection. 'Let's see if Ian stands up for what he believes in for once instead of letting Will walk all over him.'

Diana's goodwill evaporated. 'Will is the CEO, so ultimately, the responsibility lays on his shoulders, not Ian's.'

She bit back the desire to remind Rebecca that this was entirely Ian's choice. He was more than happy to be the in-house counsel and leave the heavy lifting to his older brother. Will never said a word against Ian but Diana was sure there'd been times when he wanted to. It wasn't Ian schlepping all over the world for weeks at a time. No, he stayed home with his stupid copper rangehood and his brittle wife.

'Is this your way of saying Ian wants to sell up?' Marianne asked, her mild tone belying the seriousness of her question.

Rebecca tilted her chin. 'Of course he does. Why wouldn't he want his share of twelve mill? You're not the only ones who like to travel. We could buy a nicer house, start our own business.'

Neither Marianne nor Diana reminded Rebecca that they had only just bought a much nicer house, notwithstanding the dated kitchen. Nor did they point out that, unlike his brother, Ian lacked the drive and entrepreneurial flair to build a successful business, even with Rebecca cracking the whip.

'Well, isn't it good to know where we all stand?' Marianne smiled then turned to Diana and patted her knee. 'Do you know, I still haven't seen your new studio. Any chance I can have the guided tour?'

Diana played along. 'Really? Has it been that long?' The women stood and gathered some of the empty dishes. 'It's really just the sunroom. Although, Will says the way my business is growing, he'll be building me a proper studio as well as the extension.'

Marianne laughed. 'Make sure you hold him to it.' She smiled at Rebecca. 'Coming for a sticky?'

To Diana's relief, she demurred.

As they headed inside, Marianne raised her voice so Rebecca would hear her, them, having a lovely time without her. 'Now, tell me, how is your mother going on her wonderful adventure? She's very brave, isn't she? Still, we all deal with grief in our own way.'

*

It was late by the time everyone went home. Diana could tell how exhausted Will was by the dejected slope of his shoulders. When she suggested an early night, he was quick to agree.

'Mum says you have something to tell me,' Will said from where he sat on the bed removing his shoes.

Diana stiffened. As much as she loved Marianne, when it came to her sons, she did have a tendency to meddle. 'Oh, really?'

Will came over to Diana's side of the bed. He waited while she slipped on one of his old t-shirts that she wore for pyjamas.

He rubbed his hands down her arms and drew her close. 'Why didn't you tell me you were pregnant?'

Diana looked up into those sea-blue eyes. 'I was planning to, but you came home smashed by all this business with Holworth and Harrow. A few more days wasn't going to make much difference.'

Will ran his fingers through her hair and cupped her face. He looked intently into her eyes. 'Have you done the test?'

'Yes.'

'So it's definite.'

Diana nodded, careful to hold Will's eye.

He let her go and sat on the bed, patting the space next to him. Diana sat down. Will rubbed her thigh, a gesture of comfort, not promise. 'When you were pregnant with Aiden, you cooked me a beautiful candlelit dinner.'

She went to protest but he shushed her. 'With Percy, Mrs H told us the day we moved in here.'

Diana studied her toes. They needed a pedicure but when would she find the time, especially now?

Will tilted her chin so they were eye to eye. 'Don't you want this baby, Didi?'

A shudder ran through her, as if the earth had tipped on its axis. To her surprise, she was suddenly bawling her eyes out. Will folded her in his arms and held her as she sobbed. When the crying subsided, he took the box of tissues from the bedside table and offered it to her.

Diana blew her nose. 'I don't know what's wrong with me. When I did the test, I cried like this too. I don't understand why I'm so upset. I mean, whether you sell FME or not, we can afford another baby. We have a lovely house — a new kitchen and family room can wait another year or two. To be honest, it matters more to you than it does to me. And the whole point of teaching from home is so I can be flexible. We always said we wanted four children.'

'But.'

Not a question, a statement. He wasn't a top salesman for nothing. Will knew how to read people, especially those close to him, especially her.

'The idea of going through another pregnancy, another baby, makes me feel exhausted. Just when I'm starting to get a bit of time for myself, it's all going to be taken away from me. I'm sorry, I know I'm being completely selfish but it's how I feel.'

'Maybe you should ask your mother to come home.'

'I can't, Will.' Audrey's decision to disappear in a puff of diesel smoke still hurt. Lydia thought it was because she needed space to grieve in private. A luxury Diana could not afford with so many demands for her attention. She missed her dad, and she was sure Audrey did too, but Diana agreed with Will — running away looked awfully like Audrey was celebrating her newfound freedom.

Diana sighed. 'I think I'm just tired.'

This galvanised Will. 'Okay, you get into bed and I'll make you a chamomile tea. Would it help if I slept on the couch? I don't mind, honest.'

Diana's heart brimmed over. 'I spend enough nights sleeping on my own. Stay with me.'

The way Will smiled made her realise that he needed reassurance as much as she did. A new baby, a takeover bid — it was a lot to process. She smiled back. 'But a cup of tea would be lovely.'

'Consider it done.'

Chapter 15

Then

'Ta-da!' Fi said with a theatrical flourish, depositing a platter of sushi on the kitchen bench. 'My contribution to the birthday lunch,' she declared, stepping away so they could all admire the vibrant orange flowers carved out of carrot, the seaweed green rolls and the bright white rice. 'Doesn't it look delicious? It's from the new Japanese restaurant in The Village. Near the beauty salon.'

Ruth untangled herself from the lounge and came over to see the platter of sushi for herself. 'Which reminds me, did I hear a rumour that the owner is selling the salon?'

'What?' Diana felt a visceral sense of panic slither through her. 'Where are we supposed to go for our bikini waxes now?'

Ruth regarded the enormity of Diana's body.

'Are you seriously telling me you're planning a bikini wax before the birth to impress the obbie?'

Diana laughed and rubbed circles around her belly. She might not have blown up like a balloon like she did when she was pregnant with Persephone, but there was no doubt Diana was a woman who could give birth any day now. 'No. But the moment this little sucker is breathing oxygen, I'm making a beeline for the salon. Everything below the waist has been totally neglected.'

Ruth held up a hand in the time-honoured gesture for 'too much information'.

'What's this?' Sissy asked, holding up a tub of slimy green string.

'Seaweed salad. And before you ask, they're black sesame seeds, not dead ants,' Fi replied, snatching the tub from Sissy on the pretence of finding a bowl to put it in.

Sissy's hand recoiled as if she'd been bitten, which, in a way, she had. Diana and Ruth exchanged a knowing glance. Sissy's daughter was currently Persephone's best friend at preschool. In a slightly awkward fashion, Sissy had latched on to Diana as if the girls' friendship extended to them. Diana didn't mind her company, in small doses, but Fi couldn't stand her. In private she used words like 'airhead' and 'space cadet', forcing Diana to defend Sissy who was, in truth, a bit off with the fairies. But it also wasn't reasonable that Fi expected everybody to operate at her level of competence.

On the plus side, given Sissy floated around in a bit of a bubble, most of what Fi said slid right over her. Hence why she remained fixated on the seaweed salad. 'People eat this?'

Diana picked up one of the little fish-shaped plastic containers of soy sauce. 'Aren't these cute?'

'I guess that trumps my goat's cheese and roasted asparagus tart,' Ruth said with a dramatic sigh.

'Why am I the last person to know you can get takeaway sushi around here?' Diana asked.

'It's a new thing. There's a shop in the city and that's all they sell. Massive queue every lunchtime,' Fi explained, putting chopsticks on the bench.

Diana had that fizzy feeling she got when she had a brilliant idea. 'Do you think the kids will like it?'

'You're not wasting good food on children,' Fi remonstrated. 'They are perfectly happy with baked beans on toast.'

'I'm perfectly happy with baked beans on toast,' Ruth added.

'It's a feast fit for a king,' Sissy said, gathering the salt and pepper shakers and a wad of paper napkins.

'A feast fit for ladies who lunch,' Fi tossed back, in reference to Sissy's stay-at-home status.

'Now, now,' Ruth intervened. She passed Fi a slice of quiche and gave her a look that said 'get back in your box'.

Fi rolled her eyes and sat at the head of the dining table, fluffing out her paper napkin. 'Isn't it lovely to eat a meal without children around?'

'Ooh, I forgot the champagne.' Ruth scraped her chair back and returned to the kitchen for glasses and the bottle.

For some reason, Sissy chose to sit at the far end of the table — what was known in the Forsyth household as 'the children's end'. Rather than risk embarrassing her, Diana took the seat in the middle so the women weren't spread out like members of opposing teams.

Ruth passed her a glass of bubbles. 'Happy birthday, Didi.'

'Yes, happy birthday.'

Diana raised her glass in Fi's direction. 'And congratulations on your promotion.'

'Yes, that too!' exclaimed Ruth. 'Well deserved.'

For a flickering moment, Fi actually looked embarrassed. Then she was back to her old self. 'Cheers!'

'*Salute.*'

'Bottoms up.'

'Chin-chin.' Diana took one small sip. She wasn't feeling particularly celebratory. She was more in the 'flopping on the couch moaning and groaning a lot' phase, hoping other people would do everything for her. 'I can't brush your teeth for you, Didi,' Will had said last night when she'd whinged that she was too tired. 'Yes you can — look,' she'd said. And she'd done a very good impression of Persephone standing there gaping until Will shoved the toothbrush in her mouth just to shut her up.

'How's Will?' Fi asked, always keen for a bit of industry gossip.

Diana picked up her knife and fork — she doubted she had the brain power to use chopsticks at this point in time. 'Will is in a funk over this takeover business. I barely see him. I'm usually asleep by the time he gets home. Honestly, it's just dragged on and on. The original offer was on the table for eighteen days and that was months ago.'

'He's sticking to his guns about not selling then?' Ruth asked in a somewhat bemused tone. 'You know that kind of stress isn't good for you — long term, I mean.'

Diana couldn't sit in a hard-backed chair any longer. She picked up her plate and waddled over to the couch, sweeping aside the Lego and soft toys. With a giant sigh, she sunk into it and rested the plate on her belly. 'The latest update is that Ian is putting in place some structure that prevents hostile takeovers. Marianne and Alan agree with Will that it's not the right time to sell.'

'I bet that went down well with Rebecca,' Fi said, visibly gloating at the very idea.

'Ow!' Diana clutched her side, up under the ribs.

Sissy was first on her feet. 'What's wrong?'

Diana waved her down. 'Nothing. Nothing. I'm alright.' She shifted her weight and lifted her arms above her head. 'The little bugger's got his feet buried in my liver. Every time he wakes up, he kneads my insides.'

'He?'

Diana shrugged. 'According to Mrs H.'

'And the ring is never wrong,' Fi said.

'It was last time.'

'Maybe he's on his way,' suggested Sissy, still hovering in Diana's orbit in case she was needed.

'He better not be. It's my birthday and I don't want to share it. He can have his pick of the other three hundred and sixty-four days.'

'That might be tricky,' Ruth said. 'Isn't he due in ten days?'

*

Days blurred into weeks. Cards and emails and flowers arrived from all over the world. 'You poor sweet darling thing,' texted Ruth one day. 'I bet he was the most beautiful boy,' from Fi on another. Diana left it to Will to field the phone calls, deflect the well-meaning visitors, and console those who wept on their behalf.

Diana emerged into each day, her brain like treacle — sticky, slow, opaque. On one morning, she woke to a beam of sunlight falling across the empty half of the bed. Her hand crept out from under the covers and rubbed the sheet. Was it warm from the sunlight or warm from Will? She drew her arm in and clasped it to her chest, holding herself in. She needed to go back to sleep. She was so tired she was numb.

Crying, someone was crying. Diana forced herself back to consciousness and listened hard, waiting to catch the sound again and find its source. She wiped her face on the pillow, breathed in the damp, smelled the salt. A high-pitched scream. Where was it coming from? She rolled to the edge of the bed, let her feet find the floor and pushed herself upright. She sat there, absorbed in the shaft of sunlight filtering through a crack in the curtains. 'Will,' she called, fainter than a distant bird.

The bedside clock ticked over to a nine and two zeros. That couldn't be the time. Diana heaved to her feet, took her kimono from the end of the bed and slipped it on. Bathroom. She shuffled around her corner of the bed, through the pile of dirty laundry. Diana kicked it and a plastic bag billowed on the floor. She sat on the toilet and pulled off a ream of paper, hissed through her teeth as she peed razor blades.

Children were shouting. Should she go and see what that was about? Probably. She washed her hands, opened the vanity cabinet and found the bottle of pills. Swallowed two, felt them stick in her throat. The tap was still running. She scooped up water in her hands and drank, washing down the pills so they could work their magic.

She tied the belt on her kimono and shuffled out to the kitchen. There were dishes piled high in the sink. A bottle of milk, slippery with condensation, sat lidless on the bench. Puddles of cereal, toast crusts, a half-eaten banana and a note from Will tucked under the teapot.

D,

Sorry I had to leave without saying goodbye. I know it's unfair, you have every right to be upset. The timing is terrible. Call you when I land. W

What had happened last night? She shuffled back to the wardrobe and studied the gaps in the row of business shirts. His open chest of drawers were depleted of socks and underpants. Will's favourite pair of sneakers were missing. And his club swimmers.

The phone rang, strident in the silent house. Diana followed its call through the rooms. The handset was not on its cradle.

Where could it be? The phone stopped, leaving her stranded in the middle of the lounge, not sure which direction to head next. It started ringing again. She followed the insistent clamour into the laundry and picked it up.

'Hello?'

'Didi, it's me.'

'Hello, Fi.' Diana twisted the sash of her kimono around and around her wrist, while she waited for her friend to explain the reason for her call.

'I thought I might swing by with the twins, bring something for morning tea. Ollie and James are desperate to try out your new trampoline. We can be there by ten.'

'No.'

'Oh. Are you sure?'

'Yes. I don't think that's a good idea.'

The doorbell chimed. Diana looked at the handset. 'I have to go. There's someone at the door.' She threw the handset back in the laundry basket and went to see who it could be.

On the doorstep stood Lydia, a coat over her crinkled dress. She looked pale, tired, and her hair needed a wash.

'Lydia. Aren't you supposed to be in Nigeria?'

She put down her suitcase and dragged Diana into a hug. 'It's your big sister's prerogative to lob on you unexpectedly.' Lydia pushed her out to arm's length. She bit her bottom lip and tucked Diana's hair behind her ear. 'I'm busting for the loo and dying for a cuppa.'

Against her better judgement, Diana let her in. She hovered in the kitchen while Lydia attended the call of nature.

Lydia emerged from the bathroom and grinned. 'Happiness is an empty bladder.' She dusted her hands and filled the kettle, emptied the dregs from the teapot and spooned in fresh tea leaves. 'The house seems very quiet.'

Diana stopped to think about this then said, 'Will's left.'

Lydia leaned against the bench and folded her arms. 'Yes, I know. He called me. It's only for a few weeks. I know the timing is terrible. This bloody takeover business has taken on a life of its own.'

Terrible. That's exactly what Will said. Diana regarded the puddles of cereal. She wet the sponge, wrung it out and scrubbed at the bench.

Lydia poured boiling water into the teapot then opened the sliding doors onto the deck. She stepped out and looked around the garden. She came back inside, checked the playroom then each of the children's bedrooms. 'Didi, where are Aiden and Percy?' she asked from the doorway.

Diana looked around the living room. If this were a game of hide and go seek, she'd be able to spot Persephone hiding under a dining chair. She walked over to the linen press and flung open the doors. No Aiden either. She turned back to Lydia. 'I don't know.'

Lydia seemed less surprised and more alarmed. Diana thought hard. 'They might be next door?'

Lydia nodded, her shoulders dropping in relief. She quickly made Diana a cup of tea and insisted she sit on the couch to drink it while she hurried next door to check.

Diana did as she was told and, by the time she'd finished her tea, Lydia had returned. 'Mrs H said she'd bring them home after lunch.'

'Oh, okay.' Diana tried to remember when she'd arranged this but came up with nothing. Except the way Lydia was looking at her, she felt compelled to add, 'That's very kind of her.'

Lydia didn't answer. She seemed lost in thought.

Diana decided to leave her to it. 'I think I might have a shower.'

Lydia offered to give her a hand but Diana politely declined, reminding her that she was perfectly capable of washing herself. As the water ran over her, she wondered how long Lydia planned to stay.

*

Every day, Diana woke up and saw Lydia lying in Will's spot. In a strange way, she quite liked sharing a bed with her sister. It reminded her of when they were little and would stay at their grandparents'. Somewhere else in the house she heard shouting.

'You're a cheater!'

'Am not!'

'Yes you are! I'm not playing anymore.'

Diana climbed out of bed, used the bathroom. Ever hopeful, she opened the vanity cabinet but the little amber bottle of pills was still gone. The day she'd arrived, Lydia had taken them 'for safekeeping'. She only allowed Diana to take half of one in the mornings and half at night so she could get a good night's rest. Lydia said she was weaning her off them 'because they weren't a long-term solution'. Diana disagreed. She missed the lovely feeling of being wrapped in fairy floss. Without them, she had to endure the razor-sharp edges of her grief. Every day, it was as if she were on the highwire, looking down on the crowd of upturned faces, each holding their breath, waiting to see if she would fall.

Although, now her brain was clearer, the answer to this problem had become obvious. Diana had been working on a cunning plan for days. To escape the house, to escape Lydia, the absence of Will and the ghost of Nicholas, she would go somewhere no one could find her. She was smarter than Lydia reckoned on.

All through breakfast, Diana made an extra effort to behave normally. She made Persephone strawberry jam on toast without the crusts. Lydia insisted on cooking up bacon and scrambled eggs, and Diana obediently ate them and told her they were delicious. Aiden refused the eggs and ate the bacon with his fingers. Diana let him.

When they were done eating, Diana said, 'You jump in the shower while I make the school lunches.'

Lydia seemed surprised. 'Are you sure?'

'Of course, go on. You've been running around after me and the kids for weeks. You deserve a day off.'

Diana dropped the children at preschool and waved goodbye from the gate. As she walked away, the sense of freedom grew as wide as the bright blue sky. Encouraged by Diana, Lydia had decided to catch up for lunch with an old friend from her nursing days. Diana had the whole day ahead of her.

'What are you going to do?' Lydia had asked as she slicked on a layer of lipstick and squirted her favourite perfume on the inside of her wrists.

Diana had pretended to think about it but she'd already prepared her excuses. 'I'm going to get a pedicure and then I might treat myself to a proper coffee and a bit of cake.'

Except that was not where Diana was headed at all. She drove up The Village main street, past the beauty salon, the patisserie and her favourite coffee shop. She drove all the way to the cinema complex she used to go to before she met Will. Diana couldn't wait to sit alone in the dark, safe in the knowledge she couldn't bump into anyone she knew. She bought a ticket to the ten o'clock session and a cappuccino then found a spot towards the back in the middle of the row. For two whole glorious hours, great big fat tears rolled down her cheeks, and dripped into the collar of her blouse where they trickled into the curve of her breast and the Nicholas-shaped hole beneath her ribs.

Every day the children were at preschool, Diana followed this routine to the letter. She didn't care how many times she'd already seen the movie. It was irrelevant. She could not be at home. Lydia's kindness, and Will's absence, were unbearable.

Today, a man had claimed her spot. A spark of anger almost made her tap him on the shoulder and demand that he move. Instead she shuffled along the row behind and five seats across where she could glare at the back of his head. It was hard to tell much from behind in the dark, except that he needed a haircut.

He was there again the next time — one row down, five seats across. Diana noticed something new about him, his shoulders. The familiar shudder that came in waves. The swipe of his arm across his eyes. It started as soon as the music swelled and the opening titles rolled, and continued all the way to the end of the closing credits.

The same thing happened the following time. Each of them in their own row, sitting in the dark, absorbed by their sorrow. She felt a sense of solidarity, of comfort, in their shared grieving.

Diana decided to stay after the end of the closing credits. She waited until the houselights came up. Watched him search his pockets in vain. This was her cue. She shuffled along the row and passed a packet of tissues over his shoulder. Startled, he turned around. Diana was surprised to see how handsome he was. That they were a similar age.

'Thank you,' he said, taking the tissues. He blew his nose and wiped his red-rimmed eyes. Then he stood, taller than her even though he was a row down. He offered her the tissues and she shook her head.

'Let me buy you a coffee.' The words just came out. Diana didn't want to let go of this moment of shared suffering.

His name was Ben. His wife had died from a rare form of cancer. She was not even thirty years old. He didn't know what to do. He couldn't go back, he couldn't go forward. Going to the movies each day was the only thing that got him out of bed, showered, dressed.

Diana understood completely.

Ben offered her an embarrassed smile that made her want to take his hand.

'How do you fill the afternoons?' she asked instead.

'I read a book or sometimes pick up my guitar.'

Diana lit up. 'You're a musician!'

The following day, he sat one row down, three seats across. As the movie began, he smiled at Diana then quickly turned away — polite, but no invitation. Still, Diana was prepared. When his shoulders heaved, she leaned over and dropped a packet of tissues beside him. Afterwards, he insisted he owed her a coffee.

*

Lydia had to go to Italy. She had finished in Nigeria and had another job waiting, not to mention Gabriele. She couldn't afford any more time off. She stood on the front doorstep and hugged Diana goodbye. 'I wish Mum was here.' But Audrey was in some mining town on the other side of the country, so they both knew the comment was pointless.

When Will rang, Diana kept the conversations brief. She didn't want to speak to him or hear about how he spent his days locked in boardroom meetings. He should have stayed here, where she needed him. That had been the substance of the fight the night before he left. 'You need to get your priorities straight,' she remembered yelling.

When he'd finished offloading, he'd ask, 'How are the kids?' and she'd say, 'They're fine. They're in the bath,' so there was no point in him asking to speak to them. After they hung up, she'd stick her head around the door of the playroom and say to the back of their heads, 'Daddy says to tell you he loves you.' Engrossed in their shows, they often didn't even register she'd spoken to them.

Loneliness created the space to daydream. Diana drifted into the studio and contemplated the photos on the wall, memories flooding back from her days with The Somethings. Performing had made her feel alive. That special moment when it all came together and everyone — the audience, the band — connected. It was such a big part of her life and she'd let it go. That was a mistake. She sat at her piano and played a few chords, picked out the melody. She tried to sing the verse but her voice cracked in half. Diana fell silent. Tears plopped on the keys. She wiped them away. She couldn't wait for Monday.

After she dropped the children at preschool, Diana rushed to the cinema. She parked on the rooftop and angled the rear-view mirror. She double-checked her appearance, applied a fresh layer of lip gloss, and smoothed her eyebrows. Ben was waiting for her. Neither of them said a word. He took her by the hand and they walked through the foyer, past the ticket counter, and out onto the street.

Chapter 16

Now

Diana wakes to Will's kiss on her forehead. She opens her eyes and looks into the blue sea of his. 'Good morning.'

He kisses her lips. 'Good morning to you too.'

In another time, this might have been the beginning of something but Will sits up and says, 'Coffee machine's on.'

Diana props herself up in bed and yawns. She squints at the old-fashioned alarm clock on the bedside table and retrieves her glasses from the top of her book. 'What time is it?'

'Too early.'

Diana smiles at him. 'Look at you though, all fresh and sparkly, not at all like someone off a long-haul flight.'

'Believe me, I feel it. I went for a swim to clear my head.' He pats her leg. 'You ready for a coffee if I make you one?'

It's not really a question. For thirty years, these kinds of conversations are the grease in the wheel. Will shall make eggs on toast and coffee because that's how he says *I love you*. And after a leisurely breakfast, he'll go into the office 'for a few hours' and she'll say, 'For goodness' sakes, take a long weekend, you've been on the road for three weeks,' and he'll ignore her sage advice.

He disappears into the kitchen and Diana slips out of bed. She showers, hurries to dress and towel-dries her hair. When she walks out to the living area, she notices her journal is wide open on the desk. Diana glances at Will, who's whistling to himself as he brings water to the boil for the eggs. All this secret squirrel business arranging the Big Party won't count for very much if he reads her notes. Diana closes her journal and slips it into her handbag. Remembering the sheet music, she sweeps it up and secretes it inside the piano stool.

'Do you want a juice?' she asks, approaching the kitchen bench.

'You bet.'

The kettle clicks off the boil. Will fills the saucepan and turns the gas onto high. As he waits for it to return to the boil, he flicks through the mail piled next to the answering machine.

Out of the corner of her eye, she watches Will sort through the council rates, rego papers and the electricity bill. Diana pours the tomato juice, adding a splash of Tabasco to Will's.

'That yellow envelope was hand-delivered,' she says, sliding his juice across the bench.

Will picks it up and flicks it over, searching for an address. Finding none, he puts it back on the bench, saying, 'I'll open it later,' and returns to poaching the eggs.

Over breakfast, they fill each other in on what they've been up to. Diana skips lightly over lunch with the girls, the visit to her mother, and leaves the details of the rest of her fortnight unspoken. She's had plenty of time to think about the note and on balance has decided that whatever it meant, it belonged to another time when forgiveness had been in short supply. It wasn't worth the fireworks of bringing it up. Will is more than happy to fill the void, talking animatedly about his negotiations for distribution rights for a state-of-the-art laser-imaging machine.

'Anything exciting to share on the Persephone front?' she asks as Will makes a second coffee.

'*Tout va bien.*'

Diana groans in mock horror. 'Please don't practise your terrible French on Camille and Raphael while they're here, will you?'

Will shoots her an evil look. 'You bet I will. It'll be all mirepoix and bouillon and whatever other fancy French cooking terms I can pull out of the Larousse between now and then.' He passes Diana her cup. 'And you won't have a clue what we're talking about because it'll be secret chef's business.' He taps the side of his nose and winks.

Diana smiles into her cup. 'Barrel of laughs.'

After breakfast, as she clears and stacks the dishwasher, Will picks up the yellow envelope. He tears open the flap and pulls out a wad of paper held together with a large paperclip. It's photographs. Mystery solved — he's had some of his pictures developed.

Will reads the attached post-it note and frowns like he's confused. He scrunches the note in his fist and tosses it on the bench then slides off the paperclip and removes a sheet of plain paper protecting the top photo. There's a sharp intake of breath.

'What is it?'

He doesn't answer, just shuffles through the photos, fast, like he's dealing cards. Then back to the beginning, studying one, laying it face down on the bench before examining the next. One by one, until there's a pile of photos.

The lines on his forehead knot into a frown and a tingly spidering creeps up the back of Diana's neck. She wrings out the dishcloth and drapes it across the tap to dry. 'Will?'

He straightens the edges until the pile is square. A wave of tension spasms through his body. His gaze flickers in rapid fire, like he's about to explode.

'Will? What on earth is wrong?'

Without a word, he passes her the stack. Diana glances at the first photo then starts in recognition. It's of her in the courtyard outside the beauty salon. Ian is leaning in close and she's smiling at whatever he's said. Strange. She puts it aside. The next photo shows her standing beside Ian's car outside their apartment block. She's wearing a different top. Ian wears a sports shirt. In the next, he's kissing her cheek.

Diana clamps her jaw shut, not a single sound escaping her lips. Someone has been spying on her?

It gets worse. The next set of pictures are of her and Michael. They're having coffee at the café around the corner from the warehouse. Another shows Michael clasping both her hands in his. In the next photo, they're kissing goodbye. A different day, another outfit. She and Michael holding hands, laughing, the wind whipping her hair around her face. The very image of happiness. The taste of breakfast rises in her throat.

'How long has this been going on?'

Will's words echo across the years and the past rushes up to greet her. Diana cannot answer. Her mind whirs through infinite possibilities. These photos aren't casually snapped with a smartphone. Whoever took them must have used a long-range lens. Otherwise, she'd have noticed, wouldn't she? Her throat goes dry.

With an effort, she unlocks her jaw. 'Don't be ridiculous, Will. Surely you don't think Michael and I ...'

'He's always had a thing for you.' A vein throbs in Will's temple.

'What? No he hasn't …' But seeing Will's anger surge, she quickly changes tack. 'It's not what it looks like.'

He stabs a finger at the picture. 'You're kissing him.' He shoves the photo in Diana's face. 'See?'

She flinches.

'I'm not blind. I'm not stupid either.'

Diana seethes with indignation. 'Will, listen to me. I can't explain why someone would've taken those pictures but I promise you, there's nothing to it. You're leaping to conclusions.'

'Am I just?' He tears the photos from her grasp. 'Explain to me why anyone would follow you, clearly over many days. What were you doing with my brother?'

'What? Nothing! That's beyond stupid. Ian—'

'Well, someone saw something!' Will shouts.

Diana steps away, finds the cool of the fridge at her back.

He picks up the abandoned note and flattens it out. '"*I thought you should know.*" Who thinks I should know, Diana? Or, more to the point, *what* should I know? If there's nothing going on between you and Michael, or, or,' he shuffles the photos and pulls out one of a third man, 'whoever the hell this is having a cosy wine with my wife, then why is there evidence to the contrary?'

The injustice kindles her temper. There are a lot of things she'd like to say but old hurts don't improve with fresh airings. Despite her denials, the photos have thrown her off kilter. She's not sure where to start defending herself.

Will is so angry, he is visibly shaking. 'Where there's smoke there's fire.'

'No, there's not! Trust me, there's nothing going on.'

'Trust you? That's rich. Why the hell should I if this is what you get up to when I'm not around? For all I know, this might just be the tip of the iceberg.' He takes the top photo and skids it across the bench. 'Who's this prick then?'

Diana glances at the photo of her and Ben. Will's already completely lost the plot; she can't tell him that Ben is back in her life. Will thinks he's safely in the past where he belongs.

Her hesitation is answer enough for Will. He shakes his head in disgust. 'Yeah right. I get it. At least last time you had the guts to tell me to my face that you'd slept with someone else.' He laughs. 'You didn't count on somebody snooping around watching you while my back was turned though, did you?'

'Can you hear yourself?'

'I believed you when you said it would never happen again.'

'That was a completely different set of circumstances. This has nothing to do with … with …' She can't even say it. It's too painful. It feels like a scab being ripped from a wound.

Will clenches his fist and pounds it on the kitchen bench. 'Alright then, how about another straightforward question. Are you fucking Michael?'

It's like a slap to the face. The slight is so visceral, her palm flies to her cheek. 'How dare you! I'm not fucking anyone.'

For a second he glares at her. She holds his eye. Then Will spins away, grabs his keys from the bench and slips his phone in his pocket. 'I don't know who's the bigger fool.'

'Stop it, Will. We had a perfectly civilised breakfast, then like that,' and she snaps her fingers, 'you've completely lost it. Don't use the past against me. That's unfair. I can't explain the photos, I really can't, but clearly someone is trying to make waves.'

Except Will's no longer listening. He barges past her and picks up his travel bag from where he'd abandoned it by their bedroom door. He shoulders the bag and turns to face her. 'It's not me who's dragged up the past.' Then he swoops on the photos and flings them in the air. 'It's not me in the fucking photos.'

The pictures scatter like startled pigeons in a town square. The front door slams shut and the photos flutter and fall.

Fury drives her. Diana runs after him and wrenches open the door. 'Will! Don't be so bloody ridiculous. Stay here and talk to me,' she calls down the stairwell.

But her words meet with silence. Will is gone.

Part II

Everybody has an opinion

Chapter 17

Now: Friday

Diana runs out to the terrace as Will's car turns onto The Esplanade and disappears. Stunned, she stands there, waiting for the sedan to miraculously reappear the moment he comprehends the magnitude of his overreaction. Nothing except runners, glider bikes, couples pushing prams, and a girl — arms akimbo — wobbling on rollerskates.

She retraces her steps, anger piercing her thoughts like daggers. She picks up the post-it note, smoothing its creases: *I thought you should know.*

Straight away, she thinks of the lost note. *I forgive you.* She'd all but dismissed it. Digging up the past never solves anything. Then Will opened the envelope of photos and that was that. The past came knocking anyway.

Whoever it is that thinks Will should know, Diana doesn't recognise their handwriting. She drops the note on the bench and returns to the hallway where she sweeps the photos into a rough pile. She takes them into the living room and spreads them out over the lid of the piano. She sorts them into rows. Ian. Michael. And Ben. Her heart squeezes in her chest.

She has to step away. It's a way to compartmentalise her feelings, a way to try and see the photos as if she's an impartial observer. It's impossible. Such an invasion of privacy. She feels dirty, vulnerable, exposed. Judged. And not just by Will.

What kind of hateful person would deliberately, provocatively, send Will these pictures? It's such a blunt instrument. Neither of them told a soul about what had happened all those years ago. Not Fi or Ruth or even Lydia. They'd agreed to bury it and, as far as she's concerned, it had stayed buried since. She'd kept her promises, on both counts, despite the fact that Will had never actually said the words, *I forgive you*. They had carried on as if he had; after all, they were still together, weren't they? And after this long, she thought that wound had healed. Yes, some scar tissue remained but until today, she hadn't realised that it had never really healed at all. Thanks to the photos, she's now discovered that beneath the scab lay a festering wound.

The last row. Diana runs her fingers lightly over the photos, sorting them into sequence. She and Ben are sitting in a bar — not Carlo's, it didn't seem wise to meet up locally. She holds a large glass of white wine to her lips. He has his legs stretched out under the table. Her feet are crossed at the ankles. It looks like they're touching but that's not how she remembers it.

Diana studies his face. Still handsome after all these years. A little grey at the temples, his laugh lines deeper but still the same Ben. Actually, better. He's one of those lucky men who improve with age. Seeing his face again moves a piece inside her. She recalls his face as it was. Hurt makes a person vulnerable, strips them of their skin. That's the Ben she remembers. But then when she ran into him all these years later, he was happy, relaxed, and she was glad of it. If anyone deserved to find happiness, it was Ben. She could never have given him that. Not for the long haul.

In the next photo, he holds her hand in his, the other hand rests on her forearm. He's closing the space between them, as if they are about to kiss. Diana knows they did not.

There are no more photos but there should be. Where is the one showing them leaving the restaurant? Or Ben walking to his car, turning around to wave goodbye as she walks in the opposite direction? Towards home. Towards Will. There's no proper end to this story.

Diana piles up the photos and stuffs them back in the envelope. She forced herself to look and now she's done. Pictures capture a moment — it's the viewer who interprets what it means. Does a glimpse of the past explain the present? Diana knows who she is and what she has done. She's not proud of her behaviour but she accepts why she behaved appallingly at that time. These photos are a violation — of her privacy and her dignity. Her life is her story to write, no one else's, not even Will's.

Diana takes her half-drunk coffee out to the terrace. She stands in a patch lit by the morning sun, feels its bright warmth cleanse her, calm her mind.

Why on earth would Will go off like that, and about Michael especially? It's been more than thirty years — he can't seriously still entertain the idea that Michael is a rival for her affections. If anything, all the evidence points to Ben. Except she was saved from answering Will's question because he zeroed in on Michael. Maybe knowing Michael personally had made the threat tangible.

Diana reflects on that night, all those years ago, when Will left to go overseas. Her memories are a little hazy, probably the drugs she was on, the pain she was in. They had fought, badly. It had been brewing for weeks. 'Please don't go, I need you here,' she'd begged him. 'Can't you put the trip off for a few weeks?' The look in his eye, desperation, and she realised he couldn't wait to escape the unbearable hurt at the centre of their lives. Work was the perfect excuse. 'I love you, Diana, but I can't heal you.' Those were Will's exact words, *that* she does remember. When she woke up the next morning, Will had gone. When she needed him most, Will flew off like Superman to save his precious company. Because the business meant more to him than his grieving wife and his dead son.

Her fury now is a pale imitation of the younger Diana's but the anger is there, simmering. *I love you*? Everyone knows that actions speak louder than words. Here was she, raw with pain, as if someone had split her down the middle and turned her inside out. Their son had died. Incomprehensibly, inexplicably dead. How could Will say he loved her then run away at the first opportunity? She hated him for it. God, how she hated him. Hate made her foolish. *I forgive you*? Well, he never forgave her. She hasn't forgiven herself either. And she's had to live with both those facts ever since.

The truth is, she'd been mad with grief and Ben had saved her. They had saved each other. By the time Will walked in the door, after Lydia had left, after weeks overseas, Diana had been righteous in her anger towards him. Anger made her determined to lay out the bare facts of her affair because she wanted to hurt Will as much as he had hurt her. But telling Will about Ben was the cruellest thing she has ever done. Worse, because she had done it intentionally. The moment the confession left her lips, the moment she saw the anguish in his eyes, she knew she had made a horrendous mistake. In her pathetic, misguided attempt to pay him back, she had made things worse.

Of course, once Will had told her exactly what he thought of her, he turned right around and walked straight back out the door. His parting words? 'I can't talk to you right now.'

The memory of it makes her cheeks burn afresh. She had humiliated herself twice over. Months later, when they did reunite, she made herself a promise that nothing like that would ever happen again. She has stuck by her decision and been faithful to Will ever since. Even though he never really forgave her, that wasn't the point. She was doing it so that she could look herself in the eye, for the children, not in order to earn Will's forgiveness.

*

The home phone rings. Grief has knocked her off balance. She almost trips over the step as she races inside and grabs the handset. 'Hi.'

No answer. 'Will? Are you there?' A slow beep. Did she cut off the call? Diana hits speed dial, impatient as the digital beeps of the imaginary fingers press each number. She wants to crawl through the phone and find him. The call goes straight to voicemail. It takes all her self-control not to sob.

The answering machine lights up with an incoming message. Relief floods her. *It's okay*, she tells herself and takes a deep breath. She hits play. His voice is hollow. 'I'm going to stay in town for a few days.' A pause. He clears his throat. 'I can't talk to you right now.'

The apartment shrinks around her. The exact same words he said the first time he turned on his heel and walked out. Gone. Just like that. Her confession stale in her mouth. Delivering the cruellest of blows, watching him crumble. Her horror when she saw what she'd done. She'd chased him out onto the street. She'd tried to apologise, she begged his forgiveness, begged him to stay, if not for her, for the sake of the children. Will threw his bag on the back seat, opened the driver's door. Him on one side of the car, her on the other, and he looked at her and said, 'Never in a million years.'

Night had fallen. She'd tucked Aiden and Persephone into bed, Aiden watching her with those big eyes. Wary of her, sensing that the mother he knew, who kept him safe, had disappeared.

'I want Daddy,' Persephone declared from her little sleigh bed. It had been her cot. She'd been so excited the day Diana turned it into a bed. That night, she was in and out. In and out until Diana threatened to put the sides up again and turn it back into a cot. Tears. Diana hating herself for being mean. Holding her sobbing child. 'I'm sorry. I'm sorry, I'm sorry,' until Persephone fell asleep in her arms.

Then again, 'I want Daddy.' Diana rigid with fear. Why now? Will was often not there to tuck the children into bed. So often, it was normal.

'Daddy had to go out tonight, darling. He'll see you in the morning.' She found Wabbit under the bed and tucked him in under Persephone's arm. 'Maybe if you're very good, he might even make pancakes for breakfast.'

Eyes like saucers. 'Wiv storby jam?'

'Lashings of strawberry jam.'

'Promise?'

'I promise.'

Pulling the door almost closed, so that a crack of light filtered into their room from the hallway and kept at bay the scary monsters lurking in the dark. Turning on the porch light, as if this alone would lure Will home. Back into the lounge room, turning on the lamps, one by one. Through to the kitchen, flicking light switches as she went. The bathroom lights, the laundry, the deck. Diana stood in the middle of the family room in a halo of light, her heart hammering against the wall of her chest, begging to escape. So many lights she had no shadow, because she was the shadow. The dark in the light.

'Mummy, why is it so bright in here?'

Spinning around. Aiden in the doorway. 'What are you doing out of bed?'

He went ramrod straight, little hands curled into fists at his sides. His voice aquiver. 'I need a wee-wee.'

Yes, of course. Perfectly normal. 'Let Mummy help you.' Galvanised into action, Diana strode across the room and opened the bathroom door. She helped Aiden with his pyjama bottoms, held teddy while he did a wee and washed his hands. Back in the family room, Aiden looked around the room lit up like Christmas. His hand reached up to hers. She caught it.

'Can I sleep with you tonight, Mummy?'

It was like he knew. Diana looked into those serious brown eyes. She wanted to dive in and hide there. 'Mummy would love that.'

Chapter 18

Friday

Diana catches herself, gripping the ledge of the terrace until she can breathe. For one horrifying moment, the road swims beneath her but it's okay, it's okay, her feet are on the ground. She concentrates on the waxy leaves of the figs gleaming in the sunshine, the way the slight breeze ruffles the water into choppy waves. She needs to get out of here.

Diana takes off across The Green, against the tide of students traipsing towards the senior campus. Long scarves in house colours wrapped around their necks, hands wrapped around takeaway hot chocolates, their chatter misting in the cold.

'Morning, Miss,' they chorus as they pass.

'Morning, girls,' she replies, glad for the sunglasses shielding her eyes from their curious glances. She must look a sight. Her hair's a mess, no makeup. She's missed choir practice. She should call and make her excuses.

Diana crosses The Esplanade and pretends it's the wind making her eyes water. The sea is moody — waves chop at the shore, stirring up the sand. She has the path to herself. A lone head bobs in and out of the water lapping the Beach Club.

At the car park she turns around, head bowed, the wind at her back. She'll walk to the boatshed end and then what? What is she doing? Marking time until Will comes to his senses? Or running away.

Someone shouts her name. She spins around, buoyed by hope. Fi stands outside the coffee shop, waving frantically. Her heart sinks. Not today. She needs to be alone, to think. Diana waves back and trudges over.

'You look absolutely terrible, darling. Are you coming down with something?' Fi asks as soon as they've placed their order and nabbed a table in a patch of sun. The waitress delivers a plate with an enormous muffin and two forks. 'Comfort food. It's pear and pecan.'

Diana bursts into tears.

'Oh my goodness, whatever's wrong, Didi?' Fi grabs a fistful of napkins from the dispenser and presses them into her hand.

'Will's left me.' The moment the words are out, she realises that this is the fear she's been fighting.

Fi shuffles her chair closer and huddles in to keep the conversation strictly between themselves. 'Start at the beginning.'

Diana gives her the short version. How an envelope arrived for Will while he was away. How it turned out someone had sent him compromising photos of her.

Fi fixes Diana with her trademark piercing stare. 'That seems incredibly nasty. Who else was in the photos?'

Diana opens her mouth to answer then snaps it shut. She can't tell Fi the truth. Not after all these years of keeping secrets. Instead, she offers a small morsel in the hope it will satisfy her. 'Ian,' she says. 'You know he can't keep his hands to himself.'

Fi snorts. 'That's it? Surely Will can't believe you're having an affair with his brother. That's ludicrous.' She cuts the muffin in half with the edge of her fork then halves it again. 'If what you say is true, it sounds more like Will was looking for an excuse to fly off the handle.'

Fi's words trigger memories from all those years ago. Diana couldn't believe Will had walked out that door. In the morning, she'd woken to Aiden in her bed and been shocked afresh. She'd raced into the family room, turning off lights as she went. Will wasn't asleep on the couch, nor in Aiden's bed. Persephone was still dreaming, her thumb in her mouth, Wabbit clutched in her embrace. In the bathroom, Diana searched in vain for the little amber bottle of pills but Lydia must've disposed of them when she left. She fell to the floor, sobbing.

Fi pulls her back to the present, warming to her theme. 'They say the best form of defence is attack. What if it was Will who had you followed?' she suggests, eyes growing wide at the possibility.

'Why would he do that?' Diana replies, wounded by the very idea of it. 'Anyway, I didn't recognise the handwriting. If Will had paid someone to follow me, they wouldn't write a post-it note, would they?'

Fi, though, is not easily derailed. 'Maybe that's to put you off the scent. After all, that's the bulk of what private investigators do, isn't it? Pursue partners suspected of adultery.'

Shame rises in a hot flush. The spark in Fi's eye tells Diana that her friend is enjoying herself, no doubt imagining what she'd do to Richard if she ever caught him *in flagrante delicto*, as if infidelity had all the seriousness of a bedroom farce. Never suspecting that in real life, the guilt erodes your self-esteem, drip by drip.

Fi skewers a chunk of muffin then pushes the plate towards Diana. She shakes her head. 'I'm not comfort eating. I'm already several kilos heavier than I should be.'

'You look fine to me. Eat the goddamn muffin. Life's too short to worry about your waistline.'

'Says you, who looks exactly the same as you did ten years ago.'

'It's the tennis.' Fi taps the table. 'Don't change the subject. I've got to go in a tick. If you want my opinion, then I think you need to figure out who wanted the photos taken. Once you do that, the rest will make perfect sense.'

Fi has a point. Whoever was tailing her sure got more than they bargained for. Not one lover but three? Who do they think she is, Ava Gardner? Thank goodness Michael's farewell kiss in the photos was innocent. Unlike the other week. It makes her feel guilty even thinking about it, despite knowing she did nothing wrong. Considering Will's always had a bee in his bonnet about Michael, imagine if he'd known about the proper kiss. Had her denial come over a bit too strong?

An image of the man with the whippet in the tartan coat leaps to mind. How he held up his phone and snapped her. Diana shudders. It was creepy and she'd been so unnerved, she'd scurried away as if she were the guilty party. Her and Michael at the café. Her and Michael at his apartment. And then there's meeting Ben. Will storming out. Oh, she is in so much trouble. Diana pushes aside her half-drunk coffee.

'I think you have two options,' Fi says, standing and shrugging on her coat. 'Either ring Will and confront him. Or leave it be. Give him a couple of days to simmer down. That would be my strategy. Honestly, you guys are rock solid. We're celebrating your thirtieth wedding anniversary next month. Trust me, he's having a tantrum. Underneath, men are all babies.' She bends down and kisses Diana's cheek. 'But, my love, you better find out who's stirring the pot and quick smart.'

Chapter 19

Saturday

Fi's sage advice brings Diana back to earth. She's right, Will is being an idiot. She's equally as guilty of overreacting. They both need to calm down. If Michael is Will's number one concern, then she's on steady ground. It's like the fine print in those investment brochures — past performance is no indicator of future performance. They should print that on marriage contracts.

Girded by Fi's pep talk, she rings Will. He cuts off the call, and just so he knows that she knows he did that, she leaves him a short but pointed message. 'We need to talk about the photos.' And to prove to him, and herself, that this load of nonsense will soon blow over, Diana throws herself into the rest of the unpacking.

On Saturday, she rises at an absurd hour. It's completely out of character but then again, life has thrown her a curve ball and scattered her usual routine like tenpins. She makes a cappuccino and checks the answering machine. Nothing. Will is obviously choosing to maintain radio silence. Well, good luck with that strategy. Diana takes her coffee out on the terrace, hoping the sunrise and sound of birds carolling in the dawn might lift her spirits.

She shivers. It's cold out here at this hour. She ducks inside for her drapey mohair cardigan and the slippers Persephone sent her as an ironic Mother's Day gift. They are an anaemic shade of pink with a kitten heel and this ridiculous feathery pom-pom thing happening on the front. She'd forgotten all about them until she unpacked a box of shoes last night. She slides her feet into them now, instantly feeling like some madam in a genteel brothel.

Diana wanders back to the living room, which sadly remains a work in progress. She reads the label of the box closest to her. Board games and knick-knacks. Well, that certainly doesn't belong out here. She grabs the corners of the box and pushes it down the hall to the second bedroom. When — if — Will comes back, he can put it in the storage locker.

The thought makes her anger flare. How dare he accuse her of wrongdoing then storm off without allowing her the space to defend herself. As if *he* hasn't had ample opportunity to fool around in all these years. He could have a girl in every port for all she knows. Far be it for her to throw stones but Will seems to have conveniently forgotten that his past behaviour was also less than exemplary. But has she questioned his fidelity since then? No, she has not. Mind you, don't ask questions you don't want to know the answer to, that's always been her motto.

On impulse, Diana flings open the wardrobe door. Will hangs his coats and jackets in the spare room because he has more clothes than a department store. What did Fi say? The best form of defence is attack. If he's hiding something, where would he keep it? Diana searches the pockets of the first coat. She finds a ticket for the New York subway dated two months ago. Three coats in, she's amassed the subway ticket, a ten-dollar note, and an airline boarding pass.

Oh, this is ridiculous, she tells herself. *What am I going to do about it if he is fooling around?* Yet she finds herself picking up a houndstooth jacket that's fallen off its hanger. She gives it a shake. It's one of Will's favourites — although, she can't remember the last time he wore it. Richard's birthday bash maybe? She slips her hand into the side pocket. Nothing. Same with the other pocket. She pats the inside breast pocket — there's a lump, which turns out to be a crumpled business card. She flattens it and turns it over. Caroline Fox and a mobile phone number. Suspiciously absent of a company name, a logo, an address or any of the regular hallmarks of a business card. Bang!

Diana carries the card between two fingers as if it were the smoking gun. She places it next to the phone and fetches her glasses. 'So, William Eliot Forsyth, what have *you* been up to?' She dials the number, vindication fuelling every press of the button. What will she say to this Caroline Fox when she answers? Who are you? No, too blunt. Better — she'll pretend to be Will's secretary and say she's calling to reschedule his appointment. That leaves it a bit open-ended.

'The number you have called is currently unattended. Please leave a message after the tone.'

Diana hangs up. She drums her fingers on the kitchen bench then grabs her mobile and searches the internet. Thirty-nine million entries, she could be any one of them. What she needs is another perspective. Lydia is the safest option. One, because she's on the other side of the world so has both geographical and emotional distance. Two, because she's her big sister, so her allegiances are clear. Oh and three, because Lydia was there the last time everything went wrong. That gives her the winning ticket. Lydia has context.

Rome is currently eight hours behind. She does the maths. It's late but if Lydia's not working she'll still be up.

'How are the party plans coming along?' Lydia asks as soon as they've completed the ritual greetings. 'Armando and I are already packing. Imagine, we'll be there in less than three weeks.'

The Big Party? Will there be one now everything is going pear-shaped? Diana mentally parks the alarm this raises off to one side. Best to deal with one problem at a time. 'Fine, fine but that's not why I'm calling.'

Diana hears the fizz of a soft drink bottle followed by the clink of ice in a glass. On the other side of the world, Lydia takes a sip then issues an 'aah' of satisfaction. 'Do you drink Campari? It's my current fave.'

'No because the colour reminds me of cough medicine.'

'You don't know what you're missing out on.' Lydia lights a cigarette and exhales into the phone. 'Right. I'm all ears. What's the goss?'

'Will has left me.'

'Nooo, you're pulling my leg!'

Lydia's reaction bolsters Diana. 'It gets better. Person or persons unknown decided to send Will compromising photos of me. The upshot is, he thinks I've been having an affair.'

'What? You and some toy boy having a roll? I'd like to see pictures of that.'

Diana flinches. 'I might be many things, Lydia, but I'm not some aging cougar.'

'A, that's a tautology. B, don't be so hard on yourself and C, I can name several men who would more than happily pluck your keys out of the fishbowl at a swingers' party.'

'Lydia, I'm not the sort of woman who has sex with random men, however interested or interesting they may be.' The words have barely left her mouth when an unpleasant thought springs to mind. She's made assumptions about Will's issues in the bedroom department. What if she is the problem?

'Doesn't mean you can't play away from home though, does it?' Lydia continues through her laughter. 'You and Will must be bored rigid by each other after thirty odd years. It must be like pressing buttons.'

Diana makes a moue of distaste. 'Don't talk about sex like it's a transaction.'

'God almighty, you're not going to give me that crap about the union of two souls and the sublime expression of mutual love and respect, are you? I remember when you pulled that stunt on Percy. The poor girl was only sixteen. I'm surprised she didn't rush out and find some random to lose her virginity to there and then. I know I would have.'

'There was a word for girls like you when we were her age. Any mother would want her daughter's first experience to be romantic and passionate. Not with some blond-haired surfie in the back of a panel van.'

Lydia hoots with laughter. 'My God, Didi. You've watched *Puberty Blues* way too many times. I can honestly say I've never had sex in the back of a panel van.'

'I distinctly remember that god-awful purple shag pile glued on the floor, the walls and the inside roof of Surfer Boy's car. I am positive there was also a disco ball hanging off the rear-view mirror. And you expect me to believe you two weren't up to no good?'

Lydia yawns, a big bellowing, completely unladylike kind of yawn that's so loud Diana has to pull the phone away from her ear. When she's done, she says, 'In my experience, men only leave their marriages if they have another bed to fall into or their wives kick them out.'

'Caroline Fox.'

'I beg your pardon?'

'I found a business card stuffed inside one of Will's favourite jackets. It had a phone number and the name Caroline Fox.'

'Well, did you try ringing it?'

'Next stupid question.'

'Internet?'

'Nothing interesting, if you don't count a dead diarist or a dead baroness. Both more than a century and a half in the grave. The living possibilities are too numerous to mention.'

Lydia sings out to Armando asking whether he wants a coffee, closely followed by the sound of her lighting the stove for the espresso pot.

'Coffee at this hour! Won't it keep you up half the night?'

Lydia sniggers. 'That's the general idea.'

Diana blushes. Armando is quite a bit younger than Lydia, although whether a man in his late thirties is young enough to be considered a toy boy is debatable. What is clear though is that Lydia's painter adores her. Luckily, he paints walls not portraits, otherwise she knows exactly where this would be heading. Some dimple-thighed nude taking up an entire wall of Lydia's apartment, that's where.

Now the coffee pot is on, Lydia gives Diana her full attention. 'What if this Caroline of the business card is behind the photos? Maybe she wants to get her claws into Will and sent the photos to deliberately cause a rift.'

'More like a chasm.'

'It's like that woman who used to work with Mum. Remember her? The tall one with short hair. Attractive rather than beautiful.'

Diana casts her mind back and summons a vague shadow of a woman in a white coat. 'Was it Sarah?'

'Sara, not Sarah. Remember how she ended up marrying her best friend's husband?'

Now the memory crystallises. How could Diana ever forget Sara? 'That's right. Her friend had breast cancer and Sara nursed her through the illness. I always admired how devoted she was, right up until the end.'

'What? You mean, right up until the point where she was boofing the husband while her friend lay dying. Couldn't wait to get a ring on her finger. Glad she wasn't my best friend.' Lydia lights another cigarette, exhales into the phone. 'I wonder if they're still together?'

'Speaking of which, you know how I've been worried about Will and his prostate. Do you reckon that could explain his irrational reaction to the photos? I mean, he did overreact to billy-oh. Maybe it isn't another woman, maybe he felt threatened.'

Lydia dismisses this line of reason with a curt, 'Don't be stupid. Speaking of people getting their leg over, has Mum told you about Victor?'

'The handyman?'

Lydia laughs. 'In more ways than one.'

'Really?'

'I dare you to ask her about him next time you talk. See what she says.'

Diana shifts her position on the couch. They've been chatting so long her leg has gone to sleep. She jiggles it, admiring the way the feathery pom-pom on her slipper bounces in time with the movement.

'Actually, now I think about it,' says Lydia, 'cancel the party. You don't want to be blowing your dough in case you need to live off your tuition fees now Will's left you.'

The finality of this statement shocks Diana. 'I think you're getting a bit too far ahead of yourself, Lyds. Right now, I'm quite happy in the righteous indignation phase. I never meant to imply the rift was permanent.' Although Lydia's words do raise serious questions. How would Diana stand on her own two feet? And if this was it and Will wasn't coming back, would this apartment be hers or would she be cast out and forced to live with Audrey or, worse, have to press Audrey's motor home back into service? It happens all the time to women her age. And if Will is already warming this Caroline's bed, whatever decisions he makes will be made with the wrong end of his anatomy. Lydia's right. Her future could be quite perilous.

'Party or no party, Armando and I aren't changing our plans. I haven't seen you in yonks. And drowning your sorrows will be much more fun in person. Actually, I have a better idea. Don't cancel the party. Worse comes to worse, we can turn it into a divorce party. We won't even need to change the banners. Thirty years is still something to celebrate.'

Diana cannot respond; Lydia has rendered her speechless.

'You won't know yourself, Didi, I promise. Shake off the shackles, taste the freedom.'

Diana thinks of Michael, that kiss. In truth, it was quite pleasant. She's always had a real connection with Michael. Music is their bond. Maybe if she hadn't fallen in love with Will, the on-stage chemistry might have turned into something. She'll never know. Diana looks at the baby grand. A gift from Will for her fiftieth. 'You hardly ever play anymore, Didi,' he'd said. 'I wish you'd sing for me like you used to.' But she hasn't, not really. It doesn't feel right, it doesn't sound right. But when she's with Michael, it sparks a freedom within her.

'You're better off without him.'

It takes Diana a moment to realise who Lydia means. 'I thought you liked Will.'

'I do. Despite everything, I think Will's a top bloke. And he's a complete spunk for a man turning sixty in a month. But he's past his best-by date. Trade him in. Get a new model. Someone who makes you feel young again.'

'I'm not sure I want to feel young again,' Diana objects.

Lydia snorts. 'You have no idea what you're missing.'

Chapter 20

Saturday

Dramatic is de rigueur wherever Lydia is involved but the phone call has left Diana in a bit of a funk. 'Thirty years is still something to celebrate,' she mutters to herself, mimicking her sister's flippant tone. 'Thirty years of marriage is bloody hard work,' she says more stridently than necessary since she's the only party to this conversation. 'Not that you'd know, Lydia Roberts.' *Who's the latest flash in the pan?* their dad used to shout after her as she skipped down the hall to welcome the current beau.

Flashes in the pan. Men who were more inclined towards a roll in the hay than building a barn. Being married required far more fortitude than a fling. It required compromise and compassion and yes, she'll say it — the ability to withstand a certain amount of monotony. Not always but sometimes. Diana may have her faults — let's face it, who doesn't? — but she has stayed the course. She made that decision almost thirty years ago and she's stuck to her part of the bargain ever since. *I forgive you.* 'Well, really, Will, what about you?'

Diana returns to the bedroom. The mussed-up sheets invite her back into their warm embrace but she will not be tempted.

That's a slippery slope. If she goes back to bed she'll wallow in misery, and where does that end? Not showering for days. Dirty mugs competing for space on the bedside table. Barely eating. Mind you, that might not be so bad. Curvaceous, Will calls her. Fat, she corrects him in her head. And just to rub salt in the wound, Will is still slender with a set of shoulders to make a girl swoon. It's all that swimming.

Diana changes direction and heads for the wardrobe. She has to keep her self-pity in check. When Will returns, she wants him to find a wife who's resilient in the face of adversity. And with that, she exchanges her mohair cardigan and feathery mules for leggings and an old shirt, ties her hair in a high ponytail and heads back to the living room. With the jazz channel for company, she spends the afternoon unpacking boxes of objects rich with memories — the paperweight from Murano in Venice, the platters from Siena, a silver cigarette box gifted to Will's grandfather on his retirement. Her grandmother's crazy tea set. Diana washes and polishes each piece and finds it a new home. It's dusk by the time she's done. She pushes the last box into the spare bedroom next to the board games and a box of surplus sheets and towels. Now she's on her own, she guesses it falls to her to take them down to the garage. In the words of Peggy Lee, 'Mañana'.

Diana heads for the cocktail cabinet. Inside is a box of leftover spirits from parties long consigned to the blurry pages of history. Up the back she spies an unopened bottle of Campari. Does Campari go off? Only one way to find out. Diana takes it into the kitchen. She wipes the dust off the crumbling label and reads the recipes. She doubts they have any pink grapefruit juice. There is a bottle of gin though. Mind you, it would be terrible to undo all that hard work maintaining the moral high ground by getting blotto. Diana finds a bottle of prosecco in the fridge and follows the instructions for making a Negroni Sbagliato instead.

'*Salute*, Lydia,' she says, raising her glass to her distant sister and taking a tentative sip. Not bad. She switches on all the lamps, bathing the lounge in a warm glow, and admires her day's handiwork. Displaying their familiar objects has gone some way to make this feel a little more like home. Still, the way things are going, she better not get used to it.

Diana adjourns to the terrace with her drink and leans on the ledge. The Moreton Bay figs are alive with activity. The fruit bats are going out for a night of foraging. The birds are settling down for a good night's rest. A puddle of light at the bus stand illuminates a group of teens on their way for a night out on the town. Her tummy grumbles. *Too bad*, she tells it. *He's not here*. She must fend for herself.

With a sigh, Diana returns to the kitchen. She finds a tin of tuna in the pantry, assembles tuna, tomato and cheese on a muffin and slips it under the grill. While it cooks, she sips her Campari and prosecco and gazes out the window. In the next apartment, she recognises the older woman she met the other day when she was collecting the mail — the lady of culottes and neat blouses. She's stirring a smoking wok and sipping a wine. She leans over and turns up the radio and does a little cha-cha-cha as she cooks. Diana eats her tuna melt over the sink to save on a plate. The lady of culottes takes her meal over to a dining nook, a place set for one. She opens a book and reads as she eats. When she's done, she washes up, wipes down the bench and turns off the light. Diana looks towards the next room over, waiting for her to turn on the television and settle in for the night. If Will's absence is permanent, this could be her future. Then the light goes on again. The lady of culottes has thrown on a coat. She collects her keys from a hook by the door and disappears.

Diana's mobile vibrates with an incoming video call. She snatches it up. 'Hello! Persephone! How lovely to hear from you!' She doesn't mean to punctuate every word with an exclamation mark but she's so relieved. 'What perfect timing.'

'Mum, I just got off the phone from Auntie Lydia. She assumed I knew all about you and Dad. What the fuck? You can't seriously be contemplating a divorce. You've been married forever. You guys are my role models.'

Diana takes her Campari over to the couch and adopts a calm, maternal expression. 'Don't listen to your aunt, darling. You know she never lets the truth get in the way of a good story. Although, it is true that your father's not currently speaking to me. Is he speaking to you?'

Persephone points at the glass in Diana's hand. 'Since when do you drink Campari?'

Since your father abandoned me. 'Lydia insisted I try it.'

'Are you a convert?'

'Not sure yet. This may very well be my first and last Campari ever. Turns out I'm a rosé kind of girl through and through. Now, answer the question. Have you heard from Dad?'

Persephone screws up her face as she thinks. 'Not since we had dinner. He forgot his charger. I rang to tell him I'd bring it with me but I never heard back.'

Old habits die hard. 'Your father has a lot on his plate at the moment.'

'*Plus ça change, plus c'est la même chose.*'

'Indeed. However, he seems to be …' Diana pauses and tries to find the right word. 'Flying off the handle' is the old Will, not the more mellow man of recent years. What clue has she missed? 'Under a bit of strain,' she ends lamely. It's important to remain diplomatic, especially with the children.

Persephone looks off screen, smiles. 'Yep, you too,' she says in a half-whisper then blows a kiss. 'I'll see you tonight.' Then back to camera and her normal voice. 'Sorry about that. Emile's going to work.'

'How is he?'

'Good. Great. Busy. He's looking forward to the break.' She leans in as if sharing a confidence. 'Actually, that's the other reason for my call. We've changed our flights to a day earlier. Don't worry, we've booked a hotel. I don't want to inconvenience you.'

'No, darling, we have a spare room, you can stay here.' That is, once she's moved all the packing boxes. 'On second thoughts, I'll see if I can squeeze in an extra night at the holiday house. It'll be lovely to steal a few hours of mother–daughter time before the whole tribe descends. And if the party plans go pear-shaped then I'm sure we'll find other ways to amuse ourselves.'

Persephone wriggles closer. 'Don't be silly, Mum. You're not cancelling the party. Dad's being a goose. He'll come to his senses, I know it. Either way, Emile and I are not bailing, we've been looking forward to this trip for ages.' She glances at the front door then back to the screen. 'Plus, there's something I want to talk to you about,' she says *sotto voce*, even though the only creature to overhear her would be Muffin, their Ragdoll kitten.

Diana spins through the options and lands on grandchildren. 'Don't make me wait. Tell me now.'

'No, I'd rather do it face to face.' Persephone sounds awkward rather than smug, which forces Diana to confront the option that maybe this isn't about children.

'Emile and I are now arriving on the fifteenth. Which reminds me, Camille keeps dropping hints about catering for the party. She seems to be thinking it could be her gift to you guys.'

Diana glances at the pile of *Gourmet Travellers* barricading Camille's smug little cookbook. 'But I've already booked the catering with the usual crew from The Village Providore. Anyway, it's not fair to burden Camille. She's our guest, Persephone.'

'Exactly. I've tried to explain that to her. Consider yourself warned though, Camille can be quite bloody-minded and is very good at getting her own way. I don't know, could you call her about it, or drop her an email? You're good at that diplomatic stuff.'

Diana reflects on her barney with Will. Perhaps Persephone should be employing the past tense when it comes to her skills of appeasement.

'Now, you and Dad. Let's face it, he does have form with overreacting. Remember that time I snuck out to a nightclub and we got busted by the police? Oh my God, I thought he was literally going to explode he was so mad. If this is the same kind of thing, then he's definitely being stupid. I'll call him and talk some sense into him.'

Diana almost spills Campari all over the cream lounge. 'No, don't do that!' The last thing she needs is the children lobbying on her behalf. And there is no way in hell she is getting into the tawdry details about the photos with Persephone. 'This is between your father and me. You stay out of it, please.'

Fi said to give Will time to come to his senses, but shouldn't she have heard from him by now? And thanks to Lydia's tactlessness, the children have become involved. Because if Persephone knows about this, then Aiden will too. It's a veritable hornets' nest. If anyone's going to go poking it with a big stick, it will be Diana, not Persephone. At least she deserves to get stung.

Chapter 21

Sunday

Maybe the Campari was just what the doctor ordered. Diana wakes up on Sunday feeling ready to take on the world. Dressed in her mohair cardigan and feathery mules, she takes her coffee out on the terrace. It's been two days since Will bunked off. Has she fallen in a heap? No. Has the world stopped spinning? Apparently not. It seems Helen Reddy is not the only one who can roar.

Diana sorts through the remainder of the mail on the corner of the bench. There's the latest newsletter from the Sea Breeze Retirement Village people. Surely they should be spending their valuable funds on caring for their elderly charges, not wasting money and time on glossy marketing materials. No wonder the place is so expensive to buy into.

Underneath Diana finds the article she'd kept for Will — 'Are You Having a Late-Life Crisis?' Originally, she kept it out of general interest, but now she scans the contents hoping for a clue to explain his extraordinary behaviour. The article lists illness, the death of a loved one or emotional problems as triggers. This gives Diana pause. Could it be that what's wrong with Will isn't a dodgy prostate or a dalliance, that they are the symptom, not the cause? Foxy Caroline might be a Doctor Foxy. A fresh search yields plenty of scientists and extremely qualified medicos, but unless Will is meeting her in Birmingham, Boston or British Columbia, that too sheds no light.

Yet, the truth is, whatever the cause, she and Will have been pussy-footing around each other for months. To put it bluntly, beyond the odd cuddle or optimistic kiss, Diana hasn't been getting any. Since last Christmas, Will has been a no-show in the bedroom department.

Each summer, Diana routinely clears their social calendar and stuffs the fridge with all his favourite treats. Will puts himself on a technology break and switches off notifications on his phone. It's supposed to be a proper holiday filled with lazy days, swims at the beach and afternoon naps — and therein lies the problem. Everyone knows that 'afternoon nap' is a euphemism. They wrote a whole damn song about it, for Pete's sake. A little bit of fun followed by a zizz. What could be nicer?

Except last summer, things did not go to plan. Will grilled some marinated prawns on the barbecue for lunch. They had a couple of glasses of white wine to wash them down then departed for the bedroom for a 'nap'. Things started off in the usual manner then disaster struck.

The memory is mortifying. Even now, a flush creeps up Diana's neck. There she was, her leg threaded through Will's, his hands running all over her, doing that sort of half-mutter half-growl thing he does when he laps her up. Such a turn-on. Then they moved on to phase two. Diana adjusted her hips to accommodate him, ran her hands over his buttocks, drawing him closer, ready for the fireworks to happen. Except it didn't.

They tried a different position, a bit more encouragement on her part. She even offered to go down on him, something she hadn't done in years. But that only served to make things worse. Frightened the heck out of Will. To be frank, she was a bit insulted. He'd always told her she had particular talents in that department. But on reflection, maybe poor Will was worried that if that didn't work then nothing would, and then where would he be? It's so tricky being a man, everything on display like that. No faking the fun for them.

Diana notices the time. *Goodness me!* She's due on a call with Aiden, she'd better get a wriggle on. She takes the remains of her coffee over to the study nook and turns on her laptop. While it's firing up, she ducks into the bedroom and throws on a clean shirt under her drapey mohair cardigan. No time for makeup, just a dash of mascara and wet finger through her eyebrows. She pops on the lovely set of beads Fi bought her for her birthday. There, that will have to do. No one needs to know she's in her pyjama bottoms and tizzy mules.

Back at her desk, Diana enters the meeting. Except when the video springs to life, it's not Aiden smiling back at her but Anna.

'Well, good morning,' she says. 'What a lovely surprise.' No point denying it. It's not often Diana and her daughter-in-law have a tête-à-tête.

She has nothing against Anna per se, well, apart from dragging her son over to live on the other side of the world and remaining there even after they gave Diana and Will a grandson. That aside, Anna is a lovely girl — perhaps a little too career-focused, but Diana refuses to be the disapproving mother-in-law from central casting and keeps her opinions to herself.

'I'm so sorry to hear the news,' Anna gushes through the ether. 'Aiden told me all about it.'

Did he now? Seems Lydia's tactlessness is contagious. Things really must be careening out of control if Anna is dishing out sympathy. How much has her bloody sister shared?

'I know we haven't seen the actual pictures,' Anna continues, unintentionally addressing Diana's question, 'but it occurred to me that maybe they were photoshopped. The technology is pretty good these days.'

Diana tunes out, hijacked by another thought. Whippet Man. She's seen him before that day at Michael's — the day they took Ruth to lunch. He was walking past The Boatshed. She knew she'd seen that dog before. The man? Totally forgettable, but she couldn't forget a whippet with caramel splodges. It was the tartan that had thrown her. The time before, the dog had worn a leopard-skin coat.

She tunes back in and conceals a sigh. Is there any point telling Anna that no one has photoshopped anything? It's her in the photos all right, just not doing what Will's accused her of.

'Anyway, don't worry, whatever happens, we're still coming. The airline had a sale on and the tickets are non-refundable.'

Diana hates to think how much Anna earns as an investment manager but Fi assures her it's a LOT. Even though she's willing to bet they're flying business class, airfares would be small potatoes.

'And Hugo and Ingrid have their hearts set on going scuba diving on the Great Barrier Reef before it disappears, so it's silly to change arrangements at this late stage.'

'Such a shame to ruin their holiday,' she demurs, grateful her children don't call her Diana. Persephone tried it once because a girl in her hockey team addressed her parents by their first names. Diana nipped that in the bud, *tout de suite*.

'Anyway, Lukie wants to say hello,' Anna says, pulling him onto her lap.

Diana's grandson leans forward and touches the screen. It gives her the perfect angled view of a little snot bubble dipping in and out of one nostril as he breathes.

'Hello, Lukie,' she croons, keeping her gaze firmly locked on his beautiful brown eyes. A finger appears, pops the bubble and then is shoved in his mouth.

'Hey, Mum,' Aiden calls. There's a flurry of jerky movements as her son shuffles in next to Anna and relieves her of Lucas. He moves into the centre of the screen as Anna wanders off. Diana's heart swells at the portrait of father and son. Lucas has his father's impenetrable brown eyes but the golden ringlets of Anna's father.

'I had a chat with Dad. Told him he should know, you know, in his heart of hearts, that you'd never do the dirty on him. Especially with Uncle Ian! How desperate would you have to be? No offence to Auntie Rebecca, but you know what I mean.'

Aiden reaches off-screen and grabs a beer. This startles Diana momentarily, but of course it's Saturday night there, not breakfast.

'Did I ever tell you about the time I saw Auntie Rebecca without her makeup? Her lips are the same colour as her skin. How weird is that?'

Aiden has told Diana this story. Hundreds of times. As appealing as it is to think of Rebecca as a bloodless vampire queen, the more likely explanation is that she'd matted her lips with foundation.

Aiden looms closer to the screen, his expression hopeful, questioning, worried. 'You wouldn't do the dirty on Dad, would you, Mum? There's nothing to the photos, right?'

Diana offers him a reassuring smile, pulls her cardigan a little tighter around her shoulders. 'Absolutely not. It's all a big misunderstanding and I'm sure your father will realise that the moment we sit down and have a heart to heart.' Fingers crossed.

Aiden pulls away, looking a little embarrassed that he'd asked, but comforted by her words. He takes a slug of his beer. 'Shame it's ruined the Big Surprise. I've been really looking forward to it. You should see the playlist I've created. And Percy's done this amazing slideshow. It'll be like *This is Your Life.*'

The Big Surprise. Boy, doesn't that now sound like the dumbest idea ever. In the light of recent events, what started out as a bit of fun is looking dangerously close to very poor taste indeed. 'I'm sorry, I know you've put in a lot of work. But look at it this way, the advantage of a surprise is that if we don't have the party, your father will be none the wiser.'

Aiden finishes off his beer. Diana can see his Adam's apple bobbing up and down. It reminds her of when he went through puberty. By that point, Will was measuring him against the doorjamb every month. In the space of a year, he burst at the seams and it felt like she was constantly buying him new shoes and clothes. Will called him the Incredible Hulk but the sight of Aiden used to make Diana's heart ache with tenderness. Shovelling in two-minute noodles, Weet-Bix and bread. Drinking strawberry-flavoured milk like it was going out of fashion. Constantly exhausted. Her poor man-child barely able to keep his head in the game of life. Now look at him. Mister Relaxed with a beautiful and talented wife, gorgeous son, and an easy existence. What more could a mother wish for?

He twists the top off a second beer and salutes Diana through the screen. 'For my money, I think we stick to the original plan. We've still got a couple of weeks up our sleeve. Dad'll come round.'

Aiden's perpetual optimism is such an admirable trait. Diana loves him too much to burst his bubble, so she simply says, 'You're probably right.' It's an act of kindness really, and she's always embraced her role as the family peacemaker.

Chapter 22

Monday

After choir practice on Monday, Diana ducks up to the salon for her long-overdue waxing appointment. When she looked in the mirror this morning, she swore she'd grown a proper moustache. Women and facial hair, beyond a well-shaped eyebrow, did not mix. And she is not ready to relinquish her beauty routine simply because Will's giving her the silent treatment.

Unfortunately, the first person Diana sees when she enters the salon is the last person she wishes to. Rebecca is in one of the pedi chairs, glued to her phone, completely ignoring the delightful Cherish working on her feet. Cherish sees Diana and waves. 'Samantha won't be long.'

Rebecca's massage chair finishes its pummelling, and she looks up from her phone. Diana notices the momentary hesitation when Rebecca registers her presence. Behind her back, her sister-in-law calls her Saint Diana, but it sure beats The Ice Queen.

Diana pastes on a smile. 'Hello! Twice in as many weeks! People will talk.'

Rebecca pats the salon chair next to her, grinning at Diana in a way that sends a chill down her spine. At least it answers one question — Rebecca knows Will's taken off. Seeing Diana in a tight spot is an opportunity to gloat.

'Oh, I'm not actually here for a pedi. I'm here for a wax …' Diana trails off. With a wistful glance at the curtain of the treatment room, she squeezes in beside Rebecca.

She'll need to tread carefully. How much Rebecca knows about Diana's supposed shenanigans will depend on what kind of conversation has occurred between Will and Ian. Rebecca treats her husband with complete disdain in public, but if any woman gets within three feet of the guy, her hackles go straight up. Ian is hers to torment, no one else's.

Rebecca leans closer. 'Gosh, you poor thing. It's just awful. You and Will.' She winces.

How Diana would love to scrub the smug smile off Rebecca's face, preferably with a piece of steel wool. Diana considers how to respond. She can't deny it. On the upside, it seems Will didn't confront his brother about the photos — Rebecca appears clueless. This brightens Diana's mood considerably. 'Will's been on business trips that lasted longer than this. I'm not exactly calling my lawyer.'

Not that she has one but her thoughts stray to Georgina Templeton. And it's as if Rebecca's read her mind.

'Well, do let me know if you need a recommendation. My lawyer is fabulous.' Then Rebecca picks up the latest issue of *Luxury Travel* and buries her nose in it.

Diana can't resist adding, 'Of course, you'll be wondering whether we're still going ahead with the Big Party.'

This gets Rebecca's attention. She turns and raises one eyebrow.

'As I said to the kids,' Diana continues, 'it would be a shame to ruin the chance to catch up with all the family. Everyone's organised their holidays around the dates, we couldn't possibly ask them to cancel at this late stage. I'm sure Will and I will be sailing on smooth waters by then.'

Rebecca gives her a strange smile. 'I've always loved your optimism.'

Diana maintains her positive veneer and fortunately, at that moment, Samantha rescues her. 'Morning, Diana. I'm ready now. Come, come.'

'Sorry, Becks, must go.' She's about to follow Samantha behind the curtain when she has a brilliant thought. Wearing her most charming smile, she asks, 'This lawyer friend of yours, I don't suppose she specialises in divorce?'

Rebecca lowers the pages of her glossy magazine. 'Yes, as it happens.'

Diana lets that hang for a moment, enjoying the sight of Rebecca's mind spinning into overdrive. 'I thought so.' Pause for effect. 'I assume this is the same friend I saw you having lunch with last week? I've heard she's very good.'

And she turns on her heel, knowing she has set the wheels in motion.

Chapter 23

Tuesday

Diana has barely walked into the apartment when the phone starts ringing. It's her mother. She's tempted to let it go through to message bank but that will only delay the inevitable.

'What's this I hear about you and Will?'

'Hello, Mother. How nice to hear from you. I'm well thank you, and you?'

Audrey grumbles. 'Yes, I'm good, thank you.'

'And Elsie, is she fine too?'

'What? The dog? She's perfectly fine. Why are you asking me about her?'

After what Lydia said on the weekend, Diana is tempted to ask after Victor as well but that might be poking the bear a little too hard. 'She's your companion, Mother, and a very sweet dog. Now, where were we?'

'Is this thing with Will really necessary? Divorce is such a drain and I am not just talking financially.'

Bloody Lydia. 'Let me be clear, Mother. Will and I have had an argument. We're just letting the dust settle until cooler heads can prevail. Surely you can understand that.'

This earns a tsk of disapproval. 'You always overreact,

Diana. If I could put up with a man as boring as your father for forty years, surely you can put up with Will.'

Was her father ever unfaithful? No, she can't imagine it. Her father was a workaholic — when would he have had the time? Mind you, back then, some people considered fidelity an optional extra in a marriage, especially the men.

'After all, he's hardly ever home,' Audrey continues. 'It's ridiculous to split up now. Did you know, women over fifty is the largest growing group of homeless people? Not enough super, no financial wherewithal.'

'Yes, Mum, I'm well aware of that fact,' although Diana doesn't mention that she has her eye on the mobile home should things get completely desperate. 'Although I'd like to believe that Will would do the right thing by me, should worse come to worse.'

Since he fought off Holworth and Harrow and the chance to get his hands on a lazy twelve mill, he's poured all his energy into building up FME. She has only a hazy idea of what he's worth these days but Diana hopes it's a lot, otherwise what was the point of all that sacrifice?

'If you want my opinion' — which Diana doesn't — 'you've only got yourself to blame. You let him go overseas on these work trips without you, he could be up to all sorts of mischief. There's nothing preventing you from going with him.'

'I have my students,' Diana reminds her.

Audrey snorts. 'I'm sure they'll survive without you for a term or two.'

The sting of her mother's words! Would anyone truly care if Mrs Forsyth no longer took them for music lessons? Probably not.

'This might surprise you, Mother, but I rather like the fact that Will travels. It gives me space to live my own life.' And not have to compromise or be held to account. 'And it's nice to miss him and look forward to him coming home.' Did that make her selfish? Probably. Diana takes the phone out to the terrace. She has a sudden need for fresh air. 'Anyway, what's it to you how I live my life? I don't offer you advice.'

'That's because you know it would fall on deaf ears.'

Diana bites her lip. There are about ten answers she could toss out right now, none of them kind, and despite her innumerable faults, Audrey is her mother.

'I can't help wondering if this has anything to do with Nicholas,' Audrey continues.

The shock leaves Diana tongue-tied. Will has stormed out on her twice in their marriage. Both times because of other men. But her mother doesn't know that. Of course she thinks this has to be about the death of Nicholas.

'I hope not,' Audrey goes on. 'You two survived the death of that dear little boy and that is a terrible test of a marriage. Infidelity isn't even in the same ballpark. You'd be crazy to throw it all away now, darling. Think with your head, not your heart. Yes, I'm giving advice. You cannot afford to maintain the lifestyle to which you have become accustomed on your own and you're too old to start again.'

There are so many things wrong with what her mother has just said, Diana barely knows where to start. 'Are you seriously suggesting I should stick with Will out of habit? I happen to believe I have thirty good years ahead of me, not one foot in the grave.'

'I'm simply saying that sometimes it's better to turn a blind eye to indiscretions. Whoever is at fault.'

Diana wonders how much her mother actually knows. It sounds like she's assuming *Will* has been playing away from home, which means Lydia mustn't have said anything about the subject of the photos. Perhaps she focused on the mysterious Caroline Fox and made it sound like that was the cause of the fight. To protect her sister?

'Well, thanks for taking the time out of your busy day to show me some support, Mum. It's been such a comfort.'

But the sarcasm is lost on Audrey because she's not even listening.

'I'll be with you in a minute, Victor.' Diana envisages the handset pressed to her mother's breast. 'Yes, put it down near the shed, if you wouldn't mind.'

Is Lydia right about Audrey and Victor? It seems odd to think of her mother with a man other than her father. What would Persephone and Aiden think if she and Will went their separate ways? Could she bear it if they liked Will's replacement model? Could she bear it if she had to be nice to her? There's a thought.

Audrey's voice returns loud and clear. 'Well, do let me know if you have to cancel the party,' followed by another tsk. 'I bought such a lovely gift from the Artist's Walk too. I wonder where I put the receipt …'

Chapter 24

Wednesday

'Your mother actually said that? Wowsers.'

Diana and Ruth are hiding in the courtyard out the back at Carlo's Trattoria. It's the end of the teaching day and they have snuck out for a quick wine before Ruth has to go home and make dinner for her boys. 'You keep your pantry too well-stocked,' Fi always says on the rare occasions Ruth has a whinge that surely now they're closer to thirty than twenty they should have homes of their own. 'Cut off supplies and they'll be out the door sooner than you can say two-minute noodles.'

'You've got new glasses,' Diana comments as she sips from a small fishbowl of wine.

Ruth looks pleased that she's noticed, although the hot-pink hexagonal frames are impossible to miss. 'Why thank you,' she replies, immediately removing them and polishing the lenses on the hem of her matching sweater. 'Now, where were we? Ah yes, I was saying, the problem is, we all have a tendency to think everything is about us. Sadly, most people are quite self-centred. Take me, for example. When Dave walked out, I assumed I'd done something wrong, that it was all my fault. My world had ended, blah, blah, blah. Large quantities of gin and cigarettes later, I realised it was only the end of that phase of my life. Not my choice, not my decision, but also nothing I could do about it. I could choose to be bitter and twisted or I could choose to move on. Obviously, I opted for the latter.' She raises her glass and they clink. 'To long-lost husbands. May they stay perennially in the distant past where they belong.'

'Cheers to that,' Diana replies before catching herself. 'I mean yours, not mine.'

Ruth smirks. 'Obviously.' She shivers and buttons her coat. 'Now the sun's gone it's a bit cool out here, isn't it? Shall we adjourn indoors?'

Diana couldn't agree more. They gather their handbags and move to one of the old chesterfields near the open fire.

'Why didn't we do this in the first place?' Diana asks, warming her hands in front of the flames.

'Because we didn't want parents catching us quaffing wine at four o'clock in the afternoon.'

Diana sits beside Ruth and picks up said wine. 'I don't see why. Half of them are in here every lunchtime, hooking into the chardy.'

'The difference being, they are not the school's career and guidance counsellor nor an adored member of the music faculty. It's hardly setting a good example, is it?'

'Don't be so hard on yourself.'

'Says you.' Ruth removes her coat and flings it over the arm of the sofa. 'Now, what was I talking about? Ah yes, my ex.' She wriggles back, and not being as tall as Diana, this means her feet no longer touch the ground. 'At least I can put my hand on my heart and say I tried to keep us together. And although that was a failure of epic proportions, the boys have learned that crises are an inevitable part of life and we must accept the things we cannot change.'

Ruth's words go straight to the core. 'But I can't say I've done everything in my power to keep Will and I together because it's not true.' It's such a relief to admit this out loud. Conversations with her family have revolved around either how she's teetering on the edge of divorce or how at some point he'll come to his senses and return home with his tail between his legs. No one has actually asked her how she feels or what she wants. As per bloody usual, it's all about Will.

'How long since you've spoken to him?'

'Nearly a week. I've left him countless messages.' Diana embellishes this with a flourish.

But Ruth, for all her general jolliness, is easily underestimated and not easily fooled. She peers at Diana through her hexagonal fuchsia frames. 'Really?'

Diana immediately folds her errant hand in her lap. 'Well, after the first couple of days, I did ring his parents. Marianne made all the right noises but basically said sorry but she was on Team Will. Ian just blustered and said he didn't want to get caught in the middle, which is kind of odd given that's exactly where I thought he was. When I rang to speak to Richard to see if he could shed any light on what Will was up to, I could hear Fi in the background berating Richard about not taking sides. The poor man couldn't get off the phone fast enough. You certainly discover where people's loyalties lie, don't you?'

Ruth swirls her wine and drains the glass. She seems surprised then disappointed to find it empty. With a sigh, she places it on the low table then turns her attention back to Diana. 'What's really going on between you and Will, hmm? He's run away, you're dancing around the edges. It feels like you guys have some dark history here that needs to be brought out into the light.' She pins Diana with a hard stare. A stare that says 'don't bullshit a bullshitter'. A stare that makes Diana squirm. 'Leaving phone messages isn't an action plan,' Ruth persists.

And the truth gushes out. 'There was someone else besides Ian in the photos.'

Ruth raises an eyebrow. 'My, you have been a busy girl!'

Diana blushes and murmurs, 'As if I have the time.'

'Oh, I think you have all the time in the world, my friend.' Ruth signals to Carlo behind the bar for two more glasses then settles into the lounge, quite happy to wait for Diana's answer.

It's all the years of counselling. Ruth is an excellent listener and shameless manipulator when it comes to the Art of Silence.

Before Diana can bare her soul, Carlo places two wines and a small plate of antipasto on the low table. 'My compliments,' he says, whisking away their empty glasses. Diana smiles in gratitude. Carlo winks at her. Ruth rolls her eyes.

Diana waits until Carlo has strutted off out of earshot. 'What it must do to a man's ego to spend his days being perved on by women unconstrained by husbands and children.' It takes her right back to the days of The Somethings with all those groupies clustered at the foot of the stage gazing adoringly at Michael's crutch. She picks up her glass. 'As I was saying, Ian is not the problem.'

Ruth drags her gaze away from devouring Carlo. 'I'm relieved to hear it.'

It feels good to talk about this. Diana's tired of going around and around in circles and Ruth is the perfect person to sort through the mess in her head. 'There were other photos.'

'I figured that much out.' Ruth picks up an arancini ball, bites it in half, and chews.

Diana fortifies herself with a large sip of wine. 'You know how I used to be in a band way back, right,' she begins.

Ruth's eyes light up. 'Is this your roundabout way of telling me you've been doing the cha-cha-cha with that dishy guy you used to play with?'

'What? No!'

'Not that'd I'd blame you. I cannot lie, if he walked into this bar, right now, I'd be throwing myself at him.' Ruth eats the rest of the arancini. 'He can strum my guitar any day of the week.'

Diana laughs to cover her embarrassment. 'Will's hated him pretty much since the moment they met.' Maybe it's the wine but she decides to allow a little truth to escape and test Ruth's reaction. 'You see, the reason Will stormed out was because there were photos of me with Michael. We're not doing anything untoward. Well, not *that* kind of thing. It was just a kiss. On the cheek.'

Ruth swirls her wine in her glass and waits for more.

Diana rushes on. 'Michael has been helping Aiden and me with a surprise we're planning for Will's birthday. We've been seeing each other more often than usual.'

'Ah, so Will saw the photos of you and Michael and put two and two together and got five.'

Diana squirms. 'Like I said, there's history.'

Ruth's eyes go as round as saucers. 'Are you telling me that you and Michael used to have a thing?'

Diana takes a gulp of wine. Drinking during the day has made her a little light-headed but she's come this far, she may as well go a little further. 'Not quite. There was a third man in the photos.'

'What! For the love of God, woman. How many plates are you spinning?'

Diana scrabbles in her handbag for tissues. Any second now she's going to lose it. A little truth is a lot harder than she thought. Her mother's words echo, *Has this got anything to do with Nicholas?* A sob escapes.

Ruth covers Diana's hand in hers. 'What's the matter, sweetie?'

'Something bad happened years ago. I acted foolishly. We never told anyone why but Will and I broke up for a while.'

'Are you saying you really did have an affair?'

Diana's first instinct is to defend herself. 'You know, this whole situation is ridiculous. I have no idea what Will gets up to when he's away. I'd prefer not to know, to be honest. But he's always come home to me.'

Ruth shuffles closer. 'I'm confused. What are you trying to tell me, Diana? Do you mean Will's having a fling?'

'Maybe. I don't know.' Diana shakes her head and puts down her glass. 'I'm sorry, I'm not being very clear.' She takes a deep breath and lets it out. 'Yes, many years ago, I had an affair but then Will and I patched things up and moved on.'

Ruth pulls a face that conveys what she thinks about moving on. 'But not with Michael?'

'No. Not Michael. I'm getting there, okay?'

Ruth gestures she's zipping her lips.

'Last week, I found a note that I'm not quite sure how to interpret. Then the very same day, this envelope arrived marked to Will's attention. I didn't think anything of it until Will got home and opened it to find these photos. Will went ballistic and walked out, leaving me wondering what the hell is going on. Of course, I know he assumes that I've been sleeping with someone because that's what the photos suggest. At this point in the proceedings the fact that it's not true is irrelevant. The real question is, why is Will overreacting?'

'The best form of defence is attack.'

'That's exactly what Fi said. She suggested that Will was behind the photos but that seems unnecessarily complicated. However, not believing me, avoiding my calls, that sets off alarm bells, doesn't it?' Diana pats Ruth's knee, making sure she has her full attention. 'It gets better. I did something I have never done in my life before and went through Will's pockets and guess what I find? A woman's business card.'

'Whose is it?'

'I don't know. That's another story. The thing is, Will and I haven't been, you know, so now I'm wondering whether it's because Will's having a fling and therefore lost interest in me rather than he's not able to have a fling, even if he wanted to, which is what I've been assuming. Does that make sense?'

Ruth sits staring into the flames. Diana can tell she's thinking, but not what she's thinking. It makes her nervous. Has she said too much?

'Wow,' Ruth finally says. 'You? You're always so serene. I thought you and Will were inseparable. Not much of a psychologist, am I?'

'Well, to be fair, you don't know the half of it.' Diana drains her glass of wine and leans back into the embrace of the sofa. *Has this got anything to do with Nicholas?* Audrey's words have struck Diana like an off-key note. She looks at Ruth. 'When Nicholas died, no one could tell us exactly why. I was beside myself with grief. I still don't ...' Diana shakes her head. She never discusses Nicholas, not even with Will, especially not with Will. 'The not knowing is like water. Drip, drip, drip. Wearing you down. Will had to go on a trip because of a takeover threat.'

'I remember. The timing was terrible.'

Diana nods. 'Except that wasn't the real reason he left. He left because he couldn't stand being around a weepy wretched woman. He didn't know how to save me but he knew what he had to do to save the company. So that's what he did. I wasn't in a good place. Lydia tried to help but she couldn't give me what I needed either, and then she had to go too.' Diana balls up a tissue and mops up the tears that have started to fall. 'I don't think I consciously went looking, but I found someone whose pain was as bad as mine.'

Ruth puts her arm around Diana and hugs her tight. Diana lets her, glad to be anchored. 'At first I thought that time would heal the wounds, we just had to move on, move past it. That's what I've been doing for the past twenty-six years. But you know what, I don't think Will's ever forgiven me, not deep down. That's why he's reacted the way he has to those photos. Because he doesn't trust me. All these years, he's just been waiting for me to slip up again. Now I realise that the wound has never healed.' Diana looks at Ruth, offers a glum smile. 'That's why he's deserted me a second time. I can't tell you how angry it's made me. What was the point of investing all this energy into making the marriage work, raising the kids, only for him to rack off because his feelings are hurt? He's not the only one who lives with pain.'

'Poor you,' Ruth says, kissing her cheek. 'You've been hauling around a lot of baggage.'

Diana nods and squeezes her hand. 'Thank you.'

'So, correct me if I'm wrong, this sounds like it's all been a great big misunderstanding in respect of Michael. But that can't be right because you said you've never slept with him.' Ruth's face scrunches up as she tries to put the pieces in the right order. 'I'm sorry, I'm confused, who did you have an affair with?'

Diana blows her nose and dabs her eyes with the tissue. The door of the restaurant opens and sends a blast of cold air into the room. She looks up as one of the parents from school walks into the bar. 'Holy shit.'

Ruth looks over her shoulder. 'I know, right? The George Clooney of Amberside College. Pity he's so damn happily married.'

Diana's heart feels like it is about to burst out of her chest. She quickly turns around hoping he hasn't spotted them.

But it's too late. Moments later, his hand rests on the back of the sofa behind her neck. 'Ladies, how's it going?'

Chapter 25

Wednesday

'You've caught us having a sneaky drink,' Ruth says, fluttering her eyelashes at him like the pint-sized provocateur she is. 'I'd ask you to join us but, you know, girls' talk.'

'Sounds intriguing,' Ben replies, turning on his electric smile. 'It's my turn to cook.' He cocks his head towards the bar. 'Hence why I'm picking up takeaway.'

Diana can't believe the man's timing. Here she was, poised on the brink of telling Ruth about her affair — without actually naming him of course, because that would be beyond awkward, given he's now a parent at the school — and who should enter stage left but The Man Himself.

And here's Ruth making eyes at him through those hexagonal fuchsia frames of hers. And him charming the socks off her because Ben is basically one of the good guys who genuinely likes people and can't help being nice.

Ben turns and shines his smile on her, the lines around his eyes softening a little. 'I'm glad I ran into you. Juliet tells me she's singing the solo at the school concert. I wanted to thank you. You made her day.'

Diana forces herself to maintain eye contact. Ben's not the only one who knows how to play his part. 'Please don't thank me — she thoroughly deserves it. If you want my honest opinion, I think you should encourage her to take music for her final years. She's clearly inherited her talents from you.'

Ruth sits there, with an amused little smile, for all the world as if she's watching a tennis match. Thinking Diana can't see her out of the corner of her eye.

'Ah, you're being too kind. I think a certain music teacher has been her inspiration.'

Diana smiles at him. 'I do hope so. But I can only really teach her technique. You have to have a certain *je ne sais quoi* to make it as a performer.'

It's right there, in that moment, the connection of a shared history. Diana lets it sit between them.

'I can't wait to hear her sing,' Ben says.

'I'm sure Juliet will make you proud.'

Carlo calls out Ben's order and the moment vanishes. 'That's me. I guess I'll see you at the concert. Enjoy the rest of your evening.'

He walks away, pulling his wallet from his back pocket. Diana focuses on making a selection from the antipasto platter until Ben walks out the restaurant door.

'Hooley dooley,' Ruth says, fanning her face. 'You two clearly know each other well.' She pretends to flick hair over her shoulder and puts on a sultry voice. 'She clearly gets her musical talents from you.'

'I did not do that.'

'Yes you did. You've always walked a fine line between charming and flirting.' Ruth pats her knee. 'It's hysterical watching grown men fall over themselves to impress you.

Remember that guy who ran across four lanes of traffic just to give you a rose?'

'He was selling them!'

'Not to you he wasn't.' Ruth swirls her wine and takes a sip. 'Now, where were we?'

Diana hesitates. The urge to confess melted away the moment she laid eyes on Ben. What was she thinking? Telling Ruth about the affair is one thing but based on what Ruth's just said about the chemistry between her and Ben, there's a strong chance she might guess it was him and that would make life mighty uncomfortable. What if knowledge of the affair coloured Ruth's perspective of Ben or his children? No, time to go into damage control.

'Well, Ruthie, luckily Ben's arrival saved me from incriminating myself any further. Too much of this,' she says pointing at her empty wine glass.

'I'm happy to buy you a third and weasel more secrets out of you.'

Diana laughs. 'I think you've done very well for one afternoon.' She pins Ruth with her gaze. 'And just for the record, you are very good at your job.' Diana signals to Carlo for the bill and hands over her credit card. The expression on Ruth's face reveals nothing. For a flash, Diana feels terrible. She leans over and pecks her on the cheek. 'I've had fun. I'm glad we went out on a school night. We should do it more often. And thank you for being such a wonderful sounding board. I feel loads lighter.'

Diana stands as Ruth shrugs on her coat. 'Well, as much as I'd prefer to stay and torture you until you tell me all your secrets, the hungry hordes will be baying for my blood if I don't feed them soon.' She glances towards the kitchen. 'Actually, you go ahead. I think I'll take a night off for a change and grab the boys' dinner while I'm here.'

'Great idea.' Diana hugs Ruth and smiles. 'I'll see you in the morning then.'

Outside, the night is fresh. Diana shoves her hands in her pockets and sets off. Carlo's is only a two-minute walk from home, but when she reaches the corner she hesitates. She can see their apartment from here — theirs a blank square among all the others lit up. Maybe she should go back and get a takeaway herself. Although Ruth will probably still be there.

She decides against it and instead crosses the road, tucks her chin into the warmth of her scarf and starts to walk the perimeter of The Green.

Years ago, she made the decision to keep all the emotional fallout from when Nicholas died tied up in a neat box stored in some dark recess in her mind. It was the only way she could move forward. Now everything is unravelling. Memories play across her mind. Will's face contorted with anger. Her screaming. Him storming out. *I can't keep doing this.*

Diana stops dead in her tracks. She has no idea where Will is now but she knows where he went last time. It wasn't just her affair that brought them undone. Will was gone for two months. Shacked up with Super Sally from accounts, evening the score like some bloody teenager, proving he had no idea as to why she'd ended up in bed with Ben. That it was precisely because Will wasn't available to her, in every sense of the word, emotionally and geographically. When she needed him most, he'd disappeared.

What's his excuse this time? It's been quite a year. The sudden decision to leave Turpentine Street — a place he always said they'd take him out of in a box. Setting them up for his retirement, he said, when he told her he wanted to sell up. 'But you're only fifty-nine,' she'd protested. Isn't sixty supposed to be the new forty? 'What will you do with yourself?' she'd prodded. That didn't go down well. 'Nothing,' he'd snapped back. 'That's the point.'

But he's not doing nothing, he's doing something. She's sure of it. Most men set up their mistresses in apartments, not their wives. Has Diana read this all wrong? Is she about to be replaced because she's past her best-by date? They haven't made love since last year, and fool that she is, she's been worrying about his health. Trying to keep it together when the truth is Will has simply lost interest in her.

Diana turns the corner and heads up the street towards the Sea Breeze Retirement Village. The lights that line the gentle footpaths through the shrubbery are already aglow. Not for the first time, she prays that their new apartment is as close as she ever gets to living in a retirement village. This place gives her the jitters. It's a short walk, literally, from a self-contained villa to residential care. Her family live on the other side of the world. If Will is leaving her, who then will care for her when she's no longer capable of looking after herself?

The glass doors of the administration building slide open, framing the silhouette of a man. He turns and waves to the woman on reception, calling out goodnight, then tugs down the brim of his cap and fetches his phone from his pocket. It lights up his face. Diana gasps and stumbles over a crack in the path. She can't quite believe it. It's Whippet Man.

Diana stays in the shadows as he crosses the road and climbs into a little red European car. The interior car lights prove she's not imagining this. It really is the same man from the park down the road from Michael's. The little red car reverses then beetles off down the street straight past her apartment block and around the corner.

All of a sudden, Diana feels vulnerable, exposed. Time to get home. She fumbles with her keys for the front security door, thank goodness they have a security door, and races up the stairs. Once she's inside, she makes sure the chain is on as well as the deadlock before running through the dark apartment towards the terrace. She opens the sliding door and peers over the balcony.

Diana scans the neighbourhood — up the street towards the retirement village then down the street beneath her, along past the block and around the corner. No little red cars. Of course there isn't, she's being stupid. She relaxes a little and has a proper look around. There's so much more to see standing in the dark. The people across the road are watching a quiz show on their giant wall-mounted television. The guy next door to them is barbecuing again. He's out there on his own — beer in one hand, tongs in the other — staring off into the middle distance, lost in thought. The fat sends up a flare of flame and the man snaps back to attention, rescuing the sausages before they turn to charcoal.

And suddenly, there's Will, right in front of her. Back at Turpentine Street, cooking dinner on his whizz-bang barbecue with all the bells and whistles. A man in his element. Diana turns around. There, in the corner, is the you-beaut barbecue, yet to be christened in its new home. She places her hand on the hood and the cold seeps through her gloves. She shivers.

She's not thinking straight. If Whippet Man is involved, it can only be as the photographer. The real culprit is whoever asked him to follow her and that has to be someone reasonably close. Someone who has a reason to want to hurt her, but who? It's not the first time she's seen Whippet Man in her neighbourhood, maybe it's sheer coincidence. Still, it gives her the creeps.

Diana walks into the kitchen, pours the rest of the bottle of rosé into a glass and takes it over to the bench. She's sick of all these one-sided conversations. Of second-guessing what is going on in Will's head. That chat with Ruth has really put things in perspective. This childish nonsense has to stop.

Diana picks up the phone. Miraculously, Will answers. 'Oh, you're there.'

'Yeah, hi.'

'Look, Will, I don't understand why you stormed out and why you're refusing to talk to me but we need to thrash this out. It's getting beyond ridiculous.'

He sighs. 'I can't, I'm about to walk into a meeting.'

'What? Where are you?'

'Texas.'

Texas? He's not even in the country? 'Well, I'm sorry' — although she's not sorry at all — 'but I'm pretty cranky with you right now' — understatement of the decade — 'and if you think I'm going to let you get away with treating me this way, think again.'

No answer, although judging by the background noise, he is genuinely somewhere with lots of people. A door closes and muffles the chatter. 'Look, Didi, I'm not discussing this over the phone. I'm back on Saturday. We'll talk then.'

But she's had it up to here with Will fobbing her off, always trying to control the situation, control her. 'No, Will. You're not listening. This has to stop. You've not returned a single one of my calls. The truth is, you've been acting out of sorts for months. Now you're overreacting to billy-oh over some stupid photos, which you know full well mean absolutely bugger all. What has got into you?'

More silence. Diana snaps. 'Who's Caroline?'

'Jesus Christ.'

'No, Will, I'm pretty sure she's not. For starters, she's not dead.'

'I'm not having this conversation.'

'Oh yes you are. You don't get to spit the dummy over a few photos, without answering some questions yourself. As I seem to recall, you were not blameless then and I am certain you are not blameless now. There's quite a lot of things about your behaviour lately that simply don't add up.'

'Don't be so melodramatic.'

'Tell me who she is, or don't come home.'

'You're threatening me?'

Is she? Diana's fed up with the secrets, the lies, the way Will's been avoiding her. Enough's enough. 'Actually, no I'm not. I'm telling you. Don't come home.' And she hangs up.

Diana stares at the phone in disbelief. Stunned, she replays the conversation. She really did it. She just told Will not to come home. Shouldn't she feel devastated? Heartbroken? She sips her wine. She feels elated, liberated, alive with possibilities. That must be telling her something. Perhaps she should have done this a long time ago. Maybe that's the truth she's been avoiding all along.

Diana walks around the apartment, her apartment, turning on lights as she goes. She sits at the piano, puts her wine on a coaster and opens the lid. She plays a few off-key notes and winces. Thank goodness Michael's piano-tuner mate is coming to fix it this week. She plays the opening chords of 'The Look of Love' — the sound's not great but it's about where she's at anyway. She and Michael used to do this number as a duet. Him on the trumpet, her on the keys. Diana sings the first lines of the opening verse.

Something shifts inside her and the music opens the portal into a world of possibilities. The buzz of being on stage. Up there on the highwire, in the spotlight, dazzling the audience, taking them on the ride of their lives, holding them in the palm of her hand. The sheer exhilaration. It's like nothing else. Michael feels it too, she knows he does, she's seen it in his eyes.

Diana takes her wine over to the dining table and looks at the photos of her and the band. Of her and Michael. The energy, the sense of connection. She's never felt so alive. She picks up the phone.

'Hi. It's me. Can I come over?'

Chapter 26

Wednesday

Diana steps out of the cab. The streets swarm with people coming home from work, browsing the shops and going out for dinner. The air is heavy with the scent of curry, garlic, chilli, luring potential patrons to the restaurants lining the main road.

She cranes her neck and sees the lights on the top floor of the warehouse. It feels strange to be here at night — it's not their usual practice. Diana summons the lift. Once inside she runs her fingers through her hair, a pinkie under each eye, checks her teeth for lipstick. She pulls out her phone. No messages. She switches it to silent and slips it back into her bag.

The doors open and Michael is standing right there. He leans in and kisses her on the cheek then steps into the lift. He presses the ground floor button. 'We need to eat.'

'Oh yes, of course,' she says, smiling. Although whether it's excitement, nerves, the wine, or a combination of all three, Diana's not sure she can eat.

In the lobby, Michael takes her by the hand and leads her out to the street. He heads up the hill taking long strides, but the moment he realises Diana is struggling to keep up, he slows down and matches his stride to hers.

'What do you feel like? Indian, Syrian, Lebanese, Turkish, Egyptian, Thai, Vietnamese or Ethiopian?'

'Golly, umm, whichever is your favourite, I guess.'

Michael shoots her a look.

Diana demurs. 'Okay. But I really don't mind as long as it doesn't have too much chilli.'

'No to Ethiopian then. They like it supercharged.'

They weave through the streets, the crowds pressing them together, then almost separating them but Michael never lets her go. They stop outside a restaurant on a corner with a glass shopfront. Inside are low benches and brightly coloured cushions. Behind the counter, a team of men are busy chopping, grilling, pouring wine. The air is redolent of charcoal and sizzling meat. The place is alive with people and food and music.

Michael pushes open the door and holds it for a couple who are leaving. A waiter in a tight white t-shirt carrying a platter high above his head dances around them. 'Hey Micky, how ya going?' He grins at Diana. 'Table for two?' he asks holding up the requisite number of fingers.

The guy deposits the platter on a table filled with the kind of people she could imagine as friends of Aiden and Persephone. Diana pushes the thought from her mind; she's not here as someone's mother. The waiter grabs a water bottle and two pretty orange glasses painted in gold filigree and winds his way through the crowded restaurant. They follow him out to a courtyard packed with even more tables, candles in glass jars, fairy lights and palm trees in pots. Outdoor heaters keep the chill at bay. Lively rhythms come from an oud player and a guy on darbuka set up in the corner.

The waiter hands them menus, pours the water and disappears. Maybe it's the wine she's already drunk but Diana feels heady, as if she's in a dream. She rests her chin in the heel of her hand and watches the duo. 'These guys,' she says to Michael, 'they're amazing.'

'Yeah. That's Idris and his brother Naz.' A bottle of wine appears on the table. Michael pours her a glass.

'Of course you know them.'

'I produced their last album. Do you want to have a jam with them later?'

Diana throws back her head and laughs. 'Can you imagine? Anyway, have you seen the stage? It's the size of a postage stamp. No room for a keyboard there, my friend.'

'That's okay, you can play the shaker.'

The guy in the tight white t-shirt reappears. 'You guys ready to order?'

Michael looks at her. She shrugs. 'I have no idea. You choose.'

'Since when have you been so accommodating?' Michael confers with the waiter who then whips away the menus and is off again. He reaches over and takes her free hand. 'Are you having fun?'

She leans over and kisses him. 'You're joking, right? I'm having a ball.'

Michael looks pleased and surprised in equal measure and her heart dances to the beat of guilty pleasure.

They turn and listen to the musicians play. Michael doesn't let her go until the food arrives. Out comes a mixed plate filled with falafel, pickles, flat breads and vegetarian delights. There's a rice and lentil dish and a slow-cooked lamb that smells divine. Michael puts a little of everything on a plate and places it in front of her. 'Eat.'

On a break, Idris and Naz pull up a milk crate each. 'Hey brother, how's it going?' They shake hands and settle in for a chat. Diana sees the question in their eyes and tells them, 'Michael and I used to play together.'

Raised eyebrows. 'Yeah? What do you play?'

'Diana's a singer.'

'And keyboards.'

'You still performing?'

Diana shares a look with Michael. 'Not really.'

He pokes her in the ribs. 'I'm working on her. We should get into the studio with you guys. Diana has a great sound.'

When they go back on stage, Michael and Diana continue eating and the wine slowly disappears. Eventually, when Naz and Idris finish, Michael calls for the bill. 'You ready to go?'

Diana nods. She has a fizzy feeling of anticipation, like she's teetering on the brink of exhilaration. Everyone knows the script, right? They'll go back to Michael's and, well, anything could happen. A little voice in the back of her mind asks the question and Diana tells it to shush.

Michael stands. 'Come on then. Let's grab a gelato and eat it at mine.'

They walk back to Michael's arm in arm, sharing a tub of hazelnut affogato. Despite the hour, the street buzzes with people. Live jazz drifts from the pub on the corner. There is a man in the plaza performing with flaming firesticks. They stop to watch him and toss loose change in his bucket when he's done.

Inside Michael's flat, he flicks through his collection of vinyl and selects an LP. The soft bossa nova evokes the tropical beaches of Rio de Janeiro, jazz clubs and the peak of 1960s sophistication.

'Oh my God, I love this.'

Diana puts the tub of gelato on the bench and shrugs off her coat. Michael takes her by the hand and brings her to him. She rests her hands on his chest, feels his hands settle on her hips. It's been a long time since Diana has danced with anyone.

The tune moves on to one Diana doesn't recognise. Michael sings along in English as they dance. 'I have always loved you,' he croons, his lips brushing her ear, leading her across the floor. 'I will always love you.' Diana feels dizzy. It's liberating and intoxicating, like singing in harmony, following each other's breath, the beat of their hearts synchronising. The faint smell of charcoal clings to Michael's shirt. She runs her hands over his biceps, he holds her tighter. 'Every time you leave, it breaks my heart.'

Michael's cheek is smooth against hers. One hand light but firm in the small of her back, his thigh pressing against hers, guiding the dance. She moulds herself to his hips. 'I'd forgotten what a fabulous dancer you were.'

He presses her palm, spins her away and reels her back in, following the rhythms of the music. 'Thank you. No one knows how to follow anymore.'

Diana laughs. 'I'm pretty rusty.'

'You feel pretty good to me.' And he spins her away, reels her back in again.

Michael brings his lips to hers. Diana threads her arms around his neck, feels the heat radiating off him. He looks into her eyes, surprising her with the frankness of his desire.

'I adore you, Diana.'

She catches her breath. Can she do this? Not just for tonight but for every night thereafter? She presses into him, her kiss full of intention. Michael's hands slide up under her blouse. The intensity of his touch on her bare skin is electric. A wave of raw yearning rolls over her. She lifts his shirt, runs her hands over the tight muscles of his abdomen, his lower back, his chest. Kissing him, kissing him, swamped by this burning intense need to be held, to be close, to be wanted.

He pulls away. His chest is heaving, so is hers. He takes her hands in his. 'I've dreamed of this. You and me.'

So have I, she longs to say but the words won't leave her lips. Why? There's nothing stopping her. Will has left her, twice. She told him not to come back. When was the last time he looked at her with such longing? Touched her like she was precious. Michael's no random stranger. He knows her like no one else. Here, now, she can change her future. Her and Michael, music, passion, desire.

He draws her into him, runs his hands through her hair. This slow seduction is excruciating and exquisite. She is wound up so tight that when he does finally kiss her again, the release is exhilarating. She closes her eyes, yielding to desire. It's breathtaking to be up here so high on a pedestal of Michael's making.

'I love you, Diana, I always have.'

And in a panic, Diana comes crashing back to reality. She lets go of Michael. The enormity of what she was about to let happen overtakes her. Seeing Michael's confusion, she grabs his hands in hers. 'I'm so sorry, I can't do this.'

'What's wrong?'

Nothing, everything. 'Michael, you're in love with the idea of me. You're in love with the girl on stage who sings up a storm, who breaks the audience's heart then lifts them to their feet. Hell, I'm in love with her.' Diana smiles to take the sting out of her words. 'But that's not who I am in real life.' And it's true. In some ways, the woman on stage is the best version of Diana but she's also incomplete.

Michael crumbles before her. 'But you've always said that you lost a part of you when you stopped performing. That being with me lights a spark. You come alive again.'

'Please don't say we make beautiful music together.'

He buries his head in his hands, growling in frustration. 'Okay. But we do.'

'Yes, Michael. We do. On stage.' She takes his face in her hands and forces him to look her in the eye. 'I love performing with you, I love how you make me feel when I'm there on stage beside you. Together, we're something special. Don't think I'm saying I don't feel it, because I do, I really do. But, I'm not *in* love with you. And I cannot let you think that I am.'

He places his hands over hers and she can feel the tension running through him. He's trying to hold it together and it breaks her heart to have hurt him so. 'Why did you come to me then?'

A question filled with sorrow, not anger. She draws a deep breath and holds it for a few seconds before she lets it go and feels it calm her. 'I'm sorry. I shouldn't have come here tonight. I'm a fool.'

He nods and Diana laughs. 'You're not supposed to agree with me.'

Michael gently pulls her hands from his face and holds them tight. They are standing so close she can feel the rise and fall of his chest. 'Is this it then?'

Diana gently disentangles herself from his embrace. 'No. I've known you my entire adult life. You know things about me no one else will ever know. I treasure that and I always will. I'd hate to lose you, as a friend. Please don't tell me that I have.'

Michael doesn't answer and as much as she wants to stay and reassure him, it's time for her to go. She picks up the coat she'd abandoned on the back of the bar stool and puts it on. 'I'll call a cab downstairs.'

Michael shakes his head. 'No way. If I'm sending you back to Will, I want you to arrive in one piece.' He pulls on his jacket and opens the front door, gesturing for her to pass. That he's being so honourable makes her want to cry.

Downstairs, the street is slick with rain. The temperature has plummeted. Diana shivers and Michael wraps his arms around her. She goes to protest but he insists. She relents because she knows he'll never hold her or kiss her again.

The cab pulls around the corner and Diana flags it down. She gets in the back seat and Michael motions for her to roll down the window. 'What?'

He kisses his fingers and presses them to her lips. 'Nothing, I just don't want this moment to end.'

Chapter 27

Thursday

Diana wakes up the following morning to a kaleidoscope of memories. The delicious food, the fabulous music, the atmosphere, not to mention the sizzling seduction. A girl could get used to that kind of attention. She touches her lips and remembers Michael's last kiss. *You made the right decision, Diana Forsyth.*

Even better, for once in a very long time, she did what she wanted to do. No compromise, no putting Will or the children's needs ahead of her own. That, in itself, is a milestone. She showers and dresses, makes a coffee and sits at the kitchen bench with her mobile phone. She composes a text.

I know things didn't turn out the way you hoped but I want you to know I had an amazing night. I am deeply sorry that I treated our friendship so shoddily. You are a wonderful human being. Now, forget about me and go find someone who can bring you joy. Didi.

She presses send. She may not have compromised herself but she had behaved selfishly. Using poor Michael as a distraction from her anger at Will was less than he deserved. And less than she expected of herself. It will serve her right if Michael refuses to acknowledge her message. Her phone beeps.

We will always make beautiful music together. Mxx

Once a charmer, always a charmer.

Diana throws herself into the morning's chores. It's the school athletics carnival today so she has the day off. Thoughts of Will are never far away but she has told him not to come back and if the way she felt last night is anything to go by, then maybe they both need a bit of breathing space. It's time to figure out exactly what she wants for her future, whether Will is in it or not. When she's done, she decides to treat herself to a browse through The Village shops to reward her industriousness or maybe her virtue, either or. She picks up one of the deli's fabulous individual pot pies for dinner and browses the bookstore for a nice fat bit of escapism. Diana thinks of the lady of culottes and feels buoyed by a sense of sisterly solidarity. The window display of the menswear store has a gorgeous check shirt in Will's favourite colour. Diana's half in the shop before she realises what she's doing. Will can buy his own bloody shirts. He doesn't need her input anymore. Caroline Fox pops into her head and Diana shoos her away. She's embracing freedom and being her own woman. No one is going to ruin her good mood.

As she passes the salon, she sees Samantha at the counter and waves. On a whim, she changes course. The little bell tinkles as Diana enters the shop.

'Good morning, Diana.' Samantha runs her finger down the appointment book and frowns. 'You don't have an appointment today.'

'No, I know. I was hoping you could squeeze me in for a facial sometime tomorrow, or Saturday at a pinch?'

'Of course, of course.' Samantha examines the page. 'Lucky I just had a cancellation. I can do tomorrow afternoon,' she says, crossing out a name and replacing it with Diana's.

'Oh, you're an angel, thank you. See you tomorrow.'

Samantha walks around the counter to escort her to the door. 'Your husband's here to pick you up,' she says, pointing to the convertible reversing into a space right outside the shop.

Shocked, Diana spins around. It's not Will, thank goodness. Relieved, she laughs. 'That's not my husband, that's his brother.'

Samantha turns bright pink. 'But I have seen you with him many times. So sorry, I thought …'

'Don't be silly. You wouldn't have a clue what Will looks like, he's never here. It's an easy mistake to make.' And doesn't it say a lot about her life that Samantha would make such an assumption. 'I'll see you tomorrow.'

Diana is about to step out when Rebecca strolls into view carrying a swag of shopping bags. 'Hells bells.' She shuts the door and hopes Rebecca didn't see her. She's in no mood for her gloating and given Rebecca's the last person she'd confide in, there's not a lot left to talk about.

As soon as he sees his wife approaching, Ian leaps out of the car. He flings open the boot and goes to peck her on the cheek, but Rebecca deftly blocks him with her morning's haul. The scene could be from *Pretty Woman* if Richard Gere's character was played by a balding man in his fifties with a paunch and Julia Roberts' character was a complete bitch.

'The rich lady's married to him!' Samantha says, covering her mouth in astonishment.

Diana bursts out laughing. 'Rebecca's not rich,' she says, shaking her head. What a crazy idea. She pulls a face. 'To be fair, I know she acts like it.' Diana points to the boot full of shopping bags. 'Poor Ian struggles to stay one step ahead of her.'

'You're not friends?'

'No. Though, unfortunately, she is my sister-in-law.'

Ian gets back behind the wheel and drives off, leaving Rebecca standing on the pavement. She checks her watch and scans the street, then pulls out her phone. Curiosity keeps Diana right where she is.

Samantha's gaze is also pinned on Rebecca. 'Customers always chatting, you know. My hearing is one hundred per cent. That lady is loaded.'

Diana drags her attention from Rebecca to Samantha. 'It can't be true.' Rebecca has always treated Ian like a piece of chewing gum stuck to the sole of her shoe. Every penny he earns goes to support the lifestyle she expects and enjoys. They are constantly upgrading the house and the cars. 'Some people suffer from a severe case of keeping up with the Joneses. Rebecca, I'm afraid, is one of them.'

It's almost as though Rebecca hears them talking about her. She turns around and stares at the salon. Diana snatches a magazine off the pile and hides behind it but all Rebecca does is adjust her hair and straighten the hem of her skirt.

'The sun's on the window,' Samantha says. 'She's using it as a mirror.'

'Oh thank goodness, I thought we'd been busted,' Diana says, replacing the magazine as Rebecca walks to the corner of the lane.

Samantha laughs in that light tinkly way of hers. 'Sorry, Diana, but she married her husband only because her mother said he wasn't good enough for her.'

'What? No, that's terrible.'

Samantha snatches up Diana's hand. 'You've chipped a nail. I fix it for you.' Before Diana can protest, she's ushered her into a seat at the manicure station.

Her nails are perfectly fine but Samantha has already gathered her tools and Diana has the distinct impression it might be worth her while to humour her. 'I admit that I'm far from fond of Rebecca but marrying a man to spite your mother is a new low.'

Samantha squirts cuticle softener over Diana's nails and points to the bowl of water. 'I tell you something. My English is a million times better than her Vietnamese. She should keep her trap shut.'

Diana puts her hands in the water. 'No offence, my love, but I think you're overestimating Rebecca's fortune. She did receive a modest inheritance when her grandmother died. Enough to renovate the kitchen but not enough to make her rich.'

'I listen.' Samantha mimes being on the phone. She points to Rebecca who's also on her phone. 'See? Yak, yak, yak all the time. Her stockbroker. Her lawyer. Buy this, sell that. I am a very successful businesswoman but if I had her money, I'd own a string of salons and someone else could do the Brazilians while I sat here and counted the cash.'

Samantha dries one of Diana's hands and gets to work on her cuticles. Diana regards her with fresh eyes. 'Do you know, I've always wondered what you and Cherish talk about when you switch to Vietnamese.' She narrows her gaze. 'Now I'm horrified. Here I was hoping you were just appalled at my dry heels when all the time you were gossiping about your poor customers.'

Samantha motions to Diana's other hand. 'You don't have dry heels. But, you know, it's good you worry so much about your family.'

'Cheeky.'

Samantha smiles. 'You're okay. But many women here are unhappy people, yes, even with rich husbands and big houses. So sad.'

'I suspect you're right.' Diana sighs. And she's one of them. Although she considers themselves well-off rather than rich, but it's all a matter of perspective.

Outside, a silver Mercedes pulls into the space recently vacated by Ian's Lexus. The driver reaches across and opens the passenger side door. Rebecca darts up from her post on the corner and climbs in. It's her companion from the lunch the other day at The Boatshed. Georgina Templeton, Rebecca's lawyer.

Samantha is also watching. 'Rebecca says she's going to live in Thailand. I don't know why. Plenty of places to live. Vietnam's much nicer.'

Diana raises her eyebrow at Samantha. In answer, Samantha tilts her head out the window. Diana turns just in time to see Rebecca and her lawyer entwine. Rebecca reaches behind her lawyer's head and shakes her long red hair loose around her shoulders. Georgina Templeton laughs and Rebecca pulls her close again. They kiss. It takes some time before they manage to disengage.

Diana turns to share her disbelief with Samantha only to realise that seeing Rebecca snogging her lawyer is not news to her.

'She's getting rid of the husband. Too old. Too fat.' Judging by her tone, Samantha and Rebecca are in agreement on this count. She pours cream onto the backs of Diana's hands and begins to massage one. 'You know, she hired a private investigator to spy on him. Said she knew he was having an affair but not who with.'

Time stops. The back of Diana's neck feels as if someone has pressed an ice-cold flannel to it. Samantha swaps hands. 'But when she saw the photos, not good. She says, "I'm taking the bastard to the cleaners."' Samantha does a fair impression of Rebecca.

Time starts again. Diana is furious. Her lying, two-timing, troublemaking sister-in-law must have hired Whippet Man to follow Ian and, in the process, Diana ended up in the photos. Not content to accept that she was simply collateral damage, Rebecca obviously decided to turn the opportunity to her advantage. Leaving her own marriage in tatters is one thing. Destroying the entire family is another. Granted, she and Rebecca have never got on but this is downright vindictive. What on earth possessed her? Will is going to be ropable. Damn it. *She's* ropable.

The Mercedes pulls out into the traffic, whisking Rebecca and her lover away. Another customer comes in and Samantha settles her in a cubicle and returns. 'I don't understand why she cares if her husband is unfaithful. She don't need his money. He don't know she's got any. She and her lady friend can just say bye-bye. No more men. Not such a bad thing, you know.'

Diana knows precisely why. 'Because she wants to make him suffer.'

As soon as the words leave her mouth, she understands why Rebecca sent Will the photos. By nature, Diana is not a violent person but by goodness, right now she'd like to slap that bitch's face. The day they received those photos set in motion a chain of events that led to her telling Will to never darken her doorstep again. It might have led to a few home truths being revealed but knowing Rebecca deliberately set out to poison their relationship puts an entirely different spin on things. God knows where Will is, she'll have to go for the next best option. Diana pulls out her phone and calls Ian.

Chapter 28

Thursday

Ian is already at The Boatshed when Diana arrives. Spotting her walking in, he orders a second beer for himself. He points to the empty wineglass on the table and she shakes her head, mouthing the word coffee.

They exchange pleasantries. Diana accepts the peck on her cheek but does not return it. She takes her time unravelling her scarf and unbuttoning her coat, placing them on a vacant chair at the next table. Their drinks arrive as she sits. Diana sips her cappuccino. Too hot. She returns the cup to the saucer and looks Ian square in the eye.

'This morning while I was having my nails done, I witnessed something very interesting.'

For his part, Ian looks rather nonplussed.

Diana spells it out for him. 'I was there when you met up with Rebecca.'

'Jeez, Diana, that's hardly world news. As much as I enjoy your company.' He goes to cover her hand with his but she's fast enough to get it off the table and into her lap.

'I was about to say, that after you left, another car pulled into the vacant spot. Rebecca climbed into this car and exchanged a passionate and somewhat prolonged kiss with the occupant.'

Ian is satisfyingly silent at this revelation. Diana doesn't linger on the image she's no doubt created in his mind. She's not here to revel in his misfortune, especially when she might be in exactly the same boat. 'However, that's not the reason I requested we meet urgently. I'm not sure if you realise that your wife has had you followed. I've seen evidence that Rebecca is onto your …' She pauses before delicately adding, 'indiscretions.'

He blinks faster than a fanned deck of cards. 'How do you know?'

Interesting. Not 'Who was Rebecca kissing?' Nor defending the allegation that he might be having an affair. My, my. Diana moves on.

'I'm not sure how much Will has shared with you but when he returned from his last trip, there was a package waiting for him.' Pause, but this time just for dramatic effect. Ian's face is blank. Good. 'In it were photos. Of you.'

His eyebrows shoot up.

Diana leans forward. 'And me.'

Ian's eyebrows hit the ceiling. 'What? That's impossible. I've never laid a hand on you.'

She lets that one slide on by. 'As the other party in these incriminating photos, Ian, I'm well aware of that. My concern is, why did Rebecca have a second set of photos sent to Will?' Diana sips her coffee. 'I assume she was, is, attempting to rock the boat.'

'Why would she want to do that?'

Diana rests her chin on her interlocked fingers. Outside a row of seagulls are perched on the jetty railing, preening and squawking, squabbling like children. Or warring factions of the one family. 'Try this on for size. Rebecca has never forgiven Will for not taking the offer from Holworth and Harrow, has she? She couldn't wait to get her mitts on her share of the twelve million.'

'You mean my share of the twelve mill.'

She shrugs. 'I don't think Rebecca recognises the distinction.'

Ian drains his beer and calls for another. Good. The alcohol might loosen his lips.

'Is that why Will's racked off? Because of some dodgy pictures of you and me? That seems a bit stupid.'

This is where things get tricky. In the back of her mind, a little plan is percolating. A way to expose Rebecca's actions and clear her name at the same time. Hopefully, without adding any more fuel to the fire.

'I think Rebecca hired a private investigator to follow you. He saw us together and took photos in case they proved important. When he showed them to Rebecca, she saw a way to repay Will for that decision and drag my name through the mud at the same time.'

Ian doesn't need to know the rest of her guesswork. That once Rebecca had seen the photos of Ian and Diana, she told Whippet Man to stay on Diana's tail. Touch one, touch all.

'That's a pretty outrageous accusation, Diana. Why would Becks stoop so low?'

Diana sips her coffee and lets Ian rant. Far be it from her to interrupt. Anyway, she agrees with an awful lot of what he's saying. Except, he's so busy being indignant, he hasn't stopped to consider the most pertinent fact.

She waits until he runs out of steam then treads carefully. 'I think you're missing the obvious here. Rebecca doesn't care about the photos of you and me. The point is, she knows about you and your ... friend.'

Ian sags. He picks up the damp coaster his beer glass has been sitting on and tears it in half then half again. 'Over the past few years, it's slowly dawned on me that Rebecca treats me like dirt. It's like boiling the frog, isn't it? Just creeps up on you, out of the blue.'

His mixed metaphor brings a smile to her lips. She swallows it, focusing instead on his trembling fingers tearing the coaster into smaller and smaller pieces.

'I mean, look at me,' he says, gesturing to the generous girth beneath the flap of his expensive jacket. 'It's like she sips from the eternal well of youth and I wallow in the shallows of the outgoing tide.'

'Being thin doesn't make you a good person, Ian, any more than being heavy makes you lazy or lacking in good character.'

Ian sucks on a fresh beer. 'I met Jacqueline in the business lounge on an interstate trip. She runs an essential oils empire. You'd like Jackie. Down-to-earth type like you.'

Diana imagines Will might beg to differ on that count.

'Jackie lives up the coast on a macadamia-nut plantation. She owns acres and acres of trees. Her daughter is a yoga instructor and runs a wellness retreat in one wing of the house; Jack writes the lot off as a tax expense. Smart woman, my Jackie.' Ian realises his gaffe and blushes.

Diana raises an eyebrow. 'You seem to know the place well.'

Ian frowns at the tabletop. 'Yeah, well, Jackie's done wonders for my self-esteem. She's got me to cut back on the grog and the red meat. And onto this special tea she makes on the farm. It tastes like shit but it's supposed to boost your energy and your, you know, sex drive.'

Diana sits back in her chair. They're moving into uncharted waters and she's certain this is a place she has no wish to navigate with Ian.

'Tantric sex, Diana. You and Will should try it.'

She has no words. Instead, she replies with a weak smile. The way things are going, the only person she'll be having sex with in the future is herself. She deflects further unwanted revelations with a question. 'Does Will know about Jacqueline?'

'Yes, of course. He was there when I met her.'

Yet Will's never mentioned it. Those incriminating photos of her with his brother didn't bother Will because he knew darn well who Ian was bonking. Her husband seems to be accumulating secrets at a rate of knots.

A shadow of sadness passes over Ian's face. He rubs at the label of his bottle of beer. 'I haven't made Rebecca happy in years. Ever since the sorry business with the babies. I told her I was okay if she wanted to use a sperm donor. I said, let's adopt. Plenty of babies need a family, don't they? But she made it pretty clear that she wouldn't be happy if it was my sperm and someone else's egg, so why should I be happy that it was her egg and someone else's sperm? I've got no answer to that, Diana. No answer at all.'

Nor does Diana. So much loss. Rebecca and her miscarriages. Nicholas.

'If I am being totally honest, Becks and I have never been really happy, not like you and Will.' Ian wipes his hands on his trousers, depositing tiny pills of beer bottle label on his five-thousand-dollar suit. Diana winces. Then he shakes off his blue mood like a Labrador out of the water. 'But Jacqueline is a wonderful woman. I'm leaving after the party. I'd go sooner but I don't want my marital woes overshadowing your celebrations.' He looks at Diana with those puppy dog eyes, begging for a pat on the head.

She adopts an expression she hopes conveys the right blend of sympathy and gratitude. Tempted to say, but not quite being able to, that he may as well go now. The damage is done. The party is a big fizzer. Michael might have thought he was sending her home to Will but there was no Will to come home to. Although, last night did make her realise that, despite everything, she doesn't want to be with anyone else. It's Will who she loves. The question is, does he feel the same about her or is he also moving on? In which case, Will and her are over. The easy option is to blame Rebecca but the truth is, this moment has been brewing for a long time. Ironically, Rebecca might have done her a favour by bringing it all to a head.

'Becks can have it all,' Ian continues. 'I'm sick of arguing with her about money. If it means that much to her, she can take it. I can't be arsed fighting over who gets what. Life's too short. I've got my shares in the company. I'm sure once Will's worked his magic, I'll be alright.'

Diana is unsure what trump cards Will may or may not be holding but right now, that's not her number-one concern. Clearly, Ian has no idea what is going on in his wife's calculating little brain. Diana came here with no intention of telling Ian that Rebecca seems to be independently wealthy because it's not really her news to tell. And God forbid she'd ever sink to Rebecca's level. The problem is, Rebecca would gladly leave Ian with nothing but the clothes on his back, and where's the fairness in that?

So she draws her chair closer and lowers her voice. 'Before you do that, I think there's something you should know.'

Chapter 29

Thursday

Diana walks home along The Esplanade. The weather has set in again. It's been a cold and miserable winter. It has seeped into her bones. She continues on past The Green, reflecting on her conversation with Ian. She wishes she could feel good about revealing a few home truths but the whole episode has left her with a bad taste in her mouth. This entire affair is tawdry. What kind of woman would not disclose her fortune to her future husband? Normal people insist on prenups, not go around for decades keeping it an enormous secret. It reeks of maliciousness, insecurity, or both.

A squall comes in off the sea like a tumbleweed of rain. Diana pulls her scarf up higher to cover her neck. Is there more to it? Samantha's words echo in her head. Did Rebecca want to prove to her mother that Ian valued her for who she was and not her fortune? But how on earth did either mother or daughter resist the temptation to spill the beans? Diana can't imagine Audrey managing it. Or herself. Maybe spite is genetic. Trauma can be, so perhaps it makes sense.

Diana reaches the end of the wide footpath that meets the car park of the Beach Club. Royce Carmichael's car is there.

She scans the waters in front of the club — steel grey, white caps, and among them bobs three heads, arms arced, paddling a steady rhythm. She recognises Royce's bright red cap, heading for the shore. That man's determined to make himself shark bait. Mad, the lot of them.

She turns around and heads towards home. In the end, keeping her wealth a secret has poisoned Rebecca and her relationship. Ian's face flashes in front of her — slack-jawed with disbelief, distress. Diana flushes. This is what happens when you meddle in other people's affairs. She should have left Ian and Rebecca to sort things out between themselves. She had no business revealing the woman's financial deceit. Plenty of men leave their wives with next to nothing. Surely the reverse can be equally true.

It seems Diana too is not immune to spitefulness. Just because Rebecca threw a bomb into Diana and Will's marriage, she decided to pay her back. Honestly, how old is she? And talk about pots calling kettles black. Rebecca isn't the only one guilty of keeping secrets.

Diana crosses The Esplanade and heads towards the café. Whatever had attracted Rebecca and Ian to each other had died a long time ago. Presumably the sex — it usually is. There's no reason for them to stay together. Unlike her and Will who have plenty of reasons to stay married but probably won't.

Diana pauses to admire the window displays in the florist. She spies peonies, her very favourite flower. She had them in her wedding bouquet. A thought pops into her head. Will knows about Ian's affair. Ian didn't specify how long he's been seeing this Empress of the Essential Oils but it didn't sound like a flash in the pan. Ian's visited her plantation, knows all about the daughter's yoga business. Yet not once has Will let slip a single detail. Diana's a fool. She should have asked Ian outright about this Caroline woman, while she had him on the ropes. It stands to reason Will would tell his brother.

Diana wrenches open the door of the florist shop. The wind catches it and slams it shut behind her. It's no warmer inside than it is out. Katerina, the owner, comes out of the workroom carrying a bouquet. She smiles and says hello. Diana inhales that heady scent unique to flower shops, tells herself to get a grip, and returns the greeting. She points to the buckets of flowers. 'Those peonies are utterly irresistible, Katerina. I must have some.'

'They are lush, aren't they?' Katerina picks two bunches from the buckets and holds them together. 'Enough?'

Diana nods and Katerina takes the flowers out to her workroom to cut the stems and make a bouquet. 'I've ordered the flowers for the party,' she sings out through the doorway. 'All white as requested.'

'Great!' Diana calls back. She takes her phone from her handbag and checks for messages. Nothing. No one. What was she expecting? A rant from Rebecca? A sobbing Ian? A love note from Michael? An apology from Will? No, not the latter.

Katerina pokes her head out. 'I ran into Jessie. Have you confirmed her for the photography yet?'

'No, I keep forgetting. Thank you for reminding me.'

'She's kept the date free. She just wants to know what sort of shots you want.' Katerina lays the bouquet on the counter and wraps it in brown paper and ribbon.

Life seems to perennially revolve around photographs. Capturing random moments in case they are never remembered. As proof of how much fun we had. How ridiculous we looked. How little you were. How big you've grown. We saw what you did. You are not forgotten.

'I'll call her as soon as I get home. How much for those?'

Diana taps her credit card and Katerina hands over the flowers like a cradled baby. 'Enjoy. Looks like you need them.'

Diana shoots her a quick smile and escapes the shop before the tears tumble. Out on the street she gulps in a lungful of air, head tilted back, throat bare to the sky. Don't look down.

'Ah, Diana, just the person I'm looking for.'

She spins around. There before her stands Royce Carmichael, wearing yet another of his faded corporate polo shirts and pair of stubbies that have seen better days. Does the man not feel the cold? She draws a deep calming breath and blinks away her tears. It's only once her vision has cleared that she realises, despite his words, Royce doesn't look pleased to see her at all.

He shuffles about in his worn boat shoes, switching his car keys from one hand to the other. Then he gives her a hard stare. 'Bad news, I'm afraid.'

'Oh?' Water leaks from the flower arrangement and Diana shifts it to an upright position.

'We had to call in the inspectors.'

More shuffling. Diana does her best to conceal her rising irritation. She has enough problems on her plate without adding Royce's dramas to it.

'Those little bastards have destroyed the joint. The ceiling is about to collapse any second now. It's going to cost a fortune.'

Diana finally twigs. 'I'm sorry, Royce, I just don't think I can convince Will to donate more funds. I'm pushing the envelope as it is.' Not to mention that she hasn't had a chance to tell Will about the two grand she handed over for a party that looks increasingly like a no-go.

Royce tugs at the tuft of hair sprouting from his ear. 'No, love, you've got the wrong end of the stick. It's outrageous. The council has ordered us to close until further notice.'

The Tricky Art of Forgiveness

'Ordered who closed?'

'The bloody Beach Club.' Royce drags a piece of paper out of his back pocket and waves it in front of Diana. 'Rats have been nesting in the roof. We've got to pull out the whole kitchen. The wiring's kaput. I'm sorry, but you see what this means, don't you?' He leans in closer. 'You'll have to hold your party elsewhere.'

Diana's first reaction is relief, like a load's been taken off. She doesn't have to cancel the party. The rats have cancelled it for her. 'Wonderful.'

Royce looks hurt then a bit shifty. 'It seems the insurance policy hasn't been updated for a few years. Bit of an oversight on behalf of the committee. I'm more than happy to put forward a motion that we name the new kitchen The Forsyth Memorial Kitchen but …'

But Diana is no longer listening. She's caught sight of something. Or rather, someone. She recognises those caramel-splodged hindquarters. The neat trim of his rusty beard. Whippet Man and his four-legged friend are tracking a diagonal path across The Green straight towards the Sea Breeze Retirement Village.

She thrusts the flowers in Royce's arms. 'Hold these,' she says, then charges off determined to cut the snooping photographer off at the pass.

Chapter 30

Thursday

'You! Stop right there!' Diana calls across The Green. Years of teaching gives her voice instant authority.

Whippet Man spins around. When he registers who it is, he bends over and scoops up his dog, who yelps in surprise. He's in no man's land, stuck halfway between the retirement village and his little red car parked on the other side of The Green. There is no escape.

All Diana's pent-up emotions rush to the surface. She takes advantage of his momentary indecision to bail him up against the girth of a Moreton Bay fig. 'You have some explaining to do.'

'I don't know what you're talking about.' His dog, today dressed in pink fur and a diamante collar, wriggles out of his grasp. 'This is harassment.'

She's tempted to slap that smug face but violence solves nothing. Instead she crosses her arms. 'I beg your pardon. I saw you taking my photo that day at the park. And judging by your other photos, you've been stalking me for some time. Do you know how much trouble you've caused?'

She pauses to allow him space to answer but all she gets is blue-eyed bemusement. Undeterred, she presses on. 'However much she paid you, I hope it's worth the cost of living with a broken marriage, *two* broken marriages, on your conscience.'

'You're nuts!'

Credit where credit's due, he's a good actor. If she didn't have evidence to the contrary, she'd believe him innocent. But that beard is masking something and she's determined to get to the bottom of it. Diana changes tack. 'If you're not following me, then why are you here?'

The dog whimpers and tugs on its leash trying to head for the grass between the path and the kerb. Diana may be many things but she's never cruel to animals. She lets Whippet Man go free and together they follow the dog as she snuffles around finding a desirable patch.

'My mum,' he says.

'I beg your pardon?'

'My mum.' He jerks his head in the direction of the retirement village. 'She lives at Sea Breeze. I come and visit her twice a week. More if I can, depending on my workload.'

This stops Diana in her tracks. It's a perfectly logical explanation. Although it doesn't explain the photographs. 'What do you do for work?' she asks, searching for a link.

Whippet Man stands a little taller. 'I run a grooming business.'

Looking at the man with his trim beard and eyebrows clipped into a neat hedge above his eyes, Diana wonders if grooming is just a fancy term for barber.

He picks up his dog who has now finished her business. 'I own a salon in the inner city. The top end of the market,' he adds.

Diana regards the dog cradled in his arms.

'That's why Cindy here is a short-hair,' he explains. 'The last thing I feel like doing after a day of washing and clipping other people's dogs is have to groom my own as well.' He smiles at her. 'You know, plumbers and leaky taps.'

Dog grooming. That seems plausible but her indignation has left her with a growing headache and no answers. 'But the photos,' she says, half to herself.

Whippet Man takes out his smartphone and pulls up a gallery of images. There on the screen is Cindy decked out in a range of coats and posed in a variety of places.

Diana recognises Harriet Penske's Memorial Park. 'That's where I saw you.'

He peers more closely at the image. 'It's around the corner from my place. We often shoot there, don't we, Cindy?'

Diana cannot help herself. 'Why?'

He preens somewhat. 'Cindy is an internet sensation. She has her own page, don't you, schnookums,' he says, puckering up at the dog who licks his lips. He changes screens and shows Diana. Sure enough, there's Cindy, grinning at the camera. Whippet Man points to a number: 7.5K followers. 'Cindy here is brilliant for business.'

'So you weren't taking photos of me?'

He runs his gaze up and down Diana as if considering her for best in show. He sniffs. 'No offence, but you're not my type.' With a tilt of his chin, Whippet Man gathers in Cindy's lead. 'Now if you don't mind, I'd like to go and visit my mother. We're up to chapter five of *The Lady Regrets*. She'll be champing at the bit.'

Chapter 31

Thursday

Diana watches him go. She'd like to say, mystery solved. But really, who took the photos is not the important bit — it's who paid for them that matters. Rebecca will get hers, at the appropriate time.

She walks across The Green towards the apartment. Bach's 'Air on the G String' begins to play from her pocket and Diana takes her phone out. Unknown number. 'Hello?'

'Mum, it's me, Percy.'

'Persephone, darling! Where are you?'

'We landed about an hour ago. We're just crossing the bridge now. I think we'll be at the house in about twenty minutes. I can't wait to see you. How's Dad?'

Good question. As is her wont, Diana keeps it breezy. 'He flies in on Saturday.'

'Oh. I must have got my days mixed up. Never mind.'

But the pause between the mix-up and the never mind tells Diana that Will is already back in the country. She's not quite sure how she feels about that, or rather, she's surprised to feel her heart skip a beat. Traitorous beast.

'If you go right at the next roundabout then left at the lights, we can avoid this traffic,' she hears Persephone tell the taxi driver. 'No, I promise. It's much quicker. This is where I grew up.'

Diana winces. If ever she needs reminding that her chicks have flown the nest, those words, 'this is where I grew up', past tense, are a stark reminder.

'Sorry, Mum, I'm just showing the driver the back way. The traffic's horrendous. Where was I? Oh yes — Emile slept badly on the plane so he's going to crash for a few hours. But I was wondering if I could come over and have a peek at the new place? Is that alright?'

Diana's antenna points straight up, humming like a tuning fork. 'Of course, darling. I can't wait to see you. It will be a treat to have you all to myself.'

She detects more than the desire for a cosy tête-à-tête about broken hearts and school subject choices like when Persephone was in her teens. She and Emile have been married less than two years. Surely they can't have hit their first hurdle. They seem so well suited.

As she crosses the road, she sees the lady of culottes stuffing junk mail in the letterboxes. Today's pants are a snazzy Irish-green check paired with a rain jacket in the same hue.

'Good afternoon,' Diana sings out so as not to sneak up on her.

She turns around. 'Ah ha! It's you.'

Surprise stops Diana in her tracks. She glances over her shoulder then smiles at the woman. 'Yes, it is.'

'I know I'm a stickybeak from way back, so forgive me, but you're new to the neighbourhood?'

'True.'

'My name is Dorothy but I go by Dotty.' She puts out her hand.

'Diana.'

Her grip is firm. 'Do you want one of these? Save me adding it to your letterbox.'

She passes her a glossy brochure. It's the latest edition of the Sea Breeze newsletter. Out of politeness, Diana accepts it.

'I do the letterbox drop each month. Bit of exercise. Good to help out where I can.' Her eyes have a sparkle and Diana senses a trap. 'We're always on the lookout for new faces. There's plenty to do. Some of our volunteers read to the residents. There's a marvellous chap from The Village who's teaching card tricks. That's a hoot. Bit hard to cultivate sleight of hand if you've got the trembles.' Dotty laughs at her joke, not a trace of malice. 'I'm in charge of indoor bowls. Twice a week I take over the recreation room and create havoc. You should join me some time. It's fun.'

Diana reels in horror. 'Thank you, but I couldn't possibly. I work. My husband travels.'

Dotty clasps a hand to her mouth then holds it to her chest. 'Oh, will you ever forgive me? I assumed you were widowed like me. Don't even think about it.' She pats Diana's arm, gives it a squeeze. 'But if you ever find yourself at a loose end, pop into reception at Sea Breeze and leave me a note. Everyone has a talent — I'm sure we'll find you something to do.'

Diana smiles and nods and backs away towards the security door, waving farewell. Once she's safely inside her apartment, she bursts out laughing. Imagine Dotty thinking she was widowed. 'Everyone has a talent.' She laughs again. Yes, indeed they do.

Diana uses the few minutes before Persephone arrives to tidy up a little and fill the kettle. But when she opens the door to her daughter, Persephone holds up two bottles of champagne and a grocery bag containing fancy cheese and crackers. Diana eyeballs the bubbles. What kind of night is this going to be?

'Come in, come in, darling.' Diana ushers her inside. 'It's so good to see you.'

Persephone dumps the goodies on the bench and throws herself at her mother. Diana hugs her just as hard back.

'Let me have a proper look at you.' Diana steps away and tsks. 'Aw, I can't believe it. Have you lost some weight or have you grown?'

Persephone looks at the heels of her boots then at her mother's. 'No, I think you're shrinking.'

'Shush. Don't be mean. You've changed your hair colour though. I love it — it suits you.'

Persephone's cheeks turn pink and it sends a surge of joy through Diana's heart.

Her daughter turns and drops her scarf and coat on a bar stool. 'Now, let's open one of these and you can give me the guided tour.'

And Diana sees it then — the shadow that passes over Persephone, and that surge of joy fizzes a little. 'Brilliant plan. I'll fetch the glasses.'

Champagne in hand, Diana starts at the front of the apartment. 'This is the spare room,' she says with an ironic flourish. 'As you can see, only a single bed, which is why I extended the booking at the holiday house for you. Thought this might be a bit too cosy for two. I'm thinking about getting a set of bunks but I haven't quite made up my mind.'

She glances at Persephone looking for a clue but she is reading the labels on the boxes. 'Oh look, the board games. Can I open it? I can take the Monopoly back to the house and set up a game with Aidy and Anna and Emile.' Persephone balances her champagne on the window ledge and rips off the packing tape. 'Oh!' she exclaims and pulls out Snakes and Ladders. The box is barely held together with sticky tape and an ancient rubber band that disintegrates the moment Persephone touches it. She pulls out the board and unfolds it. 'Will you look at that. This is so cool.' She grins at Diana. 'Remember what a dreadful cheater I was?'

'How could I forget?'

'You used to tell me that the snakes represented vices and cheating was one of them.'

'Which it is. Of course, you've grown out of it now, haven't you, darling?'

Persephone pretends to be contrite, nodding her head then shaking it. 'No. I haven't. You're allowed to cheat at games. Just not in real life.'

Diana's not so sure. On balance, it seems it might work the other way around. 'Come, let me show you the rest of the apartment. It improves from here.'

They end up out on the terrace with the rest of the bottle and the cheese and crackers on a plate. By Diana's reckoning it's too cold, but the chill of the evening doesn't bother Persephone. She's been watching her daughter since she arrived and it's obvious that Persephone has been working her way up to this moment. Diana lets the silence linger, enjoys her glass of bubbles, and pretends to be intensely interested in the view.

'When you were my age,' Persephone begins, 'did you know you wanted children?'

'When I was your age, you were already four years old.'

'That's so young. At twenty-five I'd only just started my internship. I can't imagine being mature enough to be a parent.'

Diana laughs. 'I don't think maturity is a prerequisite. In fact, it's probably a hindrance.'

Persephone gulps her champagne. 'How do you know when you're ready, though? I feel like I've only just started my life. I'm not even sure if I want to stick with general paediatrics or specialise further.'

Diana takes her daughter's hands in hers. 'We spend our whole lives wondering what might have happened if we'd made different decisions. There isn't only one fork in the road. Whichever fork you choose splits and splits again. Some of our worst decisions end up being for the best, and just when we think everything's perfect, the unexpected happens.' And all she can think is, *Ain't that the truth.*

That Persephone is hanging off her every word is slightly unsettling. Older isn't necessarily wiser. Witness the events of the past two weeks.

'But you stop making stupid mistakes, right?'

Diana laughs. 'If only.' Seeing Persephone's bottom lip quiver, she wraps her arms around her and holds her tight. It reminds Diana of when she was little and could fit on her lap. Many tears shed in the name of injustices, loss or frustration. Persephone's sense of right and wrong finely tuned — Diana's feelings tightly attuned to hers. 'Are you trying to tell me you don't think you're ready to have children yet?'

Persephone pulls away, shaking her head and wiping her eyes. 'What other animal can you think of that destroys its own environment? What we're doing to the planet is hideous and I don't think that's the kind of legacy I would want for my child.'

Diana looks out across The Green. How does she respond to this? When she was young, they had sex, they made babies. They were terribly selfish about their right to do that. But how to say this to Persephone without swaying her one way or the other? She has to try. 'I can't imagine the kind of person I would have been without children. It changes the shape of you.'

Persephone sags at these words. 'Emile says we can only affect our immediate world. That we have to exercise our privilege with care, but he's always imagined us as a family.'

Diana turns and leans against the ledge. There's not much light out here, she can barely make out Persephone's face but the shadow makes it easier to be honest. 'Then you are between a rock and a hard place, aren't you, sweetheart?'

'Exactly. If I agree and we have a child then Emile wins the argument. And if I regret that decision, then all three of us could suffer. If I stick to my guns, Emile might leave me for someone who does want children. And then later if I meet someone else and we have children, then I've made myself and Emile unhappy for no good reason. It's an impossible choice.'

'Part of growing up is learning to make the best decision you can on the information you have available to you. And accepting that there's as good a chance you've made the right one as the wrong one.'

'So if I don't have children, it's not a mistake?'

'Oh sweetheart, I can't answer that for you.'

Persephone gulps the rest of her champagne. 'I feel terrible. I should have told Emile how I felt before we got married. But I thought I'd change my mind, or at least that biology would take over and I'd be okay about that.'

'Don't stress about it. Your biology still has plenty of time.'

'And if I don't? Emile may never forgive me.'

Ah, those words. Forgiveness seems to be flavour of the month.

'Well, as they say, best to cross that bridge when you get to it. Right now, you don't want a baby. Neither of you has any idea how you'll feel in two, three or five years' time. That's as honest as you can be.'

*

It's past midnight when Diana closes the front door. She collects the glasses and washes them as she reflects on her conversation with Persephone. What would have happened to her and Will if she hadn't fallen pregnant with Aiden? She'd thought she was an adult at twenty-three, but really, honestly, no she wasn't. Will could easily have said he wasn't ready to be a father and then what? Either way, would they be married now? If she hadn't met Will, would she have ended up with Michael? She'd be the wife of a sound engineer, a musician, but who knows if she would be any happier. She could have left Will for Ben. God knows, the way Will behaved back then, she'd thought about it. In between all of those choices, consciously or subconsciously, lies every other possibility and more besides. You just never know how things are going to pan out.

Diana lies in her bed, the sheets striped by moonlight coming through the plantation shutters. She places her hand on the space Will has occupied for more than half her life, fans it back and forth across the emptiness. Despite her misgivings about Will never saying he forgave her, they did pull together after the affair with Ben and the retaliation with Sally. But she never imagined they'd be here having the same conversation almost thirty years later.

Her husband is somewhere out there, maybe looking at the same moon from a different woman's bed. Should she ask him to come home? Diana is certain she loves him but not in that fierce way she loves her children, nor with the same passion of the girl who could wrap her legs around him and bend him to her desires. Is loving him enough of a reason though? Enough to make him, her, them, happy? Maybe that's what she should have said to Persephone. You can't make someone else happy. Happiness is each and every person's own responsibility.

So what will it take, Diana Forsyth, to make you happy?

Chapter 32

Friday

Diana races into the arrival lounge and finds it's virtually empty. Not a soul except for a canoodling young couple who clearly haven't seen each other in a very long time. Damn it. Questions inspired by Persephone's visit had kept Diana tossing and turning and she slept through her alarm. What if her sister gave up and caught a cab?

But no, of course not. Diana spots Lydia relaxing on a couch in the airport café nursing a large coffee and browsing the newspaper. A slightly scruffy man, who must be Armando, stands nearby, scrolling through his phone.

Diana heads towards the sister she hasn't seen in over a year. 'Lydia!'

She leaps to her feet and rushes to meet her. 'Didi!' she says, diving in for a hug.

'I'm sorry I'm so late. I overslept.' She turns to her sister's companion. 'Armando, how are you? I'm Lydia's sister.' She offers her hand but he pulls her into an embrace. He's a bear of a man, and he squeezes Diana so hard she squeaks.

'Diana,' he exclaims in his swoon-worthy Italian accent then kisses her cheeks. 'Such a pleasure to meet you.'

'Put her down, Armando, you'll break her in half,' Lydia demands.

With a laugh Armando lets Diana go.

'Lovely to meet you too, Armando. Lydia has told me so much about you,' she manages, clasping her hands to avoid patting her hair like some spinster from another era.

Lydia reassures him she hasn't shared that much. A blatant lie, but nevertheless. Diana looks around and reaches for the nearest suitcase but Armando is too fast. He swoops in and grabs the handle of the large roll-on bag and takes it and the trolley of smaller bags under his control.

'Any news from Will?' Lydia asks, once they're safely strapped into the car and Diana has navigated the worst of the airport congestion.

She changes lanes, glancing meaningfully at Lydia and tilting her head in Armando's direction.

Taking the hint, Lydia switches subjects. 'Tell me more about this fabulous house you've rented for us. How clever of you to find a place so near the Beach Club but large enough for us all to bunk in together. I can't wait to meet Lucas, and I haven't seen Percy or Aidy in ages.'

The conversation remains on neutral territory all the way home — Lydia's work for Médecins Sans Frontières, the never-ending workload of a Roman painter specialising in restoration, and the upcoming centenary celebrations at Amberside College. Once Diana is through The Village and has taken the headland road, the conversation dwindles as the spectacular harbour views render Lydia and Armando speechless.

When they arrive at the house, there's a flurry of activity as they unload the car, and exclamations of delight once Diana opens the heavy front door and reveals an interior straight from a glossy magazine.

Armando spies the infinity-edge swimming pool. 'That's what I need, a dip to refresh me.'

'It's still winter, the water will be freezing,' Lydia warns him.

He puffs up and gestures at the blue sky. 'This is nothing. There's not even snow.'

'It's heated, he'll be fine,' Diana adds.

Armando shrugs. 'See? Swim, eat then sleep.' And he ambles off towards their bedroom, whistling a tune that may or may not be from a Puccini opera.

Lydia watches him until he disappears from view. She claps her hands. 'Right. Let's open the wine.'

'It's just gone nine!'

Lydia taps the face of her watch. 'Not in Rome.'

Diana leads the way into the kitchen. 'I've arranged for it to be fully stocked with everything you might conceivably need.' She points out the bowls of fruit and the fridge full to bursting, and shows Lydia where the under-bench wine fridge is located. 'Not that you'll need directions.' Lydia is a hound for wine. 'I even asked the boys from The Village Cellars to include a bottle of Campari. Who knows? You might make converts out of Ingrid and Camille.'

'They strike me as either schnapps or vodka types.' Lydia spies a large cardboard box on the bench. 'Ooh, what are these?' She proceeds to tear off the paper and reveals almond croissants and cherry Danishes.

'Looks like Persephone's been to the shops.' Diana calls out her daughter's name but gets no response. She shrugs and makes coffee while Lydia loads a plate with goodies. They take it out onto the deck to make the most of the panoramic view. The pool is not visible from where they sit but they can hear Armando splashing about.

'So, back to Will,' Lydia says, breaking the end off an almond croissant and popping it in her mouth. 'Mm, these are delicious.' A pause to wash it down with coffee. 'Bring me up to speed.'

And so Diana does. Such a relief to get the weight off her chest and Lydia is such a good listener, always has been. They drink coffee and Lydia smokes.

'And by the time I managed to speak to Will, I'd had it up to here.' Diana indicates a point north of her head. 'I told him not to bother coming home. In the meantime, all I've succeeded in doing is sticking my bib into Ian and Rebecca's business and I'm still none the wiser why Will's behaving like an idiot. I'm sick of trying to second-guess him.'

Lydia takes a long drag on her cigarette and blows smoke rings. She grins, just as pleased with the trick at fifty-eight as she was at sixteen. 'Well, the ball's in your court.'

'How can you say that? If Will's shacked up with this Caroline woman, then that's it. We're done.'

Lydia stubs out her cigarette. 'I suppose it's too early to open some bubbles?' she asks, meaning precisely the opposite.

'I have to drive.'

'It's not that far.'

'Far enough. I'll fetch some mineral water.'

On her way to the kitchen, Diana sees Armando asleep on one of the pool lounges, his hairy belly gently rising and falling with each breath. She returns bearing a tray with glasses filled with ice and quarters of lime and a bottle of sparkling mineral water.

She has barely sat down when Lydia says, 'Do you know, after what happened to Nicholas, I really thought that was the end of your marriage. Surely, if you can survive that, you can survive anything.'

'Lydia, don't. This isn't even in the same league.' The mere mention of Nicholas makes the pain flare from deep within Diana's core where she keeps her grief locked away.

'That's precisely my point. Nicholas dying *is* the worst thing. Will's behaviour fell short then and it's falling well short now. The way I recall it, you were far more forgiving of him than he ever was of you.' Lydia unscrews the lid off the bottle and fills each glass. Diana picks up the closest one, distracted by how the slight tremble makes the ice tinkle. 'Under the circumstances, I thought you were incredibly generous to take him back.' Lydia pulls another cigarette from the packet and cups her hand around the flame as she lights it.

Diana watches the flame, and thinks back to that scrap of a note hidden in the folds of Will's favourite sweater. Has she been looking for meaning when there isn't one? No, she's not wrong about this. Diana regards her sister. Lydia's opinions spring from loyalty, not facts. 'You'd already left before the proverbial hit the fan.'

Lydia's eyes narrow, as she waits to see what Diana will say next.

'I've always looked up to you, Lydia, always listened to your advice. But you've been gone a very long time.'

'Don't be ridiculous, we talk almost every day. I'm only geographically distant.'

Diana pokes at the wedge of lime bobbing in her drink. 'The way you see it, Nicholas dies. Diana's a mess. Will charges off to save FME. Lydia steps into the breach and exits stage right on his return.'

Lydia was long gone before the final scene played out. Will's and Diana's lives have grown around those months like scar tissue. Diana made a pact with herself to bury the lot and never speak of it again. Time has proven her to be a woman of her word.

'I'm sorry but I need a proper drink.' Lydia springs to her feet and returns with cold wine and fresh glasses. 'Whatever it is that you're not telling me, there's nothing to be ashamed of. We all grieve in our own way.' Lydia offers Diana a glass but she refuses, despite the fact that she'd love something to take the edge off. 'But answer me this. You forgave him once for leaving. Now he's left again. What happens when there's a third time? At what point does it become a pattern?'

Diana stares at her. She's turning into their mother. Lydia has always been tough. She's a midwife, she's worked in some of the most godforsaken corners of the globe, delivered children under gunfire and into extreme poverty. The woman has nerves of steel. Yet she goes through men as if there's always another fish in the sea.

'Why are you putting this all on Will? There are two people in this marriage.' There is so much she hasn't told Lydia. That as hurtful as Will's fling was, nothing happens in a vacuum. Diana eyes off the wine bottle, takes less than a second to change her mind.

'I knew you'd crack,' Lydia remarks with a self-satisfied grin.

'Don't be so smug.'

'I'm your big sister, it's my job.' She resumes her seat and leans over to pat Diana's knee. 'Have you asked yourself why Will keeps flying off the handle, Didi? I mean, I know he's always had a bee in his bonnet about you and Michael, but still?' She settles back in her chair and rests her feet on the table. 'I'll let you in on a little secret. For a while there, I was besotted with that man.'

'Michael? But you used to treat him like dirt.' Diana remembers Lydia in her twenties — hair long, waist slim, legs up to her armpits. 'Sex on legs' one of Lydia's boyfriends had called her. 'You said, "He bores the pants off me."'

'I know, right. He was smoking hot, he looked the part, but sadly, he was as dull as dishwater. Probably still is. But I have a well-tested theory that they're often the ones that turn out to be hot stuff in the sack. Don't you reckon? Not that you were ever going to find out.'

Diana blushes. This conversation is getting uncomfortably close to the bone. How would Lydia react if she knew how close Diana came to finding out exactly how good Michael was in bed? Fortunately, or unfortunately, Lydia hasn't noticed.

'He was completely intimidated by you. All the men were. You were a walking cliché.'

'What's that supposed to mean?'

'The moment you opened your mouth, you had the audience eating out of your hand. You'd walk into a room and it was like Moses had parted the sea. The only one with the balls to talk to you was Will. He must have thought all his Christmases had come at once when you agreed to a date.'

Diana's embarrassment deepens. 'Well, please feel free to jog his memory when you see him, won't you.'

'I'll be telling Will a few home truths at this rate. Like reminding him how good he's got it. And telling him to stop behaving like a jerk.'

Diana puts down her glass. 'Enough, Lydia. I know you're trying to be supportive but you really don't understand the issues here.' Lydia goes to protest and Diana holds up her hand. 'When Nicholas died, I hated the world. I hated myself. It didn't matter what Will said, he couldn't make it better. He was grieving too and he hadn't fallen in a heap. It's not the same for a man though, is it? A child doesn't carve a space in their body like it does a mother. A man doesn't spend months creating a human being from a single cell. He could never know how I felt. And I made sure he knew it. He couldn't save me so off he ran to save FME.'

Diana can't sit still any longer. She heads over to the edge of the balcony and leans over the railing.

Lydia rushes over, places an arm around her shoulder and anchors her by her side. 'I'm going to keep telling you this until the day I die — what happened to Nicholas was not your fault. As awful as it is, it was just an unfortunate set of circumstances.'

Diana cannot stay with Nicholas, she needs to move on to the next part of the story before the pain drags her down to that dark hole where it lives. She pulls away. 'I was so lonely. I couldn't bear living with the thoughts scrambling my brain. What if, what if, what if? Day and night. I never knew that grief was so visceral, so physical. I was frightened of myself. Frightened for Aiden and Persephone. I felt like I was walking a tightrope and any minute I was going to miss my footing and it would all be over.'

'I was there. If you couldn't talk to Will, you could have talked to me.'

Diana shakes her head, gulps back a wave of tears. She doesn't want to stay here at the edges of this moment. 'Will said we should have another child and I just lost it. You can't just replace a child that's died. From that point on, it was like we were on either side of a chasm. He's a man — they need to find a solution to every problem. Saving FME was a problem he could fix.'

Lydia releases her but only long enough to top up both their drinks. Diana doesn't protest when she hands her the glass. The pressure in her head is pounding. Wine will numb the pain, or not. It warms her throat as she swallows.

'Then I met someone whose suffering was as deep as my own. It wasn't really about the sex. I think we were two souls looking for consolation in a broken universe.'

If her revelation shocks Lydia, she doesn't let it show. 'Please tell me you didn't tell Will.'

Diana doesn't answer.

Lydia's sigh is almost a groan. 'Oh, Didi. That wasn't smart. I thought he just had an affair with Super Sally. You never told me it was payback. I can't believe you've kept that secret from me. But why on earth did you tell him?'

'Because I wanted to hurt him. I wanted him to taste the pain I lived with. But over the years I've come to wonder, did I tell him because I wanted him to punish me?'

And then she found that scrap of a note in Will's sweater. She has no idea what to read into it. 'I forgave Will for Super Sally because I knew it was tit for tat. Stupidly, I thought he'd forgive me too, the ledger would be square, and we'd move on. But he never once said those words.' And ever since, she's worn Will's blame like sackcloth and ashes.

'But how does that relate to now? What's his excuse this time? You told me the photos were incriminating but you were innocent. So, what am I missing?'

And now the moment is here. Diana's taken the circuitous route but no matter. She takes a deep breath. 'The third set of photos were of me, with ... with the man I had the affair with.'

Lydia looks at her curiously, carefully. 'From what you just said, I assumed you never saw him again.'

'And you would have assumed correctly. Except this year Ben became a parent at Amberside College. I teach his daughter, so you see, I cannot *not* see him. We had a drink to clear the air and I didn't mention it to Will because, let's face it, it's best to let sleeping dogs lie. I didn't want to revisit all the nastiness from the past. I never imagined someone was spying on me.'

'Would you have behaved differently?'

'Yes! Of course.' But as soon as she says that, she isn't so sure. Beneath the scab, the sore was festering. She had to see Ben again. And she could never tell Will that in a way that would make him believe it didn't mean anything. If he never forgave her the first time, he wasn't going to change his tune now.

Lydia leans over the balcony, staring into the distance. Then suddenly, she taps her ring on the metal bar, making it ping. 'You said Will's never met Ben.'

Diana nods. Lydia looks very pleased with herself. 'Then Will couldn't possibly have recognised Ben from the photos. He has no idea what Ben looks like.'

And Diana never answered Will when he shoved the photo in her face and asked her. She feels like she's fallen into deep water, all the air driven from her lungs.

Lydia grabs her by the shoulders. 'Ha! I knew it. He knows damn well this has nothing to do with Ian. You told him you and Michael are just friends. He has no idea the third man is the infamous Ben. So it's obvious, isn't it?'

'Is it?'

'I reckon Will's up to no good.'

'Caroline Fox.'

Lydia shrugs. 'Maybe. Maybe not. Whatever's going on, you need to call Will and thrash this out. And pronto.'

Part III

Everybody needs love

Chapter 33

Saturday

Diana takes her coffee out onto the terrace, shivering in the crisp early morning air. Her gaze catches on Ruth's orchid. It has a flower spike! Not only has she managed to keep it alive, it's clearly thriving. She takes a photo and sends it to Ruth as an insurance policy. A sort of proof of life.

It's Saturday. Will is due home. But given that Persephone virtually admitted he's already back in the country, Diana has no expectation that he'll make an appearance. Not to mention that she told him not to darken her doorstep. She regrets that moment of spite. Whether they can salvage this marriage or not, Lydia's right, they need to thrash things out. Running away solves nothing.

Cradling her coffee, Diana watches the world pass by. There's a mother pushing her toddler on a swing, a baby strapped to her chest, a life-giving coffee at her lips. Dotty from the next block is power-walking across The Green. There are some students dressed in sports uniforms heading for the basketball courts. And there is Will. Diana almost drops her cup.

He's sitting on a bench in the park, looking up. At her. When he realises she's seen him, he stands up, crosses the road and stops on the footpath below. Diana pulls the drapey cardigan close to her chest, smooths her eyebrows. Will stands there, hands by his side, staring up at her with those bluest of blue eyes. He hasn't shaved for a few days and the stubble highlights his jawline. He wears that frown that always makes him look like he doesn't quite believe you. He needs a haircut. And the handsome bastard still makes her swoon.

Will brings his hands together at his chest and mouths the word 'please'.

Diana shakes her head. She's not ready to be on the same turf as him. If they're going to talk, it has to be on neutral territory. She mimes five minutes. She doesn't wait for an answer. If she thinks too much about this, she might very well change her mind.

Her first instinct is to choose an outfit that she'd wear to school — the 'nothing to see here' look she prefers. But when she sees herself in the mirror, it feels too severe so she swaps the top for Will's favourite — an angora jumper in soft pink. She brushes her hair and decides a touch of mascara and slick of lipstick is as good as he deserves. She wants to convey 'I am strong' and 'see what you're giving up'. She has no intention of making it easy on him. When she's run out of excuses, she shrugs on her coat and heads downstairs.

Will has returned to the park bench but as she exits their building, he springs to his feet and comes to greet her. When he's close enough to hear her, Diana tells him the truth. 'You look terrible.'

He winces. He doesn't kiss her cheek, or take her hand, or give her a hug, even an A-frame one. 'Shall we walk?'

Diana buries her hands in her pockets, telling herself it's because she's cold, knowing it's to scrunch up her fists and strengthen her resolve. They cross the road and Will heads down the wide concrete steps to the beach itself. Her preference is to stay on the path. She glances at his feet — he's wearing docksides so he'll be okay, but stupidly she wore her suede ankle-boots. The heel will sink with every step. But she follows Will down the stairs because now is not the time to quibble about something as petty as aching calves and wet boots.

The grey sky has turned the water the colour of steel. White caps shoot across its surface like racing yachts. The wind teases her hair and tendrils lash at her face. In his usual fashion, Will has charged off ahead without her, head bowed into the wind. Diana allows the gap between them to widen, knowing that sooner or later, he'll realise and wait for her to catch up, apologising, but never changing his habit.

It takes an age to reach the length of concrete pipe that marks the middle of the beach. Diana watches Will, assuming he'll turn around at this point and head back to her. Instead, he steps over it and trudges ever onward like an Antarctic explorer in a blizzard.

She stops walking, not so much digging her heels in as sinking in the wet sand. 'Will,' she calls out after him but the wind snatches her words and flings them back at her. 'Will!' Her shout verges on a scream.

He turns around. Diana points to the steps. There's a moment's hesitation before he relents. Her victory is short-lived. At the top of the stairs, Will continues towards The Boatshed.

In an attempt to counter her rising temper, Diana takes a deep breath and charges after him. She grabs his arm and threads hers through his to anchor him to her. Then she tugs on said arm, hard enough to make him look at her. 'Talk.'

Will refuses to maintain eye contact but he slows his pace to match hers. They walk in silence, past the picnic tables and the queue forming for the donut van that parks here every weekend.

'It's just been one thing after another lately,' he says.

Diana relaxes her grip, encouraging him to go on.

'We've received another offer for FME. That's why I was in Texas.'

'Are you going to take it?' Telling him he should jump at the chance is just as likely to make him determined to hang in there. He's always been a stubborn so-and-so.

'I've let Ian know. He's keen. I'm considering it.'

'No more travel,' she says. She's not stupid enough to voice all the other good reasons. How he's not getting any younger, that he doesn't bounce back like he used to, and it might be best to bow out while he can still call the shots.

Yet she can still feel the tension snaking through him, the inner conflict of such an enormous decision. Whatever this thing is that's happening between them, Diana can't let him lose this opportunity to change his life. 'You don't need to work. It's not like you need the money.'

She waits, expecting the usual reply along the lines of, *What else would I do with my time?* Or *I've still got plenty of years ahead of me*, as if sixty really is the new forty. Diana hasn't seen much evidence this is as true for men as it is for women.

'Maybe I can take over from Royce Carmichael when he drops dead.'

She pulls up short. 'Oh.'

'What's wrong? I was joking.'

'Nothing. I've just remembered something.' Something that will have to wait until Monday. Royce has yet to bank the cheque, time is on her side.

Will disentangles himself from her grasp and takes her hand instead. Diana would very much like to stop now — her feet are killing her, but if walking means talking, then she'll pay that price.

'I just haven't been feeling myself lately,' Will says when they reach The Boatshed.

'Have you spoken to the doctor?'

He stops in his tracks. 'This isn't about my prostate, Didi. My PSA levels are normal.'

She tries and fails to hide her surprise.

He looks at her sharply but there's a glint in his eye too. 'I did read that article, you know.'

'Why didn't you say so?'

'I didn't want to talk about it. I know what's wrong with me. I don't need Doctor Lavinsky's help with that.'

Diana seizes her chance. 'And what *is* wrong with you?'

Instead of answering, Will steers her towards a bench facing the beach. She sits beside him, wishing she could snuggle into the warmth of his embrace instead of tucking her hands in her armpits before her fingers freeze. It's a relief to know it's not cancer but it still leaves the question around his bedroom issues unresolved.

She takes the plunge. 'Has this got anything to do with Caroline Fox?'

Will has the exact look of a man who's been caught red-handed. 'Okay. Tell me how you know about Caroline?'

Not, 'I have no idea who you're talking about.' Interesting. Diana shakes her head at him.

'She's …' That's as far as he gets. He tries to take her hand but she keeps both firmly tucked away. He has to make do with resting his hand on her thigh. 'This past year or so, I've grown to realise that I'm no longer having any fun.'

Does he mean with her? Or does Will mean he's no longer having fun in general? The last time she had fun was not with

Will. It was a guilty pleasure but also a reminder of how rarely she ever lets her hair down. She has no regrets that she didn't end up in Michael's bed because, in truth, what she was looking for was a reminder that she's still desirable. Right outcome, wrong guy. She studies Will's profile. She wasn't lying when she said he looks terrible. He's running himself into the ground. He might not be having fun, but he's also not much fun to be around.

'Sixty is such a big number, Didi. I'm past my prime.'

'Don't be ridiculous. Sixty *is* your prime.'

Across the road, a gaggle of seniors emerge from the water and head to the showers near the steps. Not a jot of care that the conditions are brutal. Peals of laughter float across the path.

'Aren't they great?' Diana says. 'Full of life. Friendship, exercise, and a reason to get up every single day. You might mock Royce Carmichael, but what's the point of being dead at sixty-five with nothing to show for it but a bucket of unspent superannuation for the kids to fight over.'

Will sighs. 'I get that the club gives Royce a sense of purpose, but I'm not sure I can do as good a job at convincing myself that president of the Beach Club is the same thing as head of a business. Apart from the monthly committee meetings and sorting out the timeslots for the weekly swim, there's not much to it, is there? There's an awful lot of hours to fill between Sundays and I don't think having the best parking spot at the beach is enough.'

Diana relents and takes his hand in hers and threads their fingers. 'Fun is about doing the things you love. Being with the people you love. Living with the one you love.' She watches Will closely, trying to gauge his reaction, giving him the space to rush in and say he chooses her. Instead he bites his bottom lip and she feels a pang. She can't imagine that his mouth may no longer be hers to kiss.

Will removes his hand from hers and wraps it around his fist. 'A woman like you never has to worry about being alone.' He rubs his jaw and stares out to sea rather than look at her. 'Those photos.'

And here they are. Diana tenses, waiting to see which direction this conversation is about to take. There are really only two options — look down or look to the horizon.

Will takes his time. The lines around his eyes deepen. The muscles in his neck are as tight as wires. All the signs suggest this is not going to be pretty. 'Do you know what the worst thing was?'

He pauses but Diana guesses the question is rhetorical. She waits him out.

'It was like a window into your secret life. It shocked me. I realised I have no clue what you do when I'm not around.' His frown deepens. 'Or who you're having fun with.'

'I don't lead a very exciting life, Will. Now the kids are gone and my services are no longer required, I just sort of drift along.' She shrugs. 'Outside of school, organising the party and moving into the apartment have been the highlights of my year. Other than that, I'm a very boring person.' The truth of this hits her afresh. Here she is telling Will he needs to find a passion to replace work and she's no better. She has a passion, she has the time, yet she chooses instead to coast along. Not taking any risks, sure, but also not having much fun.

Will's beautiful blue eyes are glassy with tears. 'I'm sorry I've disappointed you, Didi. I've been absent most of our married lives, always travelling, working long hours. No wonder you're sick of me. I have no one but myself to blame.'

She refuses to let him get away with casting her as some ungrateful over-privileged bitch telling him he's not good enough. She might be many things, but she's no Rebecca.

'Let's be crystal clear. I have no interest in being unfaithful. For starters, I can do without the drama. If I was, we wouldn't be sitting here freezing our butts off.'

'It's a new low point though when you realise other men are buying your wife drinks instead of you.'

'That's your choice, Will. You're right, you should be wining and dining me. And you should be putting on the mood music and waltzing me into bed. But you're not. Quite the opposite. So instead of feeling sorry for yourself, maybe you need to think about lifting your game.'

He stares at the patch of grass at his feet.

Now she's lit the match, she may as well light the fire. She presses her palm to his cheek and forces him to face her. 'There's only one way forward, Will. The truth. Why did you storm out?'

Thirty years is plenty of time to learn the signs. He won't maintain eye contact. He's doing that thing where he rubs circles in the pad of flesh between his thumb and index finger. He pulls her hand away. 'I've been seeing someone.'

'Caroline.'

'Yes.' He holds up his hands in surrender. 'But not in that way. She's a counsellor.'

Caroline. Diana's been thinking foxy, now she's imagining twin sets and pearls. A pleated skirt. Hair short but feminine. Slender. It's no use. She bristles.

'I needed to talk to someone who has no direct involvement in my life. It didn't feel right to talk to Ian and I don't really have those kinds of friendships. Swimming buddies, colleagues, but that's not the same thing, is it?'

'Me, Will? Isn't that my job?'

He shakes his head. 'There's stuff I needed to unpack on my own. It's not fair to dump it on you. Plus, if I'm being totally honest, I was scared I'd dig a deeper hole if I tried.'

'Jesus, Will. That doesn't say much for thirty years of marriage, does it.'

He shuffles closer. 'The truth is, those photos couldn't have arrived at a worse time. I came home from seeing Caroline and I was feeling pretty raw. I shouldn't have reacted the way I did. In my heart of hearts, I know you wouldn't be so ... I don't know ... I'm sorry. It's about trust, isn't it?' He buries his face in his hands, pressing the tips of his fingers into his eyelids. Then he sits up straight and looks at her. 'I was once very cruel to you and I got what I deserved.'

She feels like the wind off the sea is passing straight through her. 'Leave it alone, Will.'

He puts his finger to her lips. 'I can't. Not anymore.'

In a heartbeat, she's right back there. Except Will is not gently pressing his finger to her lips, he's screaming at her to shut up. She's trying to explain. He refuses to listen. Keeps cutting across every sentence, stabbing his finger in the air between them, calling her vile names. She remembers her rising terror. Not of Will — of what she'd done and how it had slipped from her grasp. She destroyed his trust, blown up their relationship. No amount of backpedalling was going to save her. All these years later and she still bows her head in shame.

'I found the note.'

There's a pause before he answers. 'What note?'

Diana snaps back her head. 'What note? *What note?* The one hidden in your cashmere sweater. "I forgive you"?'

Will looks at her blankly, then his expression shifts as realisation dawns. He looks surprised, sheepish even. It's too much. She's hollow. She scrambles to her feet and runs across the road, thoughts flying through her head like shrapnel. In the distance, Will calls her name. Diana ignores him. Ahead is their apartment block. It's the last place she wants to be. She pivots and heads towards the Sea Breeze Retirement Village. Then Will catches her. She's tangled in his arms and can't get free.

'Let go of me,' she shouts. 'Let go of me.'

He does but only long enough to take hold of her arms. 'Diana, stop it. People will think I'm attacking you.'

She pulls against him so hard that she falls on her bottom on the damp grass. Sobbing, she brings her knees to her chest and buries her head in her arms.

'Don't hide. Talk to me.'

She refuses to say a word. She's so angry. How dare he talk to Caroline about them, about her and what she did. They'd agreed. One foot in front of the other, and leave the past where it belongs.

'I can't do this anymore.'

Diana's head shoots up.

Will plonks down beside her. 'My knees are killing me.' He pulls a face. 'Fuck this grass is cold. I'll get haemorrhoids as well.'

He goes to put his arm around her again and she glares at him. He folds his arms instead and sighs. 'When you told me you'd slept with that bloke, it knocked the stuffing out of me. Then my ego got in the way and I did what young men do best and channelled all my emotions into anger. I was the wounded party. You'd destroyed my trust and for that, I would never forgive you.'

'I haven't put a foot wrong in twenty-six years. What does it take, Will?' Every day she lives in penance. Every time she looks at one of her children or sees little Lucas's face, it reminds her of what she did, of what she lost. Every day she carries the burden on her conscience.

'Let me finish. I was an arrogant prick. Me sleeping with Sally was payback for a damaged ego and dented pride. Not forgiving you was me twisting the knife. When we got back together, we agreed to rule a line under it and get on with our lives.'

'So the note, Will. What does it mean?'

'Caroline says that I can't have a proper relationship with myself, let alone you, until I forgive myself for being a dickhead and apologise for running away rather than dealing with the shitstorm.'

'I don't understand.'

Will stands up and offers her his hands. She takes them and lets him pull her to her feet. He draws her in close and pulls his jacket around her. 'I've been trying to write you a letter. To put into words how I felt about Nicholas, you, me, us. It's painful shit, digging up the past. It's even harder to express how I feel.'

He looks to Diana for understanding but she can't, she won't give it to him. Will is dangerously close to crossing the line.

'Caroline said that, even if I never gave you the letter, I had to process my feelings.'

'I don't understand. The letterhead is ancient. That hotel doesn't even exist anymore. I know, I looked it up. Where did it come from?'

Will frowns at her. 'I just found it in a drawer in my office. Why?'

That's not the answer she was expecting. 'I thought you must have written the note years ago and for some reason you'd decided not to give it to me and hidden it away.'

'That would be a bit mean. You know how I hate throwing anything out. I have heaps of old notepads I've nicked from hotels all over the world.'

Such a simple explanation. Why hadn't she thought of that? 'So, the torn scrap I found wrapped in your sweater is from a letter you wrote recently that you never intended to give to me, rather than one you wrote twenty-six years ago? Is that really what you're trying to tell me?'

Will, at least, has the grace to look embarrassed. He runs his hands down his thighs and sighs. 'You see, I did forgive you, in time, but every time I tried to talk to you, the mere mention of Nicholas would set you off. I couldn't share my feelings and you wouldn't let me in. We buried Nicholas in every sense of the word.'

She wants to tell him to shut up. He's ambushing the conversation; this is about him never forgiving her, not their dead baby.

Will opens his palms, appeals to her. 'Look what it's done to us.'

Diana feels giddy. She closes her eyes. Against Will. Against the memories.

'I knew something was wrong with my health. Like you, I assumed the worst. All that grief eating away at me. I was going nuts, I needed help. Seeing Caroline was my last desperate attempt. I had to talk to someone who didn't know me. Someone I didn't care about, who I couldn't hurt. That's why not you, Didi.'

'And the letter?'

Will shrugs, looks embarrassed. 'I gave up. I might have the gift of the gab but I'm useless at putting pen to paper. You'll have to just take my word for it instead. But in the process, I realised what was even more important.' Will takes her face in his hands and kisses her forehead. 'Everyone has come home. The timing is perfect.'

'For what?'

'We need to talk to Aiden and Persephone about Nicholas.'

With a gasp, Diana pulls away. 'No, no, no. We can't. It's been twenty-six years. Let it be.'

'Didi, they're adults now. They have a right to remember their brother. Keeping him a secret has slowly poisoned us. You've barely sung a note since Nicholas died. I've been making sure I was too busy to think. When was the last time we made love?'

Diana starts to cry. 'I thought you had cancer. I thought that was why. Or there was someone else. Or that you didn't find me attractive anymore.'

Will laughs. 'Oh darling, trust you to go to the worst-case scenario. I reckon once we've sorted through our issues and I get rid of the company, you'll be in serious trouble. That is, if you'll have me back.'

There's so much history between them. They are supposed to be celebrating important milestones, a time of joy and love. They are supposed to be raising a glass to marvel at the magnificent achievement that is thirty years of marriage. Except all she feels is tired, confused and incapable of making any decision, let alone the right one.

'I agree that we have to sort this out together, but I'm not sure that I'm equipped to deal with anything right now. I know that sounds like I'm having a bet each way.'

Will shakes his head and kisses her. 'Right now, I'll take what I can get.'

Chapter 34

Saturday

Diana studies her wedding rings. She's barely had them off in thirty years. She pulls on them now but they jam at the knuckle. That's okay. She'd feel naked without them. Unlike when she first wore her engagement ring. The weight unfamiliar. The shine catching her eye. The only shame is that if she can't ever get the rings off, then the inscription will forever remain hidden between the platinum and her skin. She and Will have the same words engraved on their wedding rings. *My heart is yours for eternity.* A bold promise.

Diana is in charge of making coffee while Will fetches his car. Their chat has left her drained but on one thing she is clear. If Will's idea of a long-overdue conversation includes talking about Nicholas, then he's in for a severe disappointment. The rest of their marriage is open slather, but Diana has no desire to talk about their son, not now, not ever. It won't bring him back.

Right on cue, she hears the key in the lock followed by the rumbling of the wheels of Will's travel bag. The sound ceases at the laundry door. After this morning's bruising round, Diana has no intention of beating about the bush. She's had all the time Will's been fetching his car to formulate her response. Now she needs to get it over and done with.

The moment he walks into the kitchen, she hands him his coffee then spits it out. 'Look, Will, I'm more than happy to dissect every day of our marriage. I am equally happy for you to air your grievances about any or all of my most annoying traits. I'm prepared to capitulate on pretty much anything you ask.'

Will goes to respond but Diana cuts him off at the pass. 'Let me finish. I was about to say, with one exception. Revisiting what happened to Nicholas is nothing but an exercise to prove that time does not, as it turns out, heal all wounds. After this conversation, I don't want to talk of it ever again.'

He turns and looks out to sea, giving Diana a perfect view of the muscle near his eye twitching. She battles onwards.

'All our family is here — we're supposed to be the charming hosts, not wallowing in the past. We made an agreement. I think we should stick to it.'

Will balances his mug on the ledge of the terrace wall. 'Didi, I don't want to dissect any day of our marriage, especially since I've absented myself from the vast majority of them. I don't have an itemised list of everything that's wrong with you, or us, for that matter. My list only has one item on it.'

He turns and looks at her. What does he want her to say that hasn't already been said? When she refuses to make it easier on him, Will continues.

'I hate to break it to you, but Caroline is adamant that we really do need to talk about Nicholas. She thinks we made a mistake back then trying to move on without dealing with the emotional fallout of his death. She thinks selling Turpentine Street has been the catalyst for all these other issues.' Again, he leaves a space for her to interject, to disagree, or to tell him he's damn right. When she refuses to answer, he adds, 'For the record, so do I.'

'Well, good for you,' Diana snaps. 'Maybe I should go and see this Caroline and explain precisely why I disagree.'

For reasons that escape her, Will seems pleased by this. 'We can go together.'

'What? No thank you. I will not be ganged up on by you two.'

'Didi, stop. No one is ganging up on anyone. Can't you see? This is part of the problem.' Will tries to wrap his arms around her but she's having none of it.

'Don't you dare think you can give me a hug and make me back down. Not on this, Will. We made a promise.'

Palms up, he steps away. 'Okay, okay. I won't touch you but I'm not going anywhere.'

The fury rises like a tide, strangling her in its clenched fist. 'I don't understand how we ended up here. This is about the photos and you storming out and me finding a piece of your letter and all you want to talk about is something that happened twenty-six years ago. Newsflash — talking won't change a damn thing. If I thought it would, I'd talk myself hoarse.'

Will advances again, slowly, cautiously, as if wary of her. Diana backs away until she's against the brick wall. She glances at the street below. The sun has risen high enough to bathe the playground in wintry light. Children shriek and laugh, swing and slide. Mothers rock prams or pat the bottoms of babies snuggled against them in their pouches. Soft beanies on their little heads, dangly legs, fat cheeks barely visible beneath the flannelette wraps. She never got to hold Nicholas in a pouch, or watch the muscles in his cheek as he suckled, or pace the halls at night rocking him back to sleep. Not once. Not ever.

And the fury grabs hold of her and Diana's gaze slips from the horizon.

*

Diana wakes up. It's dusk. But which day? She rolls out of bed. Her head is fuzzy. She's thirsty. She needs the bathroom.

She washes her hands. Fills the vanity basin with warm water and soaks a face washer in it. She presses it to her aching eyes, feels the warmth seep in. The woman looking back at her has aged ten years since this morning, if it is the same day. Her face is puffy, the colour patchy. All her features sort of blend into one, like she's blurring and becoming invisible. The disappearing Diana. She turns off the bathroom light. She has no desire to see any more of that woman.

Diana creeps out to the living room. Will is sitting on the couch. In front of him is an open packing box. He must have dragged it out of the spare room. After all the trouble she went to. In his hands is a framed picture. Diana inches closer. The light of the lamp illuminates a single teardrop as it falls onto the glass.

She resists the urge to rush to his side and comfort him even though her body yearns to. Yearns to feel the familiarity of his body close to hers. But she's not brave enough. Cowardice makes her cling to the security of the wall.

Will looks up. He seems surprised to see her there. He dashes the tears from his eyes. 'You're up,' he says, smiling, feigning jolly, despite the tears. And the photo.

Diana nods. 'I was thirsty,' she says, disengaging from the wall and crossing to the refuge of the kitchen. She takes a tall glass from the drawer and fills it at the tap. She can feel Will's eyes boring through her kimono, the questions hammering against her rib cage. This morning floats in front of her, blurry and out of focus. Snatches of what they said dance like dandelion seeds carried on the breeze, just out of reach.

The leather couch creaks as Will stands up. He's walking towards her. Diana counts each step. When the children were little, Aiden's favourite game to play was 'What's the time, Mr Wolf?' She'd stand there, facing the camellia hedge, hands over her eyes, fingers parted just wide enough to see through. Not that she needed to. The children's giggling gave them away every time.

'What's the time, Mr Wolf?'

'Twelve o'clock.'

Waiting for them to dare to edge closer. Their long shadows reaching her before they ever did. A third shadow, smaller, crawling along behind them. Startled, Diana would whirl around, searching for Nicholas.

'Mummy, we didn't say what's the time? You can't turn around, that's cheating.'

Diana frantic, running past Aiden's shadow, past her frowning son, wide-eyed Persephone. Running the whole length of the garden, hot feet over cool grass. Past the washing line, the guinea pig cage, the lemon tree, but she's too late. Nicholas had disappeared again. He always disappeared. He only ever let her see him out of the corner of her eye.

Will puts the photo on the kitchen bench. He approaches her. She holds herself rigid, elbows tucked into her waist. Arms around her, gently pulling her backwards, away from the past. He buries his head in her neck. Diana yields to him. Feels his body soften against hers. Hers against him. Outside, the horizon is a ribbon of orange against a darkening sky. They stand there intertwined long enough that Diana witnesses the sun concede and night claim the sky.

She puts the glass down on the draining board and breaks the spell. Will steps away. Diana turns to face him. The light from the lamp draws her eye. Illuminates the open box. The last box. The box she intended to store on the high shelf, right at the back where it would be dry and safe. She needs to keep him dry and safe.

Will reaches behind for the photo frame. He holds it out to Diana. An offering or a question. Diana can see him do this out of the corner of her eye, where Nicholas has always lived. It's his special place. She keeps her gaze firmly pinned on the soft halo of light surrounding the lamp to keep him there. Her nose prickles with the memory. Poor Nicholas never got to smell like a newborn baby.

'He was beautiful, wasn't he?' Will says, holding the damn photo out to her, begging her to take it. The movement breaks her focus on the lamp and Nicholas disappears again. Except not. Here he is, in her arms. Swaddled in a checked flannelette hospital blanket. All she can see is his tiny head and a little tuft of black hair. His eyes are closed. There's a tiny shadow of eyelashes brushing his cheek. She can see all that in the photo.

'I wonder what colour eyes he had?' she says, ignoring the crack in her voice. 'I've always wondered whether they'd be blue like you and Persephone or brown like me and Aiden.'

Will clears his throat. 'I've always thought he looked like you.'

Diana drags her gaze down. His head so small, cradled in her hand. The wedding rings bright and shiny, gaudy even, against his waxen skin. It's been decades since she's seen Nicholas's face — probably since the day she wrapped up all his photos, laid them in this box and taped it shut. She forces herself to look at the image of her son and gasps at the physical pain of it.

Will holds the photo a little closer. It's a question rather than a demand. Diana strokes the wooden frame. Nothing happens.

It's inert. She inspects her fingertips, expecting a film of grey dust. But the picture is clean. It's been wrapped in butcher's paper for twenty-six years. What did she expect?

Diana takes the photo from Will and presses it to her chest. It takes her straight back to the delivery room at the hospital. No lit candles or warm baths or any of that nonsense for little Nicholas. It was all business. The baby was dead and it needed to be removed. *The safest way to do that is by vaginal delivery.* The doctor's words echo in her head. Safest, maybe. Kindest, maybe not. Anchored to that bed by an oxytocin drip. Every time the midwife came anywhere near her, Diana practically snarled at her like some wild beast. But the rage was so strong. Feral even. Her body resisting the powerful contractions, trying to keep Nicholas in. The drugs forcing him out into a world where he would be taken away and she'd never see him again. The memory grips her, makes the bile rise in her throat.

Out he came. Silence in the delivery suite. Then a small weak cry. They were wrong! He was alive. A moment to realise the cry came from the suite next door. Someone else's baby had just drawn its first breath. The midwife pressed him to Diana's chest. Nicholas lay there, moving with the rhythm of her breath. Never one of his own. He never felt air in his lungs. Not once.

Diana floated away to watch over Nicholas from above. The midwife offered to wrap him in a little cotton blanket. Diana was grateful. She'd hate for him to get cold. Will's head against hers, her hair wet from his tears. Her own tears streaming down her face. Alarmed she asks for tissues. She doesn't want Nicholas to get wet as well. He needs a bath but that can come later.

The contractions start up again. Diana cries out in surprise. The midwife quickly takes hold of Nicholas, 'only for a moment', she promises over Diana's howls of pain, moving

Nicholas away from her outstretched arms. Next time she saw Nicholas he was dressed exactly like this. Her newborn son. Diana looks at the photo. 'I'm so sorry.' Will is holding her up. 'I'm so sorry.' Now she's making Nicholas all wet. Panicked, she drops the photo. The glass smashes.

Will pulls her away, crooning in her ear. 'Shh, sweetheart, it's okay, it's okay.'

Diana sobs and tries to break free. She needs to pick up Nicholas from among the shards of glass but Will won't let her go. His hand is under her chin, forcing her to look at him. 'Didi, you did nothing wrong.'

'How do we know?'

He shakes her, not hard, but enough to get her attention. 'Listen to me. I've spent so many years trying to figure out what made him die. And whether I asked myself this question two decades ago, two years ago or two days ago, the answer has never changed. Neither of us did anything wrong.'

Diana tries to break free. 'How can you say that? Babies don't just die.'

'Yes they do! That's my point. For some fucked-up inexplicable reason, babies die. Even when you live in one of the most privileged countries on the planet, in one of the most incredibly privileged corners of said country. Even though you have youth and good health and the best medical care available at your fingertips. Babies die. It's fucking unfair. I've lost track of how many doctors I've met in my line of work who I have asked, begged, to give me a good reason why Nicholas had to die. And not a single one of them has given me an answer better than "shit happens". Shit just fucking happens.'

Chapter 35

Saturday/Sunday

When Persephone calls to suggest they all go out for dinner, Will tells her that Diana has one of her migraines. 'Go ahead without us,' he urges in a tone that brooks no argument.

Diana listens to this from where she lies on the couch. She doesn't have a migraine. She doesn't even have words for how she feels.

Once he's off the phone, Will puts on an apron and gets out a chopping board.

'I'm not hungry,' she calls out, her voice raspy and raw from all that crying.

'I don't care. You haven't eaten since yesterday. You need something to line your tummy.'

Diana relents. She knows this is how Will says I love you. What does Ruth call it? Acts of service. That's Will's modus operandi. He cooks to show his love. And she will eat to say thank you, I love you too.

Dinner is soft-boiled eggs, toast soldiers and tinned tomato soup.

'How old am I?' she asks in a feeble attempt to make a joke, to sound something like herself, whoever that is.

Will taps his egg with the back of a spoon. 'I thought about an omelette but this seemed easier.'

He's tired. After travelling halfway across the world, he came home to an emotional tsunami.

'I'm sorry,' she says.

Will realises she hasn't touched her egg and reaches over to take the top off. He dips a piece of toast in the golden ooze and holds it out to her. 'Eat,' he instructs.

Diana takes the toast from him. Butter, sourdough, egg yolk. Comfort food.

'What are you sorry for this time?' Will asks.

'You look exhausted.'

'I'll survive.' He points to her eggs. 'Keep eating. It will make you feel better.'

Diana focuses on eating because it will make Will happy and she wants Will to be happy. He deserves it. For being so kind.

Later, in bed, she spoons into him. It's safe to talk in the dark where she can say truths without having to see his face. Diana can feel him listening. It's in the tension in the curve of his body, the gentleness of his hand stroking the back of her neck. They talk about times before Nicholas when they were invincible, how his loss has moulded them and shaped their world.

Right before he falls asleep, Will says to her, 'Tomorrow we tell the children. We have to do it while they're both here.'

He doesn't add the second half of that thought. That they need to stop keeping Nicholas a secret. Diana is too tired to disagree.

*

In the morning, she wakes to the sound of Will in the shower. She hopes he's not shaving — she quite likes the casual sexiness of a bit of stubble. If, when, he's done with FME, it could become his statement look. Will she be there to admire it? Maybe. There's a few more hurdles before she's sure of her answer.

After her shower, Diana carefully blow-dries her hair, applies makeup and puts on her game face. She studies the woman looking back at her and decides she's not too bad for an old sheila. This is the woman she wants the world to see, not that broken creature from yesterday.

Breakfast is a polite affair. Will reads the financial pages. Diana buys passes to the zoo for the kids to take Lucas while they're here. She checks the entertainment guide to see if there are any shows on that might be worth shouting her visitors tickets. Neither of them mention the enormity of the task ahead.

On the drive over to the house on the headland, Diana concentrates on mustering her resources. 'I'm not sure I'm up to this. What if the children react badly?' She glances at Will.

He wears that determined expression of his where his chin juts out. 'Didi, we talked about this last night. We're a team. I won't let you down.' And when he goes to change gears, she wraps her hand over his.

Before Diana even has a chance to press the doorbell, the front door swings open. There stands Lydia, car keys in one hand, a bag in the other. 'Ah! Hello! Good morning! Perfect timing. We're all just heading down to The Boatshed for brekkie. Come with us.'

Diana looks to Will. That's all it takes.

'Love to, Lydia, but actually Didi and I want to spend a bit of time with the kids. Maybe tomorrow?'

Her sister glances at her and Diana returns a pleading look. Lydia doesn't miss a beat. 'Of course, how silly of me. Wait until you clap eyes on Lucas. I don't know what they're feeding him but he's grown so much.' She turns and bellows down the hallway. 'I'll meet you in the car, Armando.' She pecks first Will's then Diana's cheek, and gives her arm a little squeeze of solidarity, saying, 'I'll see you both later.' Then she beats a tactful retreat.

Inside, Diana finds Anna on the floor tying Lucas's shoelaces. Diana knows better than to ask him for a cuddle. He hasn't seen her in six months. Already he's looking to his mother for a clue as to how to handle the situation.

Diana places a gift-wrapped box on the coffee table. 'This is for you, Lucas. It's a kind of say hello present.' The woman at Toy Town in The Village promised her it would be an instant hit.

Anna beams at her. 'Aw, Diana, that's so thoughtful of you.' She turns to her son. 'Come on, Lukie. Shall we open it?'

Aiden wanders in, fresh from a shower, pulling a long-sleeve t-shirt over his head.

'Mum! Dad!' He bounds over and squeezes Diana tight. Then it's man-hugs and back-slaps for Will. 'Percy, Mum and Dad are here,' he yells over his shoulder. 'Great timing. We're just heading down to The Boatshed for breakfast. I'm sure we can squeeze two more in.'

'Oh, it's a shape sorter, Lukie.'

'It's got a little hammer so he can bash them in. I thought he'd enjoy that,' Diana explains.

'Absolutely.'

Will clears his throat. 'Actually, Aiden, Mum and I were hoping for a bit of a chat. Could Anna and Emile go on ahead and you join them later?'

Aiden frowns and looks to Anna. She shrugs. 'Sure. No problem. I'll order you something.'

'What's going on?' asks Persephone, threading an enormous scarf around her neck and tying it in an effortlessly stylish knot. 'Hey Dad, long time no see,' she says, offering her cheek. 'Mum,' she adds, quickly followed by a hug. Diana inhales vanilla and spice and honey. 'It's so good to see you.' Persephone doesn't let go.

'Mum and Dad want to hang out for a bit before we catch up with everyone at The Boatshed,' Aiden tells her.

She frowns and releases Diana. Unlike her brother, for whom it's perfectly natural that the parents he hasn't seen in six months might want some family time, Persephone's first instinct is that something is wrong. 'You *are* getting a divorce.'

'What? No. Nothing like that,' Will rushes to reassure her. 'Are we?' he asks Diana.

Divorce. Good lord. She already feels like she's been run through a wringer backwards, is that the outcome she really wants? 'Not as far as I'm aware,' Diana promises her, conscious this might be wishful thinking on her part.

Diana takes a seat on the couch out of the way as Anna bundles Lucas in his coat and Emile grabs the nappy bag for her so she can carry the toddler to the car. At the front door, he blows Persephone a kiss goodbye. She grins and blows one back. They are alone with the children.

Will sits beside her, so close their thighs touch. He's reminding her that whatever happens next, they're in this together.

'Anyone for coffee?' asks Aiden, but all three of them shake their heads.

Diana can read him like a book. He's looking for a way to defer the inevitable. Faux cheerfulness to mask the anxiety. Like mother like son.

Glancing at his sister, Aiden sprawls on the opposite couch. Persephone hesitates before joining him, perching primly at the other end, directly across from Diana. Diana knows this is all the better to read the situation, a skill Persephone has always excelled at. To a point.

Will picks up Diana's hand and squeezes it. Just like he promised, he keeps a firm hold of her. It's her cue. If this were a show, there'd be a spotlight and she'd know to step into it, what number was first and how she was going to sing it. This time, she's improvising.

'When your father and I first met, we always said we wanted four children. One of each, then a gap of a couple of years and two more.' She forces a smile and even though she can't look either of them in the eye, she can feel the shimmering wave of tension emanating from Persephone.

Will picks up the thread. 'As you can see, it didn't work out that way.' He pauses, perhaps realising this doesn't really help him connect to the next point. He clears his throat. 'The thing is, we changed our minds.'

Diana averts her gaze. When Will says it like that, it sounds so simple. She finds a point across the room where she can fix her gaze, as if she's listening intently rather than trying to retain her self-control. Where Will goes next will be excruciating. She needs to hold it together, for the sake of the children.

Except Will falters. Being strong is hard and only a coward would make him bear the burden for both of them. Diana has to save him. 'We changed our minds after what happened to Nicholas.' She stops and allows her words to sink in.

Persephone sits up straighter. Aiden scrunches up one side of his face. As always, it's their daughter who takes the lead. 'Who is Nicholas?'

Such a straightforward question. Diana shifts in her seat. She lets go of Will's hand to clasp both of hers in her lap, steeling herself. 'Nicholas is your brother.'

'What?' It's like Aiden has sucked in all his limbs. Arms spring from the back of the couch to his chest. His feet bang the edge of the coffee table as he tucks his legs into his body. In a single moment, he transforms from a lanky relaxed young man to a tense little boy curling in on himself for protection.

Persephone exhales. 'Wow.'

Will's arm seeks the comfort of Diana's shoulder, drawing her closer. She understands his need, but strangely, she doesn't feel the way she thought she would whenever she's envisaged saying these words. She'd imagined them bombarding her with questions she didn't want to answer, or talking about Nicholas in front of other people, inviting unwanted questions from sympathetic strangers, and she couldn't bear the thought of that. Instead she feels an odd sort of calm. 'I was just shy of nine months pregnant when I realised Nicholas had stopped moving.'

Her children watch her, straining to listen with every fibre of their being. But it's Will who speaks next.

'It was late on a Sunday night. We were already in bed. It's not an excuse, we should have gone straight to the hospital.'

He places a hand on Diana's leg. She puts hers on top, a comfort, a reassurance, to him, or herself. 'But I told him no. Dad had just come back from a big trip. He was exhausted. I said let's leave it until the morning. The baby's probably asleep. I was sure we were overreacting.' Her throat swells. A hot ache in her ears. 'Turns out I was wrong.'

Aiden stares at the coffee table. His face a mask, his enormous hands clenched into fists on his knees.

It's Persephone, the doctor in the family, who makes the connection. 'He died in utero.'

Diana nods. She can't speak. To lose control in front of the children would be unacceptable. Not after spending their entire lives protecting them from this terrible truth.

'I couldn't believe how quickly it happened,' says Will. 'One minute, Nicholas was fine, the next your mother had to deliver him stillborn.' He buries his fingers into his eye sockets as if trying to erase the vision of those terrible memories. 'Sorry, this is still hard.'

'Don't apologise, Dad,' Persephone says, kneeling next to him on the couch. 'I am so, so sorry. It must have been awful.'

Diana sucks in her lips, pressing them hard against her teeth, desperate not to cry.

'How did he die?'

Aiden sits there, tears in his eyes. Of course, he's thinking of Lucas. Diana frees herself from Will and goes to her son's side. She opens her arms and he rests his head against her shoulder. Diana strokes his hair.

'We, we don't know. They never found a reason,' Will rushes out before Diana has a chance to answer. 'It's still so hard to accept. That a baby can die for no apparent reason. Maybe if the technology had been as advanced as it is now, it might have been different. We'll never know.'

'Making a baby is a complicated business,' Persephone says, trying her best to sound professional and reassuring. 'When you think about it, you go from a sperm and an ovum to a zygote then a blastocyst. At that early stage, with the cells dividing at a rate of knots, there are so many opportunities for programming errors. I find it more astounding that most babies are born pretty much perfect.'

Aiden sits up. 'What about the post-mortem? That must have given you some idea.'

A dagger of pain stabs Diana's ribs. She presses her hand hard against it. She has to be so careful what she says next. She can hear in his tone the need to find someone, something to blame. Just as his father had.

And maybe because he understands this need, Will answers. 'We couldn't agree on that. Understandably, your mother was reluctant.'

He glances at Diana and the meaning passes between them. Reluctant is an understatement. She flat-out refused to let anyone touch her baby.

They can do a limited post-mortem, Didi, Will had pleaded. *Just some swabs, some blood tests. We need answers.*

Leave him alone, she'd screamed. *He's dead. I won't see him butchered.*

And Will had looked at her like he had no idea who she was.

'It's hard to explain the shock and the grief, darling,' says Diana. 'It's all-consuming, it's so physically debilitating. You have no idea what it's like to have your whole life geared around this new arrival and then it's ripped away. I'd washed all your baby clothes in soap flakes and bought fresh sheets for the cot. Your father had bought Nicholas his own chest of drawers.'

'The ladybird sheets,' Aiden suddenly says. 'I remember.'

Flabbergasted, Diana can only nod. Aiden had been four. How could he possibly remember that?

'The cot was in that little room off your bedroom.'

Diana finds her voice. 'That's right.'

Thank goodness, the staff at the hospital were very kind. They made sure Diana and Will had time alone with Nicholas and took photos of him. They arranged a cast of his feet. And when Will brought Diana home, Lydia had warned him to make sure everything was as she'd left it. The cot with its brand-new ladybird sheets and his own teddy bear, the change table with its stack of nappies, wipes, powders and creams, the mobile of planes spinning dizzy circles in the breeze.

Will stares at the floor. 'I was angry with your mother for refusing to find out how Nicholas died. I wanted to take charge, and when she wouldn't let me fix her, I blamed her.' He looks across to Diana, and she catches a glimpse of how it broke him too. 'Young and stupid.'

She offers him the smallest of smiles. She turns to Aiden, his head buried in his hands, her husband trying so hard to be mature and in control of the situation, and her heart aches with compassion for their pain.

'I arranged for Auntie Lydia to come and stay. I decided your mother was in safe hands and didn't need me hanging around. So I left. Literally took the first plane out of there.' Will hangs his head.

In the wee hours of this morning, as they lay in the dark, they agreed not to mention her affair, his payback. No one knows the landscape of a marriage except the two people in it. Will's right, the children have every right to know about their brother, but some things you have to live through to truly understand. And what's the point of damaging their perception of either Diana or Will for the sake of complete honesty? By this age and stage of life, they both know that honesty is overrated.

Persephone folds in on her father. She looks fragile but not as fragile as Will. In silence they mourn. It's more than the death of Nicholas, it's also the loss of her remaining children's innocence. By trying to protect them, had she denied them the opportunity to learn the truth about life, to find a way to grow up with a brother they could never truly know? Would that have been so bad? Each year they could have baked a birthday cake together and celebrated that Nicholas had existed at all. They could have hung his pictures on the photo wall so they saw him every day as they passed. Instead, she buried herself in her pain and closed the door on her absent son. In a way, it is her who has denied Nicholas an existence. Grief made her selfish.

Persephone untangles herself from her father's embrace. 'Can we see him?'

Diana has prepared for this. She takes a picture from her handbag. It's in a different frame but the same decades-old butcher's paper with fresh sticky tape holding it together. She passes it to Persephone. It takes every ounce of willpower to remain seated between her two children as they see their brother for the first time. The child who should be celebrating his twenty-sixth birthday in two months and who never got to celebrate a single milestone. Never lost a first tooth, said a first word, started big school, finished high school, fell in love, or had his heart broken.

Persephone peels back the tape, careful not to tear the paper. She glances at Aiden as if asking him if he's ready. Diana presses back against the lounge. Will walks over and stands behind her, resting his hands on her shoulders. He gives her a little squeeze. Persephone turns over the frame and holds Nicholas in the palms of her hands.

Aiden reaches over and brushes an imaginary speck of dirt from his baby brother's cheek. 'He's beautiful.'

Diana presses her hand to her throat, willing the lump to go away.

'He's perfect,' Persephone adds, tracing the curl of his ear. 'Poor little thing.'

'I wish ...' Aiden begins then heaves a huge sigh. He doesn't finish the sentence. All their wishes for Nicholas, about Nicholas, who he was, who he might have been, remain the same. Unfulfilled.

'I want to meet him.' Persephone looks to Diana then her father. 'I mean, can we go visit?'

Chapter 36

Sunday

Will and Aiden lead the way. They follow the winding path through a brick archway into a garden that brims with floral abundance. Carefully maintained gravel paths and the neat hedges counterbalance the untended cottage garden feel. It opens out onto a lawn where topiary giraffes and emus and bears and a giant caterpillar frolic. Hiding in one of the flower beds is a kangaroo with a joey in her pouch. In another a sow and her piglets meander through a meadow of cosmos and freesias and seaside daisies. From the one giant tree in the corner hangs an old-fashioned swing — two chains, a plank of wood. On it sits a bronzed statue of a child. She leans backwards, hair streaming behind her, feet stuck high in the air, a grin from ear to ear. For all the sorrow contained in the children's garden, this is a place of joy.

Persephone picks some of the freesias and ties them with a blade of grass. She hands the bouquet to Diana than plucks another for herself. They walk to a sunny corner and gather around the tiny gravestone.

Diana finds Will's hand. They move closer together, the children flanking them. Though she feels pulpy and tender and raw, in a strange way, she feels more complete. There will always be a Nicholas-shaped hole inside her, except now he has his brother and sister to love him too. Long after Diana has gone, they'll be here to remember him.

Persephone places her bouquet on Nicholas's grave and presses her finger to her lips. She touches the headstone and steps away. Diana hands her bouquet to Aiden because he looks so lost and tangled up by his emotions. He kneels at his brother's grave and rests it next to the other posy. Aiden sits back on his haunches, closing his eyes. His lips move in a mumble, incoherent to anyone but himself, then he stands off to one side, swiping an arm across his face. Diana understands that it's not grief for Nicholas making Aiden sad, but the thought that it might have been Lucas.

Persephone embraces her mother. 'I'm so sorry you've been carrying this burden for so long. I wish I'd known. I'd like to have grown up with Nicholas in my life.' Then she kisses Will's cheek. He draws her into a hug and holds on to her, while he takes Diana's hand and brings it to his lips. Diana gathers in Aiden, her arm around his waist. The four of them anchored by the presence of Nicholas.

Diana studies Will — that little furrow in his brow, the bump in his nose where he broke it skiing, the little white crescent on his bottom lip from the fall off his bike when he was eight. His stubble is salted with a few more greys these days. Imagine never again waking up to see that face beside her. Who would bring her coffee in bed after his morning swim? No more gourmet dinners. If Will sets himself free from FME, who will he be without the shackles of the business? Is that a man she'd like to get to know better? Maybe yes.

Persephone catches Aiden's hand. 'C'mon, you, let's go say hello to Grandpa while we're here.'

Diana and Will step into each other's embrace and watch their oldest children leave the garden. They are alone with Nicholas, the sunshine and the twittering birds. There is a shifting inside her. It's not so much that the truth has lightened the load, it's more like the shape sorter she gifted Lucas, and the little wooden star has found the right hole.

She turns to face Will. 'I'm so sorry,' she begins but a wave of emotion swamps her and she's crying. Goodness me, hasn't she cried enough? And what use have all those tears been? 'I am,' Diana says with more vehemence than she intended. 'I've done nothing but wallow in self-pity for twenty-six years. Caught up in the why me's and what if's. Blaming me, blaming you, blaming the universe. It's done me no good at all.'

'That's a bit harsh, Didi.' Will takes her by the hand and leads her over to the wooden bench against the garden wall. 'You can't punish yourself for being heartbroken. If anyone should be apologising it should be me for being such an insensitive prick.'

Diana leans her head on his shoulder and nestles into the familiar warmth of his embrace. 'What a mess we've made of things.'

He kisses the top of her head. 'I forgive you.'

She sits up. 'What?'

Will locks her firmly in his arms. 'I said, I forgive you.'

Her antenna is twitching. She's right back to the day she was unpacking his clothes. The crumpled note falling to the floor.

'You know how I said I wrote you a letter?'

Diana nods.

'I've been thinking about our conversation yesterday. I feel like I never properly answered you and I want you to be in no doubt. I forgave you years ago, Didi. I assumed you understood that. Actions are supposed to speak louder than words.'

Acts of service. Will's cooking. Their beautiful home. An easy life.

'Now I realise I didn't give you the one thing you needed — to hear me say the words. It wasn't enough to write you a letter. Even if I had given it to you, it wouldn't have been the same as saying the words out loud. But it's hard to say what you mean, you know?'

'It needs to come from the heart.'

Will's face brightens. 'Yes, exactly. That's what I realised.' He reaches inside his jacket and pulls out a sheet of paper folded in half.

Diana recognises it. It matches the hotel stationery she found in Will's cashmere sweater. 'It's the same letterhead!'

'What?'

'Nothing, sorry, you were saying?'

He shifts in his seat, clears his throat, then unfolds the sheet of paper and takes a deep breath. She assumes he's nervous, girding his loins. What she doesn't expect is for him to start to sing.

When I first fell for you,
I didn't know what to do
About the way you made me feel.

When I first looked in your eyes,
I felt our two worlds collide
And I knew this love was real.

And Diana is back on that beach with this handsome man — younger, more headstrong, and so romantic — who had fallen at her feet. Time has changed the shape of them, age has tempered them, yet despite the hurt and the loss and sadness, she remembers that girl well and how she blossomed under this man's love.

> I knew right from the start
> That losing you would break my heart.
> And here we are at the end,
> A place where we can start again.
> And I'm begging you to
> Please forgive me,
> Like I forgive you

The words take Diana straight back. She was scraping plates, rinsing them, stacking them in the dishwasher. Spaghetti Oops and toast for dinner. Again. Aiden and Persephone were bathed, in their pyjamas, sprawled on the rug in front of the television in the playroom. Will walked in the front door. It had been two months.

The children were so engrossed in *Bananas in Pyjamas* or *Babar the Elephant,* or whatever the show was, that they didn't see their father creep back into his own home.

Neither Will nor Diana said a word, but volumes passed between them. About Nicholas. About Ben. About Sally from Finance. About Will storming out and refusing to speak to her for two months.

Then he turned and said, *Hey kids, what's happening?* And the unspoken words were swamped by squeals of excitement, a flurry of hugs and kisses. The children shouting over the top of each other to tell Daddy everything that had happened since he went away, searching his bags for gifts from whichever foreign shore had laid claim on him. The bedtime tears, Persephone's tantrums and Aiden's withdrawal all forgotten. It didn't matter now that their father had been safely delivered home again.

Diana turns away from the past and looks at Will. 'You've made me cry.'

He pulls a clown's sad face but it's his eyes that tell her the truth. That he is sorry. That he loves her.

'It's the only song I've ever written. I'm quite proud of it.' He says it in a jokey tone though, so that Diana has space to tell him how awful it is.

But she doesn't. She shuffles along the bench and snuggles into Will. She slips her hand in his but keeps her gaze firmly locked on the stone that marks the spot where Nicholas lies.

'Do you know, all those years I sang for a living, not one single person ever wrote me a song? I have sung about falling in love, falling out of love, never finding love, cheating hearts and every kind of conceivable heartache, but always other people's words. And then you, who can't sing to save his life ...'

'Hey!'

She squeezes his hand. 'You come along and write me the most beautiful song of all.'

Will wraps his arms around her and kisses her cheek. 'That's the nicest compliment anyone has ever paid me. The question is though, is it good enough to win me back the girl?'

And here they are. Will puts his hand on her thigh and the warmth seeps into her skin. He has beautiful hands. They're just the right size so when he holds hers, it feels safe. His touch is firm, gentle, kind. No one has ever, or could ever, touch her in quite the same way.

'Caroline says I didn't understand your grief because it was a different shape from my grief. Mine was a burning rage. When I said we should have another baby, I didn't mean to replace Nicholas. I just wanted to replace the hurt with love, not drive you away. I'm so sorry I broke your heart and I promise, I promise, I'll never let you suffer like that again.'

Diana thinks of the relationships around them. Lydia's a serial monogamist, running away at the slightest hint of commitment. Ian and Rebecca — my God, where to begin? Her mother, brittle beneath that carapace of calm efficiency. Her children, though, have chosen well. Hopefully, for them, love will be enough. 'The thing is, Will, you can't fly off the handle every time someone pays me any attention. Us getting back together is never going to work unless you trust me.' She looks deep into those blue yes. 'I mean it.'

Will drops his gaze. A silence grows between them and Diana lets it because their marriage has been on his terms for far too long. If he meant a single word he just sang to her, then he's going to have to change the way he operates.

Will looks at her. 'I've felt you slowly drifting away from me for years, further and further out of reach. I thought selling Turpentine Street was a way to rule a line under our past, a chance for us to start over. But instead I found out that desperately trying to hold on to someone is the best way of making sure you lose them. I guess my reaction to the photos proves that I still have a way to go with managing my emotions.'

'I'm not going to argue with that.'

Will grimaces and picks up her hand. He lightly kisses her knuckles. 'I promise I will do everything in my power to be a better man.'

'Can you hold that promise for another thirty years?'

Will starts. 'My God, woman, I'll be ninety.'

'You won't live that long.'

'What?'

'Not if you don't sell that damn business and get a life.'

Will takes her face in his hands and gazes into her eyes. 'I also promise that I'm selling the business. But be warned, having me at home all the time might take some getting used to. I might drive you mad.' He pauses to wipe a tear from her cheek, his voice softening. 'If you left me, I'd be devastated. I'm a lesser person without the love of my family. Without you.' He touches his forehead to hers. 'I love you, Didi.'

'I love you too.'

'Good.'

Diana looks up at her handsome husband with his sparkling blue eyes, how the laugh lines fan out around his eyes. She caresses his stubble with the back of her fingers. 'Ruth says the most important thing about forgiving someone is to remember that you're not doing it for them. You're doing it for yourself. On that basis, you don't need me to forgive you.'

Will grabs her roaming fingers and kisses them. Something over Diana's shoulder catches his eye. She turns and sees Aiden and Persephone have almost returned. 'Okay then,' he says, drawing her attention back to him. 'There is one more thing.'

'What's that?'

She leans towards him, expecting a secret whispered in her ear. Instead he kisses her in a way that reminds her of when they were young and life was ahead of them. The years fall away and when she is in his arms, anything is possible.

'Ooh yuck, they're pashing,' Persephone says.

'Get a room,' adds Aiden.

Now that there's an audience, Will wraps Diana tighter and she's practically smothered by his kiss.

She pushes him away, laughing. 'Enough, Will. The children are present.' And she smiles at Persephone, Aiden, and Nicholas.

*

'When you two have finished, Auntie Lydia just called. She says she ran into some bloke at The Boatshed called Reese? He thought she was you.'

Diana's heart plummets. She's forgotten to tell everyone about the rats. 'Royce.'

'Royce Carmichael? What's going on?'

Diana covers her face with her hands. 'Oh God, the party. The council has closed the Beach Club. Apparently, rats have been nesting in the ceiling and chewed through the wiring. What with everything else going on, I haven't had the wherewithal to deal with it.'

'Too easy, we'll just have everyone back to our place.'

'Will, no! It's not big enough.'

He kisses her. 'Stop worrying. Who cares if it's a squeeze? We have to christen our new home sometime. It will be perfect.'

And that's what's been missing. A house is not a home until it's filled with love. Diana has been dragging her heels on this party business for months. It's so obvious why. Until today, she and Will have had little to celebrate. Now they have every reason in the world.

Chapter 37

The Big Party

Camille has taken control of the apartment's kitchen and press-ganged Ingrid into the role of sous chef. Instructions fly through the air in French and English with the occasional response in Swedish. Diana doesn't speak a word of the language but judging by Ingrid's expression, she gathers Anna's mother is not paying Camille a compliment.

As soon as she spies Diana, Camille tosses the piping bag onto the bench and whips around the other side. 'Diana, you look divine. That dress!' She kisses her cheeks.

'Yes, it's very nice,' adds Ingrid.

'Sizzling.' Lydia licks her finger and hisses.

'Thank you. Will bought it for me for the party. It's not too revealing, is it?'

'*Non*, absolutely not. He has very good taste, your husband,' Camille says, grabbing a clean tea towel. She dampens it and washes off a trace of her red lipstick from Diana's cheeks. 'That's better.'

'Do you need help with anything?' Diana offers.

Camille's hands go to her hips, her expressive eyebrows knotted in the middle of her forehead. 'You know, I found my cookbook hidden behind some magazines in your kitchen. I told Will that it's much easier to use if you leave it on the kitchen bench.' Having scored her point, Camille grins and shoos her away with the tea towel. 'Go on. It's your party, relax and enjoy yourself.'

'Exactly,' Lydia says, holding out a champagne flute of Campari — a Negroni Sbagliato. Diana shakes her head and motions 'no way'. This early in the night, she's sticking to water. She needs to keep her wits about her.

Lydia passes it to Ingrid instead. She stops unpacking a box of goodies from The Village Providore. 'What is in it?' she asks, looking at the cocktail as if Lydia is trying to poison her.

Lydia pats her shoulder. 'Never you mind. Drink up. It'll help you cope with our Gallic gastronome.'

Diana follows the sound of oud and darbuka floating through the apartment. Idris and Naz have set up out on the terrace and by the look on Emile's and Raphael's faces, the brothers have gained new fans. She hopes Michael made sure they brought copies of their new CD.

At a kiss on her cheek, she turns and smiles at Will. He offers her a platter.

'Camille has made caramelised onion and goat's cheese tarts. Try one. They're delicious.'

'I see *you're* allowed in the kitchen then.'

Will takes his phone out of his pocket and shows her some photos. 'I asked Camille if it was alright if I posted these on my Instagram page. You know what she said?'

'I can't imagine.'

'She said they were better than some of the shots in her book. Camille reckons I might have a new career ahead of me.'

Diana bites into one of the caramelised onion tarts. 'Hmm. You're right, of course. On both counts.'

Will kisses her again and whispers hot in her ear — 'Very, very sexy' — then takes the tray over to where Audrey is deep in conversation with Marianne and Alan. No sign of her mother's handyman, Victor. Diana looks around and finds him playing peek-a-boo with Lucas under the benign eye of Anna. She rests one hand on the small mound of her belly, the other on the crown of Lucas's head. Twins! Diana can't quite believe it.

'So you're having girls?' Diana asked when Aiden and Anna broke the news.

Will had winked at her. 'Because if you're not sure, Diana knows a neat trick with a wedding ring.'

Diana goes over to say hello to her mother. 'So, Mum — you and Victor?'

Audrey snorts. 'Not you as well? As I told your sister, the only garden Victor is cultivating is my backyard, thank you very much! I have no intention of letting him move in. I like my independence. I've no need to wait hand and foot on any other person than myself.'

Diana sips her drink. 'Nice try, Mum. But I'll just say that there's nothing wrong with enjoying a man's company, as and when it suits.'

Audrey does what Audrey does best and deflects. 'You look radiant in that dress, darling.'

A tap on the shoulder. 'Diana, I'd like you to meet Jacqueline.'

She turns around and looks up at a statuesque woman. It takes her a second to recalibrate. The Empress of the Essential Oils wears a jumpsuit Catwoman would envy and towers over Ian in her stilettos. Not to mention that she's drop-dead gorgeous.

Diana regroups. 'Hello, lovely to meet you.' She offers her hand but Jacqueline pulls her into a hug.

'I've heard so much about you.'

'Oh, well, that's wonderful. I've heard a little about you too.' Diana thinks of the tantric sex and immediately swipes a cocktail from a tray Lydia is passing around.

'Fantastic,' Jacqueline says taking two and passing one to Ian. She tastes it — 'Wow, that packs a punch, doesn't it?' — and takes another gulp.

'Hello, I'm Fiona.' Fi offers the goddess her hand and shakes it like the company director she is.

Jacqueline doesn't miss a beat. 'Fi Sterling, yes? It's so nice to meet you in person. I believe my financial controller, Bevan O'Connell, was at uni with you.'

In a flash, corporate Fiona has tossed off her metaphorical power suit and let Fi into the room. 'Bevan? Gosh I could tell you a few stories about him back in the day.'

Jacqueline winks at her. 'I bet you could.' She grabs Ian's cocktail — 'Sorry, darling' — and passes it to Fi. 'C'mon then. I promise you, I operate under a cone of silence.' And she ushers Fi out onto the terrace.

Diana looks to Ian. 'My, my, haven't you landed on your feet, young man?'

Ian's grin is every shade of sheepish. 'I told you.'

'Now I understand why you were more than willing to let Rebecca have it all. I think she got the short end of the stick.'

He looks momentarily worried. 'Speaking of the she-devil, is she ...'

'No, she's not coming. She and Georgina flew out to Thailand this morning. For the record, I did ask her though. Needless to say, she was taken aback. So win-win on both counts.'

'Excellent.' Ian checks around them to ensure no one else is listening. 'Thank you for telling me what Becks was up to.

You guessed right about those photos. Rebecca confronted me with them and said how she was going to squeeze me for every penny in the divorce. You should have seen her face when I told her that if she went after mine, I'd go after hers. I owe you one.'

He goes to kiss her cheek but Diana steps away. 'I'm glad it's worked out for the best. To be honest, I ended up deciding not to confront Rebecca. Partly because I didn't want to give her the satisfaction of knowing the damage she'd caused and partly because I realised that I feel sorry for her more than anything. There was nothing to be gained by rubbing her nose in it.'

This time, Diana doesn't dodge Ian's kiss. 'My brother's a lucky man,' he says.

There's a break in the music and Diana hears a random chord. She turns to see Aiden seated at the piano, which is now — thanks to Michael — tuned. She makes her way over. 'Hey darling, are you nervous?'

He grins at her. 'Me? Nervous? Never.' He turns on the mic and tests the sound.

Michael gives him the thumbs-up. Diana looks around for Will and sees him chatting to Ruth. She made Aiden tell his father why Michael being here was mission-critical. Under the circumstances, she knew he'd take it better coming from his son rather than his wife.

'I'm glad you haven't hung any pictures on this wall yet,' Persephone says at her side. 'It makes the perfect screen for my slideshow.'

Diana looks up and sees a photo of Will and her and the kids projected onto the wall from Persephone's laptop. The kids are about nine and eight and they're on a family holiday in Disneyland. 'My goodness, look how young we were.' She leans closer. 'Have you had a chance to talk to Emile?'

For a moment, her daughter's trademark confidence dims a little. 'Yeah, I did.'

Diana waits, fearing the worst. 'Is that it? You're not going to tell me what he said?'

'I confessed that I didn't think I wanted children and that I'd understand if he wanted a divorce.'

'Oh Persephone, I didn't mean you should ...'

'It's alright, Mum. He said, "Do you think I'm crazy?"'

Diana hugs her little girl. 'I'm so glad. I like Emile.' She reaches up and kisses her cheek. 'I'm even warming to his mother.'

Aiden catches her eye and taps the back of his wrist. It's time. She goes to check her makeup in the hall mirror, stepping away to admire Will's gift. It is truly a lovely dress, although it's been decades since she's worn anything this revealing. She bends her knee and the dress falls open, split to the thigh. Diana catches a glimpse of the girl she once was. Remembers the *joie de vivre*, how she thought meeting Will meant she would never have to care or worry about anything ever again. Ah, the optimism of youth.

She makes her way over to the baby grand. Michael has positioned one of the standing lamps to illuminate her seat. It bathes Diana in its glow as she settles herself onto the stool and adjusts the mic. Michael is in front of her, his guitar strap slung over one shoulder. Aiden's beside him, his tenor sax on its stand and an array of percussion instruments at his fingertips. Will is now deep in conversation with Fi's Richard. Now that she looks more closely, cornered might be a better word for it.

Diana switches on the mic and says, 'Good evening, ladies and gentlemen.'

She waits for the chatter to diminish. Muscle memory takes over. It transports her to a nightclub, the faint smell of dry ice, cigarette smoke and stale beer. The heat and the envelope of darkness that hides the crowded room.

'My name is Diana Forsyth and these guys are The New Somethings.'

Persephone wolf-whistles, there's a smattering of applause. Much to her satisfaction, Will's expression is caught between shock and delight. Whatever Richard is saying is going right over Will's head. Diana plays a couple of chords. She looks at Aiden, her tall handsome boy, and he grins. He's excited. Months of rehearsal have brought them to this moment. She looks to Michael and he smiles that sleepy sexy smile and counts them in.

They open the set with 'For Once in My Life'. It's been a long time between songs. Diana's throat opens, her vocal cords relax and she lets it all out.

Camille, sashaying between guests, platter aloft, catches Diana's eye. She nods approvingly.

The space is so small Diana can see everyone. Her mother is perched on the arm of the lounge. Victor whispers in her ear and her smile is like the first bite of an apple.

'I Say a Little Prayer' follows 'I Know a Place', 'Do You Know the Way to San Jose?' and 'Until You Come Back to Me'.

Diana lifts her heavy hair from the nape of her neck. She's dripping and blood courses through her veins. Hugo and Ingrid are dancing. Raphael is jiving with Persephone. Ruth is making eyes at Michael. Diana glances at him — he knows it too. The sly bastard has let his fringe flop over his eye and he's watching Ruth watching him. Some things never change.

Will moves into her line of sight. She's surprised to see his camera around his neck. He holds it up to his eye, one hand cradling the lens. Snap! He lowers the camera and looks at her in a way that — if she weren't performing, if they did not have a house full of guests — would mean that man would be in serious strife.

At the end of the set, Diana thanks everyone for making this such a special night. 'I couldn't think of a better way to christen our new home than with friends, family and fabulous food. *Merci beaucoup.*' She blows Camille a kiss and is surprised to see her blush. 'I also want to thank my amazingly talented son, Aiden, for convincing me this was a good idea, and Michael for helping us give this encore performance of Diana and The New Somethings. I hope you've enjoyed it.'

Diana beams as their guests make loud their approval. How she loves the sense of connection, the power to hold an audience in the palm of her hand and bring them such joy.

Naz and Idris wander in from the terrace. Naz settles the drum between his knees and Idris picks up the shaker. Diana motions for everyone to be quiet. 'I also want to say happy birthday to my husband, Will, who turns sixty tomorrow. Happy birthday, Will. I hope you're enjoying your present. He's the father of our three beautiful children.' Diana glances at the photo of Nicholas in his rightful place on the photo wall. 'The love of my life for more than thirty years gone and thirty years to come. Happy anniversary, darling. This song is for you.'

Diana looks to Michael. He counts them in and Diana and The New Somethings launch into the cool bossa nova beat of Will's all-time favourite, 'The Look of Love'. As she sings, she can't look at Will, because whatever he's feeling right now is bound to throw her concentration. Instead she focuses on Aiden. She can't believe she's here on stage with her son. It takes all her self-control not to cry as she watches him play the sultry melancholy solo that always sends a shiver down her spine.

When she plays the final note, Will comes over and offers his hand. Diana takes it and stands. She bows to the audience, gestures to Michael, then Aiden, Idris and Naz, who have earned the generous applause that greets them. She presses her palm to her heart and mouths thank you. And, as hot and sweaty as she is, Will wraps his arms around her and whispers in her ear, 'God, I love you.'

Diana brushes his cheek with her fingers. Over his shoulder, she catches sight of that photo. The image of her, hot and sweaty at the piano. The one her mum has on the kitchen dresser, that used to hang in the studio at Turpentine Street. And Diana realises that the reason this photo fills her with so much longing is because she was young and carefree and so damn alive. About the same way she feels right now.

Will's hands slide down her hips and she presses into him, feels his heart pounding beneath his shirt. The reassurance of his touch. Nicholas is still with her, in every beat of her heart. She lost a part of herself when she lost Nicholas. She's been searching for it ever since. And here it is. In this room, surrounded by all the people she loves. With the man she loves. To feel this happy is more than she deserves.

Diana kisses Will gently on the lips. 'I have to go.'

He frowns as he releases her. She resumes her seat at the piano.

'There's one more number we want to play for you tonight.' She picks out the melody with her right hand. 'We've been working on this song for months' — Diana plays a couple of chords beneath the melody — 'but I couldn't find the words to fit, until my darling husband gave them to me.'

Diana looks at Will, who has the exact look of a man who has been surprised. Twice in one night. This could become a habit.

'Sweetheart, we've played around a bit with the lyrics, I hope you don't mind, but I think you'll recognise the song.' Diana takes her hands off the keys and waits for The New Somethings to get settled. Then she leans into the mic and says, 'It's called "I Forgive You".' She lets her gaze linger on the love of her life. 'And it goes a little like this.'

*

It's very late by the time everyone finally leaves. Diana puts on a CD and soon Peggy is singing about the boy she knows. Diana threads her arms around Will's neck. 'Did you enjoy your birthday?'

He kisses her. 'You bet I did. Especially my surprise.'

'C'mon, you must have guessed once you saw the set-up.'

Will kisses her again, a little longer, a little deeper. 'I wasn't sure.'

She runs her hands down his arms, squeezes his biceps. 'You know, you're pretty hot for your age. I think I might keep you.'

'No one else would put up with me.'

'Ooh, I don't think that's true. Anyway, why would I want to be with someone no one else wants?'

Will draws back. 'That reminds me. Now that everyone's gone, I've got something for you.'

'What?'

He disappears into the spare bedroom. 'I picked this up from the framers on Friday.' He reappears carrying a long rectangular package in plain brown paper.

'It's your birthday, not mine.'

'No, I know, but I also know you've been less than thrilled about leaving Turpentine Street. And despite all this,' — Will gestures to the photo wall and the objects collected over a lifetime — 'there is one thing we can never replace.' He points at the package. 'Open it. No need to be careful, just rip it off.'

So she does and discovers the most extraordinary thing. 'Oh Will.'

'Do you like it?'

'Next stupid question.' It is a section of the doorjamb from the architrave between the family room and the spare loo. On it, in Will's handwriting, are marked the children's ages, dates and their heights. Diana smiles at Will. 'Aren't you just the most divine human being?' She leans it against the wall, next to the photos chronicling their lives, before giving her husband the kiss he deserves. And the best bit is the way he kisses her right back.

By the time she's come up for air, Diana knows there is one more obstacle in their path before she can truly say that she and Will are back on track. Letting things fester has led them here. If they're going to make the most of however many years they have left together, there must be no more doubts and second-guessing. Those kinds of secrets do no one any good.

'There's one last tiny thing I need to tell you.'

'Hmm?' Will slides down the zipper of her dress, slips his hand around her waist and into the dip at the small of her back. He draws her closer, his lips on her throat.

She pulls away. Her first instinct is to lie but she's made herself a promise. It's important to clear the air, to be totally honest. It's the only way forward. 'The other day, I never answered your question. The third man in the photos? That's Ben.'

It's there, the hesitation. She dares not look down in case she loses her nerve. 'We were laying ghosts to rest.'

It's the truth, but Diana can see it's still hurt him, and wishes she could smooth the pain away. But that's not her job and Will must make his own choices.

Eventually, he replies, 'So I have nothing to worry about?'

She takes his face in her hands and looks into those eyes, the same colour as a tropical blue sea. 'I'm going to pretend you didn't ask me that.'

Then Diana takes his hand and leads him into the bedroom. She gently pushes him back on the bed, straddles his hips and holds his hands to her lips. 'In case you've forgotten, this is where I belong.'

Forgive Me

Lyrics by Will Forsyth

When I first fell for you,
I didn't know what to do
About the way you made me feel.

When I first looked in your eyes,
I felt our two worlds collide
And I knew this love was real.

Chorus:
I've been a fool for you
One touch and I'd die for you
Every note you sang to me,
Every smile, brought joy to me.
Being loved by you felt too good to be true
But I almost lost you
Please forgive me.

Then I went and let you down,
I didn't want to be around
To be the man you needed me to be.

When I realised my mistake,
How much I'd put at stake,
Without you there's simply less of me.

Chorus:
As the years have flown by,
I've seen the doubt grow in your eyes.
Sometimes what we lost is too much to bear
And I'd rather be anywhere
Than to face the truth
That I was losing you
Please forgive me.

Break:
I knew right from the start
That losing you would break my heart.
And here we are at the end,
A place where we can start again.
And I'm begging you to
Please forgive me,
Like I forgive you *(to the end)*

The Tricky Art of Forgiveness
Playlist

There is a blend of nostalgia and wishful thinking involved in the creation of *The Tricky Art of Forgiveness* Playlist. I grew up in a house filled with music. My parents were fantastic dancers, and jazz, bossa nova and Burt Bacharach formed the soundtrack to my childhood (as much as 2SM and 2JJ). When the Motown sound enjoyed a resurgence in the 1980s, we embraced it too. I may, or may not, have also spent a sliver of time behind the microphone singing 1960 covers, wishing I sounded as good as any of these amazing performers. What a joy that would be!

'Hallelujah I Love Him So' — Peggy Lee (1959)
'I Heard It Through the Grapevine' — Marvin Gaye (1968)
'Peter Gunn Theme' — Henry Mancini (1958)
'Son of a Preacher Man' — Dusty Springfield (1968)
'The Happening' — The Supremes (1967)
'Do You Know the Way to San Jose?' — Dionne Warwick (1968)
'I Say a Little Prayer' — Aretha Franklin (1968)
'Love Child' — The Supremes (1968)
'River Deep, Mountain High' — Ike and Tina Turner (1966)
'Signed, Sealed, Delivered, I'm Yours' — Stevie Wonder (1970)
'Is That All There Is?' — Peggy Lee (1969)

'(They Long to Be) Close to You' — The Carpenters (1970)
'Take 5' — The Dave Brubeck Quartet (1959)
'Smooth Operator' — Sade (1984)
'Mockingbird' — Dusty Springfield (1965)
'Fire and Rain' — James Taylor (1970)
'Brandenburg Concerto No. 1 in F Major' — Johann Sebastian Bach (1721)
'These Boots are Made for Walking' — Nancy Sinatra (1966)
'"A" You're Adorable' — Perry Como with The Fontane Sisters (1949)
'Mañana (Is Soon Enough for Me)' — Peggy Lee (1947)
'I Am Woman' — Helen Reddy (1972)
'Afternoon Delight' — Starland Vocal Band (1976)
'The Look of Love' — Dusty Springfield (1967)
'Air on the G String' — Johann Sebastian Bach (1731)
'For Once in My Life' — Stevie Wonder (1968)
'I Know a Place' — Petula Clarke (1965)
'Until You Come Back to Me (That's What I'm Gonna Do)' — Aretha Franklin (1974)

I've recreated the soundtrack of Diana and The Somethings, inspired by the artists who made these songs famous, on Spotify. Scan the QR code to find the playlist. C'mon! Sing along — you know you want to.

Reading Group Questions

'Marriages traverse such complex and treacherous landscapes' (page 39). Diana often refers to her marriage using geographical terms like this. What do these metaphors say about long-term relationships?

'But old hurts don't improve with fresh airings' (page 166). Why do you think Diana chooses to not bring up the note when she is confronted with the photos? Is Diana right to be furious with Will in this moment, rather than defensive? What would you do if you found such a note among your partner's belongings?

'Her life is her story to write, no one else's, not even Will's' (page 173). How does this speak to Diana's feelings that her life has been subsumed by being a mother and a wife rather than a woman in her own right?

When Diana reveals her affair to Lydia, her sister says, *'Please tell me you didn't tell Will'* (page 275). And later, when Diana and Will tell Aiden and Persephone about Nicholas, she reflects on how much the children need to know about the past and says, *'By this age and stage of life, they both know that honesty is overrated'* (page 309). Do you think Diana is right about honesty? Why do you think she feels this way?

'Don't ask questions you don't want to know the answer to, that's always been her motto' (page 183). What are your thoughts on Diana's motto? Is this a sound strategy?

It's like the fine print in those investment brochures — past performance is no indicator of future performance. They should print that on marriage contracts (page 182). Diana has a very dry sense of humour. Do you think that she uses humour to deflect her true feelings? Does this make her a dishonest narrator?

'It's ridiculous to split up now. Did you know, women over fifty is the largest growing group of homeless people? Not enough super, no financial wherewithal' (page 208). The novel touches on the serious issues around women's financial security in later years, particularly after a divorce. It also questions the choice to stay together for the sake of economic security over the potentially riskier strategy of starting over. Why do you think these issues are so prevalent at this point in life?

A central theme of the novel is the long-term impact of unresolved grief. This is an intrinsic part of Diana's story, and is also partly told through Audrey's story and her decision to sell up, buy a motor home and travel the country. What clues are given as to Diana's and Audrey's true emotional states throughout the novel?

Diana's friend Fi embraces being an empty nester, Ruth's boys still live at home, and Diana struggles to find a renewed sense of purpose now that her children live overseas and she no longer needs to keep the family running smoothly. How do these characters typify the issues surrounding those post–child rearing years in a woman's life?

The Tricky Art of Forgiveness

'Ruth says the most important thing about forgiving someone is to remember that you're not doing it for them. You're doing it for yourself' (page 319). The novel explores the question of forgiveness from many angles — infidelity, hurting those you love, and self-love. Do you think Ruth's viewpoint is true? Does forgiveness depend on the extent of the damage done?

Diana tells Persephone, 'I can't imagine the kind of person I would have been without children. It changes the shape of you' (page 263). Yet many of the female characters in the novel do not have children — Persephone, Lydia, Rebecca. In what way does the novel explore the issue of female identity, in particular societal norms around motherhood?

'... if sixty really is the new forty. Diana hasn't seen much evidence this is as true for men as it is for women' (page 282). How true do you think this statement is? In what ways does the novel look at aging, particularly when it comes to the differences between men and women?

Acknowledgments

Ideas for novels come in the strangest of ways. In this case, I had this idea of a woman sitting alone in the dark in a picture theatre. I only saw her from behind so I could not see her face. I wondered why she was there. I sensed a great sadness. Every time I drove past our local cinema, I wondered about her. Where was her husband? Dead? Away? She was very much alone.

Then one day, when I imagined her sitting in the dark, watching the movie, there was a man sitting a few rows in front. This surprised me. I wondered if there was a connection and what it was. Would they meet? What would happen when they did?

Then COVID happened and I thought about absent children, families unable to come together because of the pandemic, more loss, more sadness. I started writing notes by hand about this and slowly the two ideas merged and out of it came Diana. I'd written about thirty thousand words before I realised what the story was. Then I put aside those meandering notes and began what would become *The Tricky Art of Forgiveness*.

By nature, I'm not one who likes to dwell on sadness. Finding joy is so important. After I'd created Diana, I realised that I wanted to write a love story, a romantic drama, but not young love. A love story for people who have lived life already and have more to give. I wanted Diana to be gorgeous and charming but, in my experience, true happiness has to have the edges knocked off it. You don't truly appreciate what you have without context.

As much as this is a love story, it is also about unresolved grief, which harks back, I think, to the feeling I had about that woman in the picture theatre. Would we care about Diana and Will's marital travails if they did not have a reason to be struggling to stay together? I don't think so. I've drawn on personal experiences of loss (although, to be clear, not a stillbirth), experiences of women I know and the wonderful resources and stories shared on the internet of those who have survived a stillbirth. It was a support site that recommended the memoir by acclaimed novelist Elizabeth McCracken, *An Exact Replica of a Figment of My Imagination*, a *New York Times* Notable Book of the Year. My goodness, this is a wonderful, important book about loss and grief, and ultimately an impassioned reminder of how we live on and find new meaning shaped by that grief. McCracken's memoir underpinned the veracity of Diana's experience as did conversations with midwives who are there at this turning point in life. Any mistakes are, of course, all my own.

Side by side in every writer's life is the team that believes in them, believes in the story and wants to turn it into a book. Always I thank Tara Wynne from Curtis Brown Australia, who has been with me through thick and thin. I have so much respect for this woman and am eternally grateful that she is my literary agent.

But a writer also needs a great publisher. HarperCollins Publishers is made up of an amazing bunch of people. My publisher, Anna Valdinger, is perceptive, intuitive, hard-working and demanding (in the best possible sense of the word). She has assembled the best support crew a writer could wish for. Thank you to the editorial muscle and wit of Liz Monument, Dianne Blacklock, Rachel Dennis and Pamela Dunne. You make me look good! My campaign manager, Dave Cain, I salute you, sir. Thank you to the HarperCollins design team for the cover, and the marketing and sales teams for all the support banging the drum and getting the message out there. I ride on your coattails!

Thanks to Joanna Nell for casting her eye over the first draft, both as a writer and a GP. Again, any mistakes, blame me. Also thanks to my writing coach extraordinaire, Sophie Hannah, for keeping my head straight, and to the rest of the Dream Authors. It's true to say that a problem shared is a problem halved.

I live and write on unceded Murramarang Yuin country and wish to specifically express my respect and gratitude to the Murramarang people and pay respect to their Elders, past, present and future. I am humbled to be able to have this unique privilege and am reminded of that every time I look out my studio window at this magnificent country on which I create.

Thank you too to the wonderful team at my local bookseller, Harbour Bookshop, led by the dedicated and passionate Michelle Evans. Thank you too to all the bookshops that have let me pop in to say hello and do events, and/or that have been the bookseller at events. I'm hoping we are going to do it all again this time around. Booksellers are the best and Australian stories would be lost without these booklovers pressing them into readers' hands. The same goes for those magnificent librarians all around the country. Booksellers and libraries have been under enormous pressure these past few years and I'm sure I speak for all readers when I say, we'd be lost without you.

For everyone who has read my work, taken the time to post a review or send me an email, turned up to an event, or invited me to their book club, thank you. For everyone who let me chat with them on their podcast, radio station, blog, website, thank you. To the amazing community of writers, readers, booksellers and publishers on Instagram, thank you for your kindness and humour, and for sharing some great books. I have a teetering TBR pile because of you. Keep it coming! Thanks also to Nikki Croft for diligently keeping me on message.

Last but by no means least, my family are the backbone of this entire operation. They provide economic security, sanity checks, reality checks, and are the best cheer squad a writer could ask for. Thanks Paullie, Imogen, Matilda and Beau for your daily patience. I wouldn't be here without you.

meredithjaffé
Newsletter

If you would like to know more about what I am up to, what I am reading, listening to, and working on, or even what my bookish friends are up to, then my newsletter is the perfect place to read all the goss. It will hit your inbox every couple of months and will be about a one-cup-of-tea read. Plus, I'll sneak in a few giveaways along the way, because who doesn't love a freebie? Sign up at meredithjaffe.com

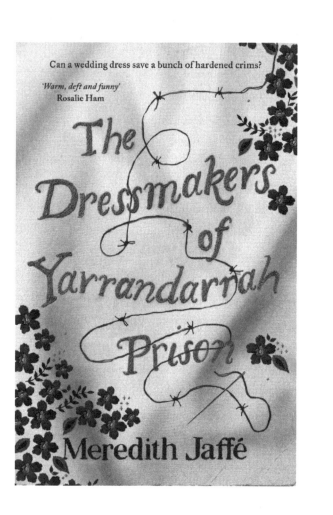

Can a wedding dress save a bunch of hardened crims? *The Full Monty* **meets** *Orange is the New Black* **in a poignantly comic story about a men's prison sewing circle.**

Derek's daughter, Debbie, is getting married. He's desperate to be there, but he's banged up in Yarrandarrah Correctional Centre for embezzling funds from the golf club, and, thanks to his ex-wife, Lorraine, he hasn't spoken to Debbie in years. He wants to make a grand gesture — to show her how much he loves her. But what?

Inspiration strikes while he's embroidering a cushion at his weekly prison sewing circle — he'll make her a wedding dress. His fellow stitchers rally around and soon this motley gang of crims is immersed in a joyous whirl of silks, satins and covered buttons.

But as time runs out and tensions rise both inside and outside the prison, the wedding dress project takes on greater significance. With lives at stake, Derek feels his chance to reconcile with Debbie is slipping through his fingers ...

A funny, dark and moving novel about finding humanity, friendship and redemption in unexpected places.

Praise for *The Dressmakers of Yarrandarrah Prison*:

'This is a deft and unlikely story in an uncommon setting about an estranged daughter, her jailed father and a very bad idea about a dress. It all makes for a warm, funny union of foes and a lovely encounter with what matters.'
Rosalie Ham

'Overflowing with humour and heart. If you like a story about misfits making good, but with the added lustre of silk and satin, then this book is for you.'
Natasha Lester

'This deliciously original, immersive and darkly funny novel is full of hope and heart. A refreshing take on the theme of redemption and second chances from an assured writer.' Joanna Nell

'Funny and moving' *Sun-Herald*

'Funny, heartfelt, and gorgeously written, *The Dressmakers of Yarrandarrah Prison* is a highly original and extremely enjoyable read' *Better Reading*